THE TRAITOR'S ALLIANCE

The Divalian Chronicles

Book 1

S. T. Hobbs

S. T. Hobbs

*Book and Cover design by germancreative
ISBN: 979-8-9857217-3-7
First Edition: February 2022
10 9 8 7 6 5 4 3 2 1*

Table of Contents

S. T. Hobbs

Chapter 1

SASHA SQUINTED, BRINGING THE distant target into focus. He drew in a sharp breath and held it. If it had been any other day, any other practice, his hands would not have this slight tremor in them, nor would sweat have been beading up on his forehead, threatening to run down into his eyes. If it had been any other day, Father would not have been watching him. It had been nearly a year since Father had taken any interest at all in Sasha and what he could do. Sasha could not miss now.

With a hiss, the arrow sped toward its target and for one brief, thrilling second, Sasha was sure it would be perfect. He hazarded a glance at his Father, but the distance was too great for him to read the expression on Father's face. He turned back to the target and watched as with a sickening thud, the arrow planted itself in the very base of the target, far from where Sasha had been trying to hit.

It wasn't fair, thought Sasha. All the hours of practicing he had done, all the days following one warrior after another around, begging to be taught anything, anything at all about fighting. And now he missed the one shot, probably the only shot that mattered. Father's brief interest would be lost, and Sasha would have little hope of regaining it, not when there were nearly thirty other sons of the Chief of Aruuk all vying for his attention and favor. It didn't help that those other sons, Sasha's half-brothers, all had mothers who were still in favor with Chief Gundar.

It wasn't fair, he thought again watching Father walk away. When Father was entirely out of sight, Sasha sent his bow skittering across the ground and then turned and kicked over the barrel of arrows he had been practicing with. A brief, savage smile flitted across his face as he watched the arrows scatter.

"Clean this up, then bring my bow to me," Sasha called out to a poorly dressed man. As Sasha walked away toward the distant, sprawling building he called home, the man hurried to obey his very young master.

Sasha slipped inside and made his way through the labyrinth of halls and doors. Each of Chief Gundar's wives had their own set of rooms that they shared with their children. As Gundar added to his household, so he had added to his house, so that it was now far larger than when Sasha was first born. The additions had not been made with any thought towards order or convenience, so the entire mass made little sense to anyone who did not frequent the place.

"Where have you been? Axel was looking for you just a few minutes ago," Agathe said. Sasha's only full sibling, she sat on a low stool in their room, allowing an elderly woman to plait her hair.

"What did he want?"

"Didn't say. He just wanted to know where you were. What is wrong with you?"

Sasha shrugged. "Zena, go get me something to eat."

The elderly woman dropped Agathe's hair and scurried out of the room, leaving Agathe scowling behind her.

"She was already busy."

"Your hair can wait. I'm hungry now."

A pout formed on Agathe's lips as she muttered something under her breath. She was older than Sasha by several years, but the fact that she was only a daughter of the Chief and not a valuable son gave his orders precedence over hers. Sasha ignored her and flopped down onto his mat to wait for his food. He shut his eyes and played over and over again in his mind the shot he should not have missed but did. Why did Father pick that moment to show up? Why did Sasha have to glance over long enough to see him there? Sasha was sure that if he had not been aware of Father's presence, he would have hit the target as perfectly as he normally did. Archery was the one thing he excelled in.

The door creaked open, and a short, red-haired man entered the room. He stood by the door, clearing his throat several times, waiting to be acknowledged.

"What is it, Axel?" Sasha finally rolled onto his stomach and faced him.

"Chief Gundar requires your presence, Master Sasha," Axel said. He bowed slightly as he finished speaking.

Sasha's heart quickened as he scrambled up. Father summoning him! That had not happened in nearly a year. Not since Mother had fallen from grace with Gundar. Sasha had been barely eight at the time, too young to understand what went wrong, but plenty old enough to feel the sudden neglect from his father. Rising now from his bed, he ran a hurried hand through his hair, making it poke up wildly, and followed Axel out into the hallway.

He didn't need to be shown the way, but there was protocol - even for a son of the Chief. He passed the old set of rooms that Mother, Agathe, and he used to share. They had been the nearest Chief Gundar's private quarters, and the great hall where any important meeting would take place. And they had been far more comfortable than the ones he and Agathe currently inhabited. As they moved down the hallway, Sasha wondered where it was that Axel was bringing him, if it was Father's private quarters or the great hall.

"This way, Master Sasha." Axel pointed toward the heavy doors that marked the entrance to the great hall. Sasha took a deep breath, wondering what exactly awaited him on the other side of the doors. He was startled to find his heart hammering in his chest, and the palms of his hands growing clammy with sweat. This was Father he was about to see. There was nothing to be afraid of.

Axel pulled open the doors and stepped fully inside before prostrating himself.

"I have brought Master Sasha to you, Chief Gundar, as you commanded."

"That will be all," Chief Gundar's voice carried across the long room. "Sasha, come in."

Sasha came all the way in, moving past the still prone form of Axel, and knelt on the rich carpet several feet from Father's chair. With his head bowed, he brought his right hand, closed in a tight fist, to his forehead and then to his chest in salute.

"You wished to see me, Father." Those words had been among the first he was ever taught to speak. Still keeping his head bowed, Sasha managed to raise his eyes enough to see Mara, Chief Gundar's new favorite wife, sitting by his side. Of course, he couldn't really see her, just the veiled outline of her face. No one was permitted to see any of Father's wives or personal female slaves. He suppressed the face he wanted to make at the sight of her sitting there, adorned in the same jewels Mother had once worn.

"Sasha, it has been a long time. Too long, I think. I must admit, I was worried that you would be tainted by your mother's disgrace. You have proved me wrong. Tomorrow, I want you to begin training with your year group. Does that please you?"

"Yes, Father." It was all Sasha could do to keep himself to the expected answer. He wanted to jump up and down with joy.

"Very well. That is all. Do well in your training and you will take your place at the warriors table when you are of age."

"Thank you, Father! I will not disappoint you."

Sasha saluted again, and backed out of the room, barely noticing Mara's glaring eyes. He was restored to a proper standing as the Chief's son. No one would ever make fun of him again. Sasha fairly raced down the halls back to his room. He could not wait to tell Agathe, although she doubtless would not share his joy. She never did.

"Agathe! Agathe, guess what!" he called out as he pushed the door open. "Agathe?"

Zena stood alone inside the room, a tray of food still in her hands. Sasha glanced quickly about the room, and finding it empty, turned back to Zena.

"Where's Agathe?"

"Master Sasha, she's gone. Chief Gundar sent orders to have her...," Zena let the words hang, shaking her head.

Silence closed in on Sasha later that night, reminding him of just what he had lost. Agathe was gone. And he should not care. She was hardly the first female in the family that Father had gotten rid of. It was what they were for. Probably Father had found a clansman that needed rewarding, and Agathe had been given to him. Sasha stared at the crack in the ceiling above his bed, willing himself to ignore the loneliness. The absence of another being filled the dark room. Sasha closed his eyes. He needed to sleep. Tomorrow was an important day. Not only was he to begin training with the sword master, but the Spring Market was set to open.

Mother's face danced before his shut eyes. The Spring Market last year was the last time he had seen her, and she had been in the possession of another man then, a stranger from some land far away. Sasha never knew where, and he knew better than to ask around. Mother was disgraced, and if he wanted to maintain a position of honor with Father, he had to forget about her. But forgetting about her was a lot harder when he was lying alone in a dark room without even the sound of his sister's breathing to keep him company.

With a groan Sasha rolled over, slamming his fist into his pillow twice before laying down again and drifting off.

It was Axel who awakened him the next morning. Sasha sat up groggily, rubbing sleep from his eyes as the old slave brought his clothes to him.

"Chief Gundar has requested your presence at breakfast."

Sasha grimaced as he remembered the one drawback to being among Father's favorites. It meant living by Father's schedule. Eating meals with him, attending whatever lessons he decided were necessary, and so on. Shrugging, he got up. It was a price he would simply have to pay. Because the alternative was what happened to Agathe.

The table in the great hall was already set, and half a dozen slaves scurried about the room serving whoever Chief Gundar had deemed worthy of attending. Sasha bowed and saluted when he came in before taking his seat near the end of the table. As Sasha waited to be served, he took in the other members of his family. Three of Gundar's wives were there, including Mara. Several of his half-brothers were there as well.

"You're starting with the sword master today, aren't you?" Boris, almost a year older than Sasha, whispered across the table to him.

Sasha nodded, his mouth too full to answer.

"I'll be there, too. Before we go, let's slip down to the market and watch for a bit."

Sasha frowned. Of all his many half-brothers, Boris was the only one who he truly got along with. And it would be great fun to go down to the Market. People from all over the world would be there, with their strange clothes and languages. There would be booths selling all sorts of exotic delicacies and trinkets. But if Father expected him to be somewhere - maybe it would be better to ask. He would have to wait, though, until Father spoke to him first.

As the meal dragged on, the knot of anxiety grew in Sasha's stomach. Surely Father didn't request him here just so he could ignore him. One by one, Gundar dismissed his wives and then his older sons until at last it was just Boris and Sasha.

"Anxious about something Sasha?" Gundar said after studying his son for a moment.

"No, Father. I mean, I was just wondering," Sasha paused, taking a deep breath. Father hated rambling. "Boris and I would like to go down to the Market this morning, if that is acceptable to you, Father."

Gundar nodded thoughtfully, his hand on his chin.

"Is this true, Boris?"

"Yes, Father."

"I had intended for you both to begin training today. You've had ten years to play and enjoy yourselves. You'll only have five to learn what it is to be a warrior." He paused, watching them carefully as his words registered. Then he smiled slightly. "However, I suppose one more morning would not hurt. It is, after all, opening day. I don't intend to miss it myself."

"Thank you, Father," they said simultaneously.

"You know, it is a poor Market this year compared to the past. You both would do well to learn all you can. I should hate for such poor raids to take place under your leadership someday."

That would be a few years yet, thought Sasha. He did not miss the threat in Father's words, though. When Gundar waved a hand to dismiss them, he and Boris bowed quickly and left the room.

"Why did you have to ask?" Boris dug his elbow into Sasha's side as they raced down the hallway.

"I just got invited back to this, there's no way I'm going to lose it doing something stupid with you."

"You'd better be glad he said yes, because if he didn't, I would have killed you for messing up my day."

Sasha only laughed.

Outside, the entire face of the town had changed overnight. Crowds gathered around the many stands that dotted the marketplace. It was the mixture of languages that always fascinated Sasha, and even now, as he and Boris made their way through the crowded streets, his ears worked to single out the different speeches and his mind tried to make sense of the sounds. One sound penetrated all the others and worked its way deep inside of him. It took longer than he realized to place. Someone was calling his name.

He stood on his toes, trying to see above the mass of people filling the street. He still couldn't see, but he knew what direction it was coming from.

"Come on, Boris." Sasha pushed his way through, heading toward the auction block.

The crowd in front thinned out enough for Sasha to finally see who it was calling him. His heart skipped a beat and the blood drained from his face. It was Agathe. And she was in the slave pen.

"Sasha, help me!" Her voice carried across the short distance, cutting through the noise of the crowd.

Without thinking, Sasha ran towards her, grabbing her extended hand.

"What happened?"

"I don't know. I don't know what I did. Oh, Sasha, I don't want to go through this. Please. Help me." Agathe's eyes were red from crying, and new tears filled them now as she clung to her younger brother.

"Sasha, what are you doing?" Boris hissed in his ear. "If Father sees this..."

"No, please, Sasha. Don't leave me. Don't. Talk to Father. Tell him I'm sorry for whatever I did." With each word, Agathe's hysteria grew.

Sasha bit down on his lip, his eyes darting back and forth searching for some sign of Father. Boris was right. If Father saw him with Agathe after he had decided she was worthless, he would end up in the same place.

"I'm sorry, Agathe, I can't help." His jaw hardened and he worked his arm free of her clutching grasp. For a moment, he met his sister's eyes, and he knew why she was there. Agathe had had the audacity to grow up to look like Mother, and Father didn't want the reminder.

Walking away from the slave pen, Sasha pressed his hands to his ears, trying hopelessly to block out his sister's cries. Somehow the fun of the Spring Market and the anticipation of starting training with the sword master was lost. He left Boris behind him and made his way to the archery range where he had spent so many hours.

This was all Mother's fault, Sasha thought as he picked up his bow. If she had tried harder, if she had done whatever it was that Father wanted her to do, none of this would have happened. He would not have had to spend so much time trying to get back in Father's presence, Agathe would not be punished for resembling her offending parent, they could all have been living quite happily together.

"Why?" The word tore out of him with as much ferocity as the arrow left the bowstring. The only answer was a dull thud.

Chapter 2

HOW MUCH LONGER DO WE HAVE TO wait?" Ophelia shifted her legs beneath her, trying to find a more comfortable bed of twigs and leaves to sit on.

"Shhh. Stop asking, or she'll hear us." Meredith did not waste so much as a glance at her sister. Instead, her dark brown eyes remained glued to the door of a stone cottage standing in the clearing. She ignored the heavy sigh Ophelia let out for her benefit. For several minutes, they waited in silence.

"Did you ask Mother about this?" Ophelia squirmed again and let her gaze follow a butterfly darting here and there about her.

"No."

"We're going to get in trouble."

"I asked Father," Meredith said.

Ophelia's face darkened with suspicion. "Did you ask him when he was busy?"

This time, Meredith did not answer.

"You did! We're going to be in trouble," Ophelia repeated, her frown deepening.

Meredith finally turned to look at her sister, an argument already rising in her throat. It was just like Ophelia to be worried about getting into a little trouble. She was always so careful about those things. But Meredith had asked Father. It wasn't her fault he had been too deep in his work to give proper consideration to her request. At least, it mostly wasn't her fault. Even

9

as she prepared to argue otherwise, Meredith was conscious of the fact that she had followed Father around for half the morning, waiting for the right amount of distraction to lay her case before him. And she had not asked directly about coming here. It was a foolproof method of getting what she wanted, one that never worked the same on Mother. Even so, she was prepared to defend herself, but the opportunity was lost. A creaking sound came from the door of the cottage, and Meredith's full attention was given back to the task at hand. This was why she was here, and she couldn't miss a moment of it.

"Shhh," Meredith put her finger to her lip. "She's coming."

With the endless boredom gone, Ophelia sat up and peered through the leafy branches she was hiding behind. From the doorway of the cottage, a strange figure emerged. Dressed in a wild assortment of colors that shimmered and shifted constantly with the movement of walking, the figure made their way down the short stone path that led to the place that had first piqued Meredith's interest.

It was a rectangle of ground, spacious, but not large enough to contain any sizable animal such as a cow or horse. Around the entire perimeter rose a high, wooden fence, quite solid. It successfully hid whatever was inside and that's what bothered Meredith. The woman reached the gate and, pulling a key from somewhere inside her vibrant, flowing garments, unlocked the gate and slipped inside.

Meredith and Ophelia let out a breath simultaneously.

"See? I told you something strange is going on," Meredith said, turning to Ophelia.

"I don't know. Nothing looks strange to me, aside from the way she dresses." Ophelia bit down on her lip. "What's inside there, anyway?"

"That's just it. No one knows. I heard Father telling Mother that there was something going on here."

"He said that?"

"Well, not quite like that, but, yes, something along those lines. I mean, look at it. Why would you build a wall like that if you weren't trying to hide something? Come on, let's see if we can get a look inside the wall."

Meredith crawled out from behind the bush that hid her from view. Keeping her attention on the gate, she crept forward, inching her way toward the far side of the walled off plot of land.

It was not until she reached the relative safety of the wall that she chanced a look behind her. Ophelia was nowhere to be seen in the open space between the woods and the wall. Meredith's face tightened into a scowl. Of course, Ophelia had not come. She was probably too scared to. Ophelia was too scared to do most things, but she still followed her twin around, most of the time.

Hidden from the gate, should it be reopened suddenly, Meredith searched the wall for a crack to peek through. She was not long in finding one. Down on her knees, with one eye pressed against the rough wooden slats, she got her first look inside the mysterious place. Meredith was not quite sure what she expected to see inside the walls, but she was sure it was not a garden. A garden was just plain boring. Everyone had one they grew to provide fresh food for meals.

For a second, Meredith hovered between disappointment and anger. She had risked being in trouble so that she could be here and all there was to see was a garden. Then a sound reached her ears. It was the woman. She was speaking. No, she was singing. Meredith cocked her head, trying to make sense of the lilting words that drifted towards her. The woman's voice was rich, and melodious, but try as she might, Meredith could not understand the words. Nor was she familiar with the tune.

"What's going on?"

Ophelia's voice in her ear made Meredith jump and emit the tiniest squeal of surprise. Horrified, Meredith clapped a hand over her mouth and peered inside the wall again, searching this time for some sign that the strange woman had heard her. The singing voice continued, and Meredith relaxed a little. The woman had not heard her. Her presence remained a secret.

A snuffling, rustling sound stole her momentary relief. A small, reddish-brown animal with a triangular face, and pointed ears that stood straight up from its head made its way across the garden on three feet, its nose twitching incessantly. Meredith silently willed it to go away, but the animal continued straight to the crack in the wall. When it was only a few feet away, the red animal let loose a series of short barks.

The woman, whose back had been toward Meredith, finally turned and looked. Meredith knew she should get up and run, but her legs had turned to lead. She felt Ophelia's hand on her arm, pulling her, but was powerless to go along, and all the while the woman was getting closer and closer. So was the strange animal. It had reached the wall and was now scratching at the very spot Meredith and Ophelia were hiding behind.

A series of unintelligible words came from the woman as she too reached the wall and knelt next to the animal. Her tone was soothing, and the animal's frantic clawing slowed but did not cease.

"Come on," Ophelia hissed in Meredith's ear at last, breaking whatever spell held her frozen in place and the two sprinted to the shelter of the nearby trees.

Meredith did not look back until the shadow of the trees was safely over them. When she did, her heart sank. There, standing just outside the gate and watching them was the woman, but worse still, was the streak of reddish-brown that was quickly catching up to them. With a shriek, both girls took off again.

"I told you this was a bad idea," Ophelia panted in her ear.

"Shut up. Climb a tree."

"What?"

"Climb!" Meredith reinforced her words by reaching for a low hanging branch above her head and pulling herself off the ground, not bothering to see if Ophelia followed her lead. Hand over hand she pulled herself further up into the safety of the tree. Whatever the animal was chasing them, she could only pray it did not climb. Several feet off the ground, Meredith paused and looked around. Ophelia had listened and was perched in a nearby tree, clinging to the trunk with her arms. Meredith grinned despite the situation. Seeing Ophelia up so high was a rare sight. She preferred to keep her feet solidly on the ground.

A squealing sound brought Meredith's gaze to the ground beneath her where the small red animal circled the tree, jumping up and down trying to reach her dangling feet. She had to get higher. Raising her hand, expecting to grab a solid branch above her head, Meredith screamed when instead a cool, squirming rope slid through her fingers and down her arm. Snake. Without a second thought, Meredith released her tenuous hold on the tree and crashed to the ground.

Gasping for the breath that had been knocked out of her, Meredith could not give voice to the cry that rose in her throat as the triangular, red face, with its wet black nose loomed into view. The squealing grew louder, and Meredith tried to push it away with her hands.

Seconds ticked by as Meredith lay on the ground beneath the tree trying to figure out what had happened to the animal. There had been a voice, she was sure of it, although she could not understand the words spoken. That voice had called the animal. And the animal had listened. If it had been a dog, Meredith could understand. After all, their own dog, Howler, would answer to his name. But that animal wasn't a dog.

"Was there a snake?" Ophelia's face came into view, her eyes dancing with amusement.

"No. I just fell." Meredith pushed herself up and attempted to regain her composure and dignity.

"Whatever. There was a snake. You just don't want to admit you're scared of them."

"I'm not scared of snakes. I don't like them. There's a big difference between disliking something and being afraid of it. And you're one to talk. I saw the way you were clinging to that tree, afraid of falling."

Ophelia shrugged.

"You're bleeding."

"What?"

"Where you tore your shirt, you're bleeding," Ophelia answered.

Meredith let out a small groan and twisted her head around to see her shoulder. Sure enough, a gaping tear was there, and beneath it, a trickle of blood. She must have caught a branch on her way down.

"Mother is going to kill me," Meredith said under her breath. The bloody shoulder she could have hidden well enough, but the torn shirt - that mother would spot right away.

"What do you suppose that was all about?" Ophelia turned to look back in the direction they had just run from.

Meredith did not answer right away. She stood up, still turning her head to try to get a better glimpse of her shoulder. There was only one thing that could be going on. Or two. Meredith was certain of it. She leaned in close to Ophelia, meeting her twin's matching dark eyes, and whispered.

"I think...I think she's a spy." Her voice dropped even lower on the last word, as though saying it would bring the sudden wrath of their strange neighbor down upon her. "Or a..."

"Witch," Ophelia finished, and Meredith nodded.

"You heard her, didn't you?"

"Yes."

"And that strange animal. She called it, and it listened," Meredith said.

"And the way she was dressed. She isn't like us at all."

"Not at all. I wonder if anyone else has noticed."

"Probably not."

"Then we have to be careful. And we have to find out more. She could be dangerous to everyone. What if she's spying on us right now?"

Both girls' eyes darted around, searching for some sign of the mysterious person. A shiver ran down Meredith's spine as a light breeze sent a whispering rustle through the trees. It could be... perhaps it was... it had to be someone moving through the trees, creeping up on them, watching them, listening to every word her and Ophelia said. Gripping her twin's hand in her own, Meredith bolted towards home.

The pain in her shoulder, and the subsequent tear in her clothing, was all but forgotten by the time Meredith, still pulling Ophelia along behind her, came within sight of the spacious clearing that contained her home. Stepping out into the open meadow gave her enough courage to stop and look behind her for the first time since taking off. If someone had been following them, they were not in sight. That didn't mean they weren't there, Meredith reminded herself, it just meant that they were good at hiding. And that seemed like something the strange woman would be good at.

"Look, Father's just coming home," Ophelia said, pointing to the far side of the clearing. "Come on."

"Wait, Phelie. Maybe we should wait."

"Why?" Ophelia turned to face her sister, wariness creeping into her eyes. "You didn't really ask him, did you?"

"I did too. I just...," Meredith bit down on her lip. "I think it's better if we wait."

"Too late." Ophelia caught Father's eye and waved her hand in greeting. "I shouldn't have let you talk me into going with you."

"I told you I asked. He said we could go to the creek."

"But we weren't at the creek." Ophelia started toward the house.

"No. But, if we don't say anything, he'll never know. And it doesn't matter, anyway. We didn't cause any trouble..."

"Aside from that." Ophelia glanced pointedly at the tear in Meredith's shirt.

"Well, yes, aside from that. But honestly, that could have happened anywhere. I could have slipped on a rock in the creek and torn it or climbed a tree by the creek and torn it, or anything. Please, Phelie, just don't say anything at all about where we were. We're the only people who know about that woman. If Father knows what we're doing, he'll stop us and no one will be watching her, and then who knows what kind of terrible things she could do to everybody."

Ophelia hesitated; her face screwed up in thought. Finally, she shrugged.

"Alright. I guess it doesn't hurt anyone. I won't tell. It'll be our secret."

It was the last in a long line of secrets the girls had shared since before they could talk. If there was one thing, they were good at together as twins it was keeping each other's secrets. Relieved, Meredith fell into step with her sister. Now the only hurdle left to cross was her bleeding shoulder and torn shirt. Maybe if she slipped in quietly enough and went straight to the room Ophelia and her shared with Priscilla, she could change and wash the blood away. And if she tried to be unusually kind to Ophelia, she might get her to stitch the tear back up and Mother would never notice. It would never work if she did it, her stitching was horrific.

Meredith's hopes for a quick escape were dashed when Mother stood facing the door as she, and Ophelia came in.

"Where have you two been?" Mother asked. "And what happened to you, Meri?"

Meredith caught Ophelia's gaze in her peripheral and heard the quick intake of breath from her sister.

"Oh, we were out playing, and I fell," she answered airily and took a step toward her bedroom door.

"Where were you playing?"

Again, there was the sharp inhale from Ophelia, and Meredith could feel her sister stiffen slightly.

"By the creek. Father said we could." She looked over to where Father was just now coming in from the barn.

"What did I say?"

"That Phelie and I could go play down by the creek. I asked you this morning. Remember?"

"Was I busy?"

As soon as the words left Father's mouth, Meredith sensed Ophelia's glare boring through her. She could almost hear the "I knew it" coming from her twin.

"Maybe. You were in the barn."

Meredith looked down at her feet, wishing with all her heart that she had climbed through her bedroom window and cleaned up before she had to have this conversation. Mother was upset by the torn shirt, and Father was upset that she had asked him when he wasn't actually paying attention to her request. At least, she had convinced Ophelia not to talk about where they had really been. That would make everything so much worse.

"Go, change into something that's not ripped up. You're going to have to stitch that back up this evening after dinner. And you, Phelie, watch Nora and Adel while I finish up supper." Mother waved them off and Meredith wasted no time in getting to her room.

Meredith dawdled for as long as she could, dragging out each step to the absolute longest. If she waited long enough before leaving her room, supper would be ready, and the moment of displeasure would be gone. Father would be the first to forget it. He always was. Mother would eventually move on too, especially if she was particularly helpful throughout the evening. Maybe she would volunteer to watch Elenora and Adelaide for a while, or wash up all the dishes, or something, anything that would bring her back into Mother's good graces.

Chapter 3

A S HUNGRY AS MEREDITH WAS, the food on her plate sat mostly untouched. She pushed it back and forth with her fork, wondering why she could not work up the appetite to eat, but every time she tried to swallow, a lump stuck in her throat. Her attention was at last diverted by the sound of Mother's voice from the now lukewarm food in front of her.

"Hamo, I almost forgot. This was dropped off for you earlier today." Mother had risen from the table and now returned with an envelope in her hand. Meredith squinted, trying to decipher the seal that closed it as Mother handed it to Father.

"Who brought it?"

"A King's courier."

"A King's courier," Father repeated the words under his breath, staring at the envelope in his hand.

"What is it? Did the king actually write something to you?" Ophelia asked.

Father did not answer right away, and Meredith knew from the look on his face that he was lost in thought. It was the expression she waited for when she needed to ask him something that would normally be answered with a no.

"Whatever it is, it's not written or addressed to any of you. Phelie, help Nora finish up. Meredith, why aren't you eating? Is something wrong?"

Meredith shook her head, staring once again at the food in front of her. She could not explain why she wasn't eating. Everyone else was already finished and Priscilla was already clearing away the dishes.

"What were you and Phelie playing at the creek?" Father broke into her reverie.

"Uh...we were just...you know, playing." Meredith glanced up in time to catch a very puzzled and perhaps even a slightly disappointed look from Father, and the heaviness in her chest grew. She squirmed in her chair. "I don't remember."

"It must have been quite entertaining. Did you see anyone while you were there?" Father was still looking at her, watching her.

"No. It was just me and Phelie."

"I see." Father held her gaze a moment longer before pushing away from the table and disappearing into their bedroom.

"Meri, help clean up and then we'll fix your shirt," Mother called from the kitchen.

Meredith's face twisted in a mixture of concentration and disgust as she bent over the torn shirt later that evening. Father had built the fire up so that there was more than enough light, but all the light in the world could not make Meredith a good seamstress or a happy one.

All her sisters were already in bed. She should be too, except that Mother was adamant that the stitches be neat and small. If it had been any other night, or if it had been for any other reason, Meredith would have been thrilled to be the only one allowed up with Father and Mother. Tonight, however, she couldn't enjoy one moment of it. It was not fair that Mother insisted on perfection. After all, it was Meredith who had to wear the shirt, not Mother. And it certainly didn't bother Meredith if the edges didn't line up properly, or the stitching were uneven and sloppy. Without looking up from her work, she caught snatches of her parents' conversation.

"I'm not saying you should do it, Hamo, I'm just saying you should think about it. Don't turn him down right away."

"What would be the point? If I turn him down now or wait a week. I don't want any part of it."

It wasn't often that Meredith heard her parents disagree and she began to follow the conversation with new interest. It was about the letter, of that she was sure. And she would be the first to know about it out of all her sisters, even Ophelia.

"But you never know what might come of something like this. It's not like it's a secret to the king how you feel about the war. Maybe he's asking you because that's the opinion he's looking for."

"Funny, isn't it? The law says the king can't declare war without the support of the war council, and yet the king is the one who decides who sits on that council."

"Which is why I think you would be good for it." Mother picked up her own sewing from the basket she kept near the fireplace. "Meredith, make your stitches smaller. Those will never hold."

Meredith made a face without looking up. Truth be told, the quality of her stitches matched exactly the amount of attention she had turned toward her parents. She anxiously awaited Father's reply, but he didn't seem to be in any hurry. From the bedroom, Adelaide began to cry.

"Just promise me you'll actually think about it," Mother said as she got up and disappeared into the darkened room.

Meredith's brow creased even deeper as she neared the end. She heard Father get up as well and startled when he sat down next to her. Her heart quickened and the fabric between her fingers blurred.

"Meri?"

"Yes?" Meredith didn't look up, but bit down on her lower lip, surprised to find it quivering.

"Where did you take Phelie today?"

"I didn't take her anywhere, she just decided to come along," Meredith answered, avoiding his question as best she could.

"She goes wherever you suggest, and you know that. But you didn't answer me."

"We went to the creek," Meredith said, trying hard to keep the tremor out of her voice.

"Do you know who else was at the creek?"

"I told you already, there wasn't anybody else there. We were by ourselves."

"I was."

The fabric in her hands swam in front of her eyes and a small dark spot appeared where a single tear fell. Meredith gave up all attempts at stitching and twisted the cloth about in her hands. She could not see to sew, anyway, with the pool of tears in her eyes.

"Since you didn't go to the creek, where did you go?"

"We went to the edge," Meredith could barely get the words out. "By the house where that woman moved last winter."

"Why?"

There didn't seem to be any point in not telling Father why they were there, not now that her lie was discovered. Bit by bit, Meredith confessed the reason for her and Ophelia's trip to the edge of the woods. When she finished speaking, Father didn't say anything. Meredith was certain he was very, very angry and that was a terrifying thing, because Father so very rarely got angry.

"I'm sorry, Father," Meredith whispered when she could no longer bear the silence.

"What are you sorry for? Lying, or getting caught?"

"I don't know. Both?"

"Go to bed, Meri. We'll talk about it in the morning."

Meredith set aside her sewing and made her way to bed, closing the door behind her just as Mother was returning from putting Adelaide back to bed.

"What was that about?"

"Edith, do you know anything about that woman who moved into that empty cabin?"

"Not really. She's not from around here, I don't think. Why?" Edith glanced quizzically at the hint of smile on her husband's face.

"Meri and Phelie think she is a spy, or a witch."

"Do they? I wonder what gave them the idea. I can't say I really blame them, though. I used to believe that the old man who rented a room above our shop was the ghost of a man who was beheaded a hundred years ago."

"Really? You thought that?"

"Absolutely. And no one could convince me that I was wrong."

"How old were you?"

"A whole year older than the girls. And very wise for my ten years. I was the only one who understood what that man really was, and no one would listen to me." Edith laughed softly at the memory. "Hamo, I think we should invite the 'spy' over to supper some night. And I think Meri and Phelie should come with me to give her the invitation."

Chapter 4

MEREDITH WASHED THE LAST dish from breakfast slowly. She was in no hurry to finish up the morning's chores and continue last night's conversation with Father. He was still in the house, probably waiting for her.

"Meri, hurry up. You're coming with me this morning. You too, Phelie," Mother called out from her room. Meredith and Ophelia exchanged a curious glance. It was unexpected, but to Meredith it was a relief. If she was going somewhere with Mother, it would give Father just that much more time to forget about how she had lied to him.

"Where are we going?" Ophelia asked when they started out the door.

"Visiting."

"Who are we visiting?" Ophelia asked again.

Meredith stared at the dirt path beneath her feet. She had a horrible feeling she knew exactly who they would be visiting, and any excitement or relief she had experienced earlier quickly dissipated. She was too lost in her own thoughts to catch Mother's answer, but she didn't really need it anyway. With every step they took, it became more obvious where they were going. Meredith searched Mother's face, hoping for some clue as to why they were making this trip. It seemed more than coincidence that Mother should choose to visit their new neighbor today, right after Meredith's confession to Father about spying on her. Her only relief was that the woman had no idea who Ophelia and her were. There was little chance of her connecting two well-mannered little girls to whoever was spying on her a day ago.

Meredith heard Ophelia let out a little gasp as the stone cottage came into view. Falling behind Mother, she dug her fingers into Meredith's arm.

"Did you tell them about her?"

"I had to," Meredith answered defensively.

"This is going to be awful. Do you think she knows?"

Meredith shook her head quickly as they reached the door and Mother knocked on it. Meredith could hear the woman inside singing, the string of words still completely unintelligible to her. The singing stopped at the sound of Mother's knock and Meredith's heart rose to her throat as she heard footsteps crossing the house and coming to the door.

"She didn't really see us," Meredith whispered as much to reassure herself as her sister. She kept her head bowed; her eyes squeezed shut. If this woman really was a witch, or a spy, they were in grave danger and Mother probably had no idea. Meredith twisted her fingers, silently hoping that nothing bad happened.

"Meredith?" Mother's chiding voice brought her to her senses. "This is our new neighbor, Taliea."

Meredith looked up at the first time and found herself staring into the darkest eyes she had ever seen. They were almost black, and they were happy, pretty eyes, brought to life by the vibrant colors she wore. Not at all what she would have expected a witch to have. In fact, the woman's whole face radiated happiness. If she were a spy, or some other dangerous person, she was good at hiding it. Now she was stepping aside, inviting them into her home. Mother and Ophelia went in right away, but Meredith hung back a little, stepping only barely into the doorway.

"You're not from here, are you?" Meredith asked abruptly, ignoring Mother's startled face. Everything about the woman spoke of kindness and Meredith had a hard time keeping up her suspicion.

"No, I'm not. I come from across the sea. It's very different there, much hotter, and less green." Taliea's voice was as rich in speaking as it was in singing, and although she spoke clearly, a hint of an accent clung to her words.

"You traveled all this way? Did it take you a long time?" Ophelia looked at her with new wonder.

"We were sailing for almost a month. Would you like to see something from where I come from?"

"Oh, yes. Please," Ophelia answered.

"Come, it's out in my garden." Taliea led the way out a back door and down the stone path that led to the walled off garden Meredith had spied on just the day before.

Reluctant as she was, Meredith was curious to see inside the garden, to actually see, not just peek through a tiny sliver of a crack. Ophelia flashed her a quick grin as Taliea pulled out the same key they had seen the day before and unlocked the gate.

What Meredith had been able to see through the crack had hardly done the place justice. Meredith, her suspicions forgotten in the moment, took in the kaleidoscope of colors that filled seemingly every inch of the place. It reminded her of the vibrant, colorful, shiny clothes the woman was wearing. And the fragrance! She drew in a deep breath, inhaling the scents of a hundred different flowers. Green ivies clung to the walls and trellises. Two small trees grew in the center, their branches weighted heavily with fruit. Stone pathways divided the space into tidy sections. It was the most pristine, enchanting garden Meredith had ever seen, nothing like their own vegetable garden.

"This is beautiful! What do you do with all of these?" Ophelia said.

"I use them. Believe it or not, every single plant in here has a purpose. I make medicines from them. I'm an apothecary of sorts."

"Really?" Meredith bent down to run a finger over the velvety petal of a deep purple flower. "What can you make with this one?"

"That one," Taliea knelt next to Meredith, "That one I do not use the flower of, but the leaves make a wonderful tea that helps bring down fevers."

"What's an apothecary?"

"Someone who makes medicines. Although, I also use them."

"You help sick people?"

"Sick people, hurt people. I try to help anyone I can. Healing is its own sort of magic, isn't it?" Taliea met Meredith's eyes with a knowing smile, and Meredith felt the blood rush to her face. But there was something about Taliea that made it hard for Meredith to stay embarrassed. With an abrupt change of heart, Meredith decided she liked Taliea.

For the better part of the morning, Ophelia and Meredith wandered about the garden, pointing to various plants and asking their use. It wasn't until Mother called to them that Meredith remembered. She was supposed to be suspicious of this woman. Almost instantly, she pushed the thought away. A witch or a spy could not possibly be as nice as Taliea had been, showing the girls around and patiently answering their questions. Maybe she wasn't a bad person after all.

"You will be coming tonight then?" Mother turned to ask Taliea as they prepared to leave.

"Of course. And if either of you girls ever feel like doing a bit of extra gardening, I would love to have you over again. I'm sure Perseus would too."

"Perseus?" the girls spoke in unison.

"Yes. You met him before, I think. I'm afraid he might have scared you, although he is really quite harmless."

Meredith felt the blood drain from her face. She knew. Taliea knew. All this time, she had known. Biting her lip, she dared a look at the woman. Taliea met her eyes with a smile, and Meredith breathed a sigh of relief. She wasn't angry.

26

Chapter 5

W HY DO YOU HAVE TO go away?" Meredith's somber brown eyes regarded Father's.

"I told you, Meri, King Darien needs me."

"Not as much as we do," Priscilla chimed in.

"You never had to go anywhere before."

"You're right, Phelie. This time is different." Hamo looked up to where Edith was standing behind the girls, Adelaide in her arms. "Told you this was a bad idea."

"No, it's not. Father won't be gone that long, girls. And he won't even be that far away." Edith smiled tightly and set Adelaide down. With her arms around Hamo she whispered, "Seriously, don't be gone long. And make them stop fighting."

"I don't know that both of those things can happen."

"Just try. Enough people have died. It needs to end."

"Al will stop by and let you know if I'm going to have to stay longer than a week. Girls, be good for your mother." Meredith dropped her eyes when he looked pointedly at her. It wasn't like she needed to be reminded. After all, it was only last week when she had been in trouble for lying about where she and Phelie had been. She would be good for at least a while.

Hamo joined Aldrid, and together they rode down the dirt path into the woods.

"I have to be honest; I can't believe you're actually doing this," Aldrid was the first to break the silence. "I thought you hated being in town and having anything to do with the war.

"I do."

"So, why are you doing it again?"

"Edith's right. Darien's reasonable. If enough people around him want to end the war, he just might do it."

"You'll have to be awfully good at convincing the other councilmembers. Most of them profit from the war. They're not going to want it to end. But then, you are pretty convincing." Al shot his older brother a grin.

"What's that supposed to mean?"

"You talked Edith into marrying you, and that could not have been easy."

"You're just jealous, because you haven't had any luck with that."

"Haven't tried," Al retorted.

A day's ride brought them within sight of Bren, the towers of the castle rising high above the rest of the town.

"I take it you get to stay there," Aldrid gestured toward the castle as they rode through the streets, "while I have to find a room at some shabby inn that's going to charge me way too much money."

"I could always ask if they have room. If the old magistrate were still around, I imagine he would find a place for you."

"No thanks. I'll see if Sabina wants a visit instead." Aldrid waved briefly before turning down a narrow road.

Hamo continued on alone, reaching the castle gate just as the sun was sinking in the west. He hesitated, steeling himself against the wave of memories he knew would come. It had been ten years since he had been inside this place, and many years before that it had been his home. The memories weren't all bad, but they were overwhelming. It was enough for him to question his own sanity in returning to this place.

A stable hand came hurrying forward, taking the reins of his horse from him. A rather harried looking middle-aged man came out of a set of doors to meet him. The new secretary, Jarvis. Hamo missed Geoffrey a little. He had been as much a part of the castle as the front gate when Hamo was growing up there. Hamo smiled to himself as he thought about the way the old secretary moved about, always in a hurry, always late.

"Mr. Serbon, the King is waiting for you. If you would be so good as to follow me," the secretary said and motioned for Hamo to accompany him.

Hamo assumed they were headed to the throne room, where the king did most of his business, or at the very least, the council room. It was neither of those places. He was surprised when the secretary led him instead into the dining hall. There, surrounded by stacks of paper and looking about ten years older than the last time Hamo had seen him, was King Darien.

"Oh good, you came. I wasn't sure you would, you know. Please come in and have a seat."

Hamo hid a quick smile. Darien was nothing like his father. Then, neither was he.

"To be honest, I wasn't going to come. I'd much prefer to stay home, away from people, and mind my own business. It was Edith's idea for me to come."

"I'm glad you did. You see, Hamo, I want to end the war." Darien shuffled a few of the papers in front of him, sliding them off to the side. "Frankly, I'm sick of it. But I need people in the Council that want to end it too. Right now, everyone on the Council are men my father appointed. They profit from the war. They have no interest in ending it."

"Probably because they've never had to actually fight."

"That'd be an idea, wouldn't it? I imagine that would bring about a very hasty end."

"Couldn't you just declare it over? You're the king."

"I wish it were that simple. Unfortunately," Darien sighed, "while I cannot go to war without the Council's permission, I also cannot end a war without their permission. That's why I'm changing who's on the Council. It's been a slow process, since those men are only appointed every five years, but it's high time we put an end to this thing."

"I think I can safely promise you that I will always vote to end it."

"I'm counting on it. And while you're at it, maybe you can convince some of the others."

Chapter 6

MEREDITH SAT UP IN HER BED, taking in the sounds all around her. Next to her, Ophelia's even breathing indicated that she was still asleep. Something had awakened her, though, and she was trying to guess what it was. A murmur of voices came from the other side of the wall - her parents. Meredith waited until she heard the front door open and shut softly, and then pushed the covers off of herself.

Tiptoeing quietly past Priscilla's bed, she cracked their door enough to see that the front room was empty. Adelaide was crying, and Meredith could hear Mother quietening her. Silently, she grabbed a blanket from her bed and wrapped it about herself before squeezing out of the narrowly opened door.

Groping her way across the dark floor to the front door, Meredith lifted the latch and stepped out into the cool night, closing the door softly behind her.

"Meri, what are you doing?" Father's voice so close to her made her jump. He was sitting on the front steps.

"I couldn't sleep. And I wanted to check on Stitch. I wanted to see if the medicine worked."

"I'm sure your cat is fine. Go back to bed, Meri. You can check on her in the morning."

"But I can't sleep. Can I sit out here with you?" Meredith sat down next to him without waiting for an answer and rested her head on his shoulder. She was sure it was Father that had woken her up. Mother told her once, when she asked why Father had such bad dreams, that it was because bad people had done terrible things to him many years ago. Meredith had a hard time believing anyone would do anything terrible to Father. "Can you not sleep either?"

"No, apparently not."

"Did you have a bad dream?" Meredith stifled a yawn.

"It's nothing you need to worry about."

"What was his name? The man who saved you."

Father didn't answer for a long time, long enough for Meredith's eyelids to start to droop.

"Drogo," Father whispered the name.

"What happened to him? Will you ever see him again?"

"I don't know. As old as he was, he could very well be dead now. Even if he's not, I doubt I'll ever see him again. I have no desire to go back there."

"I wonder if he knows."

"Knows what?"

"That he kind of saved all of us when he saved you. I bet it would make him happy to know that."

"He did, didn't he?" Father met her eyes and smiled. "Let's go check on that cat, and then you need to go back to bed."

They stood up together and Meredith slipped her hand into Father's while using the other one to hold the blanket tightly around her. Normally, she feared the dark, but there was a full moon tonight, and Father was with her.

"Taliea says I'm getting good at mixing medicines and taking care of the plants. She says that someday I could be just like her and help lots of people."

"You spend enough time over there, you ought to be getting good at something. Did you give Stitch some of your medicine?"

"Yes, but only after Taliea stitched him back up."

"Is that why you called him Stitch?"

Meredith nodded.

"You know, Meri, medicine doesn't always work."

"I know. But it will this time," Meredith said. "I want it to."

"That's not exactly how it works."

Father lit the lantern hanging up just inside the barn door and Meredith followed its circle of light all the way to the wooden crate that she had so carefully prepared for her latest patient. She had wanted to bring Stitch into the house, certain that would give him the best chance of surviving, but Mother had refused. Now, as the light shined down on the orange cat, a thrill of elation went through Meredith. He was moving, which meant he wasn't dead.

"You saved that?" Father asked, a look of doubt and disbelief written on his face.

The cat was hideous, missing an eye and half an ear. Even without his most recent injuries, it was clear from the scars that crisscrossed his body that he was the veteran of many fights.

"Of course. He's cute, isn't he? And he's still alive. I told you the medicine would work."

"Just make sure Howler doesn't find him, or the medicine won't stand a chance. Come on, let's go to bed."

Chapter 7

SASHA FOUGHT TO KEEP HIS eyes open, waiting until he heard Zena's rhythmic breathing from her mat at the foot of his bed. It did not usually take the old woman long to fall asleep. Her days were long and hard, serving not only Sasha, but anyone else in Chief Gundar's house who commanded her. Tonight, however, Sasha was beginning to wonder if she would ever fall asleep.

At long last, a soft snore told him that the coast was clear. Climbing out of bed with the greatest care, lest it should creak and awaken the slave woman, Sasha felt around for the clothes he had told Zena to lay out earlier. Almost tripping over himself trying to be quiet, Sasha threw his clothes on, making sure his dagger hung from his belt. Reaching the door, he groped for his bow and the quiver of arrows he had placed against the wall. Slinging both over his shoulder, he stepped out into the hallway.

"Finally. I thought you changed your mind," a voice whispered out of the darkness.

"Shh...I had to wait. Come on, Boris."

The two boys crept down the hallway, Sasha noting the boards that creaked and groaned beneath Boris' weight and trying to avoid them himself. It wasn't likely that anyone else was still awake, but it couldn't hurt to be careful.

Once outside, the full moon lit the yard and the sprawling town in a pale, ghostly light. A shiver ran down Sasha's back.

"Are you ready to do this?" Boris glanced back at him, a nervous grin on his face.

"Are you? Bet I'll be the first to get one."

"Whatever." Boris waved an impatient hand at him and continued.

The wooden wall that surrounded the town loomed ahead. There was a gate, but that was not where the boys were headed. Part of the fun of a wolf hunt was sneaking out and you couldn't very well sneak out of the gate. Boris reached the wall first and started testing for a good handhold. Sasha, determined to stay ahead of his slightly older half-brother, had spent most of the previous afternoon finding just the perfect spot to begin his climb. Gripping the knot of wood high above his head, he started up.

"Wait for me," Sasha heard Boris call out to him in a hoarse whisper as he dropped lightly to the snowy ground on the other side. So much for the night guards, Sasha thought with a smirk. Getting out had been easy. Boris hit the ground next to him, coming down a lot harder than Sasha had, and causing a puff of snow to fly up.

"So, where are we going from here?"

"Let's head that way. I heard one of the clansmen telling Father that a pack was hunting around there." Sasha pointed toward the dark side of a mountain.

"You brought your bow?" Boris fell in behind Sasha and noticed for the first time the weapons he chose.

"Why not? There's no rule about how you kill your first wolf, just that you have to kill one."

"But that's kind of cheating. I have to actually get close to get mine."

"Not if you throw your axe instead. But I guess you haven't practiced that."

The mountain grew larger with every step and the ground began to rise beneath their feet. Sasha cast one last look back at the sleeping town. A smile darted across his face. Tonight, he and Boris would prove that the last two years of their training hadn't been a waste. They would take their first step into manhood. His smile faded as he caught sight of a shadow moving across the ground, away from the wall.

"Boris," he grabbed his brother's arm, "look. Something's following us."

Boris squinted into the darkness for a second before his eyes caught sight of it too.

"Or someone. That's a person."

"Who else would be sneaking out?" Sasha knew they were the only two in their year group who had not completed a wolf hunt. And he could not think of another good reason to be sneaking out of town.

"Let's get closer."

"What? Are you crazy? What if it's someone dangerous? It could be a spy, or a thief, or anybody."

"You're scared?" Sasha went red at the insult in Boris' words.

"No. Come on, let's go."

Whoever it was clearly did not expect someone to be watching them from the side of the mountain. They moved almost straight towards the boys without hesitation, although they glanced furtively back at the town frequently.

"It's one of our slaves," Boris exclaimed. Before Sasha could comprehend what was happening, Boris cupped his hands around his mouth and yelled.

Sasha thought about putting an arrow to his bow string but decided against it. Already, men were coming out of the gate, and the escapee stood little chance of making it away.

"Should we keep going?" he asked Boris, who was now entirely preoccupied with watching the recapture of the slave.

"No, let's go back. I want to make sure Father knows we were the ones who caught the slave."

It was always like that, Sasha thought. No matter how good they did at anything, they were always looking for a new way to impress Father. He was just that sort of person. He commanded that kind of respect and admiration.

Reluctant to leave the prospect of the wolf hunt behind, Sasha followed Boris back to town, this time using the gate. It was so rare that a slave even tried to escape that Sasha was sure Father would be awakened immediately. Already he could see lights moving about inside the Chief's house, suggesting that someone was relaying the news.

"When he finds out that we were the ones who first saw them, do you think he'll give us a reward?"

Sasha shrugged. He and Boris lingered in the hallway, watching for some sign of Father. It would never do to seek him out uninvited. He had to see and address them first. A commotion at the end of the hallway turned their heads, and Sasha caught sight of Father coming. It was hard to imagine he had just woken up. He looked exactly the same as every other time Sasha saw him. Fully outfitted in the clothes and headgear that befitted a Chief. Father caught sight of the two standing there and motioned for them to follow him.

Inside the great hall, two soldiers already awaited Chief Gundar, and between them, lying flat on the floor was the slave. Boris drew in a sharp breath as he recognized the man as one of his family's attendants.

"He must have waited until I snuck out," Boris whispered in Sasha's ear.

Sasha couldn't tear his eyes off the man. He had never seen anyone so afraid, and he had seen a lot of frightened people. Pretty much anyone who was around Father experienced some level of trepidation. Even he had. But it was nothing compared to the pure terror this man obviously felt. Sasha was standing quite a distance from him and could still see the trembling that took hold of his body.

"Boris, these men tell me you were the one who first saw this criminal," Father's voice rang out loudly in the great hall.

Sasha's brows knit together briefly in a frown. He was the one who saw the fugitive first, not Boris. Father was not done speaking yet.

"I believe such alertness merits a reward, don't you?"

"If you think so, Father," Boris bowed his head as he spoke, and Sasha's anger grew.

"I do. And this is your reward. I want you to decide this man's punishment. And remember, it has been a long time since we have had anyone try to escape. I need an example of what others can expect if they try the same thing. Any thoughts?"

Sasha looked sideways at Boris and noticed the beads of sweat forming on his forehead and the way he ran his tongue over his lips. Boris was afraid. And Sasha was glad that Father did not know that he was the first to spot the runaway. He did not want to hold the life of this terrified man in his hands.

"I think...," Boris started out hesitantly.

"Why am I rushing you? Take time to think about it. I want you to think of something worthwhile. Go," he motioned for everyone to leave the room. "Except you, Sasha."

Sasha froze, his heart jumping to his throat.

"Yes, Father?"

"Walk with me. Now that my night has been disturbed, I might as well make the best of it."

Sasha fell into step slightly behind Father, reveling in this time alone with him. Father was always surrounded by other people and Sasha never had the chance to just be with him.

"You and Boris were planning on a wolf hunt tonight, weren't you?"

Outwardly, Sasha responded in the affirmative, although inwardly he puzzled over how Father could possibly have known about it. He and Boris had been so careful. There was no way anyone could have seen them leaving, was there?

"Sometimes I forget how old you are getting to be. It's been so many years since my own first wolf hunt." Father reached down and lifted a thin rope of braided leather from his chest. Bound into the end of it was a large wolf's tooth. "This is my talisman from that hunt. I expect you'll get yours shortly."

Sasha wracked his brain for what response he should give, before giving up, realizing that none of his training in protocol ever addressed what to do when engaged in a casual conversation with Father. There simply weren't any rules that he could recall. Father continued speaking without his response anyway.

"Do you know why Aruuk is so strong?"

"Is it because we train for war better than anyone else? Or because we raid our neighbors and keep them weaker than ourselves?"

"No. It's because we are governed by the very strictest of laws. Everyone in Aruuk has their place. There is none of this wondering what you are going to be, or what you are going to do with your life. Even the slaves know their place, and they are better off in that place. Order is our strength, and we must keep it. If we were to allow that order to slip the country would descend into chaos."

Sasha wondered where Father was going with this and held his tongue.

"You pitied that man, didn't you?" Father stopped walking and turned to look sharply at Sasha.

"No. I just...he was very afraid."

"And he should be. I hope Boris is up to the task I gave him." Father frowned for a second before resuming his walk. "But you did pity him. I saw it on your face. Stamp it out, Sasha. Compassion is weakness. You'll never be strong so long as you let pity and compassion cloud your judgement. People beneath you do not deserve your sympathy, or your thoughts. You are my son, the son of the greatest Chief this country has known. I would hate to think you can't live up to that."

"Yes, Father." Sasha lowered his head. He hated to think of what would happen if he couldn't live up to that.

"Chief Renalt was weak like that. He never realized the full potential our people had. He had us hiring out, fighting wars for other countries, dying for other causes. Take twenty years ago," Father stopped in front of a large map hanging on the wall and Sasha realized they were standing in the war room, the place the clansmen met to decide raids and campaigns. "I fought in that war. We destroyed the enemy. Chased them all the way across the great plains beneath the mountains.

And what did we get for it? A handful of slaves and a bit of money. The country we fought for was weak. If Renalt had been smart, he would have destroyed Dorsten first, and then wiped out Dival." Father's finger tapped the places on the map as he named them, and Sasha's eyes followed.

"That's all one country on the map?" he said after studying it for a moment.

"It's an old map. When it was made, those two were one country, and a formidable one at that. We most likely would not have been able to take them. But now they are divided. Their people hate each other. They spend so much time fighting each other, they leave themselves open to attack. Someday, I will take advantage of that."

"Why don't you just do it now?" Sasha could hardly believe the words coming out of his mouth. Never, in his entire life, had he addressed Father so directly, so openly.

"I'm not ready. I have spent years rebuilding what Renalt allowed to go to waste. But soon," his finger tapped the map again, absently this time, "soon, I will be. And you, Sasha, will have your chance to take part in the greatest conquest Aruuk has known in over a hundred years."

"I would like that."

"Of course, you would," Father offered a rare hint of a smile, "You're my son."

"What happens if they stop hating each other and become one country again before you're ready?"

"Sasha, people don't stop hating. That's not the way the world works. Once they have been divided, they will never come together again. They will never unite, even to fight a greater enemy."

Chapter 8

HANGING BACK FROM THE REST of the group, Hamo took a moment to take in the sight of the Dorstenian castle. A hand on his shoulder made him turn around.

"Bet you never thought you'd end up back here," Stephan said.

"It's the last place I want to be. I don't know why King Darien thought it was a good idea for me to come."

"You're the only one who has ever even met Lord Bayner. Doesn't that seem like a good reason?"

"Not good enough." Hamo shook his head, trying to chase away the memories that crept up. "I don't want to be here."

"Let's get this over and done with, then."

Inside, an elderly man greeted them with a bow.

"It is a great honor to have you meet with us. The Lord Bayner is awaiting your presence. This way." He started off down a passageway.

Hamo took a deep breath when they reached the great double doors that led into the meeting room. This was going to be a nightmare. The only thing he could hope for at the moment was a quick resolution. Both sides had already agreed that a formal peace would be beneficial. With luck, this would only take a few days, and as little input from Lord Bayner as possible.

The table in the center of the room formed a perfect circle, and around the half facing the doorway were those Dorstenians who would be responsible for their part in the treaty. In the seat just opposite the door sat Lord Bayner. Hamo wasn't sure what he was expecting.

Whatever it was, it was not what sat before him. Lord Bayner had been a young noble, not even thirty years old when Hamo had known him previously, and in good health. The man Hamo saw sitting in the elevated seat of power at the table was a ghost of the leader he had once feared. Lord Bayner's face was drawn, the corners of his mouth pulled down into a perennial frown. His eyes darted over the group as they entered, searching each face, but never lingering long enough to make eye contact. And he certainly did not look as if he enjoyed the thought of a peace treaty.

As the meeting commenced, Hamo found himself ignoring most of what was said, and found his gaze drawn again and again to his old nemesis, wondering if the man could recognize him. It didn't seem like it. Lord Bayner had no end of arguments opposing the treaty and the day dragged on. It wasn't until he saw Lord Bayner start at something that had been said that Hamo turned his mind back to the conversation.

"How dare you come in here, accusing us of such a thing. Slavery has been outlawed in this country since we became sovereign. Anyone participating in such a crime would face the harshest of consequences."

Hamo glanced at Stephan, raising an eyebrow at the man's comment. Stephan was probably the one who had brought the issue up in the first place.

"You're sure about that?" Hamo leaned forward, resting his elbows on the table. It was the first he had spoken all day and every eye in the room turned to him.

"Absolutely," a different man answered him.

"Hmm...," Hamo leaned back, "Would Lord Bayner say the same thing?"

He shouldn't enjoy it, Hamo knew, this wasn't why he was here. But there was something so satisfying about watching the color drain from Lord Bayner's face, realizing that he had lied to his own people, watching him squirm in his seat. Next to him, Hamo heard Stephan mutter something under his breath but couldn't quite catch what it was, nor did he really care. Several of the Dorstenians turned to face their lord, looking for some reassurance. Lord Bayner simply stared at Hamo. At last, he seemed to realize that an answer was expected of him.

"I want," Lord Bayner cast a nervous glance at the faces around him that were growing doubtful, "I want an audience with that gentleman" - he gestured toward Hamo - "Alone."

"Not a good idea," Stephan whispered next to Hamo. "Remember, we're trying to end a war, not start a new one."

Hamo acknowledged him with a nod.

There was a moment of hesitation before the sound of chairs scraping across the floor started. In a matter of seconds, the room had emptied. Even emptied, it took some time for Lord Bayner to put together his thoughts. Hamo said nothing.

"Who are you? What do you want?" When he did speak, Lord Bayner's voice was hoarse.

"You called me 'captain's son', remember?"

"You're alive." The words were barely audible. "How? I sent you north."

"No thanks to you."

"What do you want from me?" he repeated. "Is there some sort of compensation, money, anything? Name it, it's yours, just..."

"Just what? Not tell anyone? Let you keep lying to your people so that they won't throw you out?"

"Please, there must be something I can offer you. Something to make up for it."

Hamo hesitated. He should drop it, he knew. Nothing could be gained from this, no good would come of it. But he couldn't.

"You stole my life. You lied to me. You lied to my father. You thought less of me than the dirt beneath your feet. But you want to pay me now. Why?"

"Call it a change of heart." Lord Bayner attempted a halfhearted smile. "I want to make things right. People do that sort of thing, don't they?"

"No. You're afraid. You're afraid of what those men out there will think of you as their leader if they find out you lied. This isn't the only thing you've lied about to them, either I bet." Hamo guessed from the look on

Lord Bayner's face that the leader had built a great deal on lies.

"Please. You have no idea how difficult it is to control people, to run a country. Name your price and say no more about it."

Hamo watched him, a knot of anger rising in his chest. Pushing his chair back, he stood and began pacing.

"You know, I wanted to kill you," he said softly, and Lord Bayner stiffened in his chair, glancing at the closed doors, regretting the fact that he had sent everyone from the room. "More than anything in the world. When you showed up that day, and told me my own Father didn't want me, I wanted to be the one to take your life from you. I dreamed about it. How I would do it. What it would feel like."

There was no doubt Lord Bayner was second guessing his decision to speak with Hamo alone. His face, already pale, went ashen. At Hamo's last words he started to rise from his chair.

"So, what do I want from you now? How could you possibly make up for what you put me, and all those others, through? I'll tell you what. You can sign this treaty without any arguing and conniving your way into a profit from it, and you can end this pointless war, that way I can go home to my family because I absolutely hate the sight of this place and of you and I'm afraid if I spend too much more time around you, I'll start wanting to kill you again."

"I'll sign it," Lord Bayner's voice was small. "Send everyone back in here and I'll sign it. And you won't tell?"

Hamo shook his head, suddenly tired of the whole thing.

"I don't actually care at all about how you run your country, just quit fighting mine," he said over his shoulder as he went to open the door.

"You know," Lord Bayner's voice made him stop. A hint of his old self showed in his tone. "I'm not as terrible a person as you think I am."

Hamo faced him, his eyes asking a question.

"I know what happened between Drogo and Forbes because of you. Forbes told me all about it. But I let Drogo's choice stand. I didn't have to. And I let Drogo stay past his time because of you."

"What?"

"Drogo. He only owed me five years of service in exchange for his citizenship. He gave me many more. I could have forced him out, replaced him with another iron smith, but I chose not to."

"What did you do that made him want to serve you five extra years?" Hamo asked.

"Nothing. He stayed because of you."

"You're lying." Hamo walked away again, shaking his head in disgust. He should have known Lord Bayner would have the last word, that he would try to turn the conversation around to his favor and control. And he succeeded, just like he had when Hamo was here before. Lord Bayner hadn't let Drogo stay on as a favor to Hamo. He did it because Drogo was far and away the best at his trade, and Lord Bayner needed the best.

Everyone stood waiting outside the doors, far enough away to not be accused of eavesdropping but close enough to get a look at both Hamo and Lord Bayner's faces. Hamo caught Stephan's eye and gave him half a smile.

"I don't really care what happened in there but promise me you didn't start another war."

"No, just ended this one."

"Good. Let's get this done."

To Hamo's relief, Lord Bayner was determined to follow through. He must be really afraid of me telling, he thought, watching the man wave aside the concerns and input of his own advisors to hasten the signing. When the sun sank down to the west, the first peace treaty between Dorsten and Dival had been signed.

"Can we go home now?" Hamo asked as they stepped out of the room.

"Actually, I was kind of hoping to stick around for just a little while." Stephan thrust his hands in his pockets and stared at the floor.

"What? Why would you want to stay here?"

"I was kind of hoping to find someone."

"Who? Come on, Stephan, just say it." Hamo looked at him in bewilderment. It wasn't like Stephan to stall like this.

"I want to find my brother."

"Your brother? I didn't know you had a brother over here. Why didn't you ever say anything about him?"

"I haven't seen him since, well, since I was sixteen. I just want to see what he's up to, what he's turned out like. It'll only be a couple of days, I promise."

Hamo threw up his hands in exasperation and started to walk away.

"Do you have any idea what happened to that man you worked with? What was his name again?" Stephan called after him.

"Drogo. No, I don't know anything about him."

"Maybe now would be a good time to find out."

Hamo shrugged and walked away.

Chapter 9

THE SPRING MEREDITH AND Ophelia turned twelve was uncharacteristically tranquil. For more than fifty years, spring was most often marked by preparations for war with Dorsten. This had never bothered Meredith since Father never went to war. This year, however, everything was different, and Meredith wasn't sure what to think. Now all the other fathers were staying home and hers had to leave.

Father was gone. Not gone to Bren for war council meetings. Gone to Dorsten, along with Grandfather and Meredith had no idea how long he would be gone. Everyone talked about what a wonderful thing it was that a peace treaty of sorts was being signed, and Meredith knew she should be proud that her father had anything at all to do with it. But it was hard to feel proud when she missed him so much.

Meredith sat back on her heels, watching a swallow swoop and dive above her head. It was hot already, but the heat was not enough to prevent her from being out here, in Taliea's medicine garden. She had made a habit in the last couple of years of hurrying through her chores at home so that she could come here as often as possible. With Father gone, she had more to do and had made her appearance in the garden a little less often than she would have liked.

"How are you today, Meri?" Taliea came up behind her, a basket in her hands.

"I'm hot, and I wish Father was home," Meredith answered more crossly than she meant but Taliea only smiled.

"It is quite warm. Why look, even Perseus isn't up playing. Maybe that means you should come inside and help me today."

Meredith shrugged. It would be almost as hot inside as outside at this point but working with Taliea was always interesting.

"Do I get to pick a plant?"

"Whichever one you want. You look around and decide while I get what I need."

It was a game she and Taliea had invented. Meredith would pick a specimen from any plant in the garden and Taliea would tell her everything she knew about it, how it was used, what it could be mixed with, where it grew. Meredith stood up, stretching her back after having sat crouched down for so long. Taliea disappeared behind a bush and Meredith made her way slowly down the narrow path that separated the plants. The most vibrant and exotic ones she had picked long ago, when they first started the game. Now she was left with the more boring plants. There were bushes with thick green leaves, but no flowers. A two-toned frosty green vine that climbed a trellis in the corner. A shrub with spiny branches and glossy leaves. Meredith pursed her lips, trying to guess which one would be the most interesting. She needed something very interesting to distract her from the little ache she felt at Father's absence.

At last, Meredith settled on a bush that was covered in tiny thorns and produced clusters of pearly white berries. Twisting off a branch required more care than usual, but even so, Meredith's hand stung a little from the thorn pricks. Wincing, she turned the branch over in her hand, trying to imagine what use Taliea had for it. It didn't look incredibly promising. It must have some extraordinary properties to make it worth the pain of collecting.

Taliea was already waiting for her, spreading freshly picked leaves out on the table.

"So, what did you pick today?" Taliea held out her hand to take it from Meredith. "Ah, Snowkiss berries. That's an interesting choice. What made you pick this one?"

"The berries. They're pretty. It's like a whole cluster of pearls."

"It's deceptive."

"What do you mean?"

"So pretty, and yet they are deadly."

Meredith recoiled a little. "Deadly? Why would you grow this, then?"

"It has its purpose. A very tiny bit of juice from the berries, or if they are dried a bit of the powder, is enough to put someone to sleep for several hours. More than a drop or two, however, and it can kill a person. I only use this if I have no other option."

Meredith plucked a berry off the branch and rolled it between her fingers.

"Have you ever given someone too much?"

Taliea didn't answer right away and when Meredith turned to see why she was horrified to see Taliea's eyes filled with tears.

"Only by accident, once," she finally said.

"I've never seen this growing anywhere around here." Meredith hurried to draw the conversation in a different direction.

"No. That plant likes the mountains. Colder air. More shade than sun. I learned about it when I was living up there for about a year or so."

"You lived in the mountains? I've never seen them. Father has, but he says he doesn't really care for them."

"I thought they were beautiful, but they can be dangerous. This plant is proof of that. I had a hard time growing a specimen down here, but as long as it doesn't get too much sunlight, it manages."

"Do you use it for anything else?"

"No. Sometimes I just need something to make someone sleep."

Meredith studied the branch, noticing the shape and color of the leaves. If Ophelia had come with her today, she would have drawn a sketch of it so that Meredith could always remember it. Meredith had a whole stack of such sketches in her room. But Phelie was home watching Elenora and Adelaide, so it was up to Meredith to imprint it into her mind.

Meredith stayed the rest of the hot afternoon, helping Taliea grind dried leaves into powder and measuring the powder out into jars. She was busy enough to almost forget that Father was gone and that the house would seem big and lonely and empty without him when she finally went home. Mother said he was likely to be gone at least another week. Apparently, there was more to signing a peace treaty than just writing your name, Meredith thought, although she had no idea what could possibly make it such a lengthy process. It shouldn't have been much more difficult than when she and Phelie agreed to stop arguing about something.

"Taliea, you said you used to live in the mountains for a year. Is there anywhere else you've been?"

"I've been to a lot of places. I think it's fascinating going to different countries and seeing the way those people live."

"Is that where you learned about all these plants and how they helped people."

"That started at home, actually. My own father was an apothecary. I used to help him when I was little. When I got older, and I started to travel, I realized that there was so much we didn't know or have from where I came from."

"So, you've just gone around collecting different plants and learning about them?"

"No, I've also used my skill as a healer to help people wherever I live. What good would it do to know all of this, and not use it?"

"What was your favorite place to live?"

"Home."

"What was that like?"

"It was a desert. Dry, hot, and sandy. But it's where I grew up, so I'm used to it."

Meredith was quiet for a while as she tied together bundles of leaves to hang and dry.

"If you are always moving to different places, does that mean you are going to leave here eventually?" The thought was sad, and Meredith realized just how much she enjoyed coming over and helping Taliea.

"Unless I have a very good reason to stay."

50

"Like what? What would be a good enough reason?"

Taliea opened her mouth to answer, but the sound of hoofbeats coming up the lane interrupted her. Meredith followed her to the door.

"It's Uncle Al!" Meredith waved to the approaching young man, then stood up on her toes to whisper in Taliea's ear. "He thinks you're pretty."

"Does he?"

"I heard him say so, but he doesn't know that I did."

"Our secret then?" Taliea's almost black eyes twinkled with amusement. "What brings you here, Aldrid?"

"Meri does, actually. Her mother wants her home."

"Am I in trouble?" Meri looked up at her uncle in alarm. Mother had never sent him riding after her.

"I don't think so. All she said to tell you was," Aldrid stopped and tapped his chin thoughtfully, "that there might be someone there that you haven't seen in a while, and who is very anxious to see you."

"Father! Is he home?"

"Yes, he is. Want a ride?" Al held out his good hand and pulled Meredith up behind him.

"Make him run, please, Uncle Al." And Meredith let out a squeal of delight when the horse lurched forward.

Meredith didn't wait for the horse to come to a halt but slid to the ground and ran straight into Father's arms.

"I thought you weren't coming home for at least another week," Meredith's words were almost inarticulate since her face was buried in Father's shoulder.

"Well, we gave them a really good reason to sign quickly."

"I think threatened is a better word for it, wouldn't you, Hamo?" Stephan spoke up from where he was still mounted.

Meredith glanced between her father and grandfather and decided that there was something going on that she was not to be made aware of. Not that it mattered at the moment. All that really mattered was that Father was home. And that their venture had been successful.

"Does it mean we won't ever go to war with them again?" Priscilla asked.

"Unfortunately, no. It will only last a year. After that, we'll have to sign it again if we want the peace to continue."

"Maybe people will get used to the peace. I know I will," Mother said quietly.

Chapter 10

SASHA STARED OUT ACROSS THE mountains that were visible from the window, paying attention to everything except the man who was trying to teach him. Sasha enjoyed most of the things Father wanted him to learn - riding, sword fighting, even geography, although the maps they used appeared to be very outdated. But this, learning the language of people Father intended to be enemies, was boring. Why was it necessary anyway? If Father really intended to one day conquer the two countries to the south of them, beyond the mountains, wouldn't those people have to learn his language? That's what they already did. All the slaves they collected from their raids were made to learn Aruuk. It wasn't fair that Father made him do this, especially since he didn't make Boris.

Besides, the man who was teaching him was a slave. And Sasha wasn't in the habit of paying attention to slaves. It was unusual for one to be in this sort of role, acting as the teacher, the superior, and Sasha loathed it. Still, however much he didn't want to be there, he was making progress. He could carry on a slow, methodical conversation with his tutor.

Sasha's thoughts wandered to the upcoming raids. It would be his first year going on one. Fifteen years old. Father had asked him just that morning if he wanted to join the sea raiders or stay on land. The sea raiders went much further and left earlier in the summer. The idea of going to sea was enticing. There were so many more places he could go if he went to sea. There was only one reason holding him back. One that he did not dare tell Father about, although some of his older half-brothers knew it, for they had been the ones who had helped him discover it. Sasha hated being confined. He hated small, cramped, or dark spaces. No matter how hard he tried, he couldn't keep his breathing from accelerating, his heart from racing, the panic in his chest from rising. He had first known it when two of his older brothers trapped him in a cellar for several hours when he was little, and since that day, Sasha carefully avoided any tight spaces. He would love to go to sea - but if he did there was a good chance he would panic at the enclosed space.

It would be land raiding for him. The thought was a little sad, because he desperately wanted to see all the places the sea raiders talked about. The land raids were not nearly so interesting. They mostly took things like livestock and grain - necessary to the survival of Aruuk, but totally uninteresting.

Sasha jerked back to the present, realizing that his so-called teacher was finished and waiting to be dismissed. He also realized that he had not listened to a word the man said for at least the last fifteen minutes. It didn't matter. He would just tell Father that the man was an incompetent teacher, and Father would do away with him and find someone who was hopefully more interesting. That was what happened to his last two teachers.

"Go," Sasha waved the man away and took off himself in search of Boris.

He found him in his room, pouring over a map. Sasha had seen him doing that a lot the last few days.

"What are you hoping to find?" Sasha crouched down next to him.

"A new place to raid. Father's going to love my idea, just wait. It will make us a good profit too, at the Spring Market."

"Where are you thinking?"

"Not telling. For all I know, you're just trying to get it out of me so that you can run off and tell Father yourself."

"I wouldn't do that," Sasha protested, knowing all the while that it was exactly what he would do. Boris would too if their roles were reversed. That's just how things were done.

"You're coming with me, right?" Boris ignored his retort.

"I don't know. Will they let us go together?"

"We're Chief Gundar's sons, I think they have to let us go wherever we want. As long as the raiding gets done Father doesn't care."

"Then yes, I'll go with you - but only if you tell me your great idea."

"Not a chance. Do you think if it's a really good raid Father will give us our choice of the slaves?"

"Maybe. He sometimes does." Sasha gave up trying to get Boris to tell him. Instead, he lay down on his stomach next to him and studied the map as well. It wasn't like there were a whole lot of new options. The neighboring countries, almost universally weak and unprotected, were already prime targets. The only other feasible place was the country beyond the mountains, the one the map showed as being part of a much larger nation, the one Father said was divided. "You're wanting to go there," Sasha pointed in triumph at the map.

Boris' face darkened and Sasha let out a little yelp of pain as his brother's fist caught his shoulder.

"You're always doing that."

"Doing what?" Sasha rubbed his shoulder.

"Always trying to be better than me, and make Father pay attention to you. Can't you just let me have the idea for once?" Boris folded up the map with such aggression that it almost tore.

"That's not true. He gave you credit for finding that runaway first, even though I saw them first."

"That was one time, three years ago. Besides, you're the one he wanted to stay and talk to. All I got was to pick someone's punishment."

Sasha pressed his lips together in a thin line. Boris had a point, one that he couldn't very well argue with. It hadn't been the only time Father had singled him out and spent time with him away from everyone else.

Sasha loved it. It was all his hard work finally paying off.

"Look, I won't tell. Honestly. But you have to do something for me if you don't want me to."

Boris looked at him with suspicion and Sasha continued.

"You help me practice more with my sword and I'll let you be the one to suggest it to Father."

"You have a trainer."

"Who won't spend enough time with me. I could be better if I just had more time."

Boris thought for a moment. It was the one thing he was better at than Sasha, and better by a lot. Sasha just couldn't quite master it, not the way the Chief's sons were expected to, at least. Sasha could see he didn't really want to give up the one area of superiority that he had.

"Just until the raids start?" Sasha pressed. He could always go to Father and suggest the new raiding place after a few practice sessions with Boris. Any improvement would be welcome.

"Alright. But if you go behind my back, I'm done helping you."

Chapter 11

THE LATE AFTERNOON SUN WAS pouring through the western windows of the house, spilling into golden patches across the wooden floor. Edith stood at the counter, her hair tied back in its customary red scarf, her knife rising and falling quickly as she cut through a small pile of vegetables.

"You should come with me," Hamo said suddenly from where he was sitting at the table mending a harness piece.

"Just so we're clear, you are talking about your upcoming trip to Dorsten, right?"

"Yes. You should come. We could leave the girls with Mother and Stephan. Meri, Phelie, and Scilla are all able to take care of themselves."

"I don't think so." Edith scooped the remainder of the cut produce into a pot. "What would I do? You'd be in meetings the whole time, and I have to confess, I've never had a great desire to visit our former enemies."

"I hate going. I wish he would just sign something that lasted a little longer."

"Why don't you persuade him to? Stephan said you were very compelling that first time three years ago."

"I don't want to push our luck. It's his way of feeling like he still has some control. I'm afraid of what would happen if he felt he lost it."

"I have an idea." Edith came over and sat in the chair across from Hamo's. "Why don't you take Meri and Phelie with you instead?"

Hamo started to shake his head, but Edith held up a hand.

"Meri is dying to see the world. This would be fun for her. And if Phelie goes too they can look out for each other."

"I don't know," Hamo said after a moment, "I think it would be better if you came."

"Not a chance. Not when the baby is going to be here in a couple of months. Maybe a different year."

"Then I shouldn't take the girls either. You'll need help."

"Scilla and Nora are old enough to help, and you'll be back before she comes anyway. You're never gone for more than two or three weeks."

"She?"

"I'm just making a good guess. Maybe it will be a boy. If it is, what will you name him?"

"Hadn't thought about it."

"That's no fun. I have at least five names picked out if it's a girl. Anyway, you should think about taking them. They'd love to go."

Later that evening, when the day's work was done and supper finished, Hamo found Meredith and Elenora sitting on the front steps outside of the house. Meredith's fingers were working at untangling a knotted ball of yarn while Elenora wrapped the free part of it up into a new ball.

"Here, Nora, I'll take that." Hamo sat down next to her. "If you go inside, you might be able to talk Phelie into telling you a story before bed."

Nora handed off her part and hurried inside.

"You're not going to offer to do my part so that I can go listen to a story?" Meredith asked, laughing as she watched her younger sister disappear inside.

"I thought you'd outgrown your sister's stories, now that you're fifteen and all. Besides, I wanted to talk to you."

"Oh?"

"I have to leave again for a couple weeks."

"I know." Meredith glanced over curiously. "Nora was faster with that, you know."

"Well, I guess I don't have to talk to you. Nora can come back out and finish." Hamo started to get back up when Meredith caught his arm.

"No. You can't do that to me. You can't say that you want to talk and then just leave me hanging. That's not fair. What were you going to say?"

"I was going to say that I'm leaving. And that your mother thought you and Phelie might like to come with me."

Meredith dropped the tangled thread and clapped her hands together.

"Serious? You're being serious right now? You're not just messing with me. Did you ask Phelie yet? Does she want to go?" Meredith paused for breath.

"Not yet. Do you actually want to go?"

"Of course, I want to go." Meredith's smile faded for a moment. "Is it safe to go over there?"

"Well, the treaty has held for the last three years. I don't think there's any reason to believe it won't this year. I think everyone enjoys the peace. And, aside from the fact that I don't like them very much, it is an interesting place to visit." Hamo gave up on trying to roll the yarn neatly and set it down. "I still have to see if Phelie wants to come. If she does, we'll have to leave in a couple of days. We're meeting a lot later than usual this year and I want to be back before the snow sets in and the baby comes."

Time moved both swift and slow during the next two days. There was enough that needed to be done that Meredith had little to think of her own excitement.

Meredith knew she should be asleep. Tomorrow was going to be a very early morning. She shut her eyes, forcing her body to lie still for as long as she could stand, but it was hopeless. The excitement of going with Father was more than she could sleep with.

"Phelie," Meredith kept her voice at a whisper so as not to wake anyone else in the house. Ophelia didn't answer. Of course, she managed to fall asleep, Meredith thought. Her sister had always been better at facing things calmly and had always been a much better sleeper.

Meredith sat up in frustration, tossing aside her blankets and pulling her knees up to her chest. The farthest she had ever been from home was when the whole family had gone to Bren, a day's journey from home. Aunt Sabina and her family lived there, and Meredith had always loved the times they had gone. But this, going all the way across the Void, was so much more thrilling. Meredith wondered what the Void looked like. Father and Uncle Aldrid, and even grandfather spoke of it from time to time. Their words usually painted a grim picture, and Meredith shut her eyes trying to conjure up the image in her mind. It would be awful. She was sure of that. But it would be interesting, too, in its own way.

And then there were the mountains. She would finally get to see mountains. Keeping her eyes closed and laying back into her pillow again, Meredith thought about how Taliea described them. Majestic. Unmoving. Towering giants of rock and earth. Meredith yawned. She would get to see them. And hopefully explore them.

Meredith opened her eyes to find Phelie standing over her, shaking her shoulder.

"Wake up, sleepy. Thought you were too excited to sleep!"

Groggily, Meredith sat up. The window was still dark, but from the sounds coming outside the bedroom she could tell Father and Mother were already up.

"What time is it?"

Ophelia shrugged and disappeared from the room, leaving Meredith to scramble into her clothes. Splashing cold water onto her face from the washbasin, Meredith finally started to feel awake. Even so, she wished she had fallen asleep sooner the night before. She couldn't quite shake the sluggish feeling. Running a comb through her brown hair, she started braiding it back into a single braid as she left the room. It was shorter than Ophelia's, one of the only differences between the twins, and Meredith liked it that way. It kept people from constantly asking which one was which.

"Look who's finally up." Mother smiled as she came rushing out of her room. "I thought you might have changed your mind."

"Absolutely not. Where's Father at?"

"Outside, getting the horses ready. Here," Mother held out a plate, "you should eat before you leave. Your Father and sister already did."

"I slept that late?"

"No, they were just up that early."

Meredith tried to swallow her food down, knowing Mother was right. She would regret it later if she didn't eat now. But she could only manage to finish half of it before her own excitement overtook her and she went outside.

The morning had a crisp, damp chill to it, hinting of the approaching autumn. Above the sky was clear, revealing the stars for a little while longer before the sun came and chased them out of sight. Meredith took a deep breath of the morning air. The pre-dawn hours were her favorite, she decided. So inviting, so tantalizing, so mysterious. She should get up this early more often, although a sleepy yawn seemed to argue with that.

"I can't believe we're actually going," Meredith whispered to Ophelia as they worked to put the finishing touches on their preparations.

"What do you think it will be like? I mean, we don't actually know anyone over there. We're barely not enemies anymore."

"I don't know. There's probably a lot of people like us over there that don't really care for the war. Anyway, it will be interesting to see."

"You just want to go because of all the stories Taliea tells you about traveling the world."

Mother interrupted any retort Meredith might have made. She pulled Meredith toward her in an embrace.

"Look out for your sister, Meri. You know she always does what you suggest. Be careful and have fun." Mother kept her voice low enough that only Meredith could hear her.

Meredith nodded. She should feel sadder about leaving then she did, Meredith thought. But sadness or homesickness didn't fit in with her excitement. She was leaving home, she would see things she had never seen before, and that would make her a person she had never been before.

By the time the sun had risen fully, home was nowhere in sight. The road, dry and cracked with the summer's heat, stretched out before them like an endless brown snake. Meredith didn't bother looking back anymore. There was too much to look forward to.

Chapter 12

SASHA SWAYED EASILY TO THE motion of the horse beneath him. It was almost enough to put him to sleep. It didn't help that he had barely slept the night before. He and Boris had stayed up far later than normal, talking about their first raid. Sasha glanced over at his brother now, wondering if he was as nervous as Sasha was at the moment. Not that Sasha could see. In fact, his brother, only older by a few months, had adopted the hardened look of the older raiders. Sasha tried to emulate him now. It didn't matter that his insides were churning with anticipation, that his hands were so sweaty he could feel his reins dampen in their grasp. All that mattered was that he looked and acted the part, especially since Boris wasn't the only one of his brothers on this raid.

When Boris suggested a raid into the country Sasha had learned was called Dorsten, Father was reluctant. At least, Boris thought he was reluctant. Boris did not see the gleam in Father's eye the same as Sasha did, and it made Sasha regret that he hadn't broken his promise to Boris and made the suggestion first. Now Boris would get all the credit for it. The only stipulation Father made was that Armin lead the raid. Armin was Sasha's oldest brother. Sasha had to turn in his saddle to get a look at Armin. He rode at the very back of the group, hanging behind everyone else. Armin was considered one of the best warriors in Aruuk, but perhaps more important than that, he was considered one of the best raiders. Sasha studied his face briefly before turning back around. He certainly didn't want

Armin to catch him looking at him. His eldest brother had a temper, and more than once in his short life Sasha had been on the receiving end of it.

A sudden jolt from his horse made Sasha catch himself and turn his focus to the ground before him. The mountainous terrain was growing rockier, steeper. His horse, raised to navigate these mountain trails, picked its way carefully along the trail. Sasha had come to appreciate the quality of the little mountain horses their Father had carefully bred and raised within the kingdom. Agile, fast, and more sure-footed than any other animal Sasha had ever known, they were the safest way to travel through the treacherous mountains. They were riding up a narrow defile that did not allow more than two or three horses to ride side by side. Boris nudged his own animal into the spot next to Sasha's.

"How much longer before we reach the first village, do you think?"

"A few more days probably. The map is kind of old though, so I don't know."

Boris rode next to him in silence for a while. It wasn't until the pass opened into a wider trail that he leaned toward Sasha.

"Are you nervous?"

Sasha shrugged nonchalantly. "Not really."

"Liar." Boris' serious face suddenly split in a grin. "You're just as scared as I am."

"Maybe, but do you have to that advertise to everyone else?" Sasha glanced around at the other men who had now spread out into more of a cluster than the column they had been riding in. "We're the only new ones with this group, we have to at least pretend we know what we're doing."

"We do. It's what Father's been training us for."

Sasha let out a little sigh. He wished he had Boris' confidence. He wished he had anyone else's confidence. Reaching forward, he scratched the neck of his mount, trying to quell the thoughts that surged up in his mind, thoughts of what would happen if he somehow failed, if he brought dishonor to Father. There would be a price to pay. Mother had paid it, Agathe had paid it. Sasha didn't want to pay it. It would be worse as a son; he knew that much. In his fifteen years he could only remember one instance when a son had brought dishonor to Father. He couldn't even remember what his name was or what he had done. All Sasha knew was that he hadn't faced the slave market. He was made an example of, a horrific, terrifying, bloody spectacle. Sasha had only been seven or eight at the time, but closing his eyes now, he could still conjure up the scene in his memory.

"You look like you're going to be sick." Boris stared at him.

"I'm fine."

"You'd better be. How many slaves do you think we'll take?"

"We won't just be taking slaves, you know that, right?"

"Well, technically. But you know as well as I do that livestock isn't what makes us the most money at the Spring Market."

"True. I think it would be considered a good raid if we could take at least twenty." Sasha really had no idea, but it seemed like a reasonable number, especially considering that they had no real idea as to what they would find in the outskirts of Dorsten.

"Thirty," Boris said, glancing sidelong at his brother.

"Alright, thirty."

"Come on, Sasha, you're not being any fun. What's gotten into you?"

Sasha lifted one shoulder up in a halfhearted shrug. He didn't want to be drawn into an argument with Boris, no matter how trivial. It just did not seem like the right time. He started to answer when he felt someone's eyes on him, watching him. Turning, he caught sight of Armin. Their eldest brother was intently watching them. And from the look on his face, he wasn't happy. Then again, Sasha couldn't remember the last time Armin had looked happy. Probably never. For a fleeting instant Sasha tried to imagine Armin as a child, wearing the same scowl he did now. The image brought with it the irresistible urge to laugh, which only served to intensify Armin's glare. Sasha fought to regain control of himself. It would not do to anger Armin, not when he would be the one telling Father about Sasha and Boris' performance.

Chapter 13

TRAVELLING TURNED OUT TO BE tedious. Meredith's excitement had worn away a little with the monotony of the trip. The Void that was spoken of as something horrifying, was disappointing. And Meredith knew she shouldn't have been disappointed. It had grown over. The muddy, desolate land that had once been beautiful plains was once more growing over. Lush grass, swaying gently like the rippling waves of the sea, covered the multitudes of mounds that contained the bodies of the fallen. In fact, if Meredith had not been aware of their existence, she would never have guessed. For as far as the eye could see, there was nothing except the long, knee-high grass intermixed with a colorful assortment of meadow flowers. Meredith had thought about collecting some to take back to Taliea but had decided that would be a task better suited to their return trip.

Now, having spent the last four days and nights out in the Void, the horizon showed a dark line of trees. The border forest. Father said that it used to take longer to cross, but in the three years of peace, a highway of sorts had been constructed, smoothed out, and straightened.

Meredith shifted in her saddle. She was used to riding for only a little while at a time. This trip had certainly proved that she was still susceptible to that terrible condition known as saddle soreness. Meredith smiled to herself as she thought of the actual beds that awaited them at the end of the day. Father and grandfather both assured her and Ophelia that they would reach the capital of Dorsten by nightfall. Meredith couldn't wait.

It was late afternoon when the forest closed in around them. Even here, a clearer road had been laid in the last three years. The woods were nothing new to Meredith. She had lived in them her entire life, but she found herself inspecting this one, searching the vegetation that grew there. It came from spending so much time with Taliea, Meredith thought.

"We're so close, I can almost feel an actual bed," Ophelia spoke up from beside Meredith.

"Me too." Meredith flashed a weary smile. "I will say, this gives me a whole new appreciation for the comforts of home."

"You were the one who was so anxious to go and leave home."

Meredith cocked her head, trying to think of something to say in her own defense. Ophelia was right of course. Ophelia usually was.

"You agreed to come, though."

"Couldn't let you go and have all the fun without me, could I? Besides, we do everything together. That's just how it's always been."

Meredith pulled her horse to an abrupt stop and pointed ahead.

"Look. There's the castle, and the town, and those must be the mountains." She swung her arm in a wide arc, encompassing the landscape that opened up before them out of the trees. "They're so...so," Her brows furrowed as she tried to think of a word that could truly describe them.

"Magnificent. Breathtaking," Ophelia finished for her.

"Yes. Father," Meredith twisted around to find him, "We're going to explore the mountains, aren't we? Just a little bit?"

Father followed her gaze to the towering heights above the distant castle and sighed.

"If we have time."

Later that night, Meredith sank down into the mattress of her bed, pulling the covers all the way up to her chin. A real bed was so luxurious. A real bed inside the castle was even more so.

"I can't imagine what it must be like to live like this all the time," Ophelia whispered. "I would feel so spoiled."

"You know, Mother said Father actually grew up in a castle like this."

"I know, Meri. I heard all the same stories you did," Ophelia's voice held a hint of irritation. "I wonder if he wishes he could still live there?"

Meredith shrugged and lay silent for a while, enjoying the opulence of the room she shared with her sister. Heavy tapestries hung along the outer wall, holding back the cool night air. Wrought iron candle sconces were placed at intervals, the thick white candles in them burning slowly. A velvet, purple canopy draped the frame above the bed the girls shared. A thick carpet covered the center of the room. All of it led to a sensation of wealth and grandeur that Meredith had never encountered before.

"Phelie," Meredith's voice was barely audible. She was not entirely sure her sister was still awake.

"Hmm?"

"We should go tomorrow."

"Go where?" Ophelia pushed herself up on her elbow and looked hard at Meredith. "The mountains?"

Meredith smiled. It was one of the best parts of having a twin sister. She could read Meredith's mind like no one else could.

"Yes. The mountains."

"Father wouldn't want us to."

And there was the downside to having a twin sister, Meredith thought with a frown. Ophelia was the rule follower, the one who never got into trouble on her own.

"We could ask first."

"What? You mean when he's busy and isn't actually paying attention to what we're saying?"

"No," Meredith denied. "Maybe. I'll talk to him. He'll say yes."

"I'm not holding my breath." Ophelia lay back down and rolled over, facing away from Meredith.

"I just need to see them. I need to explore them. They're so different. He won't mind, I'm sure."

"Goodnight, Meri." It was Ophelia's way of telling her that the conversation was over. Either Meredith got Father's permission, his real permission and not his distracted permission, or they weren't going.

"Goodnight, Phelie."

Chapter 14

SASHA GLARED AT THE CAMPFIRE dancing before his eyes. His first raid. Boris' first raid. And Armin wasn't going to let them do anything. His fingers reached up to his throat and felt for the wolf's tooth that hung there. Absently, he rolled it between his thumb and forefinger, his mind busy with all the reasons why Armin was being unfair. He and Boris had trained for this, every day for the last five years in fact. They had completed every test, every requirement asked of them. They were ready. But Armin wouldn't see that, and all the thoughts in Sasha's head at the moment were ones he would never dare voice to his eldest brother. Boris had started to protest the decision earlier that day, and now he sported a black eye and broken nose.

"It's not fair," Boris kept his voice low, glancing around to make sure Armin was not within ear shot. "We're ready."

Sasha lay back on the hard ground, his eyes taking in the starry sky high above the mountains.

"We are ready," Sasha sighed. "But there's nothing we can do about it."

The moon was already high in the sky. In only a few hours they would be making their attack on the first village. Sasha had seen it from the trail, nestled into a small, flat meadow at the foot of a mountain. There were only a handful of houses built of wood, scattered haphazardly about. From the number of houses, Sasha guessed there were less than a hundred people living in the village. That would make it an easy raid, which made Armin's decision even more unfair.

Without realizing it, Sasha must have fallen asleep, laying on his back near the fire. He woke with a start as the sounds of men and horses moving about grew louder. A streak of pinkish gray showed between two mountains toward the east. Dawn was not far off.

"Sasha, you remember what I told you yesterday?" Sasha nearly jumped when Armin's voice came from directly behind him.

"Yes, Armin."

"Stay here with the pack horses and have them ready to go."

"Yes, Armin." Sasha stared resolutely at the ground. He wanted to demand that Armin let him come on the raid. He shouldn't be afraid of Armin. He was just as much one of Chief Gundar's sons as Armin was. He wasn't afraid of him. "Armin, can't I..."

He got no further than that before Armin's hand caught the side of his face.

"You'll do as I say, or you can go back home now and explain to Father why."

Sasha's hand covered the bright red mark on his face that was sure to turn into a bruise shortly. Going home right now was not an option, not if he wanted to retain Father's favor, but did Armin really have to hit him for asking? He caught sight of Boris watching him, a smug expression gracing his features.

"Did you think he was going to like you asking better than he did me?"

Sasha did not bother to answer. He rose stiffly from where he had fallen asleep and watched as the other men in the camp readied themselves for the raid. They were quiet as they arranged and checked their weapons, the saddles on their horses. Sasha deliberately avoided Armin's gaze as they mounted up and disappeared into the morning mist that hung low over the mountains. He kicked at a rock, sending it skittering across the ground and folded his arms across his chest.

"So, I guess we just wait for them to come back?" Boris stood beside him.

"I guess. We should have gone with someone else."

"We could always sneak down after them and watch at least. These horses," Boris jerked a thumb in the direction of the pack horses standing quietly tethered in place, "aren't going anywhere."

Sasha chewed as his lower lip, turning the thought over. He wanted to at least see the raid. He had no idea exactly how they were carried out. Oh, he knew the theory of them well enough - that had been part of their training - but to actually witness firsthand how it played out would be beneficial if they ever did get to participate. His hand reached for the sore spot on his face and made his decision for him.

"No. We can't risk him getting mad at us again. If he sends us home...," Sasha let the words hang, the weight of them enough to curb even Boris' recklessness.

The two stoked up one of the fading fires from the night before and sat down. Sasha didn't even have a good guess for how long they would have to wait. The minutes dragged by with an agonizing sluggishness, drawn out by complete boredom. Sasha fetched some of the hard bread out of their supplies and chewed on it, watching the little tendrils of mist dance around the rocky mountainside and finally dissipate into a cold, blue sky.

"They've been gone forever." Boris got up and checked for the hundredth time on the horses. "They should be back by now, don't you think?"

Sasha shrugged, and, squinting his eyes, tried to see all the way down the trail hoping to catch sight of them. His eyes had searched the trail dozens of times and there had not been any sign of the raiding party. Now, he saw the sun glinting off something. He sat up on his knees, searching. At last, it was more than just the glimmer of sunlight off metal. He could make out horses and riders. Another few yards and he caught sight of the faces of the riders and breathed a sigh of relief. It was their group.

Armin was the first to ride through the defile into the campsite, followed by several others on horseback and then a string of people on foot bound together with a long rope. Sasha counted them in his head as they came fully into view. Twelve captives, twelve slaves for the market. His eyes were drawn to the faces of the newly captured. Their expressions ranged from stunned disbelief to abject fear to barely controlled anger. There was only one who bore the expression of anger, a younger man at the end of the line. None of them put up any fight against the rope that held them together, though.

"Did anyone get away?" Boris forgot his anger at Armin and grabbed his eldest brother's horse while he dismounted.

"None. And the village will be burnt to the ground by the end of today."

Sasha turned back to where he knew the village lay just out of sight. Climbing high into the air were plumes of wispy smoke. The sound of a scuffle startled Sasha and he turned just in time to see the man at the end of the line pull a bloodied knife out of the chest of one of the guards and sprint away back in the direction of the burning village.

"Shoot him down, Sasha," Armin's voice cut through Sasha's mind, compelling his hands to act.

In one swift motion, he had his bow up, an arrow nocked on its string, and his fingers pulling it back. All the years of practice reasserted themselves and Sasha did not have to think twice about what to do. The string slipped from his fingertips. The arrow hissed its way off, and Sasha didn't wait to see his success before pulling another arrow free from his quiver and firing off another shot.

Both found their mark.

Jerking with the impact, the man continued several paces before sinking to the ground. Even then he wasn't dead, Sasha saw. His legs moved, and he tried to push himself up. Armin didn't wait for that to happen. Knife in hand, he approached the fallen man. Sasha looked down at the bow in his hands, suddenly reluctant to see the job he began finished. It wasn't until Armin was shoving the bloody arrows he retrieved from the corpse into his hands that he looked up.

"Good shot." Armin met his eyes. "If he'd gotten away, he could have warned all the other settlements. We would have had to turn around and head home."

Sasha just nodded. Despite Armin's sparse praise, his insides were churning. A hand slapped him on the shoulder from behind and he glanced back quickly to see one of the older men laughing.

"First kill's always the hardest, isn't that right Armin? You get used to it after a while."

The man moved away, leaving Sasha to stare at the arrows in his hand. Blood had dripped down soaking the ground at his feet, but now it was beginning to congeal. Sasha had bloodied plenty of arrows on numerous hunting excursions. He had never had to clean one. Zena or Axel always did that. Now, staring at them in his hand, he wondered just how he was supposed to do it, or if he wanted to. Part of him thought it would be better to just throw them into the shrubbery and forget all about them, and his first kill. Another part of him knew that would never happen. Even now, if he shut his eyes, he could see the spasm that went through the man as the first, then the second arrow struck him. He could hear the strangled cry. He could smell the sweet scent of blood.

Chapter 15

THREE DAYS. THREE LONG DAYS they had been in the capital of Dorsten, living in the shadow of the mountains. Now, at last, Meredith's desire was being fulfilled. Father was going to take them a little way into the mountain pass. Meredith shifted from one foot to the other in impatience. In her hand she held the bridle of her horse, next to her Ophelia waited with at least an outward appearance of indifference. Where was Father at?

"You know he really does not want to do this," Ophelia said.

"It won't be that bad. We'll have fun, I'm sure of it."

"That doesn't mean he wants to do it. Maybe we should just find something else to explore."

"No. I didn't come all this way just to be cooped up in town. We've seen everything there is worth seeing here."

"It's a lot poorer than I would have thought," Ophelia switched subjects. "I mean, I thought we were bad off after all the years of war, but I think it's been worse for them."

"Well, if it was so terrible for them, they could have been the ones trying to end it." Meredith picked at a broken fingernail, trying to distract herself from how long it was taking Father to come.

When he did finally come, Meredith saw immediately that Ophelia was right. He certainly did not share her excitement for this adventure. She considered telling him that she didn't really want to go, but the idea of riding through those magnificent landforms was so enticing. There probably would never be another time when she could go. So, she held her tongue and went to mount her horse.

"You would have thought we'd had enough riding coming here," Ophelia grumbled slightly, but Meredith could tell that she was anxious to go too.

"We won't actually be able to go that far into them," Father pointed out. "We can ride up the pass a little way, but we don't want to go so far that we can't make it back before dark."

"Why isn't Grandfather coming with us?" Meredith asked as they rode through the narrow streets.

"He's looking for someone."

"Who?"

"His brother. He's tried to find him for the last three years, but so far, he hasn't been successful."

"How did he lose a brother?" Meredith laughed a little at the idea. She couldn't imagine just losing one of her sisters.

"It's a long story."

"You say that about a lot, you know." Meredith was surprised to hear the words she was thinking coming out of Ophelia's mouth.

"Do I?" Father's eyebrows went up.

Both girls nodded at the same time.

"We do sort of have all day, so...," Meredith turned pleading eyes to him.

The town fell behind them and Meredith was briefly distracted by the nearness of the mountain range. A narrow passage between the two nearest came into view.

"He left his brother here when he was sixteen, before the war started. Before the country had even divided. He wanted to go to sea. By the time he came back from his first voyage, the old king was dead, his twin sons had divided the kingdom and war had been declared between them. He was conscripted into the army of Dival and never had a chance to come back to his brother."

"That wasn't that long of a story," Meredith laughed. "But it is kind of sad. I wonder how many other families had something like that happen when the war started."

"I think it's horrible. All those times Grandfather fought, he might have been fighting his own brother. What if his brother is dead? What if he was the one who killed him?" Ophelia said.

"No, he's not dead. Stephan knows that much. He just doesn't know where he is."

The further into the mountain pass they rode, the happier Meredith was that she had convinced Father to take them. A deep forest, alien from the one she had known, grew up the sides of the mountains on either side. Most of the trees were tall evergreens, holding onto their dark green hues in the face of the approaching winter. There was a spattering of orange, gold, and red amongst the pines as other trees shed their leaves. The ground beneath the horses' feet was rocky and rough shrubbery grew along both sides of the beaten trail. For several hours they rode, deeper and deeper, the girls taking turns chatting and sitting quietly listening to the sounds of the wildlife.

"Have you ever ridden through here before?" Meredith turned to Father.

A shadow flickered briefly over his face and Meredith saw his jaw clench before answering, "Yes, once."

Meredith hesitated, wanting to ask more, but not wanting to upset him. Bits and pieces of stories she had heard throughout her childhood put themselves together in her mind. Father and Mother never talked about it, at least, not in front of the girls. But other people had. There had been something that had happened to him, here in Dorsten, something terrible.

"This is where you came when you were...," Meredith paused over the word, unsure of what Father's reaction would be.

He nodded slightly, staring ahead.

"I'm sorry," she whispered.

Father turned toward her now, a funny smile on his face. "You shouldn't be. You had nothing to do with what happened."

Before Meredith could answer, Ophelia broke in, pointing to a barely visible cabin in the woods to the right of the trail.

"There's someone who lives up here."

Meredith followed her finger and saw the cabin as well, although to her it didn't look exactly like it was lived in. Although the trees were thin enough that reaching the cabin wouldn't be a problem, there was no obvious path leading up to it.

"I don't think anybody is there. We should go look."

"No, that's not a good idea," Father said.

"Why not? It's probably empty."

"If it's not, whoever lives there clearly appreciates their privacy. I doubt they would be happy to have three strangers intrude on that."

"We could sneak up, and they would never know," Meredith suggested.

"What, spy on them like you did with Taliea? I don't think so."

Meredith's prediction was dismantled a moment later when the cabin door swung open, and a man stepped outside. Even from a distance, Meredith could tell he was stooped with age, his hair completely white, and he walked with the help of a cane. Meredith wasn't sure if the man had come out because he had seen them, or if it was merely coincidence. He was certainly heading in their direction, but he didn't really look up at them. The closer he grew, the more Meredith realized that he must have once been a very tall man. Even with his back bent and his shoulders hunched over, he could be described as tall.

"Something I can help you with?" The man's voice was surprisingly low and soft, despite the gravelly edge that came with age.

Meredith heard a gasp, and turned from the man to Father, whose face was now devoid of all color, and then back to the man. Father knew him. And she couldn't decide how he felt about that.

"Do you need something?" The man was closer now, peering up at the trio with eyes surrounded in wrinkles.

Meredith heard Father whisper something but could not catch what it was. She and Ophelia stared at him. Aside from that whisper, he appeared incapable of speech. He only stared at the old man. After a moment, the old man met Father's searching gaze.

"Who are you?" the old man said again.

"We're just passing through; we didn't mean to disturb you. We were getting ready to turn around and head back to the town now," Meredith found herself rambling, trying desperately to end Father's trance. To her shock, the old man ignored her and continued watching Father.

"No. Who are you?" he repeated.

"Drogo?" Father's voice was husky and only barely audible.

"It is you, then. Hamo."

Father nodded, but Meredith could not read his face. She racked her brain trying to remember who Drogo was, what part of Father's story he fit into.

"Thought you would forget about me," Drogo said at last.

"How could I forget the man that saved my life?"

That was it. That was the connection in the pieces of stories Meredith had heard. Drogo was the man who saved Father from dying. No one moved for several seconds, and Meredith began to wonder just how long they would sit there, when Drogo motioned with his hand.

"Come. Come inside," he hesitated, a frown crossing his face as he looked at Father again. "If you want to, that is. You do not have to."

For the first time since they had seen the man, Father smiled slightly.

"I want to."

Meredith glanced over to Ophelia, who shrugged uncertainly. Drogo had been speaking directly to Father. Were they supposed to come inside, too, Meredith wondered. He didn't seem to even notice that they were there. Ophelia did not move, and Meredith was tempted to do the same. But she was curious, so curious. All her life she'd known there were secrets, there were parts of Father's life that were hidden. Every so often, she had seen the secrecy crack, but never enough to really know the truth. Here was a chance, an opportunity thrown into her lap to discover something of Father's past.

Reaching a decision, she swung her leg over her horse's back and slid to the ground. Her movement brought both Father and Drogo's attention to her.

"Who is this?" Drogo still directed his question to Father.

"My daughters, Meredith and Ophelia."

Drogo nodded slowly, taking in the sight of them as if he had just now seen them.

"They look like you. You may come inside as well." Drogo motioned back toward the cabin.

Father came out of the daze he had been in and tied the horses to a low hanging branch nearby before following them up to the cabin.

The inside of the cabin was sparse. The iron stove, along with a table and two chairs occupied one half of the front room while a stone hearth and another chair took up the other half. A door at the back of the room led to what Meredith assumed was a bedroom. A collection of pots and cooking utensils hung on hooks on the wall above the stove, but otherwise there was little decoration. Lying on the floor before the hearth, was the largest dog Meredith had ever seen. Only, when she looked closer, she was sure it wasn't quite a dog. There was something about it, something almost savage in its face. She turned when she heard Father's sharp intake of breath.

"Is that a..."

"Wolf. Yes, but she's harmless. I found her about ten years ago. She was a pup then. Orphaned. Starving. I decided it was nice to have someone to look after. I took her in."

The animal sensed they were talking about her, and her long, thick tail thumped a slow rhythm on the floor.

"You live here all alone then?" Meredith asked, still watching the wolf warily.

"Yes."

"Don't you ever get lonely?" Meredith bit down on her tongue as soon as the words left her mouth. She should think before she spoke, like Mother was forever telling her. Then she wouldn't ask complete strangers rude questions.

"Sometimes." He turned to Father. "How are you still alive? They sent you north. No one escapes from them."

"We never reached them. We were rescued, all of us."

"By whom?"

"An old friend of my father's and my brother. They were scouting, and they came across us. They didn't know I was there."

"I'm glad," Drogo said softly. "Very glad."

"What about you? What happened to you after we left?"

Meredith and Ophelia settled themselves on the floor near the fireplace and listened as Drogo spoke. For more than an hour, Father and Drogo spoke with little input from the girls, although, to Meredith's disappointment, most of their conversation revolved around what happened after Father was rescued. She had been hoping for more insight into what had happened to him in the first place.

"How did you two meet?" she finally spoke up.

"That's a long story. And, unfortunately, one that we don't have time for," Father answered. "We need to head back if we're going to reach town before dark. You girls go ahead and get the horses, I'll be out in a minute."

Meredith tried to cover her disappointment as she said goodbye to Drogo.

"Can we come back and visit?"

"Yes. I think I'd like that," he answered, smiling.

A tiny part of Meredith wanted to hang back and listen in on whatever Father and Drogo said to each other when they were alone, but Ophelia guessed her thoughts and tugged gently on her arm.

"There's some things you don't have a right to hear, Meri."

It was several minutes before Father appeared and when he did, his face was unreadable. The ride home was far quieter than the one coming. Meredith and Ophelia spoke only occasionally and Father not at all.

Chapter 16

SASHA COULD FEEL BORIS' GLARE from across the campfire, but shrugged it off. Boris shouldn't be mad at him just because he had done something useful, and Boris hadn't. It wasn't like it was getting Sasha any special favors from Armin. They had both been left behind to guard the bound prisoners, livestock, and pack horses again while the rest of the group raided another settlement. This one proved more successful than the last, adding to their wretched collection of slaves another sixteen people. None of them had tried to escape, a fact that Sasha grudgingly admitted he was glad of. His success at stopping the first runaway had brought with it the acceptance and camaraderie he had craved, but it also brought some unpleasant nightmares.

"Think we'll head back yet?" Boris finally broke the tense silence between them.

"Don't know. No one knows we're here yet. Armin said no one got away today either."

"We're pushing awfully deep into their country though. We can't be that far from the capital."

Sasha shut his eyes, trying to picture the map he and Boris had poured over before the raids started. It was a challenging task. The passes through the mountains wound and twisted and splintered off into new passes so much that it was difficult to maintain a good sense of distance or direction.

"We're pretty close, I think."

"I'm bored." Boris pulled his sword out its sheath and ran an appraising finger over its sharpened edges.

He'd already spent most of the morning sharpening it while the others were on the raid.

"What do you want me to do about it?" Sasha sounded more irritable than he intended. The truth was, he was equally bored. Aside from his moment of glory bringing down the runaway, the raid had been disappointing.

"Think Armin would let us go hunting?"

"Probably not."

Boris slid his sword back into its sheath and laid it aside, turning his attention to an equally sharpened dagger.

"If he raids again tomorrow, and it's successful, I'm going to ask him. If he says yes, will you come with me?"

"Sure. But he's not going to say yes."

"He might. Fresh meat is worth it. I'm tired of eating this dried stuff."

Sasha watched Boris start sharpening his knife's blade again, and then let his eyes wander over to the group of captives they had accumulated from the two towns. It was a mixed group of men and women, the youngest in the group being around ten or eleven and the oldest around thirty. Most appeared to have accepted their fate at this point, staring out of hopeless eyes, shuffling along when they moved camps. That was why Father said these people were born to be slaves. They slipped so easily into the listless, submissive state required of them.

No one from Aruuk would behave in such a manner if they were captured. Of course, no one in Aruuk would allow themselves to be captured. It was a dishonor, not only to the captured one, but also to their family. And dishonor was something you didn't want to live with in Aruuk. Looking at these people now, Sasha understood what Father was saying. Some people were just born to serve, to obey, to be weaker than others, cowards. Thank goodness he was not one of those people.

Sasha played out in his mind what he would have done if he had been in the same place as these people. He was sure he wouldn't be meekly going along. He would fight. He would take as many as he could with him. He would get away. He was born to do that.

"At this rate, I can't wait until we go home. This was supposed to be more exciting." Boris put his knife up and threw himself back on the ground. "I wonder if Father would be on our side if we told him that Armin wouldn't let us help?"

"Doubt it. He trusts Armin."

Chapter 17

MEREDITH SMILED WHEN SHE SAW the cabin in the trees. It had taken all her persuasive talent to convince Father to let her and Phelie come up here alone. But he had a meeting, the last one, and the next day they were going home. Meredith was secretly glad that it worked out that way. Without Father along, she wouldn't hesitate to ask Drogo for stories about him. Perhaps this would be her only chance to find out what was in Father's past that he was so troubled by. It was bad enough that he still had nightmares about it, although they weren't nearly as frequent as they had been when Meredith was a small child.

They dismounted and made their way up to the door, knocking on it. From inside, a short bark and the sound of someone walking across the floor came to their ears. Drogo opened the door a moment later and ushered them inside.

"Where's your father?"

"He couldn't come this time. And we were leaving in the morning, so this was our last chance to see you."

"I see."

Meredith looked around the room, noting that there was practically no change since the last time they had come.

"So, what brings you for a visit?"

"We wanted to hear stories about Father," Meredith answered.

"From when he was with you," Ophelia hastened to clarify. "He never talks about it."

"No, I don't suppose he would. I would not either."

"What happened?" Meredith asked.

"That really is a long story."

"We have time."

"Do you?" Drogo lowered himself into the chair before the fire and shut his eyes. The girls sat down on the floor nearby, and for a minute Meredith thought he had fallen asleep the way old people sometimes did. "It was more than twenty-five years ago when we first met."

"How?" Ophelia said.

"He was a slave," Drogo said softly. "And I was his master."

"What?" both girls cried out together.

"Not what you thought?"

"But he likes you? He says you saved his life?" Meredith studied Drogo's face with confusion. He was an old man, and it was hard to picture him as someone who would own slaves.

"He does, and I did. But that does not change what either of us were at that time."

"But you don't seem like someone who would do that?"

"No, and I'm glad of that. I hated most of the time we were at that mining camp. I never want to see another human being treated the way your father and the others with him were treated."

"What mining camp?"

"The one set up for the slaves to work in. They pulled the iron ore out the mountain, and I smelted it and forged it. What's left of the camp actually isn't far from here. Just up the trail a little way."

Drogo kept speaking, but Meredith only half listened. What Drogo said about the camp's nearness intrigued her. And with each passing moment, the conviction that she needed to see it grew. While Ophelia soaked up every word Drogo said about Father, Meredith planned how they would get there. She barely noticed the questions Ophelia put to the older man, barely acknowledged the answers. Finally, Drogo stopped speaking.

"Aren't there any other stories?" Ophelia asked.

"Not ones I would share. Your Father does not want them remembered, and for good reason. Some things are best forgotten."

"Thank you," Meredith said. "We should probably be leaving anyway. We promised him we'd be back before dark."

Ophelia's eyes watched her suspiciously as Meredith got up, but she didn't say anything. Instead, she thanked Drogo as well and followed Meredith out the door.

"We have hours before we need to leave. That's why we came out here early, remember?" Ophelia waited until they were on their horses again before challenging Meredith. "I wanted to hear more."

"But he said he wasn't going to tell us anymore anyway."

"You want to go to the camp, don't you?"

"You heard him. It's not far from here, and we just have to follow the trail. We could go look around and still be back in plenty of time."

"But we told Father we wouldn't go anywhere else."

"We didn't plan on going anywhere else. We didn't even know this place existed, so it doesn't count. Come on, Phelie! It's the only chance we'll ever have of seeing the place Father spent so much time at."

Ophelia thought about it. Meredith could see her working it out in her mind.

"We're not going anywhere except there, and we'll stay within sight of the trail," she finally conceded.

"Absolutely. Come on, we'll have to hurry."

Chapter 18

ARMIN WAS IN A RARE GOOD mood. A third village had fallen prey to their raid that morning and another twelve captives added. The pack horses were laden down with far more than they had made their initial journey with. The livestock filled a makeshift pen to capacity. And the best of it was, that no one outside of the three unfortunate settlements had any idea they were there. When Boris approached Armin with the idea of Sasha and him going hunting, it was Armin's good mood that came through for him.

"We're leaving in the morning, be back by then or we're leaving you behind." Sasha knew it was no idle threat.

Now, with his bow in one hand and a quiver full of arrows on his back, Sasha rode next to Boris through the woods. They weren't dense, but the low hanging pine boughs caused them to lay flat on their horses' necks frequently. Small game in woods like these, that were so rarely touched by human hands, was easy to find. Sasha had three squirrels in his game bag already, but he really wanted something bigger. A deer would be nice, or even a rabbit.

Boris, a much poorer shot with a bow, had nothing. For once though, the discrepancy didn't appear to bother him. He was just glad to have something to do other than sit around camp guarding prisoners who were too shocked or frightened to even try to run. Sasha had been increasingly disgusted by how easily these people gave up. Lesser people, just like Father said, knew better than to fight against greater ones. Sasha had never seen the truth of it until this raid.

"Father will be pleased with our raid, and he'll be pleased that this was my idea," Boris tired of the silence and started speaking.

"He will."

"Do you think Armin will tell him we served well?"

"I did serve well. I stopped the person who could have ruined this whole expedition, remember?"

Boris's face soured at the reminder.

"Honestly, if it wasn't for me, this raid might have been a disaster," Sasha continued, enjoying for a moment the hurt expression on his brother's face. "But, yes, I think Armin will say we both served well."

"You don't have to be like that, you know," Boris said quietly as a red flush filled his cheeks.

"Like what?" Sasha threw his hands up in mock innocence.

"Oh, never mind. We should probably head back. We're not going to catch anything around here after all the talking we just did."

Sasha couldn't argue with that, and he started to turn his horse's head back toward camp when a break in the trees caught his eye. There were buildings there. Old, dilapidated, disintegrating buildings.

"Let's check that out first." He pointed and Boris' eyes followed.

As they approached, Sasha grew puzzled. He had assumed it was another little mountain village tucked away out of sight. But the closer they got, the more obvious it was that it was not a village, and it was also not inhabited. Rather than a scattered cluster of houses, there was a neat row of long low buildings, bigger than the cabins that the other villages had. Beyond that, there was an assortment of irregularly shaped buildings, the furthest from them seemingly built around a massive stone chimney.

Most puzzling of all were the two saddled horses that stood near the entrance of that last building. Although it was clear that no one lived here, Sasha was also certain that he and Boris were not the only ones to have discovered it at the same time. Sasha nudged Boris' arm to get his attention and silently gestured to the distant horses.

"They must be inside the building. We could catch them by surprise and bring them back to Armin."

Boris nodded his agreement and urged his own mount forward again. Sasha followed at a distance, scanning the valley clearing for signs of more people. It was just two. A thrill of excitement washed over him as the realization of what they were about to do hit him. These would be the first slaves they took. He smiled as a girl emerged from the dark doorway of the structure and wandered toward another building, entirely unaware of the presence of strangers. They suspected nothing. This would be easier than he could have imagined. Boris, eager for the chance to prove himself, was already moving to intercept the girl. Sasha hung back and watched as his brother kicked his horse into a canter and closed the distance between them rapidly.

A scream echoed against the mountainsides as the girl turned and saw Boris riding down on her. And then she was thrown to the ground and Boris was off his horse, standing over her. It had taken less than ten seconds, and one of them was already caught. Sasha smiled and broke his gaze away from his brother and the girl, searching for whoever else was there. They must have heard the scream.

Chapter 19

MEREDITH TURNED OVER one of the dusty metal instruments in her hand. She recognized it as a file. She'd seen Father use one of these at the forge near their home. There was something surreal and almost eerie about the whole place. Closing her eyes, Meredith tried to picture what it must have been like twenty-five years ago. A fire would have been roaring in the enormous furnace. The room would have been unbearably hot, she knew from experience. More than once she had gone with Father to the forge and the heat inside was oppressive, suffocating.

A scream brought Meredith out of her reverie, and she glanced around the shadowy room. Ophelia wasn't in here. How long had she been gone? Meredith looked at the tool in her hand, considering, then dropped it into her pocket. No one was going to miss it from here, and it would make a nice souvenir. Turning her back on the huge smelting furnace, she retraced her steps to the doorway and peered outside, searching for Ophelia.

"Phelie?"

Meredith's heart stopped. A cold wave of horror washed over her. Her feet froze in place. There was Phelie, not twenty feet in front of her. But she was lying face down on the ground, and a strange man knelt over her, tying her hands behind her. Only, when he turned to look at her, Meredith could see that he was actually around the same age as herself. The realization was followed immediately by a red-hot surge of anger. Who was this person who thought he could treat her sister like that?

"STOP!" Her voice sounded loud in the silence as she started forward.

A hand clamped over her mouth. An arm wrapped itself around her, yanking her to a stop. Meredith stifled another scream rising in her throat and twisted, fighting to break free of the imprisoning grasp. For several seconds, the hold on her slipped and she threw herself forward in a final gamble for freedom.

It was hopeless. No matter how she fought and kicked and threw herself about, the hand did not leave her mouth, and the arm did not release her. Instead, it dragged her inexorably forward. A voice, coming from just behind her, spoke but the words were unintelligible to her. It brought the other young man to his feet, and he approached her, a length of rope in his hand. For one awful second, Meredith caught sight of her sister's unmoving form and all her own fear drained away giving way to the flood of horror at the thought of Ophelia dead. Meredith went limp. It was so unexpected that she slid out of her captor's grasp and sank to the ground.

Ophelia gone. Ophelia dead. It couldn't be. A numbness crept over her. She barely registered her own hands being pulled behind her, a thin rope twisting around her wrists, holding them in place.

"You killed her," her voice was a husky whisper, devoid of any feeling. "You killed her."

"She's not dead," whoever held her from behind said, his voice heavy with an accent. "She's no use to us dead."

If the words had been meant to reassure Meredith, they could not have had a worse outcome. All the fury that had died down at the sight of her sister, all the fear that had drained away into shock came flooding back.

"You monsters!" she screamed, kicking out at the one in front of her. Her foot connected with his shin, and he stumbled back with a grunt of pain. A cold prick on the side of Meredith's throat sparked a warning.

"Enough." The word, reinforced with the blade of a knife, brought Meredith to her senses. She didn't stand a chance, not now, not alone.

"What do you want with us?" she tried to twist around to get a look at the speaker, but his hand grabbed a fistful of her hair causing her to yelp in pain and pulled her to her feet instead.

Ignoring her question, he and the other young man conversed while he shoved her toward where Ophelia was just starting to stir.

"Phelie?" Meredith watched in horror as her sister was pulled roughly up and she caught sight of her face. Blood dripped down from a gash above her left eye, and even though her eyes were open, it was clear that Ophelia was not entirely aware of what was happening. A dazed, glassy expression covered her face, and she made no effort to fight against the young man dragging her to her feet.

As much as Meredith wished to get away, the realization that she couldn't without leaving Phelie behind weighed upon her. Whether that realization was visibly apparent, or it was merely coincidence, Meredith couldn't decide, but her captor's hands relinquished their grip on her. He stepped in front of her to join his companion, and Meredith got her first look at the man who'd held a knife to her throat. He was slightly younger than his companion, and his blue eyes carried a smug self-satisfaction that almost set her off again. She bit down on her lip to quell the riot of fear and anger that swelled in her chest.

Try as she might, Meredith could not decipher the words that passed between the two. Their language didn't sound a bit like the one Taliea slipped into every now and then. While the younger one walked over toward the girls' horses, the other grabbed Ophelia by the arm and motioned for Meredith to follow. Meredith hung back for a second, but even as she did, she knew she would follow. They knew she would follow. So long as Ophelia was in their hands, so was she.

Despite having both the girls' horses in hand, no offer was made to let them ride. As they started off towards their unknown destination, Meredith cast a final glance about, desperately hoping for...she wasn't really sure. No one knew they had come here. No one had seen what happened. The soonest they would even be missed was in the evening, hours from now. They're younger captor must have noticed her searching eyes.

"If you run, I will shoot you."

Meredith glared at him.

The trail they were taking was hardly worthy of that title. Rugged, narrow and steep it would have been difficult to traverse in the best of circumstances. Meredith stole another worried glance at her sister. The blood had dried, the cut scabbed over, but her sister's face was pale, and beads of sweat clung to her forehead. Her steps were clumsy, and she wobbled precariously on the uneven ground. They did not make it far before Ophelia's dizziness caught up with her. A root caught at her foot, and she fell forward onto her knees.

"She needs help. Untie me and I'll help her."

"You'll run."

"And leave my sister? No, I'm not a monster like you."

To Meredith's outrage, he laughed at her.

"It's alright, Meri." Ophelia struggled back to her feet and stood unsteadily, her eyes meeting Meredith's begging her to stop. "I'll be fine."

It took more than an hour before Meredith heard other people. As the camp came into view, Meredith felt Ophelia shrink back next to her. Every eye in the camp was turned toward them. A man stood up from the farthest fire and called out a greeting as he came towards them. His eyes narrowed as he got near and he looked first Ophelia, and then Meredith, over appraisingly. Before Meredith had time to react his hand darted out and caught her chin, jerking her face up to meet his own. Meredith met his eyes briefly, then looked down, a cold fear rising in her as she took in the hardness inside his eyes. He dropped her face and moved to Ophelia, performing the same detached inspection. He spoke to the two who had brought them.

"You're twins, right?" The younger one dismounted and came around to face them.

Meredith clenched her teeth together. There was no way she was going to answer these animals. Ophelia simply nodded. The young man turned and said something to the others that made everyone laugh. Meredith went hot all over, the blood rising to her cheeks, her breath coming heavy.

"You're a matched set. You'll make more at market," the young man offered an explanation.

"You won't get away with this," Meredith spit the words out. "We're not that far from people who will come looking for us."

"Oh really? How far?"

Meredith bit her tongue. She should have just kept her mouth shut. If they didn't know how close they were to the capital of Dorsten, she wouldn't be the one to enlighten them. Her questioner's eyes narrowed for a moment and a flash of anger darted across his face. Catching Meredith off guard, the back of his hand bit into the side of her face and she staggered back a step.

"How far?" he repeated.

"Stop. The capital's less than a day away," Ophelia intervened, her eyes staring at the ground, refusing to meet Meredith's.

An instant's satisfaction was granted to Meredith when she saw how this news was received. Her captor's blue eyes went wide, and he turned and rattled off something to the older man who in turn began barking orders. Both Meredith and Ophelia were grabbed and yanked toward a group of people Meredith noticed for the first time. Dejection and despair were written all over the faces of this group as they sat bound together. Meredith let out a little gasp of relief when her own bonds were temporarily removed. Then she was added to the rope attaching several of the others together, with her hands in front of her this time.

"Meri, what are we going to do?" Ophelia's voice whispered in her ear when the men who secured them walked away.

"I don't know."

"Father's not even going to know what's happened to us."

"I know."

"This wouldn't have happened if we hadn't gone."

"I know," Meredith's voice trembled slightly, fighting back the tears that burned in her eyes. "I'm sorry."

She couldn't cry. She wouldn't cry. Not in front of these people. Squeezing her eyes shut, Meredith willed the tears to go away, willed the burning in her nose to stop, willed the quivering in her lip to cease. But it didn't do any good. A single tear, and then another, and another slid down her cheeks. The most she could do was pray none of those horrid men were watching her. As she thought about it, her eyes flicked about the camp site. They were all too busy to notice the tears of one of their captives. Doubtless, she wasn't the first one who had shed some. Surreptitiously, she brought her bound hands up, trying to wipe away any sign and that's when she saw them. Both the young men responsible for her and Ophelia's current state were watching her and talking, almost assuredly about her and her sister. It was all the motivation Meredith needed to bring herself back under control. She glared at them for a moment, a hatred filling her that would have terrified her at any other moment. Meredith had never hated anyone in her life. Until now.

The haste with which the entire camp was dismantled was incredible. Obviously, they were not comfortable staying so close to the heart of Dorsten. As the group set off, Meredith found herself pulled along behind five or six others. Ophelia was directly in front of her, and no one was behind her. No one, that is, except for one of their captors. Meredith turned her head enough to see that it was the one who spoke their language.

Already tired, the trek became exhausting. The trail they took was less traveled, rockier, and did not necessarily stay sandwiched between two mountains. They had been walking for nearly two hours and were now being led across a particularly narrow part of the path. The sheer wall of a mountain rose above them to one side, while to the other the earth dropped away into a twenty-foot-deep ravine. They had passed several such ravines already, and with each of them, Meredith watched her sister's back stiffen, watched her press herself as far as she could against the rock wall. At least she seemed to be staying on her feet better, Meredith thought. Meredith's focus was so taken with watching her sister in front of her, that she barely noticed where she was placing her own feet. Stubbing her toe against a rock jutting out from the ground brought her eyes back to the path in front of her. Desperate to regain her balance, she reached out to grab onto the rock wall beside them. Expecting to feel the rough surface of stone beneath her hands, Meredith was in no way prepared for the cool, slippery rope that slithered through her fingers and onto her arm.

Snake.

With a scream that could have been heard from miles away, Meredith flung the creature away from her, into the depths of the ravine while stumbling backwards - straight into a horse. With a shrill squeal the animal careened backward, onto its haunches, throwing its rider free from the saddle, and into the ravine. The horse, off balanced, followed its rider in the plunge.

For one horrifying second, Meredith gaped at the spot where horse and rider had been. Her entire body trembled at the rush of adrenaline, and the rudeness with which it had all happened. A shout from the front of the group rang out. A tug on the rope that tethered her to the others jerked her almost off her feet. They were moving again. And no one bothered to check on the fallen rider. In fact, no one seemed at all disturbed at the loss. Meredith felt sick.

Chapter 20

IT STARTED WITH A SCREAM. Sasha knew that much. There had been a scream, and his horse spooked. Then there was falling. He hadn't fallen far. Not far enough to kill him, anyway, or he wouldn't be able to think like this. Then the stop. Something crunching inside his chest, slamming all the air out of them. And then there was darkness. Groaning, he opened his eyes, almost surprised to find that they worked. He tried to bring them into focus, tried to gather his wits. Slowly, slowly his eyes told him he was lying face down in the dirt. Now that he had established that, Sasha tested each limb. His legs were sore, but functional. His right arm moved at his will, but his left one struggled. His attempt to move it sent pain shooting through that shoulder and all the way down the arm into his hand.

Positioning his right arm underneath himself, Sasha tried to push himself up off the ground. Agony ripped through his chest and side as if someone were stabbing a hot knife into his torso over and over again. Even the tiniest breath was almost unbearable. Black dots clouded his vision and the pain threatened to overwhelm him as he sank down again, this time on his back. The sun, brilliant in the late autumn sky, beat down on his face, warming him.

Sasha jerked back awake, and the first thing he noticed was that the sun was no longer directly over the ravine. It was sinking lower. He had to get up. He had to move. He had to find his group. They couldn't be that far away, surely. Gritting his teeth against the pain he knew would come as soon as he started to move, Sasha braced himself and sat up slowly, moving only an inch or two at a time. It was the best he could do. The pain was simply too great, too monstrous to push through.

Once he was sitting, Sasha looked around him more closely. There, only a few feet away from him, lay his horse - dead. So much for riding back to the others, although Sasha doubted his ability to pull himself onto a horse at the moment. His left arm was pretty much useless, the pain in his chest told him that he most likely had at least one broken rib, and his head was throbbing as if it wanted to explode.

A rock jutted out above his head, and Sasha wondered if that was what had caused the impact in his chest when he fell. Whatever part it played in injuring him, he gripped it now with his good hand and pulled himself up. The world spun. The rock in front of him blurred and separated into two, then three rocks before coming back into focus as just one. When he finally felt confident enough to let go of the rock, Sasha lifted an exploratory hand to his head. It came away sticky and warm with blood.

He had to walk. There was no question in his mind about that. What there was a question in his mind was which direction he needed to walk in. If he could just bring his brain back under control, he could figure it out, he knew. But his head was splitting with the worst headache he had ever had. And his lungs were screaming for more air than he could stand to breathe in now. He took his first step away from the rock and nearly collapsed. Then another. Another. One foot in front of the other. Eyes locked onto the ground before him that swam treacherously.

The ground sloped upward, and Sasha kept going, steeling himself against the stabbing pain in his chest as his lungs required more and more air for his exertion. By the time the ground leveled out a bit at the end of the ravine, Sasha was trapped in a walking nightmare. He could put one foot in front of the other,

S.T. Hobbs

but precious little else. He started off in the easiest direction.

Sasha lost all sense of both time and direction. The only thought he could put together was that if he didn't catch back up to his group, he would die. Surely, they had stopped and camped nearby to give him a chance to catch up. They would probably even send out a search party as soon as they had their captives secured. They would not just abandon one of Chief Gundar's sons. They couldn't. The thought burned so deeply into his mind that when the soft whinny of a horse nearby roused him, he was sure he had finally made it. Staggering the last few paces toward the source of that sound, Sasha's heart filled with hope. He was saved. They hadn't left him behind.

His eyes registered the group of horsemen. His lips tried to form a cry for help. But his strength was spent. Wordlessly, he sank to the ground in a faint.

Cold water splashed across Sasha's face, waking him and causing him to gasp for air. It was a mistake. No sooner did he suck in a gulp of air then his chest began screaming in that searing agony. His gasp turned into a tortured, breathless cry. There were faces in his vision. Strange faces. Men he had never seen before were bending over him, staring at him - and speaking to him, he realized belatedly. Reducing his breaths to shallow, less painful ones, he managed to make out what was being asked of him.

"Who are you and what happened to you?" Although Sasha understood the words, his heart sank. These weren't his people. They were his enemies. The same people he had spent the last week raiding. Fortunately, they either didn't know about the raids, or they hadn't recognized Sasha's clothing. The best Sasha could do was to keep it that way.

"I fell," he said, the words eating up his energy, and the effort of speaking antagonizing his broken ribs.

"Bad fall, too, by the looks of it. Where are you from, boy?" The words were not said unkindly, and Sasha was sure if he could come up with a convincing lie about where he was from, that it would stay that way. He didn't get the chance though. Another man shouldered his way into the huddle.

"Northerner. Aruuken. Look at his clothes, and this," the man pulled the wolf's tooth talisman away from Sasha's neck, "they all wear one of these."

Sasha shut his eyes. So much for lying about it. At least he hadn't already lied.

"What are you doing here?" The first man's tone changed entirely, hardening.

"Nothing." To save his life, Sasha could not think of a better answer. The truth was too damning, and his brain refused to work properly to form a good story.

"Hmph. I doubt that."

The sea of faces staring down at him evaporated as the men stepped back to converse amongst themselves. Sasha tried to make out their words but failed. It was probably for the best. He didn't really want to hear what they were planning to do with him, since it would almost certainly result in his death. They were probably just debating on whether they should kill him outright or leave him for the wolves to find and finish off.

After what felt like an eternity, the first man knelt next to him again. His hands tugged at Sasha's clothing, pulling his shirt open and away from him. Then the man's calloused hands ran along his chest, appraising his injuries. Even that light pressure was more than Sasha could quietly bear. He cried out and tried to pull away.

"Lay still," the man told him gruffly, "You're not going anywhere. Broke at least two, maybe three. And," the man's hand traveled up to his left shoulder, "Messed this up. Must have been quite a fall doing nothing."

"What are you going to do with me?" Sasha's voice was little more than a ragged whisper and he was ashamed of the fear in it.

"Taking you with us. We'll see just how much 'nothing' you were really doing." Even as he spoke the words, he was lifting Sasha up into a sitting position and turning to another man. "Give me a hand with this."

"What are you doing with him, Norman?"

"You'll see."

Sasha was just as concerned as to what the man called Norman was planning on doing to him but decided he probably shouldn't ask. Instead, his eyes followed every move Norman made. Norman pulled a handkerchief from his pocket and twisted it up before shoving it into Sasha's unresisting mouth.

"You'll want to bite down on that. It might help."

Sasha's eyes widened but he made no effort to spit the cloth out again. Norman moved behind him and directed the second man to hold Sasha in place. This could not be done without causing Sasha a good deal more pain than he was already in. He whimpered into the cloth.

"That's not even the worst part," Norman said from behind him.

Sasha didn't get the chance to wonder what the worst part was going to be before Norman grabbed his left arm and wrenched it. The sucking pop of the bone sliding back into its joint was lost in the scream that ripped out of Sasha's throat. Norman and the other man stepped away, leaving Sasha gasping, spitting out the wet handkerchief.

"That was the worst part."

A rope materialized from somewhere, and Sasha found his hands being pulled together in front of him. Norman secured the rope around his wrists, leaving a length of it dangling free.

"Get up."

Sasha tried to obey, but even with his shoulder back in place, there was an overwhelming amount of pain coursing through him, and movement made it worse. Two pairs of hands reached for him and jerked him to his feet. Sasha saw now why the length of rope had been left. As Norman mounted his horse, he held the far end of it in his hand. Sasha was walking. He hoped they didn't have far to take him, or he wasn't going to make it alive. A tug on the rope propelled him forward awkwardly. He didn't make it twenty steps before he collapsed, face down, howling at the sudden impact on his rib cage. Either Norman didn't notice right away or simply didn't care, because Sasha was dragged several feet across the rocky ground before the horse came to a stop.

"I... can't...walk...," Sasha gasped as Norman came back for him.

The man studied him for a long moment, frowning. Then, with a shrug, he dismounted.

"No, I guess you can't."

Sasha worried for a moment that he would decide to just kill him instead, but Norman pulled him back up and helped him towards his own horse.

Even riding would have been a disaster if he hadn't been held in place by Norman. As it was, the jostling was horrible, but he at least didn't have to fight to stay conscious. He could simply yield to the blackness that dotted his eyes.

The sun sank beneath the western horizon and a damp chill settled over the night air. Sasha barely noticed the fading light, but he was acutely aware of the drop in temperature. Winter was coming and the night air hinted at it causing Sasha to shiver, which hurt. They had been moving for a long time, many hours Sasha thought. He wasn't sure how much longer he could tolerate it. Every step the horse took jarred him. He shut his eyes again.

When he opened them again, Sasha snapped fully awake. They weren't riding through the mountain pass anymore. They were riding through a town, a large town. The pale, silvery light of the moon was punctured by the yellow flicker of streetlamps. Painfully forcing his head up, Sasha tried to take it all in and piece together where exactly he was. Silhouetted against the mountains and wreathed in enough light to give it an almost ghostly glow stood the walls and towers of what could only be a castle. But that wasn't where they were going.

The horse beneath Sasha stopped, and Sasha's own hold was so weak he nearly pitched forward off the animal's back. Hands grabbed him and pulled him safely down. Sasha's legs, which he thought were uninjured, screamed in protest at the sudden burden of his own weight, and Sasha was tempted to just sit down where he was. He was not given the opportunity, though, as the same hands that lifted him down now propelled him forward to a low stone building in front of them. Sasha's eyes took in the stone walls and barred windows and although he could not read the sign that hung above the door, he had very little doubt as to the purpose of this building.

Inside, a nauseating stench assaulted his nose, strong enough to make his eyes water. It was brighter in here than out in the streets. Sasha was shoved forward, almost falling into a small desk. Seated behind it, with his feet propped up on it, was the jailer.

"What do you have for me tonight, Norman?"

Norman didn't answer right away as he was busy undoing the knots that bound Sasha's wrists. It was not until the rope came loose and fell away that he turned to the man.

"Northerner. Keep him here in holding. I've got to talk to the lord and see what he wants to do."

"Anything you say."

The man's feet swung down from off the desk. He rose and came around to where Sasha stood unsteadily.

"He understand what we're saying?" the jailer asked while his hands began searching Sasha for weapons, causing Sasha to wince. The men who had brought him here hadn't bothered, and the only weapon he had left anyway after his fall was his dagger. This the jailer took from him, throwing it down with a noisy clatter on the desk.

"Yes, he does. I'll be back later for him, I'm sure."

Sasha heard the door shut behind Norman, and then the jailer had him by the arm, leading him back through a door. Beyond the door, the smell magnified itself, and Sasha wished for probably the hundredth time that day that he could just stop breathing. A hallway, well-lit by torches mounted to both walls, opened up to them. Heavy wooden doors, reinforced with iron bands lined both sides and it was to the first of these doors that the jailer led him. For the first time he was taken, Sasha balked. It didn't take much imagination to guess what faced him on the other side of that door. He would be locked in, trapped inside a small room.

"Don't get any funny ideas." The jailer's hand on his arm tightened and Sasha noticed for the first time the two guards that stood in the hallway. Running wasn't an option here.

Pushing down the rising panic in his chest, Sasha watched the man pull out a ring of keys and unlock the door. Beyond the heavy door, the room was much larger than Sasha had imagined. And it was occupied.

A dozen faces turned to look at him, and Sasha thought that he'd seen dogs eye fresh meat with more compassion. Swallowing, he followed the jailer's motion for him to step inside.

"Here's a new friend come to spend the night," the jailer nudged Sasha all the way in, "He's from up North so be nice to him."

The tone of the man's voice hinted at the opposite, and Sasha felt sick at the effect the jailer's words had on the men he would be locked up with. As the door shut behind him, and he heard the lock click shut, Sasha attempted to gather his wits and brace himself for whatever was coming. To his surprise, no one made any move, although they still watched him. His upbringing chose that moment to resurface and a flood of anger at how he had been and was being treated filled him. He was, after all, the son of a sovereign chief. Even captured, he deserved to be treated better than common criminals, locked up in a filthy hole. Gritting his teeth against the pain that still gnawed at him, he lifted his head, ignoring the mockery and menace in the eyes of these lesser people, and made his way to an empty spot along the back wall.

His hauteur lasted all the way up to the moment he sat down gingerly. He was exhausted. More than exhausted. He was drained of both physical and mental energy. He knew he should snap himself out of it, find a way to escape this place, at the very least come up with a good story for how he ended up here in the first place, but he just couldn't. Leaning his head back against the rough stone and realized why this spot had been empty.

A trickle of water came in through the window above his head. It must have started raining. Giving up, Sasha shut his eyes.

Something was wrong.

Sasha could sense it in his sleep, but he was powerless to rouse himself out of his slumber, or to even pinpoint the source of his unease. A seed of worry dug into his mind, trying to nudge him to action. It was the silence, Sasha realized drowsily. The cell had not been silent since he was brought in - was it minutes ago or hours? There had been the murmur of voices, then the sounds of men sleeping. Now there was nothing. A void of quiet enveloped him. Frowning in his sleep, he tried to reach for some explanation.

Something thick and soft pushed up against his mouth, forcing its way between his teeth. A rancid taste filled his mouth and Sasha's eyes flew open - only to be met by total darkness. Not the darkness of night, but a smothering, blanket of blackness wrapped tightly about his face. A soft chuckle came from directly in front of him as several pairs of hands took hold of him, pulling him away from the wall.

Sasha thrashed against the grip of at least four of his cellmates. The only thing he accomplished was sending a savage pain through his torso. His cries were muffled by the foul cloth filling his mouth. The pain was awful. The thought of what was about to happen was frightening. His own powerlessness to stop it was humiliating. But worse, far worse than any of those things was the primal terror of having his face entirely encased in a thick, black hood. He couldn't breathe. He couldn't see. He couldn't escape it. Trapped. Trapped, just like in that cellar so long ago. Sasha's heart pounded. His lungs screamed for air that wasn't fast enough in coming. Blood rushed to his head, pulsing in his ears.

It was only a matter of seconds before Sasha was pinned on the floor, held down by his arms and legs, and whoever was holding the hood over his head. His lungs worked faster and faster, ignoring the pain that tore through his body. The only thought that pounded through his brain was that he had to get away, he had to break free from these men and tear that awful cloth imprisoning his face off.

The lukewarm water hit the cloth and soaked in, stealing Sasha's breath. He tried to twist his head to the side to escape it, but the hands that held the hood over his head were too strong. As more and more water poured over his mouth and nose, and his lungs began to burn for want of oxygen, Sasha renewed his efforts to get loose, jerking his arms and legs against the hands that held them firmly in place. His only reward was a man's booted foot stomping directly on his midsection. Sasha inhaled with the pain - a breath full of water.

As suddenly as it started, the water stopped. The cloth, soaked as it was, still clung to his face making breathing nearly impossible - but not quite. Sasha could hear his own muted whimpers mingled with the restrained laughter of his tormentors. Surely the guards in the hallway could hear too. Surely, they weren't going to just leave him to the mercy of these criminals.

"You know, I really don't like you Northern dogs," the words were whispered directly into his ears. "Only one way I know of to deal with you, and it's a bit messy. You're not going to like it."

A chill crept over Sasha as the cool tip of a knife brushed against his throat. He shuddered against it and the laughter of the others filled his ears again. They weren't trying very hard to stay quiet. They were enjoying this. His pain and fear were amusing to them, Sasha realized. With agonizing slowness, the speaker slid the knife down from his throat to his chest. Paralyzed now with horror, Sasha felt the blade travelling down his body, digging in every now and then. Not enough to cut, but enough to make him tense and flinch. The man was toying with him. His body trembled. His breathing hitched. He wanted to beg, to plead, to offer these men anything in return for this to end, but the rank cloth in his mouth turned his words to garbled noise. The knife continued its journey down his stomach, into his groin. The paralysis snapped as realization of what they were about to do dawned on

Sasha. Screaming against his gag, he threw himself from side to side. The laughter swelled. The knife pressed in.

And then it was gone. The knife disappeared from his skin. The hands released him. A new set of hands grabbed his arms. He was pulled backwards. Voices rang out, but he couldn't understand them. All he understood was that he was being sat up against a wall. His arms were dropped. He brought them up again quickly, clawing at the hood over his face. It came off easily now, and he spit the filthy rag out with it.

Sasha didn't look around. He didn't try to make sense of what had just happened. He leaned against the wall, his body quivering, his breath gasping, and tears spilling out of his eyes and running down his cheeks. Sasha was crying. Sasha hadn't cried in years, not since the night Mother was taken away. He had no idea how long he sat there, allowing the tears to flow. He gradually became aware of an argument taking place above his head.

"If they'd killed him before we questioned him, you would have been held responsible." Sasha looked up to find Norman standing only a foot or so away from him, his back turned to him, and the jailer just beyond him.

"They weren't going to kill him. They were just having a bit of fun with him. Look at him, he's already feeling better. Just think of it as a bit of softening him up. You know you're going to put him through it when you question him anyway."

"It's not the same and you know it."

"If that's what you need to tell yourself. You know as well as I do, the lord will get his answers, and he doesn't care how they come."

Sasha tried to push away the despair that washed over him. Here he thought he was being rescued. His torment was just being postponed. The thought made him ridiculously angry.

"You can't treat me like this." Sasha surprised himself at his own boldness.

"Oh, and why's that?" Norman turned, eyebrows raised, and faced him.

"I... I'm the chief's son. He'll make you suffer if you hurt me."

"Good to know. I'll keep that in mind if I ever see him. Let's go 'chief's son'." Norman reached down and pulled him to his feet. "You've got some questions to answer. And I'd suggest you think twice about how you speak to us. I'm sure the chief would be thrilled to hear his son cried his first night in prison."

Chapter 21

"GLAD THAT'S OVER FOR ANOTHER year," Stephan said as he and Hamo exited the council hall early in the afternoon. "And not a day too soon. I'm ready to leave."

Hamo nodded absently.

"Where are the girls at?" Stephan asked.

"They wanted to visit Drogo again before we left."

"Funny how you found him again after all these years. Maybe I should pay him a visit too."

"Why?" Hamo glanced over.

"Seems like a good person to get to know." Stephan shrugged.

"We could ride up there and meet them, if you wanted. It'd be better than just sitting around here all evening."

"Still don't enjoy this, do you?"

Hamo shook his head, turning his steps toward the courtyard. The two men crossed it quickly and entered the stables. A quick glance reassured Hamo that the girls' horses weren't back yet. Saddling their own, it was only a short time before they left the castle and town behind.

"No luck finding your brother yet?"

"None." Stephan shook his head in frustration. "I'm beginning to think he's avoiding me."

"Here it is," Hamo gestured toward the nearly hidden cabin, "But I don't see their horses anywhere."

"Maybe he's got a barn out back they put them in."

"Maybe." Hamo frowned, a germ of worry implanting itself in his mind.

"One way to find out." Stephan moved to get off his horse just as the door to Drogo's cabin swung open.

"Hamo, is that you?" Drogo's stooped frame still nearly filled the doorway. "The girls said you wouldn't be able to come."

"We finished up earlier than we thought. Are they in there with you?"

Drogo shook his head, stepping aside to let Hamo and Stephan in. When neither did, he turned to see the reason. Hamo's face paled, and his forehead creased in the worried lines Drogo was so familiar with.

"You thought they were still here?"

"We did," Hamo answered.

"When did they leave?" Stephan asked.

"Hours ago. They said they needed to get back. I'm sorry, Hamo." Drogo looked at his former slave with concern.

"I'm sure it's alright. They probably got back early and decided to go out in the town. You know how Meri can be when she gets bored," Stephan said. "By the time we get back, they'll probably be there wondering what's become of us.

"You're probably right. I guess we should get back, then." Hamo nodded as he spoke, as much to convince himself as anything else.

"I am sorry," Drogo repeated. "I hope all is well with them. They are very sweet girls."

Hamo smiled his appreciation. "I'm sure it'll all be fine."

Riding back toward the castle, Hamo tried to push away the nagging worry. Worrying didn't do any good, anyway. But still, Hamo's mind jumped around, seeking out the worst possibilities. What if they had become lost? Or attacked by wild animals? Hamo berated himself for letting them come up alone. But Stephan was right. The most obvious answer was that they had gone back out after they returned to the castle. It was something they would do, especially if Meri got it into her head that there was something worth seeing or doing.

It was dark by the time they passed beneath the massive entrance of the castle. Hamo went directly to the stables. They weren't there. Meredith's and Ophelia's horses weren't there. And when he asked the stable hand, the man assured him that they hadn't been there all day. Hamo felt the blood drain away from his face.

"Something's happened. I know it."

Stephan stood behind him, his face grim, his hands jammed down into his pockets.

"What are you thinking?" he finally asked.

"They're up in the mountains still. They have to be." Hamo buried his face in his hands. "Why did I let them go? This is all my fault."

Chapter 22

THIS IS ALL MY FAULT," Meredith whispered through chattering teeth. The night air in the mountains was biting and cold. "None of this would have happened if I hadn't insisted we go."

Ophelia lay quietly next to her. Meredith could feel her sister shivering with the cold as well.

"I'm not going to say we shouldn't have gone, but in all fairness, Meri, there was no possible way you could have thought this would happen. So, no, it's not all your fault. It's their fault for being the sort of monsters who kidnap other people."

Ophelia's words were strangely comforting to Meredith, who had spent most of the day berating herself. At least Ophelia didn't hold this one against her.

"Is it sort of selfish to say that I'm glad you're here with me?" Meredith turned enough to see her sister's face.

"It is, but I'm thinking the same thing so..." Ophelia met her eyes, "How are we going to get away?"

"Can we? They've kept us tied together all day, and it looks like that won't change tonight."

"We have to." Ophelia turned away. "Did you see the way they acted when one of their own fell? They didn't so much as blink an eye. They don't care."

"It was one of the ones who took us."

"What?"

"The one who fell. He was the one who put a knife to my throat. I'm glad he fell, he deserved to."

"At least it makes one less that we have to get away from."

For several minutes, Meredith lay still - as still as she could with the cold making her whole body shake. The captives had all been bunched together, still tethered in their groups, to the center of the camp. Fires formed a ring around them, keeping the area well-lit. Their captors stayed on the far side of the fires, able to monitor every movement among the captives. Meredith just wished the fires were actually close enough or big enough to keep them all warm.

"Do you think Father will find out what happened to us?" Ophelia broke the silence.

Meredith felt a tear slipping out of the corner of her eye, running down to her ear as she stared straight up at the night sky.

"I don't know. No one saw what happened."

"That's what I was afraid of."

"Just that?"

"Well, that, and belonging to one of these animals."

Chapter 23

TWO GUARDS ACCOMPANIED Norman and Sasha through the darkened streets. For once Sasha was grateful for the shadows. It gave him the time and obscurity he needed to collect himself. His heart was slowing down from its frantic hammering, he was able to regulate his breathing to the least painful rhythm possible, and the throbbing in his head receded as long as he avoided any sudden moves. Still, he couldn't quite shake his fright. After all, the jailer seemed quite certain that he was going to face more torment wherever they were taking him. His stomach churned at the thought. He already hurt so much. Why did they have to keep hurting him? What could they gain from it?

The heaviness of his eyes told him that it was either very late at night, or very early in the morning. Either way, he hadn't got nearly enough sleep after the punishment his body had taken in the last twenty-four hours. He hoped they would at least allow him a few hours of rest whenever they reached their destination.

His wish was granted when they entered the castle, and he was led to a small room on the first floor. It was mostly bare. The only furnishing being a hard wooden cot. In that moment, it was the sweetest bed in the world, especially since there was no one else in the room to threaten him. He barely registered the lock clicking into place behind him as he laid himself down and shut his eyes. If he laid on his back and breathed very carefully, he could almost forget his battered ribs. It was bliss.

Not even five minutes passed, Sasha was sure of it, when a bright light shone on his face, and a voice was telling him to get up. Groaning, Sasha tried to turn away from the light, bringing an arm up to shield his eyes. That arm was promptly grabbed.

"I just laid down." Sasha couldn't keep his complaint quiet and was rewarded by a resounding slap across the face. It stung more than anything and reminded Sasha of the way Armin had treated him. He could handle that.

Held between two guards again, Sasha was pulled along a long hallway and down a staircase.

"What are you going to do with me?" Another slap across the face, and no answer.

Sasha twisted around enough to see that door at the top of the staircase stood open still. Wherever they were going, whatever they were planning, Sasha was sure it would not be pleasant for him. Gathering himself together mentally, Sasha pulled back against his guards, throwing them off balance. Spinning around - and regretting it instantly as his head threatened to explode with pain - he made a dash for the stairs. Weakened by his ordeal, he tripped on the first step, but managed to recover himself. He didn't dare look back. Forcing one aching leg in front of the other, pushing down the stabbing in his chest, he made it halfway, three quarters of the way. Only a few more steps to go. He was out the door. And straight into a third man. The impact sent him flying back, and he would have fallen down the stairs he'd just ascended if the man hadn't been quick enough to reach out and catch the front of his shirt.

"That was a terrible idea." Looking up, Sasha recognized Norman, and his heart fell to his feet. So much for escaping.

"You're going to regret that," a thin voice came from behind Norman, and Sasha saw another man, this one dressed much finer than the others.

"Sorry, my lord. He wouldn't have got far," a guard apologized as he clamped his hand over Sasha's arm again.

"I'm sure he wouldn't have. Take him down and prepare him. I'll be there shortly."

Once down the stairs, Sasha was marshaled to a room that was unlike any other room he had ever seen. There was a table with three chairs lined up along the far side of it facing the door. The main feature of the room appeared to be two stone pillars nearly a foot in diameter and adorned by several iron bands positioned at various heights. From each of those bands protruded an iron ring on the inside of the pillars. Sasha froze.

"You can't...you can't do this to me," he said, his voice high pitched, almost squeaking. "You can't. You don't know who I am."

The guards made no acknowledgement of his words. One of them disappeared from sight behind one of the pillars, and the other forcibly helped Sasha out of his shirt. He let out a low whistle as he took in the sight of the numerous cuts and bruises that already covered his torso.

"A word of advice, boy. This'll go a lot easier if you just give 'em what they want."

Sasha blinked in disbelief at the sudden sympathy in the man's voice.

"What are you going to do to me?" Sasha dared to repeat his earlier question.

"Ask some questions. If you answer them, it won't be too bad."

Sasha didn't have time to ask what happened if he didn't before the other guard reappeared, two heavy chains in his hands. He passed one off to his companion and then took Sasha's right arm. The clamp of the iron cuff over his wrist sent a chill through him. The feeling was replicated on his other wrist, and he was led forward to the spot between the pillars. He noticed as he stepped forward that the place they were making him stand was not the same as the rest of the floor. Instead of smoothed stone, it was bits and pieces of cut rock. It didn't exactly hurt his feet through his boots, but it wasn't fun to stand on either. The chains were fed through the rings nearest eye level with him, and then pulled tight and secured. His left shoulder was quick to protest. Having been dislocated and relocated in less than a day's time, the soreness was still present. With his arms stretched out to either side of him, Sasha struggled to draw a relatively painless breath. His arms weren't pulled tight enough to be painful. In fact, if it hadn't been for his broken ribs, they would have just been uncomfortable.

The two men went behind his back, and for a moment Sasha thought they left the room. A black object flashed in front of his eyes, and the next thing Sasha knew, his face was covered in much the same way it had been by the criminals he'd been locked up with. He let out an involuntary cry of shock and panic and twisted his head from side to side trying to rid himself of it.

"It's not coming off, and if it does, we'll just tie it on next time," it was the kind guard who spoke.

"How many is he supposed to get?" the other guard queried.

"Ten. Just soften him up a bit, you know how the lord likes it."

Ten? Ten what? Sasha stopped trying to get the black hood off and listened carefully. He wasn't going to like it, whatever it was. A whistling sound came from behind him, and a moment later a whip connected with his bare back. It wasn't the first time Sasha had been around a whip. Everyone in Aruuk felt they were necessary for keeping slaves in line. It was however, the first time he had ever felt one himself. It was awful. He clamped his mouth shut, determined to not cry out. He only had to get through ten lashes. Nine. Eight. Seven. He silently counted down through clenched teeth. It was agony. He felt blood trickling down his back. Five. Four. It was almost over. Two. And one. He let his jaw go slack, released the tension from his body as best he could, letting out a shuddering breath. And then he realized that the men were gone. He was alone. Immobile. Blind.

It was his worst nightmare.

The discomfort in his arms and shoulders grew, morphing into actual pain as the minutes ticked by. Sasha tried shifting from one foot to the other, hoping to find some relief from the taut aching. It was no use. Beneath the hood, his eyes grew heavy again, his eyelids sliding shut. He was tired. He couldn't keep himself awake. His head slumped forward. He let his entire body sag, and then snapped back up with a cry as his weight hit the chains holding his wrists, sending spasms of agony up his arms.

Again and again it happened, and Sasha began to wonder if he had been completely forgotten about down here. If so, this would be a horrible way to be abandoned. He couldn't even hope to sleep. It was cruel. He had just shifted his weight again when he became aware of the presence of another person. He couldn't hear anything, but they were there, standing close to him. He sensed them.

"I assume you have a name?" said the same thin voice of the richly dressed man he had briefly encountered at the top of the staircase. Something in his voice, in the arrogant authority of it, reminded Sasha of the way Father spoke. Whoever this man was, he was used to being obeyed - and probably used to punishing disobedience. Sasha thought briefly back to the words the guard had spoken to him. He was already miserable, but he had no doubt it could get worse if he proved himself difficult.

"Sasha Gundarson."

"One of my men informed me that you are from Aruuk, that you claim to be the son of their chief. Is that true?"

At least these were easy questions to answer, Sasha thought.

"Yes."

"What are you doing in our land?"

Sasha floundered internally. He couldn't tell this man why they had come; it would spell out his own death. And should they get the idea to pursue, the rest of his raiding group would be endangered. He couldn't betray them. That was cowardice Father would never forgive.

"Are you comfortable, Sasha?" The sudden change in tack caught Sasha off guard. He was tempted to lie, but it didn't make any sense to. The man already knew the truth, he just wanted it admitted.

"No."

"You should think carefully about your own position here before refusing to answer my questions, Sasha Gundarson. I can assure you, I have the means and will to make you a lot more uncomfortable. Now, again, what are you doing in our land?"

"Raiding," Sasha whispered the word, his head hanging.

"Alone?"

"No."

The room fell silent, and Sasha wondered if he was alone again. If he was, how long were they planning on leaving him like this? It was growing more unbearable with every passing moment.

"So, you came with a raiding party into our lands. Why?"

He wasn't alone. Sasha almost felt relieved to find that out.

"To take slaves, and..." The man cut him off.

"No. I mean why, after all these years, is Aruuk entering our land. What is it your Chief wants?" A note of impatience entered the man's voice.

"It was just a raid. He doesn't want anything, aside from what we took on the raid."

"I don't believe you. He's trying to start a war, isn't he? He's wanted our lands for a long time."

"No," Sasha barely got the word out before his feet were swept out from underneath him, throwing all his weight onto his arms. He screamed and scrambled to regain his footing.

"When will he invade?"

"He's not..." Again, his feet were knocked out from underneath him. Again, he screamed.

"He's planning something. You can either tell me about it now, or later."

"There's nothing else," Sasha panted.

"I don't believe you. Later, then. I'm sure given enough time in here to think about it, you'll come to see it's best to just cooperate."

"You're not...you can't leave me. I don't know anything else. I'm telling you the truth," Sasha's voice broke over the last word as it echoed through the empty chamber and was met with terrifying silence.

He was alone, again.

Chapter 24

STEPHAN PACED BACK AND forth in the courtyard, hands thrust deep in his pockets, stopping every now and then to watch the road coming up to the castle gate. There were few people about so early in the morning, and most cast curious glances in his direction. Hamo had been gone all night, along with a local man who said he knew his way around the mountains. The only reason Stephan stayed behind was on the slim chance the girls came back. So far, he had not seen either the girls or Hamo and his companion. His pacing paused when a door opened, and Lord Bayner stepped out into the courtyard. The lord's face was set in hard lines, his lips pressed tightly together, his hands clasped behind his back. Stephan eyed him as he hurried across the stone yard, brushing past the handful of servants who got in his way.

Stephan resumed his restless pacing. Whatever was bothering the lord didn't have anything to do with him. Every now and then, Stephan would sit on a bench overlooking the road, drumming his fingers on his leg, watching the sun rise and dispel the frost. The frost. Stephan sat up straighter as the full import of that realization came to him. Winter was on its way. Last night was the first frost, and here, this close to the mountains, snow wouldn't be far behind. They only had two or three weeks at best before the winter closed in on them. They had to find the girls before that happened.

The appearance of two horses, heads hanging low, coming up the road toward the castle brought Stephan back to his feet and walking out to meet them. One look at Hamo's face was enough to know that the search was unsuccessful. Stephan grabbed the bridle of Hamo's horse, wishing there was something he could say to alleviate the pain and guilt his friend felt.

"Nothing?" It was a pointless question, but Hamo asked it anyway. If the girls had come back to the castle, Stephan wouldn't look like that. "What do I do?"

"We'll keep looking. You should get some rest, though."

"I can't. Stephan, I can't. What if they're hurt, or dead out there and we just can't find them? How am I supposed to go home and face Edith?"

"We'll find them, Hamo. We won't leave until we do."

Hamo nodded mutely, looking away. Stephan followed his gaze toward the same door Lord Bayner had come out of less than an hour before. Two castle guards were just entering it. Stephan frowned thoughtfully and he turned to lay a hand on Hamo's shoulder.

"One hour. Get some rest for one hour while I get some new horses, and then we'll go back out together. You won't be any good searching for them if you're too tired."

Hamo looked like he wanted to argue, but there was truth in Stephan's words, and he knew it. Without another word he turned and walked away.

Stephan watched him go. He watched the door open, and the two guards emerge, leading a third person with a black hood pulled over their face and head between them. Feigning disinterest, he started pacing again. There was something going on. He had sensed it earlier that morning in the servants' whispers and darting eyes. Lord Bayner's troubled face deepened his conviction that something was off. Now, this confirmed it. When the men disappeared through another door, Stephan followed at a safe distance.

When he saw that the trio were headed into the council room, Stephan hung back waiting. A moment later, the two guards exited alone, and Stephan slipped inside. He leaned back against the wall, half hidden in the shadows, and his presence went unnoticed. From where he stood, he could make out Lord Bayner as well as several of his advisors sitting around the far half of the circular table. Closer to the door, and seated with his back to Stephan, was the prisoner the guards brought in. Stephan could make out the shackles that held his arms to the arms of the chair. Puzzled, Stephan searched the room again, and his eyes widened in surprise at the sight of another man entering through a side door. It had been many years since he had seen that face, but he knew it anyway. His brother was here, in the council.

"Well, Norman," Lord Bayner said, "Go ahead."

Chapter 25

WHEN THE HOOD CAME off, Sasha found himself blinking in the sudden light. He tried to bring his hands up to shield his eyes, but they were secured to the chair he'd been sat in. The relief he felt at being allowed to sit was quickly destroyed when his eyes adjusted enough for him to see the row of faces in front of him. There, directly opposite him, was the finely dressed man who had been addressed as lord by the guards. And arrayed on either side of him were a half a dozen others. Sasha dropped his eyes.

"Well, Norman, go ahead," said the lord that had interrogated him before.

Turning his head enough to catch sight of Norman, Sasha grimaced. His shoulders ached abominably from the hours he had spent chained in one position.

"All I know is what I've already told you. I was with a hunting party, and we found him, passed out. He was alone when we found him, there wasn't any sign of a group."

"Very good. I have personally questioned him since then, and he has admitted to being part of a raiding group. As we know, the Aruukens raid mostly for slaves - an abhorrent practice that has long been outlawed in our lands."

Sasha kept his eyes down. Hearing them talk about him as if he weren't even there was humiliating. Having them discuss his so-called crimes was worse. They made it sound like he was nothing more than a criminal.

"I personally believe, although he has refused to admit to it, that there is more to this than just a raid." There it was again, the ludicrous notion that Sasha knew about an upcoming battle plan that did not exist. "As I'm sure all of you are aware, rumors about the raids have already begun."

"And how are people handling those rumors, my lord?" an elderly man seated at the very end asked.

"They are calling for reprisals, of course. Word has gotten out that we have in custody one of the men responsible."

At this Sasha squirmed a little. People were angry. People wanted revenge. Sasha understood both those things. He had seen them. Now, he would be on the receiving end of them.

"Sasha Gundarson." Sasha's head snapped up, his eyes meeting the lord's. "You have already admitted to taking part in raids that resulted in the capture of other people with the intention of owning or selling them. The punishment for such crimes is death by hanging."

The words sank in. Sasha felt sick.

"But I didn't," he said. His own voice sounded high and breathless in his ears.

"Excuse me?"

"I didn't do that. I was only along to guard the horses." Sasha breathed a small prayer of gratitude that Armin had consigned him to such a task. "I didn't take anyone." Anyone, that is, aside from the two girls he and Boris stumbled on. That hadn't been on a planned raid though. It didn't count.

"Perhaps not. But you claim to be the chief's son." At this there was a collective gasp of surprise. "As such, your death would make a poignant example of what your father can expect should he pursue an invasion."

Sasha gulped. He had been so stupid, giving them all of this. He should have kept his mouth shut. He should never have even let them know he spoke their language. Then they wouldn't have known who he was or anything about what he was doing.

The order of the meeting dissolved into a frenzy of conversation. Sasha let his head sink to his chest, the weight of his circumstances combining with his sleeplessness. His mind felt thick and dense. Only bits and pieces of the conversation made any sense to him. There were some who argued against hanging him, fearing that would only anger the northern chief. Sasha wasn't sure how much weight they carried in the council, but he was desperate for them to win the argument. It was a reasonable argument. Sasha tried to imagine just how Father would react to the news that one of his favored sons had been executed by an inferior country. He would be beside himself with rage, Sasha was sure. That alone might be enough to cause a war. As much as he wanted it to, the thought of Father's anger over his death did little to comfort Sasha now. Even so, he hoped those voices would win out.

Father. Just the thought of him brought on an ache that went deeper than any broken rib. He was never going to see home again, not unless he contrived to find a way to escape. He was never going to see Boris again. Sasha's fatigue showed itself as his vision blurred with unshed tears. He stared at his lap, not daring to look up at his accusers. Gripping the arms of the wooden chair he was chained to hard enough for his knuckles to whiten, Sasha blinked the tears away. He was the chief's son. He had to be brave. He had to be strong. That's what it meant to be Aruuken.

"Sasha Gundarson." The cacophony of voices died away and Sasha looked up to find everyone looking at him again. It was the man sitting on the right hand of Lord Bayner that was addressing him now. "By order of this council and Lord Bayner, protectorate of our throne, you are sentenced to death by hanging in one week's time."

Sasha heard the words but couldn't quite believe them. He shook his head slightly in a helpless gesture. His mind went blank, drained of any thought or emotion. Dumbly, he saw the men in front of them, but none of them would meet his eyes. While Sasha reeled at the news of his sentence, Lord Bayner turned toward Norman.

"Take him back," his hand waved in Sasha's direction, "and then get some soldiers together to go after these raiders. We've lost enough time with this. I want you riding out in an hour."

Sasha looked up as Norman unlocked the manacles and lifted him to his feet. His legs, having enjoyed their brief reprieve from the hours of forced standing, trembled weakly beneath him now. With great difficulty he moved forward with Norman's hand firm on his arm. He stumbled out of the room, completely oblivious of the man standing in the shadows.

It was the cold air outside that first brought Sasha out of his stunned stupor. He was going to die. Hang. Thinking about it made him nauseous. There was only one thing he could do, and now was his best chance to do it. Norman was the only one with him. He could get free of his grasp easily enough. But Sasha had his doubts about how much he could demand of his abused legs, let alone his other injuries. It didn't matter. If he couldn't run away now, he would be dead in a week. They were getting close to the doorway that would lead him back down to be questioned.

Sasha ran. His chest burned. His legs burned. He knew he wouldn't make it far. But he ran. It was a desperate, poorly planned gamble that ended almost before it started. Sasha crashed into someone coming across his path, and by the time he regained his balance, Norman and two others were on top of him. A savage kick in his stomach made him curl up, groaning.

"You're making this worse than it needs to be." Norman's face was inches from his own as the man grabbed him by the front of his shirt and pulled him up. He shoved him toward the other two men. "Take him back down and get him ready for the lord."

Chapter 26

STEPHAN TOOK THE STAIRS two at a time, brushing past whoever was in his way. When he reached the door to Hamo's room he didn't bother knocking but threw it open. Hamo sat in a chair, his face covered in his hands, and Stephan knew he hadn't rested. Not that he really expected him to.

"Hamo, I think I've got it."

Hamo looked up, hope briefly replacing the anguish on his face.

"They just held a council meeting to decide the fate of a prisoner."

"What does that have to..."

"I'm getting to that, but can you be ready to go again in an hour?"

"Yes."

"He was from up North, Aruuk. They were raiding down here, and he ran into some sort of trouble, got separated from his group and caught."

"What are you saying?"

"I'm saying I don't think they got lost. I think Meri and Phelie were taken. The boy they just sentenced was picked up pretty close to Drogo's."

Hamo's face, already haggard, went completely white and he sank back into the chair with a low moan.

"No, no, no, no. It can't...that can't be what happened to them...they...," his voice died away. "I have to go after them. I have to get them back."

"Well, that's the good news. The lord's sending out a party within the hour to overtake the raiders and rescue his people. I think he's afraid of what the people here will do if he doesn't act."

"I'm going. Who's leading it?" Hamo was up again and halfway out the door.

"My brother."

"Who?"

"My brother, Norman. He's the one leading it."

"I thought you hadn't found him."

"I hadn't. He doesn't know I saw him yet. I think he's been avoiding a meeting on purpose, but he'll let us go with them, I'm sure."

Stephan followed Hamo back down into the courtyard where a group of soldiers were already gathering. Hamo stood, scanning the milling crowd for someone who looked to be in charge, his eyes finally coming to rest on a man that bore a strong resemblance to Stephan. Without waiting for Stephan, Hamo hurried toward him.

"I'm going with you."

"No, I already have who I want." Norman tried to step around Hamo. "Besides, you're not even from here, this isn't your problem."

"I'm going. I wasn't asking. My daughters are out there, and I'm going to get them back."

Norman's face softened a little. "I'm sorry. I didn't know. Of course, you can come, but we're leaving in ten minutes."

"Fine."

"Is he coming too?" Norman jerked his chin to where Stephan was standing, pointedly looking anywhere but at him.

"Yes."

"Guess I'd better get this over with then."

Hamo watched as Norman moved through the crowd of people and stood in front of his brother for the first time in decades.

"Why didn't you want to see me?" Stephan spoke first.

"Why would I want to?" Norman snorted, "You're the one who ran off and left me all those years ago."

"I didn't plan on leaving you and you know it. This whole little war got in the way of my coming back."

"You chose to fight for them."

"It was the side I was caught on." Stephan shrugged.

"And what would you have done if we'd met in battle? Would you have killed me? Maimed me? You were willing to risk that."

Stephan looked away but didn't answer.

"Let's just get on with this," Norman said. "Your friend says his daughters were taken by the Aruukens. I hope for his sake we can get them back. The Aruukens are not kind to their slaves, especially the girls."

"I don't think he needs to be reminded of that," Stephan said softly, glancing back to where Hamo was now waiting with both horses.

Thirty men rode out of the castle. By the time the sunset that night they had already reached the scorched remains of the nearest settlement. For all the men knew about their northern neighbors, most were still taken aback by the brutality of their raid. Charred corpses littered the ground and the haze of smoke and ash hung over the entire place, trapped by the surrounding mountains. Hamo wandered about, taking in the sickening sight of it all, and his despair grew. The people who were capable of such things would be capable of a great deal more against two young girls.

The next day they passed two more villages, obliterated in the same manner. And then the trail went cold. Beyond the known borders of Dorsten, no one had a clear idea of where to go. And the frozen earth was little help. Tracks ran in all directions. Paths ran between mountains, and others skirted up their sides. As night fell the second day, Norman came to a decision. They would turn around and go home in the morning.

"I'm not going back," Hamo said, sitting across from Stephan. "Not without them."

"I hate it too, but he's right. If we wander around without any idea where we're going, we're not saving anyone."

"I'm not leaving them, Stephan. You know. You know what they'll do to them."

"I know."

"It'll be worse than anything I went through, and I wouldn't wish that on my worst enemy."

"I know."

"Is that all you can say?"

"We don't know our way through those mountains. Norman was hoping to catch them before they got back into their own land. We failed at that."

"We can't."

"We did. They're gone. We have no way of tracking them." Stephan held up a hand to ward off the anger rising on Hamo's face. "We don't have the supplies we need to be out here this long. Face it, Hamo, the lord didn't plan on this trip being successful, he just wanted to put on a good show for his people, the same as he's doing with hanging that boy."

"So, what are you saying we do?"

"We ride back with them. And then we get our own stuff, enough to last us for a few weeks. We find a map or something to navigate the mountains. They have to have something like that in Dorsten. And then we come back. It will take a day or two longer, but it gives us a chance. It gives Meri and Phelie a chance."

Stephan watched Hamo's face as he worked out his words. His forehead creased and his jaw worked back and forth. At last, he nodded.

"Good. Now, do you think Drogo would let us leave from his house?"

"Probably. Why would we?"

"It's closer. When we get back, you get together a couple of pack horses and whatever supplies we'll need."

"What will you do?"

"Find a map. I've got a couple ideas, just not sure which one will work yet."

"Alright."

"We'll get them back, Hamo."

Chapter 27

MEREDITH WASN'T SURE HOW to feel about reaching the stockade. There was some comfort in the fact that they would no longer be required to walk for many miles every day. But that comfort was eaten up by the finality of their captivity.

It was strategically placed. The mountains met to form a box of sorts. Three sides rose in sheer cliffs, impossible to scale, and the fourth side was a rugged wall of rocks with a narrow opening. Inside this corral of nature, four makeshift wooden huts stood out against the gray rock. A smattering of trees and dozens of little shrubs covered the otherwise barren ground.

The pace their captors had set for the last few days had been grueling. Meredith marveled at the fact that no one had dropped dead from the amount of sheer walking they had done. Although she hadn't had the opportunity to check, she was sure her feet were covered in blisters and sores. They certainly hurt enough to be. Ophelia stumbled a little in front of her now, and Meredith reached out automatically to catch her. As she got close to her sister, Ophelia's hand tightened on hers.

"We have to think of a way out of this place," Ophelia whispered.

Meredith bit her lip but nodded. From the looks of it the place had been carefully prepared to support the entire group through the winter months, although Meredith wasn't sure why they would keep them here in such a place. A commotion up ahead of them grabbed her attention.

A couple of men waited by the doors of two huts. Another couple were untying the first string of captives and pushing them toward their new homes. Boys and men were shoved one direction, girls and women the other. Meredith stood patiently while one of them untied her rope. It was the first time she'd been free of it in days. Gratefully, she tried to rub the soreness out and followed Ophelia into the hut.

It was small and completely bare. The wooden floor creaked ominously beneath Meredith's feet as she and Ophelia tried to find a place to sit together. Other women had already spread out and claimed their spots.

"Let's go sit by her." Ophelia pointed to the youngest girl. "She doesn't have anyone else."

Meredith had noticed her on their forced march. She couldn't have been more than twelve, and none of the other captives appeared to be related to her. Shrugging, she followed Ophelia. It felt so nice just to sit, with her hands free. Meredith leaned back against the cold wall and closed her eyes, allowing the exhaustion of the last few days to wash over her and lull her to sleep.

"What's your name?" Meredith opened her eyes and saw Ophelia was talking to the young girl.

"Una."

"That's a pretty name."

"Thank you," Una's voice shook a little.

"Are you all by yourself here?"

"Father and Mother were...," Una sniffled and didn't go any further. "But my brother is here, too."

"I'm sorry. My name's Ophelia, but you can call me Phelie. And this is my sister Meri."

"You're twins?"

"Yes. You look cold. Do you want to sit between us, that way we can all keep each other warm?"

Una didn't take any extra encouragement. She scooted into the spot between the sisters and nestled in tightly against Ophelia. A moment later great, hiccupping sobs filled the air. Ophelia wrapped her arms around Una.

"There, there. It's alright. We'll stick together, the three of us. And we'll figure out a way to get out of this place."

Meredith watched her twin with something akin to wonder. Here in this wretched place, in these wretched circumstances, her sister was managing to comfort this poor child.

"Really?" Una looked up, her eyes filled with both tears and hope.

"Really."

The conviction in Ophelia's voice strengthened Meredith's own resolve. They would find a way out. They had to. The alternative was too horrible to contemplate.

Chapter 28

THE CELL DOOR CLANGED shut and the bolt slammed into its place. Huddled against the far wall, chained hand and foot and connected to the wall by a collar and chain that did not allow him to lie down all the way, Sasha tried to rest. He was acutely aware of how much of his current situation was his own fault. After his attempt to run away from Norman he was taken to questioning again. It lasted many hours. Rather than return him to the moderately comfortable room that they had first put him in, he was brought to this cell, in the dungeon. Thanks to his attempts at escaping those two times, he was fastened to the wall by the iron collar. The chains on his wrists and ankles came later, after a third botched escape. Sasha hadn't dared attempt a fourth.

He had no idea how many days had gone by. There was no window in his cell, and even if there was, he spent so little time there that it wouldn't have helped. Most of his time was spent in the chamber, as he heard it referred to by the guards. Stretched painfully between the two pillars for hours on end, with only a handful of brief reprieves, Sasha still failed to come up with a satisfying answer for Lord Bayner.

This last time had been the worst. Sasha had been too tired to notice the brackets mounted onto the insides of the pillars, too tired to see the torches set inside them. It hadn't been until after the black hood was in place, after his back had been ripped open again by the whip that he became conscious of the heat. Far enough from his bare skin to not scorch it, but near enough to be excruciating, the torches were lit. It wasn't until they had burned down several hours later that Lord Bayner had even come in to question him. By then, his sides and underarms felt like they were on fire. And still he had no answer for the lord. Even now, in his chilly cell, heat radiated from the damaged skin.

The accumulated effects of spending so much time in the chamber were felt throughout his entire body. He'd barely slept in days, his injuries were aggravated rather than healing, and food and water had been sporadic at best. One guard thought it hilarious to put his food and water just beyond the reach of his neck chain. Sasha had made the mistake the first time the man did it of throwing himself forward, desperate for the water, only to fall back choking against the iron band on his throat.

Now, having just been returned to his cell after hours of being in the chamber, Sasha leaned his shoulder against the wall. His back was torn up by the whip Lord Bayner ordered used on him at the start of each questioning. His chest still hurt terribly at the slightest pressure. Adding his newly burnt sides to all that made his pain unbearable. Sasha shut his eyes, hoping that they would leave him alone for at least an hour or two to rest. Sometimes they did.

Sasha was too tired to notice the bolt being drawn back, and the rusty hinges groaning in protestation as the door opened. A rough hand shook him awake.

"Not again," Sasha murmured, his eyes refusing to open, "please. Just let me rest."

The guard ignored him, as usual, and unlocked the collar from his neck. Free of it, Sasha slumped all the way down to the ground, letting his weariness take over. They were going to pull him out anyway, so why put forth any more effort than necessary? Sure enough, he was being hauled to his feet. Sasha swayed unsteadily, whimpering.

"Don't make me do this again. It hurts." He finally opened his eyes and looked up at the guard through the murky gloom of the dungeon. It was Norman. "I don't know anything. Honestly."

It didn't work. It never did.

"Let's go." Norman's voice sounded gruffer than usual, Sasha thought, or maybe he was so miserable it made everything sound worse.

Sasha stumbled forward, tripping over the short chain between his ankles that prevented his running away again. Forget running with it on, he could barely walk with it.

"The lord's not going to let him get any sleep before he swings, huh?" The guard at the end of the hallway stepped aside to let them start up the stairs.

"No," Norman answered shortly. Sasha thought he must be angry about something. Norman was usually more talkative to the guards.

The guard's mention of him swinging jolted Sasha fully awake. How many days had it been since he was sentenced? It had been several, he was sure. He tried to count them up, but his brain was muddled and his memory hazy at best. What if this was it? What if this was his last day? The thought filled him with cold dread.

Sasha hated stairs the most with his ankle chains. They were nearly impossible, but none of his escorts ever thought so. They tried to ascend or descend at a normal pace, and Sasha usually ended up being dragged, unable to keep his feet under him, a scenario that guaranteed battered and bruised shins. Tonight was no different and Sasha gritted his teeth against the inevitable pain.

When they reached the landing that the chamber was on Sasha automatically turned towards the door only to be thrown completely off kilter by Norman heading the other way. They were going away from the chamber, back up the stairs that led to outside. This really was it. Norman was taking him out to hang. An irrepressible cry escaped his parched lips. He was too weary to even try to put on a brave face. He was wretched and starving and exhausted and hurting and lonely, and he just couldn't muster the energy to be strong anymore. Father would be ashamed of him, but then, Father wasn't here to see him die. No one was.

"Hurry up." Norman had taken hold of the chain between his wrists and tugged on it now making Sasha stumble once more.

Why was the man in such a hurry to hang him? What had Sasha done to make him so hateful towards him? He had run from him, but wasn't that understandable? The door to the outside swung partially open and Norman stepped out first, leading Sasha behind him. The cold night air hit him like a slap in the face. It was paradoxically painful and refreshing at the same time, especially to his singed skin. Sasha tried to take a deep breath that ended in a pained gasp as his lungs pressed against the broken ribs. Since no one had bothered to give him back his shirt, the cold bit into his bare skin making him shiver. Norman didn't give him a chance to take anything in or adjust. He kept walking and Sasha was compelled to follow him.

He was a little puzzled to find that it was still clearly night, the stars cold and distant above his head. Were they going to hang him at night? Sasha thought he would prefer that to being hung in front of everyone during the day. He couldn't imagine how humiliating it would be to see a crowd gathered for the mere purpose of watching him die. Quietly in the dark had to be better than that. They were crossing the courtyard of the castle quickly. The gate loomed up before Sasha's eyes, and a sentry moved in front of them.

"That you, Norm?"

"Yes."

"What're you doing with him?"

"Taking him to the executioner's square. He's hanging in the morning."

The sentry nodded and stepped aside to let them pass. Having Norman confirm that he was indeed heading toward his own execution turned Sasha's blood to ice. He stopped abruptly halfway across the short bridge.

"Come on." Norman jerked on his arms, but Sasha balked.

"I don't want to go," he said. His voice quivered shamefully. "I don't want to die."

Norman studied him for a moment in the darkness. Sasha tried to hide the trembling that took hold of him. Norman stepped closer to him, something silver and shiny in his hand and the next thing Sasha knew, the tip of a knife buried itself in the soft spot under his chin. He recoiled.

"You're coming. And if you don't want to come willingly, you're going to come in a lot of pain. I'm not going to kill you here because everyone wants a show in the morning, but I can make this a lot more painful than it is."

Sasha's entire being slumped with defeat. He took a shuffling step forward, and then another. Satisfied, Norman put his knife away and led them on. They turned away from the castle, across the empty meadow that lay between them and the town, and finally down a dark street. The streetlamps that kept the main road illuminated did nothing for this little alley. Sasha was a little surprised that they were taking it. Maybe it was a shortcut to the executioner's square.

Sasha's head was spinning by the time they passed the last house in town and the black silhouette of the gallows rose before them. He was shaking uncontrollably now but couldn't decide if it was the cold or his imminent death. Probably both. They walked toward the gallows. Sasha could see the thin shadow of a rope hanging down, ending in a noose - a noose meant for his neck. Sasha's heart hammered in his throat. Beads of sweat trickled down his forehead. His breath came fast and shallow. He considered begging Norman to just let him go.

They passed by the ominous structure. Sasha twisted around, looking at it behind him.

"Where..." The knife was at his throat again. Sasha tried to pull away but Norman's grip on him was firm.

"Shut up and do exactly as I say. Understand?"

Sasha nodded stiffly, eyes blinking rapidly.

"Good. Sit down."

Sasha sat awkwardly. Norman reached down to his feet and a moment later the irons that had forced him to take such painfully small steps fell away with a soft clatter.

"Now get up."

This was harder. Sasha struggled to get to his feet but couldn't quite manage until Norman reached down a hand to help him. When he was standing, unsteady and swaying, Norman threw something around him. Sasha flinched until it settled over his now freezing shoulders. It was a cloak, Sasha realized as Norman secured it around his throat and pulled the hood over his head. The warmth of the soft fabric was delicious.

The soft whinny of a horse came from the shadows around a thicket nearby. Norman led him in that direction and Sasha saw that two horses stood tied to the branches.

"Up."

Sasha tried to lift his arms to grab the pommel, but after all the hours of being stretched in an uplifted position, his muscles refused to cooperate.

"I can't use my arms."

"Of course not." Norman sighed and helped him up before getting on the other one. "If you fall off, I'm not coming back for you."

With that, they set off leaving Sasha more than a little befuddled.

Chapter 29

HAMO SAT AT THE TABLE in Drogo's house, drumming his fingers across the wood. Every whisper of wind that reached his ears caused him to jump and look at the door.

"He's not here yet," Drogo said, sitting across from him. "She would let us know if he was."

The gray wolf in question lay flat on the floor, stretched out before the blazing fire. Hamo shot an impatient glance in her direction and went on drumming his fingers.

"What's taking him so long? He should have been back by now."

"He will be."

"We need to get back up there; we need to find them before something happens."

"Hamo, you should rest until he gets here."

"I can't."

"You need to, or you won't be able to help anyone. I will make sure you are awake when he comes."

Hamo frowned, then pushed away from the table.

"I'm going to check on the horses, and make sure they're all ready."

A gust of wind blew in as Hamo stepped outside. Drogo stared after him, shaking his head sadly. Only a few minutes went by before the wolf lifted her large head off the floor and emitted a low growl.

"And there's the rest of our company, eh?" Drogo patted the shaggy head as he made his way to the door.

Stephan stepped inside, a grim smile on his face, followed by another smaller figure who made it about

144

five steps into the room before sinking to his knees on the floor.

Drogo raised his eyebrows as he appraised this third visitor. Aside from a cloak thrown over his shoulders, he was bare to the waist and covered in numerous cuts and bruises. The skin along his sides was a deep, blistered red. His face was hidden beneath the cloak's hood, but his hands were not. Drogo took in the heavy iron shackles binding his wrists together and turned a questioning gaze toward Stephan.

"Who is this?" he asked at last.

"Yes, who is it?" Hamo repeated, coming through the doorway behind them.

"Our map."

Hamo walked up from behind and yanked the hood off the person's head. The boy didn't move until Hamo reached around and forcibly lifted his face up. He was limp and unresisting at Hamo's touch. Beneath layers of tearstained grime, his blue eyes, dull with fatigue, met Hamo's.

"Name's Sasha, and he's going to be our map."

"Yes, but who is he?" Hamo let Sasha's head drop and looked up at Stephan.

"He's the one I was telling you about. The Aruuken they picked up. He's supposed to hang tomorrow, but I figured we had a better use for him."

"But he's in no shape to go anywhere." Hamo's eyes traveled from Sasha's face to the rest of him.

"Sure he is. We'll let him rest tonight, patch him up a bit, and he'll be fine in the morning."

"The morning? We're not waiting for morning. I'm ready to leave now. The sooner we get started the sooner we find them and get them back."

"We'll be lost before we're gone an hour if we try to find our way around at night. And we have no idea where exactly they might be taking the girls."

"Hamo, he's right," Drogo said gently. "Leaving in the morning is the best if it means you have a guide. And if you really are going to use him, he needs to rest first."

A moment of tense silence followed as Hamo stepped back and turned to face away from them.

"Fine. We leave in the morning. But we leave at first light, no later."

"Good. We'd have to anyway before they miss him and start looking for him." Stephan nodded firmly. "And now for you," he said as he undid the cloak from Sasha's neck and let it slide to the ground. He made no effort to get Sasha to stand, a fact Sasha was grateful for. "We're going to have a little talk before I let you sleep."

"You're not Norman," Sasha murmured, his voice hollow, lifeless.

"No, I'm not. Though luckily, I look and sound enough like him to fool the guards when it's dark out."

"What do you want from me?" Sasha asked as Stephan turned a chair around and sat facing him.

"I'm going to make you a deal."

Sasha lifted his eyes to meet Stephan's, confusion battling against hopelessness.

"You see, your raiding party kidnapped that man's daughters, who also happen to be my granddaughters," Stephan gestured to where Hamo stood watching. Sasha's eyes looked away guiltily. Hamo must hate him, he thought, just like everyone else, apparently. "We want them back. We're going after them, and you are going to lead us to them."

"I can't."

Stephan leaned back, pursing his lips as he considered Sasha's response. After a moment's thought, he slapped his hands on his knees and made to get out of his chair.

"If you can't, then I guess I'd better get you back to the dungeon before morning."

"What?"

"If you can't help us, we don't have any use for dragging you around. You can go back and face your sentencing. Come on." Stephan rose and reached for Sasha.

"Wait." Hamo came over and crouched down in front of Sasha so that they were on the same level. "Sasha, do you know where they took my daughters?"

Sasha wanted to lie. He wanted to deny that he had any part in it. But he was so tired. Tired, and unsure. The truth didn't require as much effort. "Yes."

"If you will help me find them, we won't hurt you. We'll let you go, and you can return to your home instead of being hung here. I give you my word."

Treason. That's what they were asking of him. Treason came with a high price. But so did going back to the dungeon. It was his life either way, but at least going with these two men meant a slightly longer life. Sasha shut his eyes, wishing that this was all some sick nightmare that he could wake from.

"I'll help you," he whispered at last.

"Thank you."

Sasha sat as quietly as he could, but it was difficult. They had moved him to a chair by the table and he was able to rest his head on his arms there. He might have been able to go to sleep as well, except that whatever they were doing hurt. The only comfort he found in the pain was that they were taking care of him. His wounds were being washed, a thick, herbal scented salve was being administered, and they had promised to let him sleep until morning - a promise that Sasha couldn't quite bring himself to believe. After all, the guards had regularly promised such a thing as well, usually accompanying the promise with laughter. They never kept that promise and Sasha had the same faith in Stephan and Hamo's promise.

"What do you do with the slaves you capture?" Stephan asked him. "Tell me the truth, don't leave parts out just because you think I won't like it."

"We take them back through the mountains." Sasha grimaced and sat up as Hamo reopened a deep cut across his shoulder blade. "There's a stockade there. Each raiding party has their own. It's hidden, except from my father." A cry of pain interrupted his answer briefly. "They'll spend the winter there. And when the snow melts, they'll move them to Illsen for the Spring Market. Nothing happens to the slaves before that."

"Nothing? They aren't hurt in any way?" Hamo paused what he was doing to ask.

"No. My father doesn't allow spoiled slaves to be sold at the Spring Market." Hamo stiffened behind him, and Sasha decided it was better not to mention what happened the first night of the Spring Market. Most of the raiders participated in the orgy that followed the first day of sales. For the fifteen-year-olds who were participating in the raids and Market for the first time, it was the night that sealed their manhood.

Stephan studied him, and Sasha could tell he was debating whether or not to believe him. From across the room near the fireplace, the oldest man was watching him intently as well. Sasha leaned forward again, resting his head and letting his eyes close. They probably weren't going to believe him, but there was nothing he could do. He just hoped they wouldn't resort to torture to extract their own version of truth from him.

"He is telling the truth. That is how it is done in Aruuk," said the old man from across the room. "Who is your father, child?"

"He's the Chief," Sasha murmured half asleep already. If he'd been awake, he would have been rankled by the man calling him a child, but that took more effort than he could muster now.

"I know that, boy. Who is he?"

"Chief Gundar."

"Gundar, huh? So Gundar made it after all."

Sasha frowned in his drowsiness. Something was off about what the man said and the way he said it. It was odd, but Sasha was in no shape to puzzle over it. His wounds were treated, a strip of cloth wound tightly about his chest to keep the broken ribs in place, and he wanted nothing more than to doze off. Another second and Sasha was oblivious to anything else.

Standing behind Sasha, Hamo watched Drogo with as much curiosity as the boy had felt. Seeing Sasha asleep, Hamo moved away from him and sat down on the floor near Drogo, his back against the warm stone side of the fireplace.

"You know the Aruuken Chief?"

"Once, I knew him very well. But that was a long time ago."

"How?"

"He was my nephew," Drogo sighed.

"Wait," Hamo looked from the sleeping boy to his old master, "If he was your nephew, then you're Sasha's great uncle."

"Yes, I suppose I am. But family relations matter very little in a country where wives and children are bought and sold on a whim. Gundar was a ruthless and ambitious young man back then. I can only imagine what he is now. Hamo, you must be careful."

"I'm going to do whatever it takes to get Meri and Phelie back."

"I understand. You bear the mark of a slave." Hamo's fingers automatically went to his forearm, tracing the brand that Drogo himself put there so many years ago. "In Aruuk, slaves are never freed. If you are caught, they will do terrible things to you."

"That's a risk I'll have to take."

"I know."

"But, if you were Gundar's uncle, then you must be..."

"From Aruuk. Yes. I grew up there. In the Chief's house. I was one of many of the Chief's sons. When my father died, there was no clear heir to his power. Renalt assumed the position and killed most of his brothers. He and I reached an agreement of sorts. I publicly renounced all claims to his power, and he let me live."

"Nice deal. But why'd you end up here?"

"It worked. For a while. I left the Chief's home and took up a trade rather than raiding. Then Renalt grew suspicious and banished me."

"And you came here." Hamo leaned his head back against the stone. The last few days were catching up with him and he hadn't slept nearly enough. Still, something nagged at the back of his brain.

"I came here. Lord Bayner offered me citizenship in exchange for a few years of work. I didn't think I'd get anything better elsewhere, so I took it."

"Why'd you do it, Drogo?"

"Do what?"

"Why'd you stay past your time? Lord Bayner told me you gave him five extra years."

Drogo smiled. "I meant to quit. Every single day. When my time with him was up, I was going to leave. I was going to set up a nice smithy somewhere. Be a free man. But then there was you. I got up each morning thinking I was going to send word to the lord to replace me. And you came in every morning, and I knew it would be murder for me to just leave you. And each morning, I couldn't do it. Always told myself, I'd do it the next day. Next thing I knew, five more years were gone, and I was still working there."

"So, he wasn't lying about that part," Hamo said softly.

"He wasn't. I never had a real family, any more than that boy has," Drogo nodded toward where Sasha still sat asleep at the table, "You were the closest thing I had, and I couldn't stomach losing you. Now, you should get some rest, so you don't lose yours."

Chapter 30

A HAND SHOOK SASHA BY the shoulder, rousing him from deep slumber. When he opened his eyes, he couldn't remember where he was. With his eyes still bleary with sleep, he looked around. It wasn't the dungeon, or the chamber, or the prison.

"Come on, we've got to get going." The man who had shaken him awake urged him up.

At the sight of Stephan's face, the memory of last night came crashing through him. He had been rescued, sort of. He was supposed to be hanging this morning. Instead, he had just spent the last five hours sleeping - something he had not been permitted to do for days. Lifting his head up, Sasha realized his hands were still chained together.

"I suppose you're hungry," Stephan said, putting a plate of food in front of him.

Sasha's answer was lost in a mouthful of food. It had been at least two days since he'd had anything at all to eat. He couldn't get the food to his mouth fast enough now. When his plate was scraped clean, Stephan pulled out a key and, unlocking one of his wrists, thrust a shirt into his hands.

"Put this on. Can't drag you through the mountains only half dressed."

Sasha pulled it on over the bandage wrapped around his chest. Even with the bulge of the bandage underneath to help fill it out it was too big for him. At least it was something, Sasha admitted to himself, remembering just how cold he was last night by the time they reached this cabin. A heavy jacket came next. Stephan replaced the manacle and motioned for him to follow him. It was still dark out. Once again Stephan helped him onto his horse. Sasha gripped the pommel desperately, unsure of how long he would be able to stay up here. Even with the few hours of sleep and a plateful of food, he was weak - terribly weak and sore. It took everything in him just to stay upright.

Hamo and Stephan exchanged a few words with Drogo before joining him on their own mounts. Stephan grabbed the reins to Sasha's horse and led the way, Hamo following with the two pack animals.

Sasha must have fallen asleep on his horse if that was even possible. With a jolt, his head snapped up. Drogo's cabin was nowhere in sight. The sun was high overhead, and mountains towered above him on every side. Stephan glanced back at him long enough to establish that he was awake again before returning to the quiet conversation he and Hamo were having. Sasha tried to listen in, but their words didn't reach his ears and he didn't feel up to the effort of straining to catch them. Instead, he turned his attention to his surroundings. Apparently, they knew where they were going at this point. They weren't asking him for directions.

Sasha stiffened in his saddle when the faint smell of smoke wafted through the air. He looked from side to side, searching for the source of it. It didn't smell quite like a campfire. There was something heavier, almost putrid about it.

As they rounded a bend in the trail, the scent strengthened, and a faint haze filled the air. Spread out before them was what Sasha assumed were the remains of a village. Blackened timbers pointed accusing fingers at the sky. Piles of ash shifted in the slight breeze. Scavenger birds circled and landed among the charred piles, their haunting cries filling the air.

Sasha's horse tensed beneath him and tried to sidestep away from the devastating view and Sasha was too weak to even consider trying to stop it. Fortunately, Stephan's hand on the reins was firm. There was no easy way around the village and the deeper they rode into it the more Sasha had the intense urge to vomit. He relinquished his tenuous grip on the pommel to bring his hands up over his mouth. His horse stumbled over what Sasha saw too late was a corpse and he watched the shriveled remains disintegrate beneath his horse's hoof. Sasha's stomach lurched and he gagged, swallowing down the bile that rose in his throat.

"You don't look so good, Sasha." Stephan was half turned in his saddle, watching him curiously.

"It's awful."

"You're the ones who did this. Did you never think about what happened to all these people when you burnt the place down?" The accusation in Stephan's voice was hurtful.

"I didn't do this. I never even got to take part in any of the raids. I had to stay behind and guard the horses."

"But you would have if you'd been allowed?"

Sasha was taken aback by his own reaction to the question. His immediate answer in the face of these men was no. A voice in the back of his head said yes. It had been Armin's command, not his own squeamishness, that kept him from participating. When they set out on the raid, he had set out with every intention of participating. If he had gone, what would he have done? Would he have been one of the ones to put a torch to the place, sealing the fate of anyone alive inside? A vision of himself setting fire to one of these buildings, heedless of the helpless, terrified cries of those condemned inside rose up in his mind and Sasha found it disturbing. He shook the image away. That was who and what he was. He'd been born into it. That's what Father would tell him. Born to rule over others and to take what he wanted. He couldn't change that, and it shouldn't bother him. He looked up to find Stephan, his face quite unreadable, looking at him and realized he hadn't answered Stephan's question. Hamo was staring at him now, too.

"It doesn't matter."

"I'm not sure about that," Stephan said quietly.

"I didn't do anything. This wasn't me." A rising desperation to defend himself overcame his better judgement. Everyone he had seen in the last few days hated him, hated what he represented, hated what they thought he had done. He wasn't a criminal. He wasn't a bad person. "It doesn't matter, because you're going to hate me just like everyone else, even though I didn't do anything." Except shoot a man in the back as he ran, and kidnap two girls that voice in the back of his mind accused him. "Please, can we just get away from here?"

They made it about an hour past the burned ruins before Sasha reached the end of his very limited strength. Hamo was the first to notice as Sasha teetered in the saddle, his face graying with exhaustion. In fact, if Hamo had not moved quickly enough to catch and steady him, Sasha would have fallen straight off. They veered off the trail and Sasha allowed himself to be helped down. He made it the few steps from his horse to the trunk of a nearby tree and sank down, leaning sideways against it and surrendering completely to the sleep his body demanded.

Two hours later, he was awakened to a plate of food being pushed into his hands.

Stephan waited until he was fully roused before saying, "Hurry up. We've still got a few hours of daylight to use."

Sasha took the food and ate, a task that was made more difficult than necessary by the irons still locked about his wrists. He wondered if they meant to leave them on, or if they had just forgotten about them. Even with them on, this was the most freedom Sasha had experienced in over a week and there was a measure of comfort in that.

By nightfall, they had passed the second burnt out settlement. This time, there was a way around it, much to Sasha's relief. He was in no hurry to view the handiwork of his countrymen up close, especially not under the scrutiny of two men who already thought very little of him.

Chapter 31

MEREDITH LOOKED DOWN at the three drops of blood oozing out of her pricked fingers. She hadn't seen the thorns on the bush before trying to break off a few branches for the fire.

She glanced over at the man standing guard. Thankfully, his back was turned toward her, and he had failed to notice the break in her work. Keeping a careful eye on him, Meredith pressed her bleeding fingertips against the hem of her shirt.

Mother would have scolded her for ruining her clothes. Meredith blinked back the burning tears that filled her eyes. She wasn't going to see Mother again at this rate. And the worst of it was that Mother would likely never know what happened. Meredith crouched down behind the thorny bush, obscuring her face from the guard's view in case he should deign to look in her direction. He was not going to get the pleasure of seeing her weep. Brushing an angry hand across her eyes, Meredith tried to find something to distract her from thoughts of Mother, and Father, and home.

Drawing on the many long afternoons spent with Taliea, Meredith studied the bush hiding her face. Without leaves it was impossible for her to place. The branches were thick and, as she had painfully discovered already, covered in thorns. It was working. Already her vision had cleared. That was when she saw them. Clustered near the tops of the branches, shriveled and dried, hung a handful of white berries. Forgetting completely about the task at hand, and the guard who could at any moment show up next to her to enforce it, Meredith plucked off an entire cluster of the berries. She turned them over thoughtfully in her hand. She'd seen them before. Back in Taliea's garden. Shutting her eyes, she tried to remember what they were.

A shout from the guard forced her eyes back open and she noticed belatedly that the man was coming toward her. Shoving the berries into her pocket and reaching for a fallen stick to add to her diminutive pile of kindling, she braced herself for the blow she knew would come. She felt a trickle of blood coming from her bottom lip after he backhanded her across the face. He scolded her through a string of unintelligible sounds and Meredith went back to work. Apparently, none of these men, except for the one who had captured her and who had subsequently fallen to his death because of her, were able to speak her language. That did not mean they did not expect to be understood, a fact that Meredith found more than a little annoying.

It was late in the afternoon when she and the two other women sent with her were brought back with their loads of wood. Meredith threw hers down on the heap and automatically went back to the hut that housed all the female captives. Her captors were intuitive enough to figure out that Meredith or Ophelia alone didn't pose a threat. One wasn't going to run without the other. And they used that knowledge in their favor. One or the other was selected every single day to carry out the mundane tasks that sustained all their lives in this barren prison. The male prisoners were never brought out to work, Meredith assumed because their captors thought they would be too much trouble. Cowards, she thought, as she walked past a group of them. Cowards, and animals, she added, noticing the way the men watched her.

The chain holding the door shut was unlocked by one of the men guarding it, and Meredith hurried past him before he had time to run his hand over her. The girl behind her wasn't as fast and Meredith tried to ignore her sharp intake of breath as the man grabbed her. So far, fondling had been the worst these men had done to any of them. Meredith hated to think what would happen when they tired of it and wanted something more exciting.

"Got on someone's bad side?" Ophelia looked up as Meredith came over and sat down beside her and Una.

Meredith put her hand up to her lip. To be honest, she'd forgotten all about it.

"I got distracted by something I found and stopped working." She shrugged her sister's concern off.

"What did you find?" Una's big eyes widened hopefully. "Something to help us escape?"

Meredith looked away and shook her head sadly. She couldn't bear to watch the hope die out of Una's eyes. She believed so completely that they could find a way out of here. Meredith hated disappointing her every single day.

"What did you find?" Ophelia repeated, more to break up the intense boredom of being locked up constantly with nothing to do than actual curiosity.

"Just these," Meredith pulled the berries out of her pocket. "They're growing on some of the bushes. I think I remember Taliea having something like this in her garden, but I don't remember what they were or how she used them."

"Can we eat them?" Una asked.

"I don't know. Maybe."

"Not if we don't know what they are," Ophelia said. "I'm not going to accidently poison myself."

Poison. Meredith frowned. Now that Ophelia said that she was convinced there was a very good reason to not eat these berries. In the fading light of day, she held them up, studying them. What was their name? Snowdrops? Snowberries? No. Those weren't it.

When the door opened, and another slave entered carrying a large pot of stew, Meredith put the berries back in her pocket and joined the others for their evening meal. That was one thing she had to give their captors credit for. They clearly did not intend for any of their slaves to go to market emaciated. The food might not have been quite as much as she was used to, but it was more than enough to keep them from starving.

Sleep, when it came later, was troubled. Meredith tossed and turned in her spot next to Una, only able to doze off now and then. There was a nagging thought that she couldn't quite get a hold of. It was there, taunting her just out of mental reach. It was infuriating. A lonely howl ripped through the quiet night, and a dozen mournful howls rose to meet it. Wolves were nearby. Just the sound of them sent a chill down Meredith's spine.

Snowkiss. The name came to Meredith in a flash of memory, and she sat up, her hand already reaching for the berries. Snowkiss. The berries Taliea used to make someone sleep. The berries she said were deadly if someone consumed more than the tiniest bit of their juice.

"Phelie," Meredith leaned over Una carefully and shook her sister's shoulder, "Phelie, wake up."

"Hmm?" Ophelia rolled over, squinting at her. "It's the middle of the night, Meri."

"I know. I remembered what those berries are."

"Tell me in the morning."

"No. It can't wait. I think I found our way out."

Ophelia's eyes opened all the way, and she sat up, peering at Meredith through the darkness.

"Our way out? How does knowing the name of some fruit help us get out of here?"

"It's not the name, it's what they do."

"And what's that?" Ophelia drew her knees up to her chest and wrapped her arms around them and Meredith knew she had her full attention.

"Taliea uses these to put people to sleep. She said it's good for when someone needs to be cut into and stuff like that."

"Ugh, gross. Still not seeing how that helps us."

"If we could somehow get those men to eat some of them, and they were put to sleep, we could make a run for it."

Understanding dawned on Ophelia's face.

"There's just a couple of problems."

"Finding a way to convince them to eat something that will incapacitate them for a few hours and getting rid of the chain that holds the door shut," Ophelia supplied. "It's not like we can walk up to them and say, 'Here you go, eat these so we can run away from you because we don't actually want to be your slaves. Oh, and while you're at it, unlock the door, please.'"

"Yes." Meredith wanted to add one more thing to that list of problems but thought better of it.

"I have an idea about that."

"You do?"

"You're going to have to volunteer for extra work."

Meredith considered Ophelia's words for a moment before understanding dawned in her eyes. For not the first time in her life, Meredith appreciated the bond that she and her twin had. Without Ophelia needing to explain a thing, Meredith knew exactly what they needed to do.

Chapter 32

COMPASSION IS WEAKNESS.
That's what Father always said. Sasha lay awake, curled up with his face turned away from Hamo and Stephan. He didn't want them to know he was awake already. For the last four mornings he had slept until they roused him, his body demanding the rest that had been so rudely stolen from him in prison.

This morning was different.

He was getting better. He was getting his strength back. Which brought him back to Father's words. Compassion is weakness. He was healing because these men felt sorry for him and took care of him. They let him rest when he needed it, kept his wounds clean, fed him every time they ate, gave him water every time he asked for it. Their compassion was clouding their judgement, just like Father explained it would. If they were smarter, they would have kept him in the same condition they had rescued him in - starving, hurt, and too exhausted to think clearly. That would have kept him docile and obedient. That's what Father would have done. It's what he did with any of his slaves that needed to be broken. It always worked.

Careful to regulate his breathing so that they would think he was still sleeping, Sasha tried to piece together the beginnings of a plan. One thing he was sure of, he couldn't take them to the hidden stockade.

Even if these men kept their word, and Sasha thought there was a very good chance they wouldn't because no one kept their word about something like that, and they set him free, he couldn't just run back home and pretend nothing happened. If slaves were lost, Father would want someone to blame, and that someone would be Sasha. Father would invent an exquisitely painful and terrifying punishment for him that would be performed in public.

No, revealing the location of the slaves was out of the question. But his life was forfeit the minute his traveling companions discovered his intentions. Stephan at least would not hesitate to kill him, Sasha was sure. Up to this point, Sasha's directions had been accurate. Even if he had no intention of revealing where the slaves were kept, he had to at least get close enough to give himself a chance.

The germ of a plan began to form in his mind. He would wait another day or two. By then, his recovery would be almost complete, and they would be close enough that he could make it to the stockade on foot. He couldn't let on that he was feeling better, though. For all he knew, they were only being lenient with him because of how weak he was. If they thought he could run, they would most certainly take more pains to guard him.

Sasha heard them up now. They would cook breakfast over the fire and saddle the horses and only when all was ready would they wake him. Laying there, pretending to be asleep was harder than Sasha imagined it would be. Now that he had to lay still, he was unaccountably restless, his position suddenly unbearable and uncomfortable. He fought down the urge to just sit up. Did it always take them this long to get ready? His patience was slipping away when he finally heard footsteps coming up behind him and felt a familiar hand nudging him awake. Feigning sleepiness, he sat up slowly, pushing away the blanket they gave him every night.

"Feeling better?" Stephan crouched next to him, watching him, and Sasha's heart skipped a beat. Stephan knew.

"A little," he said. Sasha hoped his voice sounded as small and weak as he wanted it to.

"Good. Maybe we won't have to stop during the day for you to rest."

Sasha nodded, yawning.

"How far is it from here?"

"Three, maybe four days."

It was Stephan's turn to nod before stepping away, leaving Sasha to eat. Sasha frowned behind his back. Maybe he couldn't wait a day or two. He was feeling much better, better than he'd felt since his tumble down the ravine. But he still had to plan it just right. He had to convince them to go the wrong way so that he could go the right way when he ran. He shrugged mentally. The best he could hope for was a good opportunity. If that arose, he would take it regardless of how he felt.

Sasha managed to push through the entire day without needing to stop and sleep for a few hours. Toward evening they reached another split in the path, and Sasha saw his opportunity.

"It's that way." He kept his eyes averted as he pointed out the narrow defile leading off to the left.

"You're sure?" Stephan asked him.

"I'm sure."

"Right. We'll camp here for now and take it in the morning."

Sasha masked the smile he felt. It was exactly what he was hoping Stephan would say. He managed to dismount on his own and shuffled over to a spot away from the horses. He was really tired after riding straight through the day. Maybe he should have pretended like he needed to rest earlier, then he wouldn't be so fatigued now. But his exhaustion was mellowed by the elation he felt at his imminent freedom.

This wouldn't be like his foolish attempts at running that he made at the castle. Those had been desperate, ill planned, and doomed before they started. This was different. He planned it, calculated it, thought it through. It would succeed. Of course, it would be difficult. He hadn't worked out a way to steal a horse so he would have to travel on foot. And his hands were still connected by the shackles, but he was getting pretty adept at living with those on. He lay down like he did every night, waiting until they gave him food. It wouldn't do to run before he had something to eat.

Hamo was loosening the girth on his horse when Stephan stepped up close.

"He's lying," Hamo said softly so that his words wouldn't carry.

Stephan nodded slightly. "And he's going to make a run for it."

"What should we do?"

Stephan didn't answer right away. Frowning thoughtfully, he moved to one of the pack horses and began removing its load, casting a glance in Sasha's direction. The boy was sitting against the trunk of a pine tree, his eyes shut, but Stephan was sure he wasn't asleep. The tiniest hint of a smile tugged at the corners of Stephan's mouth, and he stepped close enough to Hamo to whisper his answer.

"Let's let him think he can."

Hamo looked perplexed for a moment, then shrugged.

"I assume you have some sort of plan."

Stephan smiled broadly now. "As a matter of fact, I do."

Darkness could not come fast enough for Sasha. He chafed at the sluggishness of the setting sun. Now that his mind was made up, and his plan enacted, anxiety ate away at him making it difficult for him to even swallow his food that evening, a fact he had to work hard to disguise. The waiting made him restless. He tried not to show it. Stephan had already figured out this morning that he was feeling better. He turned away enough that his face was mostly hidden from the light of the fire and shut his eyes again. They should think he was asleep. He needed them to think he was asleep.

The sky was heavy with low, dense clouds so the moon was invisible when it rose. Sasha very nearly dozed off and missed his chance as he sat waiting. His head slid forward and then jerked back as he realized his mistake. Stephan and Hamo were still talking by the fire. They were too quiet for him to hear their voices, but it didn't matter. For the most part that's how all his days with them had been. They ignored him most of the time, although when they did speak to him, usually to ask the way, they were polite, and even kind.

He heard them get up and opened his eyes just enough to see Stephan disappear into the darkness beyond the fire's light and Hamo checking something with the horses, his back to Sasha. Stephan was walking in the direction of the false trail Sasha had given them. Perfect. A thrill of exaltation ran up Sasha's spine as he realized this was even better than what he had planned. He was going to just wait until one of them fell asleep.

Inching his way up off the ground, careful not to make any noise and hoping the pounding of his heart was not as loud as it sounded in his own ears, Sasha made his move. He had a good idea of where exactly the mouth of the trail opened up on the right, and he crept toward it. No cry of alarm came to his ears. No footsteps ran behind him trying to catch up.

He moved faster, going from a walk to a jog. He was leery of sprinting off in the darkness with all the rocks and trees in the way, but the more distance he could put between him and those men the better his chances were of making it out of this whole mess alive.

With freedom at his fingertips, Sasha considered for the first time what he would do when he got home. He would lie, of course. That was not even a question. If Father knew he had allowed himself to be captured, or that he had agreed to such a treasonous enterprise his life would be over. But what would he tell Father? It would have to be very convincing.

Sasha still couldn't hear any sounds of pursuit. It was a glorious moment. One that made up for all the humiliating moments at the castle when he'd tried to run.

Sasha slammed into another body and went flying backwards, landing with a sickening thud on his back, the wind knocked out of him. He gasped, not fully grasping what just happened. He heard a scuffling sound, and then an unbearable weight pressed down against his chest. With a groan, Sasha realized his ribs were not quite as healed as he thought they were. There was a hot wave of agony and with a frantic effort he tried

164

to push the weight off of himself. His arms were grabbed and pinned down above his head.

"Now where are you off to in such a hurry?" The voice was horribly familiar. So was the knife that slid against his throat.

"Stephan?" Between the weight driving the air out of his lungs, and the excruciating pain, and the knife pressed tightly against his windpipe, Sasha could barely produce a whisper.

"That's right." Stephan lifted the knife away slightly, but his knee still dug ruthlessly into Sasha's chest. "Figured you might be trying to pull a stupid stunt like this. Guess that's why they had you all chained up in the dungeon."

"You knew?" Sasha croaked.

"Have to be an idiot not to know. Get up." Stephan rose and pulled Sasha up with him. "You've got some explaining to do."

Sasha groaned again, a plaintive sound of mingled pain and frustration, and hunched over as the pain stabbed through him. He didn't resist as Stephan jerked him forward. So much for his well thought out plan. So much for getting himself out of this mess. Now he had just dug himself in deeper, much deeper. Whatever kindness he had experienced at the hands of these men was about to evaporate.

"Well, that didn't take long." Hamo looked up from where he sat by the fire as they approached, a mildly amused expression on his face.

Understanding dawned in Sasha's eyes. They'd known all along. They'd known and they'd set him up. Why, Hamo hadn't even gone in pursuit of him! Impotent rage welled up inside him. Stephan led him to the tree he'd been sitting against earlier.

"Sit down."

Sasha hesitated, glaring at him, too furious to see the way Stephan's lips pressed together.

"Suit yourself then." Stephan shrugged and the next thing Sasha knew, Stephan undid one end of his shackles, looped them over a branch high above his head and then resecured them to his free wrist. Sasha cried out in shock and pain as his arms were pulled tight above his head. "Enjoy the rest of your night."

"What? No. You can't do this. You can't make me stand all night like this."

"I gave you the opportunity to sit."

"But it hurts," he said, unable to keep his voice from rising.

"Should have listened then." Stephan turned away from him and then turned back and added, "Oh, and while you're standing there maybe you can take some time to think about the benefits of telling us the truth. Leading us on a wild chase out here will only make your life worse, because you *will* accompany us every step of the way on that chase."

"What are you talking about?"

"To your credit, Sasha, you're a really terrible liar," Hamo spoke up from his seat by the fire. Sasha looked over at him, and seeing his amusement, felt hurt. Hamo hadn't so much as smiled on the entire trip, probably, Sasha thought, because he was too worried about his daughters. It wasn't fair that the first time he should find something funny was at Sasha's expense. "You should probably avoid it in the future."

"I hate you both," Sasha spat the words out, jerking on the chains as if he had any chance of breaking them and regretting it a moment later as the pain in his chest spasmed.

"I know," Stephan said. Turning to Hamo he continued, "I'm going to get some sleep now. Wake me up when you want to switch."

Sasha opened his mouth, then clamped it shut again. Anything he said was apparently going to be brushed aside or mocked. Stephan was already laying down, content that Sasha's hopes and plans lay in ruins at his feet. Sasha had no doubt he would sleep just fine despite it. Sasha, on the other hand, wasn't going to get any rest. It was just like being in the chamber.

It didn't take long at all for Sasha's shoulders to remember the cramped tension of his hours in the chamber. The old, familiar ache began within minutes. Sasha gritted his teeth, determined not to say anything. That would only serve to fuel their mockery of him. The best he could do now was try to act like it didn't bother him. It was going to be a long night. A very long night.

Sasha was sure at least an hour had passed. He was sure that Stephan was asleep. He shifted from one foot to the other, trying to ease his discomfort. His legs were remembering his time in the chamber as well. They ached wearily. His arms were throbbing. His entire body screamed for rest and his eyes were blurry with the need for sleep.

Hamo sat on the opposite side of the fire, facing his direction but ignoring him. Sasha waited a few more minutes, his will power draining away with each second. Maybe if he asked Hamo, he would let Sasha sit. Hamo had always been the more sympathetic of the two. And Sasha wasn't quite as uneasy with him as with Stephan, mostly because Hamo had never pressed a knife against his throat. He suffered quietly for a few more minutes.

"Hamo," he said softly so that he wouldn't rouse Stephan, "please, can I sit down now?" The meekness in his own voice surprised him.

Hamo looked up at him, a hint of a smile on his face and Sasha lowered his own eyes. It was the sound of hearty laughter that made him look up again. Hamo had risen and gone over to where Stephan lay. And Stephan, wide awake and laughing, was holding up the key to Sasha's irons.

Fury wasn't a strong enough word to describe the emotion coursing through Sasha at Stephan's outright laughter. He almost failed to sit when Hamo undid his shackles. It wasn't until he caught the 'you're sure you want to do this' look on Hamo's face that he remembered. Stephan was still laughing when Hamo secured Sasha to the tree sitting down.

"You didn't last long, did you?" He finally stopped long enough to ask. "It hasn't even been twenty minutes."

Sasha elected to ignore him.

Chapter 33

HOW ARE WE GOING TO get through the door though?" The older woman's face was torn between hope and skepticism.

"We're still working on that part," Ophelia admitted. They had been forced to take this woman into their confidence. She was the one who cooked all the meals for their captors.

"Actually," Meredith put her hand in her other pocket, feeling for the file that she had dropped in as a souvenir back on the day they were captured, "maybe we're not. It'll take a lot of time, but we can file the inside of it away with this. We'll have to do it when there's enough noise to cover it."

"Perfect," Ophelia said.

The older woman looked from one girl to the other, weighing their proposition.

"If we're caught, I don't know what they'll do to us but I'm sure it won't be pleasant."

"We won't be caught," Meredith said.

"Alright. When do we do it?"

"I'll collect some more berries today." Meredith was sure she would be picked for the task of wood collecting, Ophelia had been picked the day before. "And we'll start on the chain. If we can work on it enough, we should be able to try for tomorrow."

"Tomorrow it is then. You'll help me cook and serve. They won't think anything of it because I always have one of the girls help."

Ophelia flashed Meredith a conspiratorial grin. Meredith tried to return it as the woman moved away back to her spot.

"What's wrong?" Ophelia asked.

"Nothing."

"Liar. I can tell something's bothering you."

"It's just. I hope we're doing the right thing, Phelie."

"What? No offense, but when have you ever been worried about doing the right thing?"

Coming at that moment, the words stung far more than Ophelia intended. Meredith blinked several times, feeling the blood rising in her cheeks.

"I know I'm usually the one who gets us into trouble."

"Always."

"Stop, Phelie. Just stop." Meredith wrapped her arms around herself. "This is different. If we do this, there's a really good chance people are going to die."

"Who?"

"The guards."

"You're worried about killing them? Meri, you do realize what they will end up doing to us, right?"

"I know, I know. It's just...it's something Taliea always says. You're not supposed to use medicine against people. That's what I'll be doing if we go through with this. I'll be using medicine with the intent of hurting those men."

"They deserve it."

"Probably but..."

"Do you want me to do it?"

Meredith looked up at her sister. Ophelia, the one who always followed, the one who lived mostly in the shadow of Meredith's big ideas and plans, was not the same Ophelia who sat before her now. Meredith wondered how she could have lived so long with her twin and not seen this part of her. The part that acted, even if it meant someone might die, the part that offered to bear the weight of Meredith's burden. She'd taken advantage of Ophelia so much.

"I'm sorry."

"It's alright. I get it."

"No, I mean, I'm sorry for everything. For always getting you into trouble and making such horrible decisions. And I'm not, 'I got caught,' sorry. I mean it, Phelie." Meredith buried her face in her hands.

"Thanks."

For a while they sat side by side, Ophelia putting her arm around Meredith's shoulders while Meredith cried until she couldn't cry anymore.

"So, do you want me to do it?" Ophelia asked when Meredith was finally quiet.

"It's alright. I can do it. We should probably get to work on that chain though." Meredith vigorously rubbed the remnants of her tears away. "You'll have to get as much done as you can today while I'm out gathering wood and berries. I'll take a turn at it tonight."

"You know, there's no way to keep that secret from them," Ophelia nodded toward the other occupants.

"They must want to get away too. They'll keep it a secret. Maybe you can even get them to keep up a good, loud conversation so the guards won't hear anything suspicious. Or get some of them to take turns when you're tired."

The planning was cut short by the crash of the door being thrown open. It was the same man who always came to pick slaves for work. He made a pretense of looking around the room, but in the end, he picked Meredith, just like she knew he would, and two others who were always selected. Apparently, they had a good reason not to run away by themselves either.

For the rest of the day Meredith collected armload after armload of wood, along with handful after handful of berries. She wasn't sure how many they would need, but if they were really going to try tomorrow, she wanted to make sure it was enough. By the end of the day, her pockets were as full as she dared make them. She laid her last pile of wood in the wood heap and darted inside the hut.

Ophelia was sitting in the back with Una. With the guard opening the door to let them in, no one could work on the chain, so Meredith assumed that was the reason for the break. When she got closer, she noticed the odd light in Ophelia's eyes.

"We did it."

"What do you mean?"

"Everyone helped. It's almost completely worn through. It will only take about ten more minutes and it'll be gone."

"This might actually work." Meredith let out a little sigh.

"I really hope it does," Una said. "If it does, we're going to get my brother, too, aren't we?"

"Uh...Of course we are," Meredith assured her, while locking eyes with Ophelia. They hadn't thought about the male prisoners. There was no way to file the chain off their door.

Meredith's sleep that night was troubled. Waking up from time to time, she fingered the stash of berries she and Ophelia had made over the last three days. Should she use all of them? Would that be so much that it killed everyone? Meredith wondered what Taliea would think of her using them this way. In their conversations she had been so adamant about using medicine to heal, not hurt.

When she followed the older woman, Fiona, out later the next afternoon, the berries seemed to have turned to lead in her pockets. She shuffled along behind Fiona like a good, meek slave, hoping that none of their captors had the supernatural ability to see through her pockets. The bulge in her pockets was practically screaming to be noticed.

Fiona directed her on what to put in the giant pot of stew that simmered over the fire. Meredith added each ingredient and then surreptitiously began adding the berries. Once her pockets were emptied, Meredith realized she had no idea what the berries themselves tasted like. What if they were nasty? Or strong? Maybe the men would take one bite and realize they were being poisoned. Meredith shuddered with the thought. Methodically she stirred the stew, trying to crush as many of the berries as she could, releasing their juices into the concoction. Then it was time to serve it.

Meredith began to regret her haste in telling Ophelia she would be able to do this. Her hands were trembling as she spooned it into the bowls. Her stomach twisted in knots, and she thought she would be sick as she carried the heavy tray from man to man, handing each a bowl, including the ones guarding the huts and entrance. There had been only twenty men in the raiding party. Without the one Meredith sent down the ravine with her scream and the one who had been sent ahead, presumably taking a report to whoever organized the raids, there remained only eighteen. It took very little time to serve eighteen men.

Meredith's eyes never stopped moving, watching for some sign that her plan was working. Taliea hadn't told her how long it took for the berries to take effect. She helped Fiona clean up. Nothing. The foreign chatter around the fire hasn't diminished at all. She went around and collected the empty dishes. Still nothing. She took them toward the shallow creek that flowed nearby to wash them. Still...wait, no. The man guarding the male slaves slumped forward. By the time Meredith finished her task, she almost couldn't believe the extent of success her plan had.

Sitting or lying where they had been, every one of the eighteen men were asleep - at least, Meredith hoped they were asleep. She wasn't about to check to find out otherwise. Running across the stony ground toward the female captives' hut, she called out to Ophelia.

"It worked! It worked," She reached the door breathlessly and saw Ophelia was already working on the last few fibers of the chain. "Hurry."

"I'm going as fast as I can. I thought you said we'd have at least a few hours before they wake up."

"We do."

Meredith swallowed back her impatience. The plan was working. It had already worked. Still, the ten minutes it took to finish filing through the chain felt more like ten years. When it finally fell away, the clatter of it made Meredith jump but no one dangerous was awake to hear it. Ophelia and Una were out the door first.

"We did it. Now let's get out of here." Ophelia started toward the tethered line of horses.

"What about my brother?" Una froze.

"Una, we don't have time to get the chain off."

"You promised." Una's eyes started to fill. "We can't just leave them."

"There's got to be a key around here. It's probably on one of them," Meredith looked around at the guards. She was starting to feel truly ill at the sight. What if she had just killed all of them? The last thing she wanted to do was search them for a key.

"Come on, Meri, she's right. We can't just leave them." Ophelia turned away from where some of the other slaves were grabbing horses to make their escape on. Rather than stop to search the first one she reached, Ophelia looked around for the one who had clearly been the leader. "Let's start with him."

Meredith gingerly reached into his first pocket. Nothing. Ophelia had her hand in the second one and shook her head. A young man's voice called out from the men's hut.

"He doesn't have it. It's on the guard."

Una reached the man first. She pulled a ring of keys out of his pocket and fumbled around trying to get one to fit in the lock that held the chain in place.

"Una, is that you?" It was the same voice that had guided them to the key. "How did you get out?"

"It's me." The lock came free. "Karl," Una threw her arms around the young man's neck as the door swung open and he stepped outside. "We got out. We got out. We can go home now."

"How?" Karl looked from his little sister to Meredith and Ophelia standing behind her.

"We sort of poisoned them," Meredith looked away, "We should probably get going. I don't know how long they'll stay like this."

"We're going on foot," Ophelia wasn't watching them. She was watching the last of the horses being ridden away by another escapee. "I hated walking all the way here."

"That's not fair," Meredith cried, "This was our escape. It was our plan."

Karl disentangled himself from Una's arms and took in the sight of the sleeping guards for the first time. His eyes widened.

"Come on. We're wasting our chance. Let's just get out of here." He started toward the only opening. After exchanging a quick glance and shrug, Meredith and Ophelia followed.

Chapter 34

SASHA WAS MISERABLE. Worse than miserable. His chest hurt horribly again, although Hamo had been kind enough to rewrap the tight cloth that helped hold the broken bones in place and helped relieve some of the pain. That surprised Sasha, but not enough to break through the cloud of wretchedness that hung over him.

His plan had failed, disastrously.

They had laughed at him.

And they had guessed his lie.

Instead of heading down the wrong path that morning, they were getting closer to the hidden stockade with every step. Sasha knew they were only two or three days away at the most by now. He was running out of time to turn this in his favor. There was one plan, well not a full plan, more like one idea left if he could manage it. The fact that he no longer had any freedom whatsoever made his chances slim.

The trail climbed higher, skirting yet another chasm that reminded Sasha all too much of the one he had fallen down. He shuddered with the memory of it. His life had fallen downhill as precipitously as his body had at that moment. It had yet to stop spiraling out of his control. Aside from asking for directions, Stephan and Hamo relentlessly ignored him, giving Sasha more than enough time and silence to think about his predicament. He wanted to ask them what they planned on doing with him now but could not work up the courage.

When they were past the steep drop off and the trail widened out a bit, Stephan pulled his horse to a stop. Sasha looked up long enough to catch Stephan's eye, and quickly lowered his own.

"Get down."

Stephan's hand was already clamped over Sasha's arm, ensuring his cooperation. Sasha lowered himself to the ground, keeping his eyes down, and allowed himself to be led to a nearby pine. The branches formed a low canopy, and it was to one of these that Stephan secured him to. The chain still held his hands up above his head, but at least Sasha could sit.

He turned miserably away from the two men, closing his eyes, trying to ignore the despair that was growing in him. The tiny part of him that had hoped they truly meant to let him go at the end of all this was dying. Even if that was their intention before, he was sure they would no longer do it. The smell of food drifted toward him, making his mouth water. At least they weren't withholding that from him.

"Sasha?"

The question in Stephan's tone made Sasha bristle as he opened his eyes. He didn't want to be asked more questions. Still, it was the first time either of the men had addressed him when not asking for directions and there was a small part of him that was curious.

"What?"

Stephan decided to overlook the sullenness in Sasha's tone.

"What's your family like?"

Sasha blinked. Of all the possible questions Stephan could ask him, why that? What could he gain from that? And how was he supposed to answer?

"What do you mean?" he countered cautiously.

"You have brothers? Sisters?"

"I have lots of half-brothers. I had a full sister, too. But Father sold her a few years ago because she displeased him." It was the first time Sasha had even thought about Agathe in ages.

"Your father did what?" Hamo asked.

"He sold her. He wasn't happy with her. He sold my mother too." Sasha looked up to find both men staring at him in horror and added quietly, "You don't do that sort of thing, do you?"

"No," they both said simultaneously.

"And what did your mother and sister do that made him decide to sell them?" Stephan continued.

"I don't know what my mother did. I was too young. He just took her away during the night and I never saw her again. I think he sold Agathe because she looked too much like Mother."

"Your father is a horrible person," Hamo said softly.

"No, he's not. He does what he must to keep Aruuk strong."

"Is that how you felt about it when he took your mother away?"

"That's different. I was young. I didn't understand what was right."

"I don't think you do now, either," Hamo said.

"I know what's right for Aruuk," Sasha answered hotly. Why were they trying to confuse him, and make him question Father? "Father did what he had to."

"What about your half-brothers?" Stephan interjected, "You said you have a lot of those. Are they the ones who end up leading raids?"

"Mostly. Armin led ours."

"Hmm." Stephan leaned forward, staring into the fire. "Is Armin one of your brothers?"

"The oldest." Why did Stephan care about this at all?

"And how many men does he need for raiding?"

"He only took nineteen, but everyone except Boris and I had gone before."

"I see. And all of them winter at the stockade?"

"Yes. Except for whoever was sent ahead with a report for my father."

"Thank you, Sasha," Stephan said, smiling oddly at him.

"For what?"

"For answering my questions."

Sasha went cold. They'd set another trap for him, and he just walked straight into it without blinking an eye. By making it a casual conversation, they had caught him completely off guard. They didn't even need to threaten, bribe, or torture him. He'd given them every answer they asked for. His consternation must have been evident.

"Don't be too hard on yourself, Sasha. We would have found out what we needed to know anyway," Stephan said. "This way was just easier."

Sasha turned away again, trying to hide his anger, disgust and burning shame. They'd made a fool of him again. At least they were gracious enough not to laugh outright at him tonight.

"Sasha?" This time it was Hamo. Sasha might have tried to ignore him, except that there wasn't even a hint of malice or mockery in his voice. He turned his head enough to meet Hamo's eyes. "What happens to you when you go home? What will your father do to you?"

The words hung in the air for a moment while Sasha considered them. At last, he answered, "I don't know."

The silence was smothering. Sasha was relieved when he felt himself getting drowsy enough to fall asleep even in his uncomfortable position. At least asleep he didn't have to think about any of this.

He'd been asleep for a long time when a shout awakened him. Sitting up, Sasha realized that the three of them were no longer alone around their fire. He huddled closer to the trunk of the tree, shielding himself in the shadows of it, watching and listening. At the sound of their words, the blood drained away from his face.

Chapter 35

MEREDITH CLUNG TO OPHELIA'S hand and followed the dark shadows before her that were Karl and Una. Her ears picked up every stray sound and made her heart quicken with the fear that they were being pursued.

As tired as she was, she was sure they had been up moving for most of the night. Surely their captors were awake now - if they were going to awaken. Karl didn't think they would. He had stopped long enough in their camp to strip two or three of them of their weapons and he was sure they were dead. Meredith knew she should be relieved by that. If they were dead, they couldn't come after them. But the thought turned her stomach. She hadn't wanted to kill anybody.

Well, at least not them.

If the two who had captured her and Ophelia had still been in the camp, Meredith thought she might have felt a little differently. But neither of them were still around. One because her scream had sent him plummeting down the side of a deep ravine, and the other because he had been sent ahead alone.

Meredith was tired. Even walking, she could barely keep her eyes open. She stumbled more and more, her feet catching on rocks or roots or sometimes nothing at all.

"Maybe we should rest for a while?" she whispered.

"No." Karl didn't bother to turn around. "We put as much distance in between them and us as we can. There's no telling if some of them survived and are hunting us down now. Besides, winter is almost here.

We have to get home, or we'll be trapped and die out here."

"Oh. I hadn't thought about that."

"Did you have a plan for getting food?"

"No. I hadn't thought that far ahead."

Meredith could sense Karl shaking his head in frustration even in the darkness. That was hardly fair of him, seeing as he wouldn't be free without her help.

"We should have taken whatever we could carry from the camp," Ophelia said.

"Yes, we should have," Karl agreed.

"You know, you don't have to make it sound like it's our fault for not doing it. You could have grabbed stuff too. I mean, at least we thought of a way to get out. That's more than you did," Meredith lashed out.

Karl stopped suddenly and Meredith walked right into his back.

"You're right. I'm sorry. It's just, there's really no point in getting away if we're just going to starve to death out here."

"You know how to hunt and trap," Una said, her voice dull with weariness.

"I'll try. But I don't exactly have what I need for that. Una, are you alright?" Karl's voice changed completely as Una sank to the ground.

"I think we need to rest," Una whispered. "I don't think I can keep going."

Meredith had a twinge of guilt at the selfish relief she felt for Una's exhaustion. Karl wouldn't stop for her or Ophelia, but he would for his little sister. Sure enough, he was already looking around for a good place to hide. Meredith was surprised at how much she could see in the darkness. Her eyes had adjusted well over the hours of running and although nothing was clear, she could identify the shapes of rocks and trees. Karl led them to a stand of pine trees. Meredith finally released her death grip on Ophelia's hand and sank down, letting her eyes shut at once.

"I'm going to have a look around. See if anyone's following us." Karl disappeared before anyone had a chance to protest.

"One of us should stay awake, in case something happens," Ophelia said when he was out of sight. "I can do it first, if you want."

"Fine. Wake me up when you get too tired."

Meredith didn't remember falling asleep. The next thing she knew was a hand being clamped over her mouth. She tried to scream, but the hand effectively muffled any sound she made.

"Meredith, it's me. Karl." He waited until she relaxed a little and then pulled his hand away.

"Why did you do that?" Meredith hissed.

"We're not out here by ourselves. I didn't want you screaming and letting the others know that."

"What are you talking about?"

"I had a look around, just like I said I was going to. Up ahead, around the next bend, there's another group. But I don't think they're escapees."

"Why not?" If they weren't escapees, then they couldn't be anyone good. Not here.

"It was at least two men, and I didn't recognize them."

"Maybe you just missed seeing them all this time."

"Meredith, I spent days locked up in one room with all the other men, I think I'd know if they were from our little group."

Meredith swallowed. She hadn't thought about that.

"Who do you think they are, then?"

"I don't know. They're not Northerners, either. Not by their dress, at least." Karl sat back on his heels, a puzzled look on his face. "To be honest, they look more like they're from Dorsten."

"Take me." Meredith sat up all the way.

"What? Are you crazy? No."

"I want to see them."

"And we're just going to leave them," Karl nodded toward where Ophelia and Una were sleeping. Meredith realized for the first time that Ophelia was supposed to be awake, keeping watch to make sure no one snuck up on them. That had worked out well, she thought wryly.

"Wake them up and bring them. If those men aren't Northerners and they might be from Dorsten, then they might be able to help us. We have to at least try."

Meredith could see Karl was at least considering her idea. If they weren't in such desperate straits, he probably would have just brushed it off as a ridiculous plan. Without any food, or means to get food, he had to at least weigh the possibility.

"Fine. But we just watch. We're not going to let them know we're here. Even if they can't help us, we might get a chance to steal something to eat."

It took several minutes to wake the other two girls and explain enough of what was going on to convince them that it was a good idea. By the time they had done that, Meredith was having her own doubts. What if this destroyed all their hopes of getting away? Not that those hopes were very big now, without food and with winter on its way.

It took another thirty minutes to make their way silently around the bend of the trail as it wrapped around the base of one mountain. The light of a fire in the distance reminded Meredith of just how cold she was. In the last couple of weeks, she had almost gotten used to the persistent cold. The fire made her long to sit next to its warmth. She shivered.

They crept closer, staying in the shadow of the trees. Karl put a finger to his lips, motioning for them to be quiet for the tenth time. Meredith had to smile a little. She made less noise than he did moving through the trees, and they were still far enough away that she was sure the man sitting by the fire couldn't hear a thing.

Meredith squinted, trying to get a good glimpse of the figure by the fire. There was something oddly familiar about him. Beside her, Ophelia let out a tiny gasp and tugged frantically on her sleeve.

"It's Father!"

As soon as Ophelia said it, Meredith was sure her sister was right. She was so sure that she completely ignored the horrified look on Karl's face, and the hand he reached out to try to stop her and she started toward the fire, Ophelia right behind her. They must have made some sound approaching because Father looked up and searched the darkness. Throwing away the last ounce of caution she possessed, Meredith ran. She ran straight into the light of the fire and before Father had a chance to grasp who she was, she flung her arms around his neck and cried.

"Meri? Phelie? How?"

Meredith couldn't answer. Just the sound of his voice made her cry harder, the sobs working their way up from somewhere deep inside her. Ophelia was in his arms too, and Meredith could hear her speaking garbled words and phrases in between her tears.

"...Got away...never see you...so scared."

Meredith clung harder to him, never wanting to let go.

"Meri? Phelie? How did you get here?"

Meredith lifted her face enough to see Grandfather standing there now. With an effort she swallowed back the flood of happy, relieved tears and managed a shaky smile.

"We escaped." She noticed Karl and Una standing awkwardly a short distance away. "It's alright, you two. You can come closer."

Father and Grandfather turned to see who she was talking to as Karl and Una came up. Una looked on the verge of tears and Meredith felt a pang of sympathy for the poor girl who was forced to watch a reunion she would never be able to have. Karl was simply watching the entire thing with suspicion.

"Karl, this is my father and grandfather." Meredith brought her sleeve up to her face, wiping away the tears that wet her cheeks. "And this is Karl and Una. They escaped with us."

"Hamo Serbon." Father reached for Karl's hand in welcome.

Chapter 36

SASHA WATCHED THE REUNION from the shadows, forgotten and unnoticed. He had retreated as far from the light of the fire as his chained wrists would allow him to go.

There was something painful about the unashamed happiness at being reunited that tore at Sasha's insides, although he didn't know why. He watched as the girls, their faces hidden from view, clung to Hamo. No one, in his entire life, had ever held Sasha that way. The other two were apparently strangers to Hamo and Stephan because he caught their introductions. It wasn't until they finally sat down at the fire and started exchanging stories that Sasha sat up, his ears catching every word of it.

"How'd you get away?" Hamo asked.

"It was Meredith's idea. She found berries that would poison all the guards and put them to sleep."

"Or kill them," Karl added.

"Yes, or that," the one called Meredith said. At least Sasha thought it was her, he still couldn't get a good look at their faces, "Anyway, I found the berries, and we put them in their food. And then we got away. But what about you? How did you find out what happened to us?"

"Or how did you find us, for that matter?" Ophelia added.

"Oh, we had a little help with that," Stephan said, a smile evident in his voice.

Sasha cringed and shrank back farther. The last thing he wanted was to be pointed out to a few escaped slaves. Stephan, he was quite certain, would find his discomfort and humiliation amusing. Tense, he waited for Stephan's next words, knowing they would draw everyone's full attention to himself.

"Who helped you?" Meredith asked.

"He did." Stephan jerked his thumb in Sasha's direction.

Sasha lowered his head, staring resolutely at the ground. He sincerely wished the ground beneath him would swallow him up and spare him the humiliation of being a spectacle for his former captives. The ground wasn't very obliging.

"That's him," one of the girls, Sasha wasn't sure which, cried out. "That's one of the ones that took Phelie and I."

At her words Sasha's head snapped back up and for one awful, nightmarish second his gaze met the girl's. Sasha hadn't thought his situation could get any worse, not after his failed escape attempt. This was worse. So much worse. Why out of all the slaves they had taken did Hamo's daughters have to be the two, the only two, that Sasha was personally responsible for capturing? He couldn't even bring himself to look over at Hamo, although he felt the man's eyes on him.

"Are you sure, Meri?" Sasha winced at the tone in Stephan's voice. "He told us he didn't have any part in the raids."

"Of course, I'm sure. It was him and one other one. He threatened me with a knife and pulled my hair and he told Phelie and me that we would be sold for more at their market because we're a matched set."

Sasha's face burned. He wished his hands were free enough to cover his face with. He wished he was dead. Dead, or invisible, or anywhere in the whole world but right here, listening to Meredith tell her father what he had done and said. And Meredith didn't even know the worst of it. She hadn't understood the conversation he and Boris had about claiming both girls for their own use on the opening day of the Spring Market if Father allowed them to. Oh, he was so glad she hadn't known about that.

The silence that followed Meredith's words was suffocating. Sasha couldn't decide if they were waiting for him to speak or not. He didn't have anything to say. No way he could defend himself. He was sure they were all still watching him. He could feel their eyes, accusing and hating him. It was such a cruel coincidence. He really hadn't participated in the actual raids. Now they believed he lied about that too.

And Sasha knew he was dead.

They might not kill him this second but kill him they would. Hamo would never let him live knowing what he had done to his daughters, knowing that he was the one responsible for their entire ordeal.

"How did you get him to help you find us?" Ophelia asked at last, and although Sasha didn't want to be talked about like he wasn't sitting right there, he was glad the silence was broken.

"It was either that or be hung back in Dorsten," Stephan answered.

"He deserves that," Meredith said.

"Probably." It was the first time Hamo had spoken since his daughter's revelation and Sasha's fears were all confirmed in that single word. He slumped against the tree, turning his head so that no one could see the wave of despair that washed over his face. He was going to die.

Sasha only caught fragments of the conversation after that. He heard something about Stephan and Hamo and the girls not being from Dorsten but from Dival. He heard their worries about the nearness of winter. None of it mattered to him. Not anymore. None of it was important. All that mattered was that this was truly it. The end of his life.

He wondered how they would kill him. The easiest way would be to just slit his throat and let him bleed out. But that was relatively painless. What if they wanted to make him suffer first? What if they decided to torment him before ending his miserable life? It would make sense that they would. Nausea filled him at the thought.

At some point he fell back asleep, a troubled, restless sleep full of awful nightmares. The nightmares, mostly dredged up memories of his brief time in prison, dragged him out of the oblivion of sleep and back to his reality.

He sat up a little, gasping and sweating. This wasn't how he wanted to spend his last night alive. Casting a furtive glance towards the rest of the group, Sasha went hot all over again. Everyone was asleep, except for Hamo who was watching him intently, his face unreadable. Sasha turned away again. Eventually sleep came again, as haunted as before.

The sun was still a distant promise when a collective stirring roused him once and for all. The others were awake. They were clearly making preparations to leave, which meant that whatever end they had in mind for him would be enacted soon. Sasha tried to steel himself for it. He was the son of Chief Gundar. He had to die bravely. But everything inside him screamed out that he didn't want to die at all. He had to be strong. But his heart was racing, and his breath was shallow, and his limbs trembled.

The horses were readied. The little group had eaten. Sasha ran his tongue over his dry lips over and over. They were discussing how long it would take them to get all the way back to Dival, and if they even had a chance before winter set in. Sasha vainly tested the chains that held him in place. He almost wished they would just get on with whatever it was they planned rather than drag this out. Karl was offering them a place to stay if they thought they couldn't make it home in time. Sasha's eyes darted about searching for something, anything that would enable him to escape. He heard them mounting up.

A single set of footsteps approached him, but he didn't dare look up. He was afraid to see who it was. He was afraid to see what they had in their hand. Maybe they would just use the knife. Maybe they would at least give him a quick, painless death. That would be mercy, right? It was the most he could hope for. Sasha blinked, realizing his eyes were full of tears, blurring the frostbitten ground before him. He couldn't cry. He couldn't meet his death crying. But he wanted to live.

Sasha jumped and let out a pitiful cry at the touch of a hand on his arm. The blur in his eyes swelled to completely blind him and he felt rather than saw the key unlocking one iron band and then the other. His arms dropped to his lap. So, this was how they would do it. Let him think he was free, wait for him to run, then chase him down and kill him. Father had done that many times. He made a game of the victim's death, toying with them, enticing them with the promise of freedom. It made death, when it did finally come, that much more horrifying and disappointing. The game only worked if he played it, though, and Sasha was determined to not give them the satisfaction. He didn't move. He barely even looked up enough to see that it was Hamo who removed his shackles.

He heard the horses move away. Still, he didn't move. They were probably just trying to trick him into running so that they could chase him down. They wouldn't just let him go. Not after what he'd done. No one in their right mind would let him go.

Chapter 37

MEREDITH SENT ONE LAST curious look back at where Sasha still sat under the tree. He hadn't moved since Father set him free which was strange, she thought. If it was her, she would have taken off the second the chain was gone.

"I still can't believe you just let him go like that," she said, turning to look at Father.

"I gave him my word, Meri. I had to keep it."

"Even after what he did?"

"It wasn't about what he did, it's about keeping my end of the bargain. Like it or not, he did help us get to you. We would've been completely lost without him. Besides, you're safe now." Father smiled at her. "That's all that really matters to me."

Meredith nodded, a smile spreading across her own face. She spent the last two weeks thinking Father had no idea what had happened to her and Ophelia. How nice it was to be wrong about that. All the times she had thought they were alone and abandoned, Father had been coming for them. The thought brought immense comfort.

A few flurries of snow drifted towards the ground, dampening the mood of the otherwise happy group. The reminder that winter was imminent and that they had days of riding to do before they were safe hastened their steps.

"You really could just come with Una and me. My Aunt wouldn't mind, I'm sure," Karl reiterated his previous offer.

Meredith hoped it wouldn't come to that. As much as she hated to admit it after all they had been through together, she found Karl terribly annoying. The thought of spending an entire winter cooped up in a house with him was quite distasteful. She really wanted nothing more than to be home, with Mother and Priscilla, Elenora, and Adelaide.

"I'm afraid that's not a good idea," Stephan said. "We sort of...well, let's just say I impersonated my brother to break Sasha out of prison the night before he was supposed to be hanged, and I don't think it would be wise for us to go showing our faces around Dorsten if we can help it."

"You did? I bet your brother was really happy to find out about that," Ophelia laughed. Meredith had never seen her sister laugh so easily. "Why would you go through all that trouble for someone as horrible as him?"

"Like I said before, we knew who had taken you. We just didn't know where. Sasha was our best bet for finding you. We had to take the risk. As it turns out, I think it was a pretty good risk."

For five days they retraced their steps back to Dorsten. And with each day the threat of snow grew. The flurries came off and on, sometimes sticking to the ground, sometimes melting.

"I can't decide if it was harder walking or riding all this way," Meredith said to Ophelia as they finally approached Drogo's cabin on the sixth day.

"Walking was way worse," Una, riding double with Ophelia, answered for her. "Walking was hard."

"It'll be so nice to sleep under a real roof," Ophelia murmured, looking longingly at the cabin ahead.

"If he'll let us, we'll stay for the night. Tomorrow we'll start for home," Father said, dismounting as he spoke. "Wait here while I talk to him."

Home. Meredith closed her eyes and let her mind wander back home. It was such a nice, cozy place. She tried to imagine what Mother and each of her younger sisters were doing right now. It was evening, so Mother was probably getting supper ready. Meredith smiled at the picture of Mother. It turned to a frown.

"Father, how long have we been gone?" she asked suddenly as he came back from speaking with Drogo.

"Almost three weeks."

"Do you think Mother's had the baby yet?"

A pained look crossed Father's face, and she wished she hadn't brought it up. He'd spent the last two weeks worrying about finding her and Phelie. It wasn't fair to remind him of what was going on at home too.

"Maybe. Let's go inside and get some rest. When we leave tomorrow, we're heading straight home. Karl, if you and Una want to stay with us tonight you are more than welcome to. I'm afraid we'll be parting ways tomorrow, though."

"Thank you. We'll do that," Karl said.

Meredith took one last look at the mountains rising up behind them. By nightfall tomorrow they would be deep in the Void, the mountains little more than a jagged line on the horizon. She would be so happy to see them disappear.

Chapter 38

SASHA WASN'T SURE HOW LONG he sat there, waiting. The sun rose fully into a sky broken up by many clouds and he still hadn't moved. He couldn't believe that they had just left him. No torture, no death. It was the ordinary sounds of the mountain woods that finally convinced him that no one was lurking nearby to chase him down if he made a move.

Stiffly, he rose, his hands taking turns rubbing his wrists. For the first time in two weeks, his wrists were free of the heavy irons. He almost felt lost without them. Dazed, he looked about, trying to get his bearings. A small canvas bag sitting nearby caught his eye. He walked over and opened it, stunned to find some food and a full flask of water in it. They not only didn't kill him, but they also ensured that he wouldn't die of hunger or thirst either. Strange people. The gesture was heartening, and Sasha started off.

It was tiring walking all this way, but Sasha didn't dare sit down and take a break. There was no one with him now to make sure he wasn't devoured by wild animals while he slept or to wake him up after an hour or two and make him move on. He needed to reach the stockade by nightfall. He could only hope that he would find someone still alive there. Having heard bits and pieces of what Meredith had done, he wasn't sure what to expect when he got there. The young man who had escaped with them had been quite confident that most of the guards at least were dead.

Sasha wrapped his arms around himself tightly as the temperature fell steadily through the day. From time to time, he brought his bare, freezing hands up to his mouth to blow on them. A loud snorting made him look off to the side. A small, black horse stood tangled in a thicket. Sasha couldn't see anyone around the animal. It would be nice to have a horse instead of having to walk all that way. He approached it. The animal's reins were caught in a branch above its head.

As Sasha got closer, he realized there was a person there. Lying face down, a dark stain sprawling across the ground from beneath their head, was a woman. He hesitated. It was most certainly one of the escaped captives. Turning her carefully over with his foot, Sasha found himself gagging again. There was nothing left of her face, it had been completely crushed by her fall. Sasha let her fall back and went for the horse. The animal was well trained and docile, waiting patiently while he freed it from the thicket and led it back toward the trail.

Mounted now, he made much better time. He pushed on through the afternoon and was rewarded for his perseverance when, an hour or so before sunset, he spotted the naturally built mouth to the stockade. Digging his heels into the sides of his horse, he hurried the last few yards overcome with anxiety over what he would find inside.

Sasha's eyes widened as he rode in. There was something grotesquely peaceful about the way the men sat or lay sprawled out around the camp. He slowed his horse and brought it to a stop in the center. Without getting down, he could count the bodies. Eighteen. Eighteen raiders dead at one stroke. Sasha wondered if Father had ever had an entire raiding party wiped out. He sat on his horse for a long time, unsure of what he should do. He couldn't bury all these men. He also couldn't make it back to Father tonight.

Finally, swallowing back his own squeamishness, he slid to the ground and began going from body to body. If he didn't know any better, he would have thought they were asleep. No face was twisted in pain or fear. At least it hadn't been a horrible way to die. The knot of anxiety inside him slowly dissipated as he looked at one man after another and still failed to find the face he was searching for. Armin was there, looking far more serene in death than he ever had in life. But Boris was not. Armin must have decided to send Boris ahead with the report. Boris was still alive.

As the last light of day fled away, Sasha grew more uncomfortable with the idea of sleeping alone in this place. The quiet was far from peaceful. It held an eerie, ghostly quality that sent a shiver down Sasha's spine. Even his horse was skittish, jumping at every shadow.

At last, Sasha decided to bring the horse into one of the huts with him. It was only an animal, but at least it was another living being. The guards' hut was the most comfortable, and still had a latch on the door that he could lock from the inside. He led his mount in through the narrow doorway and secured the door behind them.

There was a lamp in there, and Sasha felt around for the flint and steel to light it. Some of his jumpiness disappeared when he had a light going. He dug around in the bag of food that had been left for him and found something to eat.

Pulling out some of the blankets they kept there, and a straw filled mattress, he made himself a bed and laid down. He was tired, but even so it took him quite a while to fall asleep. Every noise made him start. He was thankful for the lock on the door, keeping the creatures of the night out.

A shrieking whinny from his horse made Sasha sit straight up. Where the night had been quiet, now it was bursting with sound. Sounds that Sasha would much rather not have heard. A howl from directly outside the hut sent a shiver down his spine. The answering howls were worse. His horse pranced nervously from side to side, eyes rolling back in her head and showing white, her body trembling and sweating. Sasha pulled the blankets tighter around him.

Then came the wet, tearing, slobbering sound of the wolves feeding. There was only one thing they could be eating out there. Sasha pressed his hands over his ears, trying to block out the sickening noise but he heard it anyway.

All night it continued, mingled with the snarls and spats of the wolves fighting for their share. Sleep was out of the question now. Sasha kept his hands over his ears and the blankets pulled up around him, hoping desperately that the wolves would finish their gorging and move away by morning.

When morning did at last come, and Sasha thought it couldn't have come any slower, a disappointing sight met his eyes. Peering through a crack in the wall because he was afraid to open the door, two things were immediately obvious. First, it snowed last night. Not enough to threaten his day's ride back to Father, but enough to cover the ground in a couple inches of powdery whiteness. At least, some of it was white. The rest was a sickening shade of crimson. Second, the wolves had indeed finished their feasting. But instead of moving off like Sasha needed them to, they lay around dozing.

For most of the day nothing changed. Sasha ate the last of his food. He tore open one of the straw filled mattresses and let his horse nibble away at the straw. Finally, late in the afternoon as more snow began to fall, the wolf pack moved away. Sasha couldn't see where they went from inside the hut, and he still didn't dare open the door and step outside to look around. The mare remained antsy, so he assumed they weren't far. He couldn't leave now anyway. He'd never make it home before dark, and he wasn't going to be caught out in the open alone at night.

He managed at least a little bit of fitful sleep that night. His horse at last quieted and Sasha was sure that in the morning it would be safe to leave. By tomorrow night he would be home, safe beneath Father's roof. The thought was not quite as comforting as he would have liked.

Sasha was more than ready for the sight of Illsen in the distance when it finally came into view late the next evening. The wooden palisade surrounding town rose in stark contrast to the white landscape surrounding it. The newly risen moon cast strange shadows across the snowy ground. Beneath his horse's hooves, the snow crunched softly, alerting anyone at the gate that a rider approached. Sasha had never had to worry about that though. Stifling a yawn, he tapped his heels against the mare's sweating sides and approached the gate. The watchman stepped in front of him, holding up a hand to bring him to a halt.

"Who are you, and what's your business in Illsen?" It was an older man, too old to participate in the raiding, but still young enough to serve usefully.

"It's me, Sasha, son of Chief Gundar." Sasha's name alone was enough to get him into the town after dark when the gates were usually kept shut.

"Sasha Gundarson," the man bowed quickly, "Forgive me for not recognizing you, but we thought you were lost on your raid."

"Well, clearly I'm not. Open the gate," Sasha snapped. He was cold and tired. He really didn't want to be out here explaining to someone beneath him what had happened, especially since he hadn't sorted out just what he was going to tell Father. The man bowed again and hurried to signal the gate open. Two other watchmen stood on the inside and watched him with curiosity as he rode past. Sasha ignored them with all the disdain his upbringing required of him. It came easily when he was already out of sorts with exhaustion.

The sprawling structure of the Chief's house was the centerpiece of the town. Upon arriving at its front door, Sasha dismounted wearily and led his horse to the stable. The slave in charge of the horses was asleep. Sasha nudged him awake with his foot.

"Take care of her," he said, tossing the reins to the man.

With that taken care of, Sasha stumbled wearily through the labyrinth of hallways to his room. It was empty. Sasha did a double take. Aside from the bed, stripped clean of all its bedding, there was not another thing in the room. They had already cleared out all his things. It was hardly the homecoming Sasha had been looking forward to. He had spent the last few hours dreaming of crawling into his own bed, safe from wolves and cruel people who wanted to hang him and sleeping uninterrupted for hours and hours. Letting the door close behind him, Sasha sank to the floor against it, drawing his knees up to his chest.

"Master Sasha." A soft tapping on the door behind his back startled Sasha. "Master Sasha."

Sasha scooted away from the door allowing Axel to open it.

"Excuse me, Master Sasha, for the intrusion. Chief Gundar requests your presence," the man bowed low as he spoke.

Sasha groaned in frustration. Father wanted to see him already? He had only just arrived, and everyone thought he was dead. How had word gotten to Father that quickly? One of the watchmen must have gone straight to him, Sasha realized. The fact that Father wasn't going to wait until morning left Sasha with mixed feelings. Either he was angry enough with Sasha to lose sleep over it, or he was so relieved that Sasha had returned that he could not wait another minute to see him. Somehow, Sasha didn't think the second option was realistic.

With his thoughts in chaos, he dutifully followed Axel down the hallways. They were headed to the great hall, he realized with a heavy sigh. It would be a completely formal meeting then. Axel pulled the heavy door open and fell to his face on the floor inside.

"I have brought Master Sasha to you, Chief Gundar, as you commanded." Axel's voice was muffled by the carpet he lay on.

Father ignored the slave and beckoned for Sasha to enter. Sasha stepped around Axel's prone body and came within a few feet of Father's chair before dropping to his knees and bringing a closed fist up in salute, lightly touching his forehead first and then his chest.

"You wished to see me, Father?"

"Boris told me you were dead. How is it that you are not only alive but here?"

Sasha's heart turned to lead, and blood pounded in his temples. A memory flitted across his mind - Hamo being reunited with his daughters. Sasha hated to admit it, but some tiny corner of his soul longed for Father to feel the same unrestrained joy at seeing him or to feel any happiness at all at his return. He knew better than to think that would happen. Father never showed any emotion. Still, the comparison threw him off and left him a little sore inside.

"They believed me to be dead when my horse stumbled and threw me over the edge of a ravine."

"Tell me everything. No lies," Father added the last two words as an afterthought.

Hamo had told Sasha he was a terrible liar. If that was really the case, lying would make things worse, much worse, with Father. But perhaps he could just tell enough of the truth to keep himself out of trouble. Sasha took a deep breath to steady himself.

"I was found, unconscious, by men from Dorsten and taken by them." Sasha didn't need to look up to feel Father's frown. "They kept me in the castle dungeon and questioned me. I didn't tell them anything. They sentenced me to hang but I escaped." Sasha decided that the means of his escape were unimportant to the telling of his story. "And made my way first to our stockade."

"Why did you leave the stockade? As a raider, you are to winter there. The bounty taken on those raids is worth more than your life, and yet you abandoned them to come home."

"Father, forgive me." A lump of fear stuck in Sasha's throat. "There was nothing left to guard."

"What?" Father's voice conveyed such anger, such deep rage in that single word that Sasha shuddered.

"It's true. When I returned to the stockade, every raider was dead, the captives gone, and the livestock freed."

For a long time, Father did not speak, and Sasha did not dare move. He kept his eyes on the ornate carpet in front of his knees. The colors began to swirl and swim in front of him, and Sasha remembered just how tired he was. Couldn't Father have waited until morning to sort all this out? A few hours wouldn't change anything.

"Axel," Father's voice was steely when he did speak again, "Bring Boris to me."

Sasha heard the slave get to his feet and scurry out of the room. Still, he did not lift his eyes.

"Sasha, you were held in the castle?"

"Yes, Father."

"Tell me everything you saw, everything you remember about it and Dorsten in general. What were the people like? Did you see any sort of standing army? Did you meet anyone in leadership?"

As if his life depended on it, and Sasha knew very well that it might, he relayed everything he could remember about Dorsten, holding back only his own part in leading Stephan and Hamo so close to the hidden stockade. He heard Axel and Boris waiting just inside the doorway, but he didn't pause. Not unless Father wished him to, and Father said nothing. At last, he exhausted his limited knowledge of the foreign country and fell silent. Then, and only then, did Father address the others.

"That is all, Axel. Boris, come."

Sasha sensed Boris' approach and caught sight of him in his peripheral vision as he knelt next to Sasha and saluted Father.

"You wished to see me, Father?"

Sasha guessed Boris had just been woken up. His voice was still thick with sleep, but even so there was a slight catch in it. Sasha glanced sidelong at his brother and saw how pale he was. At least he's as scared as I am, Sasha thought.

"Boris, who is that next to you?" Father said.

Boris met Sasha's eye briefly, his own widening in shock and - was it guilt?

"It is Sasha, Father." The hitch in his voice was more defined this time.

"What did you tell me about Sasha?"

"I told you he had died," Boris' voice dropped to a whisper.

"Speak up. Did you or anyone else actually confirm Sasha's death?"

"What do you mean, Father?"

"I mean, did you find his body?"

"No, Father. We did not look for it."

Sasha glanced at his brother again without moving his head. No one had even tried to find him? Not even Boris? The sore spot inside of him grew a little.

"Boris, what report did you bring me of the raid you were in?"

"I brought word that it was successful. That we took forty captives." Boris began to sound uncertain, making it more like a question than a statement.

Another long silence stretched before them. Father got up and paced back and forth and Boris and Sasha both pretended to ignore it. Sasha's head began to hurt, and his legs fell asleep beneath him. He wanted to go to bed. No, he wanted Zena to fill a hot bath for him, and then he wanted to go to bed. At last Father stopped just in front of them. He clapped his hands together three times, summoning the two guards who accompanied him everywhere.

"You have brought me two false reports, Boris. First, your brother clearly lives. Second, there are no forty captives. Such dishonesty must be punished, don't you think?"

Boris swallowed hard. "Yes, Father."

"Since it was Sasha you lied about, it will be Sasha who chooses your first punishment. Well, Sasha?"

All thoughts of bed and rest fled from Sasha's mind as the full meaning of Father's words sank in. His heart skipped a beat, then beat wildly out of rhythm. This was Boris, the only person he thought of as something of a friend. Boris, who had not even gone back to see if he survived his fall. Boris, who had taken the time to help him with his sword lessons. Boris, who was constantly trying to outdo him. He could feel Boris' eyes searching his face, begging him for what, mercy? Compassion? Compassion is weakness. Sasha tightened his jaw and took a deep breath.

"I choose," he turned his head ever so slightly so that he couldn't see Boris at all, "I choose flogging, thirty lashes."

"Very good. Confine him to his quarters until the morning when Sasha will carry out his punishment publicly."

As the guards moved to obey, Sasha wanted to run. There was no way he could carry out the sentence he had just pronounced. He wished Father had made that part clear before pressuring him for a decision. It might have changed his choice. He waited until Boris was gone and it was Father and him alone in the room.

"Why?" he asked.

"You two were too close. Your friendship would only lead to weakness. It is better this way, Sasha, trust me. What have I told you about this sort of thing before?"

"Compassion is weakness," Sasha quoted lifelessly. "You're punishing me too?"

"Good. Very good. I'm teaching you. Stamp it out, Sasha, or it will destroy you. Now, although I do not approve of any of my men being taken alive, I think your case may prove to be an exception. It is time, I think, to put these lesser peoples in their place. It is time to plan for a war. And I am going to need your help. Make yourself useful to me."

So much for rest, Sasha thought.

Chapter 39

WHEN IS FATHER GOING TO be home?" Priscilla came inside rubbing her red hands together to warm them.

Edith forced a smile. "I'm sure he'll be home any day. Why don't you come sit down here and help me?"

Priscilla sat down on the floor by the basket of scrap fabric, her worry forgotten for the moment.

"What are you doing with these?"

"Piecing a quilt for the baby when she comes."

"Do you think it'll be another girl?"

"Oh, I don't know. A girl seems like a good guess, doesn't it?"

Edith didn't really need another blanket for the baby. What she did need was something to keep her busy and her mind occupied. Hamo and the girls should have been home two weeks ago at the very latest. Not only were they not here, but no word had come about them. Alina had been over just the day before and although there had been a regular flow of couriers stopping by to switch horses on their way either to the castle in Bren or to the border forts, not one of them had heard what had happened.

"I bet Father wants it to be a boy," Elenora spoke up from where she and Adelaide were playing with their dolls.

"Will he be home before the baby comes?" Priscilla asked.

"I hope so." Edith tried to keep her voice light. It wouldn't do to worry the girls anymore. "What should we name her if it is a girl?"

"Snowy, because she'll be born when it's snowy outside," Elenora said firmly.

"That's not a real name, silly," Priscilla laughed, "We should name her Chloe."

"Chloe's a pretty name," Edith said.

"I want it to be a boy. I want a brother," Adelaide piped in.

The sound of horses approaching ended the discussion entirely as all three girls ran to the nearest window.

"Is it Father?" Adelaide stood on her toes trying to see past her older sisters.

"Uncle Al! It's Uncle Al and Taliea!" Priscilla abandoned the window and raced to the door.

Edith followed her. Sure enough, Aldrid and Taliea rode up the lane, deep in conversation and oblivious to the shouted greetings of her three daughters. Edith smiled for real this time, watching the girls' excitement and the couple's oblivion.

"Still not back I take it?" Aldrid finally disengaged himself from whatever conversation had kept him so rapt as they came up to the house.

"Not yet."

"And no word even?" Taliea's face softened with concern. No wonder Meredith liked spending so much time with the woman, Edith thought. She radiated empathy.

"None. Why don't you come inside for a while?"

Aldrid frowned as he got down and offered Taliea a hand.

"Mother hasn't either. We just stopped by there. Want me to go look for them?" he asked.

"Yes. But no, you shouldn't. I'm sure everything's fine. We would have heard something if it wasn't, don't you think?"

"Of course," Taliea answered smoothly. "How are you feeling?"

"Well for having a baby due any day, I suppose I'm alright."

"You're only just now due?" Aldrid asked in mock surprise, grinning. Leave it to him to make her laugh, Edith thought.

"So, what were you two doing out today? It's awfully cold for a nice ride."

"Oh, Al invited me to check his traps with him. And he's been telling me all the reasons why I should stay here."

Edith glanced at her younger brother-in-law and smiled.

"I'm sure he has lots of reasons for you to stay."

"Many. I haven't decided if they're good enough yet or not."

"You know, I'm standing right here," Aldrid said.

Aldrid and Taliea spent the next several hours visiting. Edith was glad of the diversion but the nagging worry that something was amiss with Hamo and Meredith and Ophelia was not easily banished. It hung like a storm cloud everything they did.

Lying awake in bed later that night, Edith listened to the rhythmic breathing of the three girls in the other room, painfully aware of the stillness in her own room. The tightening pain in her back filled her with dread. The contractions had started earlier that evening. They were getting closer now, and harder. Her hopes of making it until Hamo came home were fading with each one. Where was he? What could possibly be delaying them?

As the pain of the last contraction subsided, Edith got up. The door to the girls' room was cracked open and she made her way to Priscilla's bed.

"Scilla, wake up." The girl rolled over, squinting up at her. "Scilla, I need your help." Edith paused as another contraction came on. "I need you to go get Taliea."

"It's dark out."

"I know. The baby. It's coming. I need Taliea. I need you to get her. Can you do that for me?"

"I'm scared."

"I know." Edith wanted to scream that she was too. She was terrified. Hamo was gone. Hamo had always been there when she'd given birth. If Taliea didn't come, she would be all alone. "But I need you to be brave. I really need Taliea. Take Howler with you. He'll keep you safe. And I'll get you a lantern."

Priscilla got up. Without Meredith or Ophelia to help, she had already taken on a lot more responsibility in the last few weeks. Pulling her clothes back on, she went out into the main room where Edith was lighting a lantern for her.

"Are you going to be alright?" she asked, watching as Edith gripped the edge of the table.

"I'll be fine. Just hurry."

Priscilla disappeared into the night. Edith could only hope she came back with Taliea in time.

Chapter 40

SASHA GROANED IN RESPONSE to the light flooding across his face. He just wanted to sleep. Father had kept him up until the early morning hours, discussing their possibilities and drawing out the lay of the castle and the town around it. By the time Father allowed him to retire, Sasha's head was throbbing, and he'd forgotten all about his part in Boris' punishment, including the part he had yet to play.

Blinking in the dazzling sunlight, he remembered. That was probably the reason for the persistent knocking on his door that he just now became aware of. Pushing off his thick blankets, he got up. The clothes he had worn for the last several weeks were still crumpled in a filthy heap on the floor. A new set had been laid out for him, which meant Zena or some other slave had been in while he was sleeping. He hurried into the fresh clothes and opened the door. Axel bowed almost as soon as he got the door open.

"Master Sasha, your presence is requested in the Market Square."

Sasha smiled wryly at the use of the word 'requested'. From anyone else it might mean that there was an option to comply or not. Coming from Father, it was unquestionable. Failure to do as requested ended in punishment. His smile faded almost immediately. The Market Square. That was where all public punishments were conducted. The auction block doubled as a platform for punishments to be carried out on, allowing a larger crowd to witness it. His summons there could only mean one thing.

A crowd had already gathered. Sasha shouldered his way through, heedless of the scowls he caused behind his back. As one of the Chief's sons he had every right to a front row view. He would get more than that today, and the thought of it made him queasy. Father was on the platform, seated in a chair that slaves must have carried all the way out here just for the occasion. Father caught sight of him and beckoned him up the stairs. Sasha straightened and started to climb. Every step up his feet made, his heart made one in the opposite direction.

Boris was already there, which caught Sasha off guard. He thought he'd at least have time to steel himself for the first moment he laid eyes on his brother. He blanched at the sight of his brother's face. It was set in hard, defiant lines. At least Boris wasn't going to make a fool of himself by groveling. A twinge of guilt tugged at Sasha. Boris was facing his punishment far better than Sasha had in Dorsten.

Sasha knelt and saluted Father. Whatever he was thinking he shoved aside. He couldn't let Father think he was weak. That was the whole point of putting him through this. It was as much a test for Sasha as it was a punishment for Boris.

Father rose and addressed the gathered crowd, but Sasha didn't hear a word he said. He barely noticed when Boris was brought forward and secured. Someone clearing their throat loudly just behind him drew his attention and he saw one of the men who had brought Boris holding out the whip to him. Why did he say thirty lashes? Why didn't he make it twenty instead? Twenty wouldn't have been so bad. Sasha's hand closed around the braided leather handle, it's weight unfamiliar in his grasp. He took his place just to the side of Boris.

At a nod from Father, Sasha raised his arm and, half shutting his eyes so that the entire scene became a blur, brought it down again. He felt it connect. He heard a stifled gasp from Boris. His mind focused on counting. He was almost surprised by how quickly he reached thirty and by Boris' ability to stay quiet. When they had beaten him before each questioning, he had only made it through the first time without a sound. By the third time, he not only cried, but begged them not to hit him anymore. It helped, too. The man felt sorry for Sasha and only hit him twice that time.

Looking at Boris' back now, Sasha realized two things. He wasn't nearly as strong as the man who normally carried out floggings, nor was he practiced enough. He had only broken skin twice. His own shoulder was aching though, and the now familiar soreness in his chest came roaring back from his exertion. He held the whip out for someone to take and looked to Father for dismissal. Surely Father would be satisfied with him. He did what Father told him to. He passed his test, didn't he?

Father didn't catch his gaze for several seconds, and Sasha worried that there would be something more. At last, though, Father motioned for him to go. With a sigh of relief that Sasha had to cut short due to the pain in his chest, he fled. His part was over. Whatever else Father may choose to do to Boris was out of his hands.

Sasha was lying on his back half dozing when the noise started. It was too muffled at first to make out what it was. But it grew. Sasha tried to ignore it. But he knew what it was and where it was coming from. His brother's room was on the other side of that wall. And his brother was crying. Sasha sat up, unsure of what to make of the hot weight that settled over him. He'd felt the same when Meredith accused him in front of Hamo. It stripped away any pride he might have been enjoying, leaving him hollow and wretched inside.

Slipping quietly out into the hallway, Sasha made sure there was no one else standing around. He walked the few steps to Boris' door and found it slightly ajar. He stepped inside, unheard and unseen by his brother. Boris lay on his stomach on his bed, his face turned to the wall. Sasha could clearly make out each red, swollen welt upon his back. Here, in the confines of familiar space, they looked far worse than they had outside.

Compassion is weakness, Father's voice forced itself through the tumult of Sasha's thoughts. He had already proved to Father that he was strong enough, though.

He was the one who did this to Boris. He stepped closer to the bed, the wooden planks of the floor creaking beneath his shifting weight. Boris' head whipped around at the sound.

"What are you doing here?"

"I heard you," Sasha floundered. What was he doing here? Father would be angry if he found out.

"And now you're going to make fun of me."

"No, I wasn't." He needed to get out of here before someone realized where he was. "I just...you know, I don't even know why I'm in here. I didn't mean for this to happen."

"Get out of here." Boris turned his face back to the wall. "Go, see how long you can keep Father happy. He wasn't even upset that you were gone, you know."

"This isn't my fault, Boris," Sasha said. "You're the one who didn't even bother to look for me."

"Armin told us not to. You wouldn't have gone against him for me."

Sasha bit back a retort, knowing full well that Boris was right.

"Maybe not, but that still doesn't make this my fault."

"You should have died."

Blood rushed to Sasha's face as he stood, unable to speak. How could Boris say that? They had been friends. Wordlessly, he turned on his heel and left the room, slamming the door shut behind him, ignoring the broken whimpers of pain that followed him.

"Master Sasha," Axel came running toward him, "Chief Gundar requests your presence." Sasha was surprised at the annoyance he felt at the summons.

Chapter 41

THE NEW FALLEN SNOW MUFFLED the sound of the horses as they approached the house. Meredith lifted her head up enough to catch a glimpse of it between the barren trees. She regretted it as a wisp of cold air snuck beneath her hood and a few snowflakes found their way to her face. She tucked her chin back into its warm spot in her scarf.

A light in the front window cast a welcoming golden rectangle out on the white ground. Meredith thought it was the most beautiful sight in the whole world. Three weeks ago, she thought she'd never see it again.

"They don't know we're coming, do they?" Ophelia's voice sounded far away coming from beneath her own scarf.

"I don't think so," Father said.

"I wonder who's up then."

Meredith risked the cold again to look at the window. Sure enough, a person's shadow moved around the room.

"Probably just Mother." Meredith stifled a yawn. It would be so nice to fall asleep in her own bed again, to pull her warm, thick, soft blankets up to her chin, and listen to Ophelia and Priscilla's soft breathing.

"You girls go inside; I'll take care of the horses," Father said as they stopped in front of the barn.

Meredith was tempted to go without a word. She could get inside into the warmth and let Mother fuss over her for a few minutes before collapsing into bed. But Father was as tired as she was.

"I'll help."

Ophelia was already heading into the barn behind Father. Even the barn had a comfortingly familiar aroma. The cow and her year-old calf looked up at them with sleepy, docile eyes. Meredith thought they were beautiful just now. Stitch, with his scarred face, ran over and rubbed himself against her leg. He'd never looked better to her.

"Did you miss me, Stitch?" She bent down and scratched the spot under his chin.

"The only thing that cat misses is all the food you give him," Ophelia said.

Meredith loosened the girth to her saddle and slid it off her horse. Father was breaking the ice that had formed over their watering trough, and Ophelia was throwing some hay into the stalls. Meredith hurried to finish. Finished, they made their way to the house. Huge, fluffy flakes of snow were drifting down now, and even though it was night, the world was strangely bright.

"I think I could sleep for a week," Ophelia whispered as Father opened the door and they stepped inside. "Taliea?"

Meredith recognized the woman in the room as soon as Ophelia said her name. She looked away from her, not wanting to meet her eyes. She had almost forgotten what she had done to escape.

"What happened?" The anxiety in Father's voice reminded Meredith that Taliea shouldn't be here.

"Everything's fine," Taliea hurried to say. "Edith and the baby..."

"She had the baby?"

"Only hours ago. They're fine, Hamo. She's just resting."

Meredith's guilt grew as she watched Father hurry across the room and disappear into the bedroom. None of this would have happened if she'd just done what she was supposed to do instead of going off exploring.

"Now, I'm sure you two have a fascinating story to tell, being gone so long, but perhaps it should wait until morning." Taliea was practically herding them toward their own room and Meredith forgot everything when she saw her bed.

In the other room, Edith lay mostly asleep with the baby wrapped up in a blanket and cradled in her arm. The sound of the front door opening, and shutting was not enough to alarm her. Taliea had told her she would stay for a few days and Howler wasn't barking so it couldn't have been an intruder. The sound of her own bedroom door opening woke her a little more.

"Edith?" Hamo whispered her name.

"Hamo, you're back. You're home." Edith was wide awake.

The bed shifted as Hamo sat down on it.

"I'm so sorry, Edith. We tried to get back in time. How's the baby?"

"Light the lamp, and you can see for yourself." Edith adjusted the baby in her arms so that she could sit up as Hamo lit the lamp next to their bed. The soft yellow glow spread across the top of the bed. "What happened? You were gone for so long. We thought you were supposed to be home weeks ago."

"Something came up. What's her name?" Hamo traced a finger along the infant's sleeping cheek.

"He doesn't have a name yet."

"Why not? I thought you said you had at least five picked out."

Edith paused, smiling oddly. Then she handed him the baby.

"I did. But I didn't have any picked out for him."

"But you said..."

"Hamo, what do you want to name him?"

"What? Him? You mean..."

"You have a son. Yes," Edith laughed a little, "I've been trying to tell you. So? Any ideas?"

Edith sat up enough to lean against him, resting her head on his shoulder and looking down at the baby.

"What about Maurus? After your father," she suggested.

"Sabina already named her second son that. It'd be too confusing to have more than one in the family at the same time."

"True. That could make things difficult whenever we're together."

"Drogo."

"Drogo?" Edith cocked her head to look up at him. "After the man who saved you? I think it's a wonderful name."

"I found him, you know."

"You did? You'll have to tell me all about it. And why it took you so long to come home. We were worried sick about you all. Are Meri and Phelie alright?"

Edith didn't get an answer. When she looked at him again, Hamo was asleep. Taking baby Drogo out of his arms, she pulled the blanket over him and lay down. Tomorrow would be plenty of time, she supposed, for storytelling.

Chapter 42

SASHA RUBBED HIS TEMPLES, trying to push away the lingering effects of the headache that had plagued him all day. Father insisted that he attend the war council, again. Sasha wasn't sure what the point was. Father had extracted every ounce of useful information Sasha held about Dorsten, and he seemed uncommonly pleased with the coincidence that his son had been not only captured by their erstwhile enemies, but also held in the castle, their very seat of power.

Sasha remembered being excited by the prospect of partaking in the war council meetings. If only he had known how tedious and boring they were. Some days it almost felt like he was back in Dorsten being questioned. The leading clansmen peppered him with queries he couldn't possibly know the answers to. But it made Father - proud? Happy? Sasha wasn't sure but he did not dare deny Father.

He passed by Boris' door. Old door, that is. Father had banished Boris from the Chief's house until he could prove himself worthy of returning. Just what that meant, Sasha didn't know and had been too afraid to ask. The sight of the empty room was disheartening. Sasha could never tell anyone, but he missed Boris. He hurried on to his own room, surprised to find the door already open and Zena just standing there, her back to him.

"Don't you have work to do?" Sasha said as he came into the room behind her.

"Master Sasha, you will no longer require my services." She bent over in an awkward, stooped bow, keeping her face lowered as she spoke.

"What are you talking about?" Sasha threw off the heavy overcoat he'd worn to the meeting and tossed it to the floor. Zena would get it later and clean it if it was dirty. For as long as he could remember, Zena was the one who had seen to all his wants and needs.

"Chief Gundar has provided you with a gift, Master Sasha."

Sasha frowned. In his entire life, Father had never given him a gift. The only time he gave anyone anything was when the raids were exceptionally good, and he would select one or two young female captives out of each group to give to his best raiders. It's what Boris had been hoping for when they went on their raid. Sasha spun around.

There, kneeling on the ground, was a young girl. At least, he thought it was a girl and that she was young. Her face was hidden behind a heavy veil. An equally thick and shapeless robe covered the rest of her. She wasn't just a serving girl, she was a personal slave, a companion slave.

"Dagmar will serve you now in any way you see fit to use her," Zena spoke the words as if reciting them.

"It is an honor to serve you, Master Sasha," Dagmar said, voice quivering.

Sasha looked from the girl on the floor up to Zena whose head was still bowed.

"Chief Gundar wishes to know if she pleases you?" Zena said.

"Get up," Sasha commanded and Dagmar rose gracefully to her feet.

Sasha reached out a tentative hand and lifted the veil. Father was the one who picked Dagmar out, a thought that rankled him unreasonably. She was beautiful in the exotic, unusual way Father liked. And young, fifteen at most. Large blue eyes set against almost olive skin, light brown curly hair framing her oval face, she looked almost doll-like.

His hand went down and undid the clasp to the robe she was wearing. Her outfit underneath it had been selected with as much care as she had been, covering very little of her and making the most of her body.

"Tell Chief Gundar that she pleases me. Tell him thank you."

"Very well. Chief Gundar wished me to tell you that your absence will be excused until tomorrow morning." Of course, Father did. That was all part of the gift.

Sasha stood still, staring at Dagmar. He wasn't sure what to do. Well, that wasn't quite true. He knew what to do. He and Boris had talked about it plenty before they went on the raid. They had planned on either asking Father for one each or buying one of their own with their share of the raids. Was that only two or three months ago?

His eyes went over her well-shaped yet petite body one last time before meeting her eyes. As beautiful as they were, they were terrified. Haunted and pleading. She said it was an honor, and so it was supposed to be, being picked to serve as the companion slave to any of the Chief's sons. But it wasn't honor he read in her eyes. It was sick, hopeless fright. When he reached out to run his hand along her bare shoulder, she flinched but tried so hard not to.

Try as he might, all Sasha could think about was the one moment in his own life when that fear had been his own, pinned to the floor of his cell, helpless to defend himself, at the mercy of men who could violate him in the worst way possible.

His hand ran down her bare arm and the heat coming off her forearm drew his attention to it. He lifted it up for inspection. The brand on there was fresh and marked her clearly as his. His. Sasha shook his head and turned away. What was wrong with him? Three months ago, this would have thrilled him. Three months ago, he wouldn't have had any idea what it was like to be that afraid. The fear in her eyes made him sick.

Sasha sat down on the edge of his bed, his thoughts in turmoil. He tried to push away the recent memories of his own suffering and humiliation. Those things had been done to him by people who were inferior to him in every way. They had no right to treat him that way. Dagmar was different. She belonged to him. He had every right to do whatever he liked with her, didn't he? Father would say he did.

He looked back up at where she stood still. From where he sat, he could see she was trembling. Sasha had seen people that frightened of Father. No one had ever been afraid of him like that, though. Father always seemed strongest when people cowered before him. But seeing Dagmar, who knew nothing about him except that she belonged entirely to him and every whim and desire he had, nearly paralyzed with fear didn't make him feel very strong. It made him uncomfortable.

Heaving a sigh that ended in a groan, Sasha made up his mind.

As the days fell into a monotonous rhythm, it was hard to believe that he'd ever really left. War meetings, lessons, more meetings. Round and round it went until Sasha couldn't wait for the few moments of freedom that arose and wasted no time in taking advantage of them.

Pulling his hood closer to his head, Sasha stared at the snow-covered town spread out below him. He was nestled into a spot high up in the mountain on the pretense of hunting. In truth, he was hiding, and he wasn't even sure why. Nothing was right. Nothing fit. Not the way it had before he went raiding.

He hated being in his room, watching Dagmar flinch and cower every time he came near her or told her to do something - it was a never-ending reminder of his own recent fear. He was bored with the endless meetings planning the war. He was distracted in his training, a point his sword master had painfully made on his knuckles, repeatedly. Even sitting up here, pretending to watch for deer, felt wrong without Boris.

He ran his fingers up and down the limb of his bow, watching the smudges of chimney smoke stain the sky above town. Maybe being out here alone wasn't the best idea. His thoughts scattered in too many disturbing directions.

A small deer crossed his line of vision only a short distance away. He almost missed seeing it at all and when he did finally notice it, the thought crossed his mind to just let it go. It wasn't like they needed it for food. Drawing back the arrow he already had resting on his bowstring, he shot it down anyway. As the arrow flew free of the bow, all Sasha could see was the back of a man running away, stumbling as the arrows hit him, falling to the ground and struggling to get back up. He blinked several times, trying to drive the image away. The deer ran on a few paces before falling, its legs buckling beneath it and a trail of blood blotting the snow behind and beneath it. Sasha left his spot and, pulling out his knife, went to finish off the dying animal.

Reaching the Chief's house, Sasha sent a male slave after his kill and went to his room.

"Clean it," he said, tossing the bloody arrow he'd retrieved into Dagmar's lap and pulling off his cloak.

He watched as she scrambled to obey. Even after three weeks, she was terrified of him and he hadn't touched her, wouldn't touch her, at least not yet. Not until he could make her not afraid of him anymore. Not until her face stopped being a mirror of his own terror in the past. A knock on his door reminded him that he was supposed to attend yet another of Father's war meeting's.

Axel opened the council room's door and Sasha stepped inside. He was early. No one else was in the room except Father, and someone kneeling before him, Sasha couldn't see who. Father motioned him forward and he quickly knelt and saluted before moving to his customary place. His eyes widened as he realized that it was Boris before Father. Father turned to Sasha, ignoring his other son, but Boris kept speaking.

"Father, please, allow me to go in with the first soldiers. I'll prove myself worthy." Boris never even looked up at Sasha's entrance.

The first soldiers. They almost all died in the initial attack. Boris was begging for a chance to die. And for what? For Father? Sasha glanced at Father. Father was pleased. Of course, he was. Boris would die heroically, and Father would be rid of a troublesome son. And his death would mean absolutely nothing.

"Boris didn't know what happened at the stockade," Sasha was blurting the words out before he knew it. "Armin sent him with the report before it happened."

"Oh? Please explain, Sasha?" Father's voice was cold.

"There was a girl, Meredith Serbon, among the captives. It was her plan. She poisoned all the men and let everyone go. Boris couldn't have known, Father."

"How do you know all this? You said the men were all dead."

"One of them was barely alive when I got there, he told me as he was dying." It wasn't a good lie, and Sasha knew if Father had been looking at him and not watching Boris, he would have seen through it instantly. "She wasn't even from Dorsten, she was from their neighbor, Dival."

He had Father's full attention now. Sasha squirmed a little in his seat waiting for Father to speak again, wondering why he was even bothering to stand up for Boris when Boris wished him dead. When he did, the coldness was gone.

"Dival? Very interesting. Not that it really changes anything. We're attacking them as well. They'll both fall before the end of summer. I'll want to find this girl, though. She should be brought here alive. I think I would enjoy punishing her myself."

The words hit Sasha like a whip. What had he just done? Compassion is weakness. The mantra pounded through his head. But compassion was the only reason Sasha was still alive today. And he had just betrayed the daughter of the man who had shown it to him. He knew what Father would do to Meredith if he ever found her. Meredith had called Sasha a monster for capturing her. Father would make him look like a lamb.

"Boris, I will allow you this chance to redeem yourself," Father was speaking again.

The words took on a whole new meaning in Sasha's mind. Boris was going to die. And Father wanted him to. The honor Boris thought it would bring him would never be given to him. Sasha met Boris' eyes as he rose to leave. They were hopeless. And young. So young to be thrown away at the whim of a man who couldn't care less.

"I forgot to ask you before, Sasha. How are you enjoying my gift?"

Sasha barely recovered his thoughts in time to register the question.

"She's very beautiful." There was no way he could tell Father that he had yet to do what he was supposed to with her, that he had yet to take her to bed with him.

"You'll tire of her eventually, I'm sure, but by then you'll have bought more of your own. I should warn you, though, enjoy her as much as you want but if you get her pregnant, you kill the baby. I won't have half-bred slave born children in my house."

Sasha went hot and then cold. "Of course, Father."

He was glad when clansmen began to arrive. His own mind was in such turmoil that he paid little attention to the conversation whirling around him. Father was going to attack Dival. He was going to seek out the very people who had been kind to Sasha. And Sasha was quite certain he would kill them all. On top of that, Father had just approved Boris' death.

It wasn't until near the end of the meeting, when Sasha became aware of the fact that the plans being discussed involved the attack on Dival, that a seed of an idea came to him. He sat patiently through the remainder of the meeting, turning the idea over in his mind and letting it fester and grow. The idea didn't belong in his head, yet it took root there, defying everything he'd ever been taught.

"The troops embarking for Dival have already been assembled at port. They wait only for the winter weather to clear before setting sail," one of the clansmen said.

The last piece of Sasha's plan fell into place. When the meeting was over, he waited until everyone else had left and it was just Father and him.

"Father, I have a request."

"Go on."

"I wish to serve with the troops sailing to Dival."

"Looking for revenge for a failed raid?" Father asked with a smile that never went to his eyes.

"Yes."

"Very well. You'll have to ride to the coast to meet them. The sooner, the better. But remember, Sasha, if you find that girl, she's mine. Take your revenge out on someone else."

"Yes, Father." Sasha saluted and hurried from the room, heading straight for his own room. There was a lot he needed to do.

Chapter 43

MEREDITH KICKED AT A DRIFT of snow, sending a puff of white flakes into the air. She had been pacing back and forth here for at least ten minutes, her feet stamping down a line in the snow.

Between the trees, the forge was visible as was the smoke billowing out of its fat chimney. Father was working on something. Meredith usually loved coming with him to work. Today, however, she waited until she knew he was busy before walking over here. She still hadn't made up her mind to talk to him.

"He's not going to be mad if you just tell him and tell him how sorry you are," Ophelia had reassured her the night before, when they had lain in bed talking over the events of the last couple months.

Standing here outside the forge, Meredith wasn't so sure. Father almost never got angry, but when he did Meredith hated it. She kicked at the snow again. The guilt wasn't going to just go away, she knew, and it was making her miserable. Taking a deep breath, Meredith turned one last time toward the forge and made her way over to it. The door was open to help alleviate the heat inside and Meredith went in.

The roar of the fire always surprised Meredith no matter how many times she came in here. Trapped inside the furnace like a raging monster in its cage, it spat out its heat and filled the air with a noxious odor. Meredith pulled off her hood and scarf, no longer needing them to guard against the cold. Father was half hidden behind the furnace, his back to her, bent over his work. Meredith knew she could say everything she had come to say, and Father would be too distracted to catch most of it. It would ease her conscience without too much discomfort. But, for once, she waited. Giving the furnace as wide a berth as the forge allowed, she made her way around it and sat down on a stool next to Father. He glanced over at her briefly then went back to work. For several minutes Meredith watched him work, biding her time until he could listen to her.

"What are you making?" she asked when the silence became too much for her patience.

"Something your uncle asked me to."

"It's for Taliea, isn't it?"

"He didn't say, but I think that's a safe guess."

Meredith fell silent again. Her interest in Father's work changed as she remembered what Drogo had told her and Ophelia. She supposed most people learned a trade of their choice. All her life, she'd assumed Father found something appealing about working in the smothering heat and sootiness of the forge.

"This isn't what you wanted to do, is it?"

Father looked up at her puzzled, and she hurried to clarify.

"You didn't want to do this kind of work."

"No."

"Why do you still do it, then?"

"I'm good at it. Drogo made sure of that."

"Was it hard, coming back home and doing the same thing you had to do over there?"

"Very. I didn't do it for a long time."

Meredith had Father's full attention now. Taking a deep breath, she abruptly changed the conversation.

"There's something I have to tell you."

"Oh?"

"When Phelie and I were taken, we weren't at Drogo's."

"I know."

"We went somewhere we weren't supposed to. It was my idea." Meredith picked up a small tool from the bench in front of her and began fiddling with it in her hands. "Drogo mentioned that the place you were kept at was really close to his home. And when we left, we...I mean I thought it would be a good idea to go and see the place. If we hadn't gone there, those two would never have found us and taken us. And you wouldn't have had to spend two weeks looking for us. And we could all have been home when we were supposed to be, and we wouldn't have missed being here when baby Drogo was born. I'm sorry. I'm really sorry. I should have listened. I shouldn't have talked Phelie into coming with me."

Father was quiet. Meredith looked down at the tool in her hands and set it back down on the workbench. Whatever Father said, she was better for having finally confessed.

"Thank you, Meri. If you had never told me, I probably would never have known."

"You're not mad about it?"

"To be honest, yes. But you and Phelie are safe, Mother and Drogo are safe. While I wish you hadn't done that, it's over now, and I'm glad you told me yourself. Now I know you're not just sorry because you got caught."

Meredith leaned forward, her elbow on the bench, and rested her chin in her hand, watching the bright flames inside the furnace. If she closed her eyes, she knew she could replay the events that happened in Dorsten. Here, in the safety and comfort of her homeland, they seemed almost like a bad distant dream. She almost smiled.

"You know, it's my fault you were even able to find out what happened."

Father looked at her curiously.

"I was the reason he fell and got left behind."

"Who?" Father was too busy to put the pieces together.

"That boy. The one who helped capture Phelie and me. I touched a snake, and... well, you know how I am with snakes. It made his horse throw him down the ravine." Meredith twisted a strand of hair around her finger. "You know, they didn't even go back and look for him. It was like they didn't even care about one of their own."

"They don't."

"I was glad when he fell," Meredith said softly, her face clouded with the memory. "I've never actually hated someone like I did him and the other one that helped kidnap us. I still sort of hate him."

"And you're still sort of upset that I just let him go?" Father put whatever he was working on down and faced her.

"A little, I guess. I mean, I didn't want to see you kill him. But would it really have been wrong to let the Dorstenians punish him like they were going to? It wasn't an unfair punishment. He deserved it."

"It would have been wrong not to keep my promise, but I don't think I would have done that even if I hadn't made him that promise."

"Why not? He was a monster."

"Meri, have you ever been afraid that your mother or I would be so angry with you that we'd just give you away to someone else?"

"No." Meredith laughed a little at the idea. "That's ridiculous! You wouldn't do that."

"No, I wouldn't. But his father would and did. He sold that boy's mother and sister off because he wasn't happy with them anymore."

Meredith's eyes widened in horror.

"I know what he put you girls through was terrible, but I can't help but think that he's a monster of someone else's creating. Besides, if we were to be completely fair, he spent as long in captivity as you did. And judging by the condition he was in when your grandfather got him out, no one had gone out of their way to make his time easy."

"I guess. How could anyone do that to someone else?"

"By forgetting that they are people, too. Take away someone's humanity and it makes it easier to treat them like you would a horse or a dog."

Chapter 44

REACHING THE DOOR TO HIS room, Sasha paused, his hand resting on the latch. What was he thinking? And more importantly, why? Father hadn't raised him to think this way. He'd never known anyone to think this way. It was pure madness. It could end in his death. There was still time to reconsider, to change his mind and forget about the whole affair. Only, Sasha was quite certain that abandoning his plan would not allow him to forget, and as long as he remembered he would have that troublesome weight resting upon him.

He leaned his forehead against the cool wood of the door, mulling over the idea once more. It would work. It wasn't the fact that he feared its failure that made Sasha hesitate. It was the fact that he had thought it at all. It didn't fit with anything he knew, but somehow it was the only thought that made any sense in the last month.

At first glance, his room appeared empty, and Sasha frowned. He had a lot to get done. At least, he had a lot for Dagmar to get done. He must have been quieter than usual coming down the hallway and entering the room. A second, more thorough search of the room showed him that she was asleep on the mat that used to be Zena's. Looking down at her now, Father's words came back to him, and Sasha flushed with the memory of them. Father spoke the words as if they meant nothing to him, but Sasha had a fairly good idea of how many slave girls his father had kept throughout the years. How many of his own offspring had he killed before they even had a chance in the world? It had to have been a lot.

Shaking the thought away he nudged her awake with his foot. Her sleepiness was gone in an instant, replaced by a flash of fear. It was the same every single time he woke her up, or even just came into the room. It was as if every time she saw him, she expected him to visibly transform into a hideous monster and tear her to pieces.

Exasperated, he rattled off a list of orders. Dagmar's trembling ceased as she realized he was only in there to give her work to do.

"Yes, Master Sasha," she murmured when he was done speaking.

Sasha threw himself back onto his bed, going over his plan yet again. He would have to leave tonight. Father expected him to. It would only take two or three days to reach the coast where the ships lay waiting for calm weather. With the detour he was planning, it would take him more than a week. That wouldn't be a problem. Winter still had a tight grip on the world. He could make his side trip and still make it to the harbor with time to spare.

Sasha was mostly ignored at supper, which was fine with him. It made it easier to act as if nothing was wrong if he didn't have to talk to anyone. When it was over, the sun was already gone. Sasha made his way to the stable and ordered his horse saddled and then went back to his room.

A couple of bundles lay on his bed, full of everything he could think of that he might need on the trip. Not bothering to light the lamp by his bed, Sasha pulled on his warm outer clothes and gathered his weapons. Now that it came down to it, he was reluctant to ride out alone at night. He would take a lantern and that would help deter wild animals, but still... He looked down at Dagmar, asleep again. He could take her. No one would think anything of it since he would be spending the rest of the winter waiting. Besides, if Father found out anything, the chances of him taking it out on her were high. The idea didn't sit very well with Sasha.

"Dagmar, get up," he said, his voice was loud in the quiet room.

Dagmar sat up, startled. She looked up at Sasha in the darkness and a quivering hand traveled to the laces that kept her clothes on. Sasha pulled it away in irritation.

"Stop. That's not what I want right now." Sasha sensed her relief but ignored it. He scooped up a bundle and shoved it into her arms while carrying the other. "Come."

Dagmar fumbled with one hand to bring her veil back down over her face before following him out of the room. Sasha didn't bother to make sure she followed. He knew she would.

Reaching the stable, Sasha looked around for another horse he could take. His eyes fell on the little black mare that had carried him back home after Stephan and Hamo had released him. He had brought her home, so she was fair game for him to take again. Pointing her out to the stable slave, he fastened his gear to the waiting pack animal. The man led the freshly saddled horse up and Sasha motioned for Dagmar to mount up as well.

Through the gate and out into the open mountains, Sasha turned once to look back at Illsen. The last time he had ridden away from his home had been a disaster. Sasha hoped that was all behind him.

By the first light of morning, Illsen was far behind Sasha and the knot of tension in his stomach began to loosen. No one had questioned him at the gate, no one had followed him. They didn't suspect anything. When he arrived several days late at the harbor, he would just tell everyone he ran into bad weather. He didn't have to be a good liar to make that convincing. Winter in the mountains was unpredictable. Everyone knew that.

Twisting around in his saddle, he remembered Dagmar. The girl still had her veil pulled over her face. Of course, she did, Sasha thought, remembering that it was required anytime a companion slave left her master's quarters. She wasn't allowed to be seen by any other man besides him, just like Father's wives and slave girls. It seemed a little ridiculous out here where there was no one else to see them. Sasha shrugged to himself.

He missed Boris. When he had made this ride the first and only other time, Boris had been there, and together they had whiled away the endless, boring hours of riding.

Sasha unslung his bow and started studying his surroundings. He would have to hunt along the way if he was going to have enough to eat. If he had packed more than a few days' worth of food, it would have aroused suspicion.

By late afternoon, the carcass of a rabbit hung from his saddle, and Sasha decided he was too tired to keep going. He'd been riding all night and through the day. A cluster of pine trees offered promising shelter for the night, and he turned his horse towards it. Sasha dismounted stiffly after so many hours of riding and secured his horse.

"Get down and find something we can burn." Sasha was already digging around in one of the packs to find his flint.

"I'm sorry, Master Sasha," Dagmar whispered. Sasha turned around to see her crumpled on the ground. "I can't walk."

Sasha stared down at her for a minute before he really comprehended her words. Of course, he thought, slapping his forehead with the palm of his hand. She wasn't used to riding. Why hadn't he thought of that?

Worse, now that he was looking at her, he realized he hadn't thought about the cold either. He was bundled up in layers of winter clothing, but she was wearing only her outer gown and the scant outfit she'd been given to him in. She was shaking violently, and although Sasha was sure some of it had to do with her fear of him being angry with her, it was also a result of the cold. Stepping close to her, he lifted her veil up. Dagmar flinched. Her skin was tinted blue with cold. Her eyes were full of tears that she was trying vainly to blink back. She thought he was going to punish her for not being able to walk. And the worst of it was, Sasha considered it. It's what Father would do.

Sasha raised his hand to hit her when his own memory stopped him. The first day of his trip with Stephan and Hamo he had collapsed with exhaustion, too spent to even hold himself on his own horse. Instead of punishing him, they let him rest. The memory restrained him. He lowered his hand.

"I'll get the fire started." He went back to his horse and retrieved the rabbit's carcass and tossed it on the ground in front of her. "Get this ready to cook."

Dagmar stared at the carcass for just a second before reaching out and pulling it to her lap. She looked back up at Sasha.

"How?"

In that single word Sasha could hear her begging him not to be angry. Now that she had asked, he realized he had no real idea how it was done, either. All the many times he had been hunting, all the animals he had killed, and he had never, not once, been the one to gut and clean the kills. A slave always did it for him. But Dagmar wasn't the type of slave that would have been taught how to do it.

"I don't know." He shrugged, tossing her his hunting knife, "Figure it out."

Surrounded by trees, it wasn't hard for Sasha to collect enough wood for a fire. Getting a fire started was another matter entirely. After nearly thirty minutes, the most Sasha could create was a smoking pile of sticks without a single flame. Sasha stood and gave the entire pile a savage kick, sending the sticks flying wildly about. How had Stephan and Hamo made this look so easy? It had never taken them so long to get a fire going.

The temperature continued to drop as the sun sank lower and desperation drove Sasha to recollect all his firewood and try again. Glancing at Dagmar, he realized she was making better progress at her task then he was at his. At this rate, they would be eating raw rabbit, he thought with a grimace of disgust. There were drawbacks, he realized for the first time in his life, to having someone do everything for you.

The first stars were starting to show themselves in the darkened eastern sky before his efforts were finally rewarded by a tiny flame. It was a feeble excuse of a fire, and Sasha watched anxiously, coaxing the tongue of fire to grow. At least they wouldn't be eating raw meat.

"Cook it," he told Dagmar when he was confident it would burn steadily for at least a few minutes. He went in search of more wood.

After they had eaten, Sasha built the fire up some more and unrolled the blankets he'd brought. He also pulled out a change of his warm clothes and tossed them to where Dagmar huddled as close to the fire as she could trying to get warm.

"Put those on and watch the fire. When the moon reaches there," he pointed to a spot overhead, "wake me up."

Rolling himself up in the warm blankets as near to the fire as he dared get, Sasha went to sleep.

The cold crept up on him gradually, stealing over him while he slept. At first, it only made him restless, but at last it grew uncomfortable enough that he awoke. Sasha sat up. It was completely dark. There was something not right about that. Sasha pushed away the grogginess of sleep trying to think of what was amiss.

The fire.

He'd built a fire and it should still be burning. Looking up, he saw the moon was well past its zenith in the sky. He was wide awake, his eyes searching the darkness around him. Where was Dagmar? She should have woken him up. Raising himself up on one knee, he caught sight of her on the other side of the smoldering remains of his fire. She was asleep. Sasha stared at her for a long minute, annoyance giving way to anger. No fire meant he could freeze to death. No fire meant there was nothing to keep the wild animals at bay. No fire meant he would probably die.

"You worthless idiot!" He grabbed her by the shoulders, shaking her awake roughly, his voice carrying loudly through the cold night air. "You could have killed me going to sleep like that. I told you to keep it going. Do you know how long it took me to get it going in the first place?"

She was limp in his grasp, her big eyes staring, uncomprehending, at him. That blank, frozen stare only served to infuriate him. Drawing back his hand, he hit her once, twice. His own strength in the blow surprised him. She flew backwards out of his now loose grasp and sank to the ground, a mewling sound coming from her.

Sasha ignored her and turned back to the pitiful remains of the fire it had taken him so long to build in the first place. At this point, it probably wasn't even worth trying to make a new one, he decided. The sun would rise in only two or three hours anyway. They might as well get started now.

It took him only a few minutes to saddle the horses. That, at least, was something he knew how to do. Dagmar had gone quiet, and Sasha began to wonder if she fell back asleep. He looked back at where he had left her and saw she was sitting up.

"Get up. We're leaving."

Dagmar rose to her feet unsteadily and limped toward the horses, clearly suffering still from the many hours of riding she'd already done. Sasha didn't care. He waited for her to mount clumsily and started off. As difficult as this trip was proving to be, Sasha was on the verge of throwing away his plan entirely and heading straight for the coast.

The hours slipped away in uncomfortable silence, but Sasha couldn't figure out why it felt so uncomfortable. After all, they had ridden in silence the day before as well and it hadn't irked him the way it did now. Sasha tried to ignore the occasional soft moan from Dagmar. It was her own fault. She should have done what she was told. He wouldn't have hurt her if she had.

As the world softened into a predawn gray, Sasha noticed for the first time that the place was familiar. Where he was riding now was exactly the same place where Hamo was reunited with his daughters. It was in that grove of trees over there that Sasha listened with burning face to Meredith's accusations. It was there that he was so sure his life was over.

And yet... they'd let him go.

They'd given him food. Even knowing that he was the architect of their entire ordeal, they hadn't unleashed on him the anger they had most assuredly felt towards him. He couldn't fathom how they managed such a thing.

Sasha turned enough to see Dagmar. The veil covered her face once more. He pulled his own horse up and waited for hers to come abreast of it. He brought his hand up to lift the veil, and Dagmar shrank back, a frightened whimper escaping her. Beneath the veil, Sasha saw the damage he had done. Dagmar's lip was cut and swollen; dried blood smeared on it. A faint discoloration across her cheek just beneath her right eye promised a deep bruise would take its place within a day or two. The skin beneath the eye was puffy, prohibiting that eye from opening all the way.

Sasha stared at her, holding her chin in his hand so that she could not turn away from his gaze. He had done this. Not Father. Not Armin. They had done things like this, but this was his own handiwork. Meredith had called him a monster. Looking at Dagmar's face, watching the renewed terror in her eyes, he realized exactly what Meredith had meant. Compassion was weakness, Father said. But it hadn't taken any strength to hurt Dagmar. In fact, if Sasha was honest with himself, it was one of the weakest things he'd ever done.

With that realization, came the one that he could not abandon his plan. That would be weakness as well. If he couldn't survive a few days on his own, what kind of Chief's son was he anyway?

"I didn't mean to hit you that hard," Sasha said at last. It wasn't an apology either in words or tone. You didn't apologize to a slave. But Sasha couldn't look at her and say nothing. Not while he was standing in the very spot where his own life had been given back to him. Dagmar's eyes shifted from fear to confusion and Sasha turned to move on.

When, after three more days, they passed the first burnt rubble of a village Sasha realized just how slow he had made Stephan and Hamo's progress. The layer of snow covering most of the remains was a relief. Sasha really did not want to witness the entire thing again. The cold helped mask the smell of any decaying bodies, and even the horses passed by without skittishness.

The last of the three burnt and decimated villages marked the extent of Sasha's knowledge of the land. He'd come this way twice. Neither time was he aware of anything around him. Fortunately, the pass through the mountains here was obvious. There were no other easy ways to go other than to follow it as it snaked around between the towering giants of rock.

It was only midday when they passed the final settlement, and if Sasha's memory served him right, they were less than half a day's ride from his destination. They could reach it by nightfall and then by morning they could begin the return trip going back up to the coast. It would all work out just like Sasha had planned it.

Chapter 45

SASHA ALMOST MISSED SEEING IT. His eyes were tired from his constant scanning of the wooded mountain slopes. In the gathering gloom of dusk, he despaired of finding it at all and was about to just give up for the night when he saw the faint glow of light deep in the shadowy woods.

Turning his horse's head towards it, a new trepidation filled him. Now that he found what he was looking for, what if it didn't turn out the way he wanted it to? After all, there was no reason for the man on the other side of that door to trust him. He really didn't even have a good reason to let Sasha into his home.

Motioning for Dagmar to get down as well, he left the horses a short distance from the cabin. His closed hand hovered in the air before the door for a moment while he worked up the nerve to knock. The door swung open before he had the chance. Framed in the rectangle of light now flooding outside was an old man.

"Who are you?" The man's voice was soft, and he spoke unhurriedly. "What do you want?"

Sasha's heart leaped to his throat. The door opening so suddenly threw him completely off stride and the speech he had carefully prepared in his head for the last week vanished. He opened his mouth, then shut it.

"I'm Sasha." When he did at last manage to get the words out, his voice squeaked over them.

"Who?"

"Sasha. I'm the one who was brought here a few weeks ago by Stephan," the words tumbled out now, "I need to talk to you. It's very important."

The old man squinted at him, and then peered past him into the darkness taking in Dagmar's veiled face as well. After what seemed like an eternity to Sasha, he stepped aside and motioned for them to enter. Sasha slowly let out the breath he was holding. He had made it this far.

"What do you need to talk about?" The old man certainly didn't waste any time getting straight to the point.

"First, who are you? You spoke before as if you knew who my father was."

"My name's Drogo. That won't mean anything to you. I was gone long before your father came to power."

"But you knew him?"

"He was my nephew. Now what is it you came to say?"

"I," Sasha stammered over Drogo's statement, nearly forgetting why he had come all this way, "I... you're related to me?"

"Yes." Drogo didn't seem to be in any hurry to elaborate.

"Oh, well, I had no idea," Sasha paused, trying to piece together the plan he had laid out in his mind, "You're a friend of Hamo's, aren't you? That's why they were here, wasn't it?"

"Why are you asking?"

Drogo was not an easy man to talk to, Sasha decided. He forged ahead anyway.

"His daughter, Meredith. My father knows that she is the one who helped everyone escape. He knows she killed all the raiders. He's coming after her. There's going to be a war, and I have to go, but I thought since you were a friend of theirs that you could reach them somehow. That you could warn them."

"Come. Sit down." Drogo motioned him toward the table and chairs. "Tell your girl she can sit too."

Sasha gestured for Dagmar to sit down. With the veil over her face, Drogo couldn't see the mess he had made of her, and Sasha was suddenly very relieved about that. He didn't want anyone seeing it.

Drogo turned away to tend something on the stove. Sasha wasn't sure if he should say anything else. What else was there for him to say? If Drogo couldn't warn Hamo that they were in danger, there was nothing more Sasha could do. He had to get back before someone noticed he was missing.

Drogo returned to the table, two steaming cups in his hands. These he set in front of both Sasha and Dagmar. Sasha felt Dagmar's questioning eyes looking at him through her veil. She was supposed to be serving, not being served. Drogo must have been away from Aruuk for a long time if he had forgotten the role of a slave.

Sasha brought his own cup to his lips, savoring the warmth of the tea. It had been days since he'd had anything so comforting to drink. He nodded to Dagmar, indicating that she could drink hers as well.

"So," Drogo said as he settled into the chair by the fire, "you want me to warn Hamo for what? What is he supposed to do?"

"I don't know. I hadn't thought of that."

"Why are you concerned about what happens to Meredith?"

"I'm not. I," Sasha swallowed, "He let me go. He let me live. After he found out that I was the one who...well, you know." The words were a lot harder to get out than Sasha would have thought. They stuck in his throat. "Anyway, even when he knew that I was the one, he still let me go."

"And you thought you owed him?"

"I don't know. I guess? I mean, it's kind of my fault that Father found out about Meredith too."

"Oh?"

"I told him." That was all Sasha wanted to say on the subject.

"So, you're the reason Meredith's in danger. You want someone to warn them. And while that happens, you're going to go back and join the army on its way to obliterate his country?"

"I have to. It's where I belong."

"You are a fool, Sasha." Drogo's voice carried no animosity, no hate. He just said it, like it was the most obvious thing in the world. And that hurt. Sasha recoiled internally.

"What do you mean? I just thought he should know."

"You are a fool because you think you can do both." Drogo leaned forward, the earnestness on his face quelling the rising anger in Sasha. Whatever this man said, he meant it, and he didn't mean it cruelly. "How long do you think you can play both sides?"

"I'm not."

"You are. And you know it. So, you warn one family of the danger that is coming. What about all the others that you will help destroy? Do they not deserve a warning? A chance? What do you think will happen to them? You saw the villages after the raids, didn't you? The same thing will happen over and over again in whatever country your people take over. And you are going to be a part of that destruction."

"It won't," Sasha protested weakly, "It won't be like that."

"Do you really believe that?"

Sasha stared down at the now empty cup in his hand, surprised to find it trembling slightly. Why was Drogo saying all this? Didn't he realize what Sasha was risking just coming this far? He had to. If he'd lived in Aruuk at all, he had to understand.

"What happened to her?" Drogo's voice made him look up again and he followed Drogo's eyes to Dagmar. She had fallen asleep, her head pillowed in her arms on the table, her veil sliding off enough to reveal the now hideously discolored bruise around and under her eye. Sasha couldn't even bring himself to reposition the veil correctly.

"I did."

Sasha shoved his chair away from the table and fled, slamming the front door behind him as he exited the cabin. He sank down on the front step, his face buried in his hands and tried desperately to quiet the myriad of voices screaming inside his head. It was too much. None of it made sense. Drogo was just making things worse.

"Why?" he moaned the single word aloud.

"It's hard, isn't it?" Sasha jerked his head up, looking behind him where Drogo had quietly followed him out.

"I don't know what you're talking about." Sasha turned away again, staring into the darkness. "I just want this to end. I want to stop feeling guilty for everything."

"Sasha." Drogo sat slowly down next to him. "If you go back and help your father destroy innocent people, you are never going to stop feeling guilty. You can't have both, not anymore. Not now that you know the truth."

"Then I don't know what to do."

"I think you do. You just don't want to do it, because once you do, you can never go back. Do you even want to go back?"

"Yes...no. I don't know. I should. It's home. He's my father. Right?"

"A father who would kill you in less than a second if he knew what you were doing right now. A home that is built on suffering and pain. No, I don't think you should want to go back there."

"I can't just leave it."

Drogo shrugged. "I cannot warn Hamo. I'm too old to try to cross the Void."

"The what?" In all of Sasha's study of geography he had never heard of such a place.

"You would know it as the great plains. The flatlands between here and Dival. It would take days to cross, and I cannot do it. If you want him warned, you will have to do it yourself. Otherwise, you can leave in the morning and help your father butcher the people over there." Drogo rose and disappeared inside the cabin.

There it was. In those last few sentences, Drogo gave Sasha exactly two options. There had only ever been just those two choices, though, Sasha realized. With unusual clarity, Sasha knew that whichever he chose, it would dictate the rest of his life. He could betray everything. Leave home and everything he knew behind. They may or may not welcome him in Dival. After what he'd done, his chances of a welcome seemed slim. Even if they believed his warning, there was no way they could forgive his previous actions. Or he could turn back. Go with Father's army. Do what he had been raised to do. Slaughter and enslave, like all the other men in Aruuk. He would grow up to be just like Father – strong, ruthless, cruel. It was what he'd always wanted, wasn't it? It was the thing he'd spent so many waking moments working towards. He couldn't just abandon that, could he?

Chapter 46

I T'S BEAUTIFUL. WHEN ARE you planning the ceremony?" Ophelia fingered the pendant hanging from a thin gold colored chain from Taliea's neck.

"Summer. That gives me time to make a dress," Taliea answered.

"I can't believe it took him this long to ask you! I mean, he's only liked you for what? Five years?" Ophelia laughed.

Meredith watched from where she sat. Part of her wanted to run up and throw her arms around Taliea and share her happiness. The other part of her was the one that had been winning out most of the winter.

She had done the one thing Taliea said never to do. She had used her knowledge of medicines to hurt and possibly kill people. It haunted her so much that from time to time she dreamed of it. The picture of all those men, sprawled in a trance like sleep, or death, would weave its way into her sleep. Father had nightmares because of what other people had done to him. Meredith got them now because of what she had done to other people.

"Why are you being so quiet, Meri?" Mother glanced back at her.

"No reason." Meredith got up and quickly examined Taliea's necklace. "It's very nice. I'm going to go for a walk, Mother."

Meredith ignored the stares of the others as she wrapped her cloak about herself and went outside. There was no way she could be around Taliea, knowing what she had done. Several times, she had come close to telling Taliea. But each time, she thought of how hurt Taliea would be, of how angry she would become knowing that Meredith had thrown aside her instructions.

The cold air had a clearing effect on her thoughts, as usual. Meredith had taken to these long, lonely winter walks ever since they had returned from Dorsten. The exertion helped take her mind off of the turmoil in her mind. Today, a fresh layer of snow clung to the branches of the bare trees, enchanting the woods with its sparkling purity.

Meredith made her way to the creek. Despite winter's hold on the land, a thin trickle of water still flowed freely through the middle of it, although the edges were ragged with ice. Meredith crouched down, watching the water dance over the rocks, listening to the gentle gurgle of the stream.

"You know, I'm beginning to think you're avoiding me." Taliea's voice right behind her caused Meredith to fall back. Sitting on the snowy ground she looked up to find Taliea next to her.

"I haven't." Meredith averted her eyes.

"Phelie already told me."

"She did?"

"She did."

"She wasn't supposed to. I told her not to."

"I've missed having you over. I asked her why you weren't coming to visit anymore, and she told me."

"I'm sorry, Taliea. I didn't mean to hurt anyone. I just couldn't think of any other way. And, if we'd stayed there..." Meredith's voice faded. She tried not to imagine what would have happened to her and Ophelia if they had not gotten away.

"If you'd stayed there, terrible things would have been done to you. I know. Walk with me, it'll be warmer than sitting in the snow."

Meredith stood up, brushing away the snow that clung to her, and fell in step with Taliea.

"Are you angry with me?"

"Why would I be?"

"I did what you said not to do. I took something that was supposed to help people and I used it against them. I used it to hurt them."

"Or you could say that you took something that was supposed to help people, and you did help those people. It wasn't even just you and your sister who got away, it was all the others too. I think if you could ask them, they would say that you used it well."

"But I might have killed those men."

"You might have. And death is an awful burden to bear, even if it is justifiable."

"You say that like you know something about it?" Meredith stopped walking and turned to look at Taliea.

"I do." Taliea stopped, too. Rather than face Meredith though, she stood with her back to her, staring into the distance. "But that is not something I want to talk about. Not today."

Meredith hung her head. Here she was dragging Taliea through all this on the very day of Taliea's engagement. On the very day that she should be happy and celebrating.

"I'm sorry. I shouldn't have said anything at all. I'm sorry for ruining such a special day for you."

"It's hardly ruined." Taliea smiled at her. "I will tell you, sometime, and perhaps it will help you. You should know, though, that your guilt would be far worse if you'd done nothing. For now, though, I miss your company. I was hoping that you and your sisters would help me with the wedding."

Meredith met her eyes, and seeing the sincerity in them, smiled in return. Taliea wasn't just saying all this to make her feel better, she really meant it.

"I'd love to help. And I'm really happy for you and Uncle Al. I'm sorry I didn't say so before."

"Understandable. It's been an unusual few months for you."

Chapter 47

THE WIND WAS MORE THAN just a part of the weather here. It was a living being, full of fury and rage that it unleashed continually upon the unresisting world, driving everything before it. It cut through Sasha's clothing as if it weren't there. It bit into his skin, chapping it. Sasha had never known a wind that could be so fierce. It was never like this in the mountains, and Sasha had always thought the mountains got the worst of winter. The only good thing about the ferocity of the wind was that it prevented the snow from piling up too deeply. Only a thin, windswept layer covered most of the road and the long, brown grass that covered the great plains.

Drogo had been able to bring them to the entrance of the great plains, or the Void as he called it. From there, he had told Sasha, if they kept the wind to their backs, they would know they were heading the right way.

That was four days ago.

In those four days, Sasha had repeatedly questioned his own sanity. If he had thought surviving a few days on his own in the mountains was difficult, surviving out here was well-nigh impossible. He turned his head barely enough to see Dagmar and regretted it immediately as his clothing shifted and a blast of cold worked its way against his previously protected skin.

It was getting late in the day, and Sasha knew he should be looking for some sort of shelter to spend the night behind. Almost invisible unless you knew what you were looking for, mounds rose and fell all over the plains. Some of them were big enough to block the constant wind and provide a semblance of protection against the weather.

Finding one that seemed sufficient, Sasha turned his horse off the road and Dagmar followed. Sasha turned his head to the side to keep the wind from stealing his breath away. He could tell they reached the shelter of the large mound when he felt the sudden absence of the wind's pressure on his body and his horse. Sliding down, he quickly undid his horse's saddle, letting it fall to the ground.

"Get some food," he said to Dagmar.

He scraped the snow away from a large enough patch to sit down and pulled up handfuls of the dried, brown grass that grew everywhere. Once he had collected a bit, Sasha set about trying to get a fire started. It would burn out quickly, but at least for a few minutes it would be something. By the time he got a weak flame going, Dagmar still had not come over with any food. Sasha looked over at the pack horse to find her still fumbling with the ties.

Sasha pulled his gloves off and cupped his hands over the fire. The heat was almost excruciating. When it became less so, he replaced his gloves and pulled up a few more handfuls of grass to feed the fire.

When Dagmar finally came over with the dwindling bundle of their food and handed it to Sasha, he noticed for the first time her swollen, purplish fingers. Just one more thing he hadn't given any thought to, Sasha sighed. If Sasha was cold, Dagmar was freezing. Even wearing his clothes that he had given her the first night, she was ill dressed for this weather.

The warmth of his gloves condemned him.

He looked down at them, snugly encasing his hands and keeping the cold at bay, then back up at Dagmar who was now sitting as close to the fire as she could get, her arms wrapped tightly around her drawn up legs. Even so, she was shivering and her eyes, no longer covered by the veil that the wind repeatedly tore away, were glassy with the cold. Sasha sighed again. He pulled off one glove, and then the other. He held them for a moment. He shouldn't care, he knew. It shouldn't bother him to see her like that. But it did, and he couldn't deny it. He threw the gloves to her.

"Put those on for a while. My hands aren't really cold right now."

She stared at them for several seconds before clumsily trying to pull them on. He got up and retrieved the blankets from the pack horse. By the time he returned the fire was already dying. He hurried to get more grass onto it. The longer he could keep it going, the better it would be.

Sasha pulled out some dried, and now frozen, meat from the bundle of food. He held it over the flames, almost scorching his fingers. When it was thawed out enough to chew, he wrapped himself up in the blankets and ate.

Only after he had eaten would Dagmar make any move to get herself food. Sasha started to doze off. Out here, he didn't bother to tell Dagmar to keep the fire going. It wasn't possible.

He had only been asleep for a short time when a particularly loud howl of wind woke him back up. Exposing just enough of his head to look around, he scanned the land around them for signs of a threat. It was more of a habit than anything else. Nothing seemed to live out here. Still, you couldn't be too careful. All he saw was the forms of all three horses, hobbled and lying down, and Dagmar a few feet from him, curled up asleep.

Sasha watched her for a moment. The idea of telling her why he was dragging her all this way had crossed his mind a few times before in the last few days but always he had decided against it. It wasn't her place to know. If she thought him crazy, she certainly hadn't shown it. If anything, she had just grown more afraid of him. Sasha suspected that it had something to do with his hitting her.

A sudden stab of fear went through him as he watched her now. She wasn't moving. Her incessant shaking was stilled. Leaning forward, Sasha touched her face, and recoiled. Her skin was icy.

"Dagmar," he said as he held his hand in front of her mouth and nose. "Dagmar, wake up." His voice grew more insistent, and he shook her shoulder. "Wake up. You have to wake up."

Sasha's fear grew into desperation as he shook her, gently at first and then harder. He failed to register the soft moan that came from her.

Many times in his life, Sasha had been afraid for himself, but he had never been afraid for someone else. The panic rising in his chest wasn't for him, though. Not entirely, at least. That Dagmar would die out here and leave him utterly alone was a part of his fear. But more than that, Sasha realized he didn't want her to die because she didn't deserve that. She had done everything he'd told her to do. She didn't even know why they were out here. And if she died it was completely his fault. The thought weighed down on him crushingly.

"Come on, Dagmar. Wake up. Please." Sasha pulled her forcibly up into a sitting position, horrified at the limpness in her body. Her head drooped forward. "I didn't mean for you to die. I didn't mean any of this. I'm sorry." The wetness on his face surprised him. He was crying? Over a slave? "I'm sorry I drug you out here through all of this and hit you. Just, please, wake up. Don't leave me alone."

He stopped shaking her now and pulled her closer to where his blankets lay in a heap. Another soft moan came from her, and this time he fully understood it. She wasn't dead. Not yet at least.

Sasha drew on every memory he could think of for what to do with someone freezing to death. He built another fire, making it as big as he could with the grass at his disposal. Then he pulled her close to him and wrapped the blankets around them both. He wasn't that warm himself, but the heat from his body trapped inside the thick blankets would help some.

Holding her frigid body pressed against his own, he was relieved to feel the slight rise and fall of her chest with each breath. But it was slow, much slower than Sasha thought it should be.

Sasha lost track of time. He became gradually aware of Dagmar's deepened breathing. From time to time, he crawled out of the blankets enough to add to the fire, but every time he did so he allowed cold air into the cocoon of warmth. Eventually, the fire simply died out. Sasha's eyes grew heavy. He tried to stay awake, afraid of what he would wake up to find if he didn't. His eyes refused to stay open.

Dagmar stirred against him, and Sasha was wide awake. He brought a hand up to her face and the weight of despair that hung over him lifted a little. There was a faint warmth emanating from her skin.

"Dagmar, wake up." He shook her again, careful to keep the blankets wrapped up tightly around the two of them. "Come on, wake up."

This time, she responded. He felt her stiffen and begin to shiver once more. She raised her head from his shoulder with a heavy sigh. Even in the darkness, Sasha could sense her looking at him, confused. He was tempted to just let her go back to sleep now, and himself as well, but that was too risky. The best thing to do would be to get up and move.

Groaning against the cold he knew was awaiting them beyond the blankets, Sasha stood up. More time must have passed than he'd thought. There was a touch of pinkish gray along the broad eastern horizon.

"We have to get going," he said, pulling Dagmar up with him.

She collapsed the instant he let go of her. It had been on the tip of his tongue to order her to get their food, but looking down at her now, he knew that task was beyond her. Leaving her huddled in the warmth of the blankets, he readied the horses and built yet another small, short-lived fire to warm their food over. Once again, she stared at him in confusion when he handed her some food. Sasha ignored her bewilderment.

"We're going to walk for a bit," he announced when they had both eaten.

"Yes, Master Sasha." Dagmar's voice was feeble, and she looked doubtful of her own ability to walk any distance.

Sasha didn't really want to walk. It would make their progress much slower than it had already been. But walking assured that they were moving enough to keep their blood flowing and after the scare of that night, Sasha was willing to do whatever it took to not go through that again. Besides, they had to be getting close, if Drogo's words could be trusted. In fact, Sasha thought as he tried to count up the number of days they had been out here, they might even reach it today.

A dark brown line broke the white and gray horizon in the distance early the next morning.

Sasha really didn't have any idea what to expect when he finally reached Dival. The line of earthworks, broken at regular intervals by squat, sturdy forts was not it. Having ridden straight through the border of his own country and into Dorsten, Sasha never expected to encounter any sort of obstruction at the border of Dival. He had not taken into account the fact that Dival, unlike Dorsten or Aruuk, was confronted by the easily traversed plains rather than rugged mountains.

The earthen walls and forts protected from any army that chose to take advantage of such an easy advance. As his understanding of them increased, Sasha wondered if Father how well protected this side of Dival was. Not that it mattered. Father's plan didn't hinge on taking this wall.

They were riding now, having just walked some distance. Since Dagmar's brush with death, Sasha had been far more careful. They walked and rode by turns, and he had decided that for as long as they were out in this bitter cold, Dagmar would sleep next to him, wrapped up in the same blankets. She was more than a little frightened by it the first night he told her to, but since sleeping was all they did, she had relaxed. If you could call the state Dagmar lived in relaxed, Sasha thought wryly. She still flinched when he got close to her. Sasha didn't think it was very fair of her, considering he'd saved her life.

As they got nearer, Sasha could see that the forts were manned. He could make out the movements of men along the upper walls of the forts. At the sight of them, Dagmar pulled her veil down, and held it in place against the wind.

The road they were on, if it could be called a road, led straight to the entrance of the largest fort. A knot of anxiety grew in Sasha's stomach as they approached. At no time during his trip did he consider being confronted like this.

The heavy gates in front of him were a clear indication that the soldiers didn't let just anyone through. Already he could feel the eyes of the men on him, watching his approach. What if they turned him away after everything he had gone through to get here? It had taken everything in him to even decide to come all this way.

It was too late to turn back. Sasha straightened his shoulders and nudged his horse forward with a confidence he didn't quite feel. To his surprise, the gate swung open at his approach and the men guarding it stepped aside to let him pass.

"What's your business here, boy?" A man in his thirties stepped up and took hold of Sasha's horse.

"I came to see a friend." It was a stretch. An enormous stretch, Sasha knew, but he didn't have time to come up with something better.

"Funny accent you've got there. Where are you from?"

"The mountains." Sasha was reluctant to admit just exactly where he was from in the mountains. These people may or may not have heard of Aruuk.

"Hmph. Friend have a name?"

"Yes."

"Well?"

"It's Hamo Serbon."

The man studied Sasha, considering his words. Sasha couldn't decide if the name was familiar to him or not.

"That's one of the ones that helped put an end to the war, isn't it?" Sasha looked over at the new speaker, a younger man holding a saddled horse in hand.

"Do you know where he is?" Sasha asked the second man.

"No. But I'm just getting ready to head to someone who does. I'll take 'em with me, sergeant. See they don't get into trouble." The man nodded to the one holding Sasha's horse.

The sergeant hesitated still, looking at Sasha intently. Suspicion lined his weathered face, and Sasha found it difficult not to squirm in his saddle. Finally, the man nodded slightly and stepped away, releasing his grip on the reins.

"I'm leaving now, if you're ready to come." The younger man swung onto his own mount and started off, not waiting for a response.

Sasha stared after him for a second before realizing that the man meant for him to follow. Belatedly kicking his horse into action, he caught up as the man reached the far gate, the one that opened into Dival.

"So, how far is it exactly?" He guided his horse up next to their guide's.

"About eight hours. We'll stop every four hours so I can switch horses. Yours will be the second stop. Name's Leon, by the way."

"Sasha. And someone who knows where I can find Hamo will be there?"

"Yes. What's with the girl?" Leon looked over his shoulder at Dagmar, still wearing her veil.

"What do you mean?" Sasha blurted the words out before he could stop himself.

Leon glanced at him oddly. "Why's she got her face covered up like that? Scars or something?"

"Oh that. Yes. She," Sasha paused, frowning. He hadn't even considered how Dagmar's appearance might be taken by these people. "She's, um, sick. And she doesn't want anyone to see the rash. It looks terrible. She's really upset about it."

Leon raised his eyebrows. He glanced back at Dagmar again, and then at Sasha.

"Can she talk?"

"No. She lost her voice, being sick."

Leon nodded and shrugged, but Sasha knew he didn't believe him. At least he didn't care enough to question Sasha further.

The hours passed quickly with Leon doing most of the talking and Sasha only answering when necessary.

In those few hours, Sasha grew more and more pensive. It had been easy to forget, battling the wind and cold as he had been, why he was here and what the implications were for him. His conversation with Drogo now seemed like a distant memory, clouded over by the difficulties of the last few days. Drogo made it seem so simple and clear.

Now, drawing nearer by the minute, Sasha tried to quell the nervous tremor inside. There was every chance in the world that they would slam the door in his face when he showed up. And he couldn't really blame them if they did.

At last, Leon left the main road and turned down a smaller, less traveled path.

"This'll be your stop. He should be able to take you straight to your friend."

Sasha nodded, not trusting himself to speak at the moment. His mouth was unnaturally dry. His hands fiddled with the leather reins, twisting them up mindlessly. His horse, sensing his uneasiness, grew skittish under him.

They rode past the house and straight to the stable beyond it. A spare horse was tied to a hitching post, waiting for Leon. A man with his back to them put the finishing touches on the animal's tack.

"Evening, Stephan," Leon called out.

Sasha's heart dropped like a stone to his feet. Stephan? Why did it have to be Stephan? Maybe it was a different person by that name, Sasha hoped. No, it wasn't. The man turned around, raising a hand to acknowledge Leon's greeting, and Sasha saw immediately that it was the same Stephan who had held a knife to him, and laughed at him, and tricked him into revealing information. Sasha felt the blood rising to his cheeks in a deep flush as Stephan's greeting died on his lips.

"What in...," he left the words hanging.

"He said he's here to see Hamo. I told him you could help him." Leon was too busy switching saddle bags to notice the stony expression on Stephan's face as he took in Sasha. "You don't mind, do you?"

Stephan never took his eyes off Sasha. "No, I don't mind. I'll take care of it. Thanks, Leon."

Leon, still oblivious to the tension, waved his hand in farewell as he rode the new horse down the drive and out of sight.

"Get down," Stephan said, his voice terse. Sasha winced at it but did as he was told. "Who's that?" Stephan jerked his head toward Dagmar.

"A friend." Sasha couldn't bear to tell Stephan what Dagmar really was.

"Right, a friend. Tell her to get down too." Once again, Sasha obeyed, and Dagmar joined him on the ground. "What are you doing here?"

"I need to talk to Hamo," Sasha whispered. "Please, Stephan. It's really important."

"He's the one who decided to let you go in the end, you know. I wasn't going to. Not after what you did. Not after you lied. You deserved to go back and hang. So, if you're planning on causing any trouble..."

"I'm not. Honestly, I'm not."

"Give me one reason I should believe you." Stephan crossed his arms over his chest.

"I can't." Sasha's shoulders slumped forward in defeat. He'd risked everything, given up everything for this moment and Stephan wasn't going to let him get any further. "Please, Stephan. It's important."

Stephan grunted noncommittally then started to walk toward the stables, leading away Leon's tired mount.

"Don't move. I'll only be a moment," he called over his shoulder.

Sasha shifted from one foot to the other, conscious of the way Dagmar was watching him from beneath her veil. He certainly wasn't acting like a master or a chief's son at the moment. When Stephan returned, he had his own horse.

"Come on. Might as well see what's so important."

"You're going to take me?" Sasha looked up at him incredulously.

"Hurry up before I change my mind."

Stephan didn't say anything in the brief ride from his house to Hamo's. And Sasha wasn't about to try to start a conversation. He kept his head lowered, his eyes downcast, avoiding the occasional stare from Stephan. If he had known that Leon was going to deliver him to Stephan, he might very well have refused to come.

The western sky was a flaming orange as they came into the clearing. If he hadn't been so nervous, Sasha would have felt the fatigue of his trip more sharply. Coming to a stop before the house, Stephan dismounted and knocked on the door. Sasha didn't move. A woman with a baby in her arms answered it. She looked past Stephan to Sasha and Dagmar. Sasha couldn't hear what they were saying. A little girl of maybe five or six peered out from behind the woman, her eyes wide at the sight of the strangers.

"Stephan, what are you doing here?" Hamo came around from the side of the house.

"Brought someone to see you," Stephan gestured toward Sasha. "Says it's important."

Hamo froze, looking at Sasha. By the look on his face, Sasha was pretty sure he was trying to decide whether or not to be angry at the sight of him. The expression didn't bode well for Sasha's reception.

"Please, I just need to talk to you," Sasha broke the silence quietly.

"Come on." Hamo motioned for him to get down and reached a hand out to Dagmar to help her down.

Dagmar recoiled with a little cry.

"No. You can't touch her. She," Sasha wasn't really sure how he was going to explain about her, "she doesn't like it."

Hamo stepped back, exchanging a quizzical look with the woman at the door. Sasha wondered if Stephan intended to hang around to hear what he had to say as he followed Hamo into the house. To Sasha's intense relief, he didn't. He and Hamo exchanged a few words at the door and then he left.

"Sit down." Hamo gestured toward the dining table and chairs.

In the other room, Sasha could see at least two other girls, older than the one at the door but not old enough to be Meredith or Ophelia.

"I think I can honestly say I never expected to see you again." Hamo sat across from him at the table, along with the woman Sasha assumed was his wife. "Why are you here?"

"There's something I came to tell you."

"Who is she?" Hamo's wife spoke up, "Why is she keeping her face covered?"

"She's," Sasha paused. He thought about continuing the same story he had told Leon but decided against it. Hamo would know he was lying, and that would just make things worse. "She's mine."

"Yours?"

"Yes. My father gave her to me, as a gift." Sasha decided the table in front of him was very interesting. His eyes remained glued to it as the blood rushed to his face.

Understanding turned to horrified disgust on the woman's face.

"It's alright. I haven't done anything to her," Sasha hurried on as Hamo put a hand over his eyes, shaking his head.

"Except drag her all the way here, poor girl."

"I had to. If Father found out what I'd done, he would have punished her." Sasha thought it best to leave out the fact that he initially brought her along because he was afraid to travel alone. The entire turn of the conversation was very unsettling. Never in Sasha's life had he been spoken to so directly by a woman, not even his own Mother when she was around. Women and girls in Aruuk didn't act like that. He wasn't quite sure how to react. "Anyway, I didn't come all this way to talk about Dagmar."

If Sasha thought the conversation disturbing, it paled quickly in comparison to what he saw standing in the doorway. Meredith's face was white, and not from fear. Sasha squirmed, looking down at the wooden table. Meredith had made her own opinion of him clear, several times and the passing of time had done nothing to alter it.

"What's he doing here?" Meredith's voice stung.

"Go, Meri," Hamo said quietly and Meredith looked for a moment like she was going to argue with him before turning sharply on her heel and walking away. "Sasha, your horses need put up still. Come on. Leave your girl in here."

Sasha nodded and pushed away from the table, motioning for Dagmar to stay put. He followed Hamo back outside, avoiding Meredith's glare from the other room.

The quiet of the barn was a pleasant comparison to being in the house, Sasha thought as his fingers worked to undo the girth of his horse's saddle. Horses and cows weren't capable of glaring. Hamo didn't say anything until they had finished.

Leaning back against one of the stall doors, Hamo finally asked, "Why are you here, Sasha?"

"Why'd you let me go?" Sasha ignored Hamo's question and asked the one that had troubled him since that day. "Stephan said you were the one who decided to. Why?"

"You came all this way just to find that out? I thought you said it was important."

"Well, no. It is important, the reason I came. But I also wanted to know why you did it."

"I told you I would. Remember? Besides, after what you'd said about your father, I couldn't very well hold anything against you. Now, why did you come all this way?"

"My father is planning an attack on Dorsten in just a few weeks, as soon as the weather breaks. They don't have any idea it's coming."

"That doesn't explain why you're here. You're not expecting us to come to their aid, are you? We have a treaty with them, not an alliance, Sasha."

"There's more. It's not just Dorsten. He's coming here too. After he takes Dorsten, he's coming here, and he's..."

"Sasha, wait," Hamo held up a hand to stop him. "You know what you're doing right now, don't you? You tell me all this, and I will have to tell the king. Are you sure that's what you want to do?"

"I know. Drogo said it was the only way."

"You spoke to Drogo?"

"Before I came here. He's the reason I came all this way. I wasn't going to. I'm supposed to be joining the army waiting at the coast." Sasha's face fell a little as he remembered his own abandoned duty.

"So, your father is planning an attack. You came all this way just to tell us that? Why?"

"Well, there's more." Sasha took a deep breath before continuing. "He was, is, furious about what happened to my raiding party. He knows it's Meredith that did it, and he wants to take her."

"Take her?"

"Alive. He wants to be the one who punishes her."

"And how does your father know who she is?" Hamo's face darkened with suspicion.

"I told him," Sasha whispered, his hands picking apart a piece of straw. "I wasn't trying to cause trouble for you or her. I just...I wanted him to stop punishing Boris. I thought if I told him what he wanted to know he would stop. But he didn't. He still punished him, and now he wants your daughter too."

"And that bothered you enough to come here and risk your father's anger just to tell me?"

"I guess so."

"What happened?"

"I just told you what happened." Sasha looked up from the piece of straw in confusion.

"No. When you were with us in the mountains, you thought your father could do no wrong, remember? What made you change your mind?"

Sasha didn't answer right away. The truth was, there wasn't an easy answer and Sasha wasn't sure he could put it into words even if he tried.

Clumsily, he began. He described his own homecoming, and the hint of disappointment at Father's carelessness regarding him. He felt sick all over again when he told of his night at the stockade listening to his fellow countrymen being devoured. He stumbled over the parts with Boris and his own hand in punishing his brother. Then he told about Dagmar, which led back to his imprisonment and the things that had happened there.

One thing led to another and in a rare spirit of honesty, he held nothing back. The longer he spoke, the easier it came. In fact, by the time Sasha was nearing the end of talking, he had said far more than he initially intended and Hamo now knew pretty much his entire life story.

"Nothing was right when I went back home, and Drogo said it never would be again. I'm just tired of being confused and miserable, and I don't even know why," he finished. "I don't think I want to be like Father anymore. And I know that I was probably the last person you wanted to see, and that was way more than you needed to hear, and that you don't have any reason to believe anything I say. But it's true. Especially the part about my father coming. You have to believe that, even if you believe nothing else."

"You certainly said a lot," Hamo agreed. "I'm not really sure what to think, honestly. I will have to tell the king what you've told me of the invasion. And I think you're probably going to have to come with me."

"You believe me?"

"I don't know yet. Come on, it's getting late." Hamo turned to leave, and Sasha followed him back to the house. "Oh, and Sasha?"

"Yes?"

"What you told me about what happened to your raiding party. Do me a favor, and never tell Meredith any of that."

"I won't."

It was quite late, Sasha saw, as they went into the house. The only other person still up was Hamo's wife who looked up curiously when they came in.

"I saved supper for you and him," she said to Hamo.

"Thanks. By the way, this is Sasha. And Sasha, this is my wife, Edith."

"I've heard a lot about you, Sasha." Sasha had little doubt what she'd heard about him.

He flushed and looked down at his feet.

"She fell asleep," Edith said as she motioned to Dagmar still seated at the table, her head resting on her arms. Once again, her veil had fallen to the side, uncovering what remained of the bruise he had given her. When Edith handed him a plate of food, Sasha slid into the chair next to Dagmar. Dagmar was familiar. Dagmar interacted with him the way he was used to. He was sure of her in a way that he wasn't sure of these people, especially the women and girls.

Every other thought flew out of his head when he started to eat. He was hungry. And compared to the meager, tasteless food he and Dagmar had shared the last couple of weeks, this was a delectable feast.

Hamo and Edith were sitting at the other end of the table, far enough away that Sasha couldn't make out their lowered voices, although he could clearly see they were in deep and serious discussion.

His hunger sated, his eyes were drawn again and again to the couple. Whatever they were talking about - probably him, Sasha thought - they both had a mutual voice in the conversation. Sasha had never seen such a thing. He tried to picture one of Father's wives addressing him as an equal. It didn't end well.

Edith was the first to notice his open staring. She looked over at him, an odd smile on her face. "Is something wrong?"

"No. Nothing," Sasha said. "It's just...you actually like each other."

"That's sort of how it works," Edith said, laughing a little.

"Not where I'm from."

"Then you come from a really sad place and for that, I'm very sorry."

Chapter 48

"DAGMAR STAYS."

Sasha thought about protesting. Dagmar was his. Dagmar was a piece of home, and he'd grown used to having her about. In this strange country where people behaved so differently, it was nice to have someone he could trust. He knew she would do whatever he told her. Even her fear of him was predictable, although he'd spent weeks trying to make her less afraid. But Hamo wasn't going to change his mind. He'd made it very clear the night before that as long as Sasha was there, Dagmar wasn't a slave and wouldn't be treated like one. Sasha chose not to push the point, especially when Hamo told him that the punishment for practicing slavery in Dival was the same as in Dorsten. Sasha hadn't come all this way just to hang.

"She won't understand," Sasha said. "Slaves aren't freed in Aruuk. Ever. If she thinks I'm turning her loose, it just means she's available to any man who wants to use her. That's worse than belonging to me, and that's what she'll think. She'll be terrified."

"You'll have time to convince her that she really is free when we get back. She's not coming with us now, though. I think she's had enough traveling."

Sasha shrugged. She had been through quite a bit with him, that was true. And since he'd come clean with Hamo last night, Hamo knew exactly what Sasha had done to her. It was probably for the best that she stayed behind. Still, there was a part of him that hated to give up his one last possession.

He looked down at where she lay, still asleep. She'd automatically moved to the spot at his feet when they had gone to bed the night before. When Edith tried to intervene, it was Hamo who stopped her and said to let Dagmar be. Her face was completely uncovered, and Sasha could see how thin she'd grown on their journey. Hamo was right. She shouldn't have to go through anymore.

"Dagmar," he said loud enough to wake her, but not anyone else who was still asleep in the house. She sat up slowly, hiding her face behind her loose hair when she caught sight of Hamo. Sasha continued in his native tongue, "I'm going away, and you're going to stay here..."

Sasha was entirely unprepared for the onslaught of pleading tears as Dagmar shifted to her knees and grabbed his hands, pressing them to her forehead.

"Please don't, Master... I've been good and... you haven't... you haven't even tried me... please, I don't... want another... master." Her words were broken between hiccupping sobs.

Sasha felt his face go hot. He was glad Hamo, and Edith who had just come in the room, could not understand what Dagmar was saying. He wasn't even sure why she was saying it. She was still wearing the bruise he'd given her. But he hadn't done anything else to her. He hadn't done the one thing she was mortally afraid of. He hadn't raped her. Sasha's frustration with Hamo's insistence on letting her go dissipated as he watched her. Dagmar was only a year or so younger than him, and yet her entire life was shaped by this fear.

"Dagmar, stop." His voice was harsher than he meant but knowing that Hamo and Edith were both watching this display was disconcerting. "I'm not giving you to anyone. You just can't come with me. Not this time."

Dagmar tried hard to quiet herself but even so it was another minute before Sasha thought she was actually capable of comprehending his words.

"You're going to stay here, and they are going to take care of you while I'm gone. It'll be only girls, so you don't have to cover your face. Just do what they tell you to, and I'll come back." He disentangled himself from her hands and turned to Hamo. "I'm ready."

"Well, I guess you weren't lying about her not understanding," Hamo said. "What was that all about?"

"It was nothing."

"You're still a terrible liar."

"Fine. She thought I was giving her to you. And she didn't want me to because she must think I've been a good master."

"That's horrible," Edith said. "The poor girl."

Sasha remained silent. He didn't think it was so horrible. If she didn't want to be given to another man, didn't that mean he'd been a good master?

Sasha had been on the verge of falling asleep sitting up when Hamo and Edith finally finished talking the night before. While Edith prepared a place for them to sleep, Hamo told Sasha that he was leaving in the morning and that Sasha was coming with him. If Sasha had a choice in the matter, Hamo certainly hadn't made it sound like it.

Now, in the predawn darkness, Sasha thought he would be glad to never see the back of a horse again. He was sick of traveling. He was sick of riding. Even after sleeping better this past night than many nights previously, he was weary. It wasn't the sort of weariness that sleep could cure. As the plodding of the horses settled into a rhythm, Sasha turned to Hamo with a question he'd forgotten to ask the night before.

"How long is it going to take to get there?"

"Less than a day. You're sure you want to go through with this?"

"I already can't go back home at this point. But what exactly do you want me to do?"

"You don't have to do anything. I'm going to tell the king what you told me."

"So why do I have to come?" Sasha thought it was a little unfair after the great distance he'd already gone. He would have liked to stay in one place and recoup for a few days. Everyone felt sorry for Dagmar traveling all that distance, but no one seemed to realize he had done the same.

"Do you really have to ask that?" Hamo turned to look at him. "I think you might be telling me the truth. But that hardly means I'm leaving you alone with my family while I'm gone. Since there's not another place for you to go, you're coming with me."

"But I gave up my entire life in Aruuk by coming here," Sasha replied, making no effort to conceal his disappointment.

"Which is good. And before that you had a very direct hand in kidnapping my daughters. And lied to us. And tried to run away after making a deal with us. And you're forgetting that you're the one who told your father who killed the raiding party."

While Sasha internally conceded that those were all good points, it still hurt.

"What would you have done if I didn't come with you?"

"You did."

"Yes, but if I didn't."

"You did," Hamo repeated.

Realizing that there would be no forthcoming answer, Sasha lapsed into silence. Maybe he should have given a little more thought to his choice. He'd been so quick to believe Drogo when he'd said he could start over. Maybe starting over wouldn't work.

"You don't have to be so offended by it," Hamo said, laughing a little. "If I didn't trust that you were telling the truth just a little, I wouldn't be doing this now."

"I guess so. Drogo made it sound easier, though. You know he's related to me?" Sasha decided it was time to change the subject.

"I know. He told me. You were asleep."

"Oh. Why didn't you tell me?"

"He said it didn't matter. That family didn't matter where you came from. A point you made very clear when you told us what your father had done to your mother and sister. Telling you wouldn't have made any difference."

Sasha acknowledged him with a nod. Talking about family made him think of Boris. Boris would be there, at the very front of the attack on Dorsten. He would most likely die. Sasha missed him. He missed what they'd had before Boris had abandoned him for dead, and before he had punished Boris for Father. He fell quiet for some time.

Chapter 49

MEREDITH STOOD IN THE DARK doorway, watching Father disappear down the road with Sasha. Mother and Ophelia were the only others up that early. And Dagmar, Meredith realized. Dagmar hadn't moved from the spot she'd been in when Sasha told her he was leaving. She was frozen in place aside from her large blue eyes that darted about, catching every movement in the room.

"I can't believe he just trusts him like that," Meredith whispered, not really intending her words for anyone.

"It's because he doesn't trust him that he's taking him," Mother said, standing just behind her.

"But Father's still listening to him. He believes him. Or he wouldn't be going."

"Your Father can't just ignore a warning because of the one who gives it. If what Sasha was saying is true, King Darien needs to know. If it turns out to be false, there's still no harm done."

"I can't believe he had the nerve to show up here at all," Ophelia said. "And with his slave girl."

Meredith looked back at Dagmar. That could have been her, or Ophelia. She wouldn't have been like that, Meredith decided. Dagmar cringed meekly at Sasha's every word. She cowered when his hand came close to her. Meredith had watched her. It was disgusting.

"Poor thing. She doesn't even understand what we're saying. I tried to talk to her last night," Mother said. "She was really upset, though, when she thought Sasha was giving her away. I wouldn't have believed it, except that I saw it."

"How could you be upset about leaving someone like that."

"I don't know, but she was. Why don't you take her to your room and see if you can get her to change into something clean? I think she's worn the same clothes since they left home."

"How are we supposed to do that when she doesn't even understand us?" Meredith asked, but Ophelia was already approaching Dagmar, motioning for her to follow. A little ashamed, Meredith tried to make up for it. "I have something she can wear."

Inside the bedroom, Meredith dug out one of her better outfits and laid them out on her bed. Dagmar followed Ophelia into the room. By a series of hand motions Ophelia communicated that the clothes were for Dagmar. As soon as it was obvious that Dagmar understood, the twins left her to herself.

"It's going to be really hard having her around when she doesn't understand anything," Ophelia said. "I wonder how long she's been his slave."

It was more than an hour later, as Mother was setting everyone down to breakfast, that Meredith realized Dagmar was still in the bedroom. Knocking softly on the door before pushing it open, she was surprised to find Dagmar, changed and sitting on the edge of a bed. Dagmar looked up at her in a mixture of fear and bewilderment.

"Come on. We're ready to eat," Meredith said as she gestured for Dagmar to follow her.

For most of the morning nothing changed. Dagmar was a statue, and one that sought to take up as little room and attention as possible, unless she was told to do something. And always her haunted blue eyes followed the slightest movement. Meredith found it unnerving at first, but as the day progressed so did her annoyance with Dagmar's behavior.

"Uncle Al and Taliea are here!" Priscilla stuck her head in the front door long enough to yell inside.

Meredith caught sight of the two through the window. The idea of Uncle Al getting married finally still hadn't quite sunk in, but the more she saw them together, the more she liked the idea. Especially since it meant Taliea wasn't leaving. As they came into the house, Meredith could see that Uncle Al carried a bundle of something in his arms. After a warm greeting, Taliea took the bundle and laid it on the table.

"Look at these and tell me what you think," she said, spreading out an assortment of colored fabrics.

"Where's Hamo?" Uncle Aldrid asked, looking around.

"Long story," Mother answered.

Meredith ran her hand over the smooth surface of a deep green cloth. It reminded her of the color of the pines in the mountains. She only half listened as Mother explained how Sasha had shown up on their doorstep the night before.

"Who is she?" Taliea glanced over at Dagmar, who was hiding her face behind a screen of hair.

"She's the slave girl Sasha brought with him. She belongs to him," Meredith answered. "Her name's Dagmar, but she doesn't understand anything we say. Sasha was the only one who could talk to her, but Father made him go with him."

"Poor child. I wonder where she's from."

Meredith shrugged. "So, I take it green is the color you're getting married in?" she said, still comparing the different shades of green that each fabric was. "That's different."

"Not where I come from. Green is the color every girl gets married in. It's the color of life, growth, new beginnings. And, since we live in a desert, it's a color that we don't see very much of."

"I like that. This dark one's my favorite. It'll look good on you."

"Mine too." Ophelia came over to join them. "It's so soft. It reminds me of the evergreens in the mountains."

Meredith smiled a little. Her and Ophelia thought alike so much - except, of course, when they didn't. She ran her fingers one last time over the smooth, silky surface of the fabric.

Singing softly to herself the way she often did, Taliea began folding the fabric up and replacing it in its bundle. Meredith always loved when Taliea sang her native songs. The words were softer, more musical than her own tongue.

From the corner of the room where she sat, no one noticed Dagmar staring fixedly at Taliea, her lips parted in mute disbelief, a single tear tracing its way down her still dirty, bruised cheek.

Chapter 50

A T THE SIGHT OF THE CASTLE rising up in the heart of the town, Sasha stiffened. Aside from the fact that it was not backed into the side of a mountain, it differed very little from the one in Dorsten. Its dark gray exterior was like an ugly scar against the blue sky.

"They're not," Sasha hesitated. The last thing he wanted was to let Hamo know how nervous he was. He decided to start over. "When we get there, they're not going to, like, lock me up or anything, are they? Like in the dungeon?"

"No. Why would they?"

"I don't know. I just really don't like being locked up."

"I can imagine. It didn't go so well for you last time. But they have no reason to lock you up."

That was a relief to hear, but even so the castle held an ominous air. Sasha hadn't been able to get a very good look at the castle he was imprisoned in while in Dorsten. He'd been brought there in the middle of the night, and Stephan had broken him out in the middle of another night.

If the exterior of the castle was cold and uninviting, the interior was the opposite. After handing their horses off to a stable hand and being ushered inside by a middle-aged man who seemed very familiar with Hamo, Sasha found himself gaping at the opulence inside the place. The one time he'd been brought into the council room of the Dorstenian castle, he'd been blindfolded. His eyes traveled all around the room and he was oblivious to the fact that Hamo was in deep conversation with the man who had brought them inside. Hamo's voice coming from right behind him startled him out of his reverie.

"You want to come in with me or stay out here?"

"Come, I guess. Where are we going?"

"To speak with King Darien."

"Already? You can just show up and he'll see you like that?"

"I told him it was urgent."

Sasha fell in step behind Hamo and the middle-aged man who's name he'd heard Hamo say was Jarvis. His thoughts were torn between taking in all the sights the place had to offer and wondering what King Darien would be like. Sasha had only really met two leaders in his life. Father, and Lord Bayner. Both ruled the same way. He was the son of one and a prisoner of the other, and those facts directly played into all his interactions with them. How, exactly, was he supposed to act with King Darien?

He had not yet made up his mind as to how he would behave before Jarvis pulled open an inconspicuous looking door.

Whoever Sasha thought King Darien might be, it wasn't the man sitting in front of them now. The room itself didn't have the official aura of something like the council room. It looked more like a library. The man sitting at the table, less so. Smiling, he rose to his feet at their entrance and came around the table to clasp Hamo's hand in his own.

"My secretary surprised me with news of your arrival. I was not expecting to see you for several weeks. Come, sit down."

Hamo and Sasha joined him at the table, Sasha still trying to decide whether this was really King Darien or not.

"Who is this?" King Darien asked.

"This is the reason I'm here. His name's Sasha."

"Any friend of Hamo's is welcome here, Sasha."

"Thank you, um, Your Majesty." Sasha thought it a stretch to claim that he was a friend of Hamo's but didn't feel like contradicting a man who could lock him up if he chose.

"So, what is it that brings you here?" King Darien's face grew somber. "I wager it wasn't just to introduce me to him."

Hamo looked at Sasha, eyebrows raised. "Want to tell him?"

"I don't...I thought you said I didn't have to."

Hamo shrugged. "You don't. The truth is, King, Sasha's from Aruuk. He came on his own to warn us of what is coming. His father's the chief up there, and he's planning on making war with us this spring."

King Darien nodded slowly, absorbing the seriousness of the news. If he was surprised, he hid it well, Sasha thought. He turned to Sasha.

"Is this true?"

"It is," Sasha said quietly. It was one thing to tell Hamo all this, it was quite another to share his country's plans with the enemy's king.

King Darien leaned back in his chair, fingers drumming lightly upon the table. "It's what we've been expecting."

"It is?" Hamo said.

"Yes. We've received word from our network of spies that Aruuk is amassing an armada and an army to fill it. It makes sense that we're a target. I've already sent some of the fleet up to the mouth of the channel to keep an eye on things."

Sasha was oddly relieved by King Darien's words. His warning didn't seem like so much of a betrayal since King Darien was already aware of what was coming.

"According to Sasha, that's not the only attack we have to worry about." Sasha's feeling of relief disappeared at Hamo's words. "They're planning more."

King Darien frowned as Hamo disclosed the rest of Chief Gundar's plan. It was a good plan. One that would be devastatingly successful.

Rising from his chair, he walked over to a shelf and rummaged through a stack of folded papers before returning to the table with one in hand. King Darien laid it out across the table and Sasha could see it was a map. By the amount of detail, and the still crisp lines, it was quite a bit newer than any of the ones he had studied in Aruuk. He leaned forward, intrigued by seeing all the places he'd traveled in such a short time drawn out on a piece of paper. The great plains, or the Void as these people called it, looked so small and harmless marked out on a piece of paper.

"The only reasonable place to attack us by sea is here, and here." King Darien tapped a finger at two different points along the coast, one of which Sasha could see was the harbor to Bren. "They are the only harbors that would hold a sufficient number of large vessels to make an attack successful. Most of the rest of the coast is either cliffs, or jagged rocks. You couldn't get one ship close enough to land people ashore, let alone a dozen or more. There're the little fishing ports, of course, but those would hardly serve an entire fleet. If we could cut them off at the mouth of the channel, we could keep them from ever reaching either harbor."

"He'd attack here," Sasha volunteered, pointing to the harbor of Bren. "It's the capital. If he takes it the rest of the country falls. Especially since he'll be attacking here" - he ran his finger along the border of the great plains - "with his other army."

"If he takes Dorsten," King Darien reminded him.

"He will."

"What makes you so sure?"

"They don't know what's coming. And they'll be fighting alone."

"What are you trying to say?" Hamo asked.

"It's something he said to me a long time ago. He said that your two countries were so busy fighting each other that they could never unite to fight a common enemy. He said it made you both weak."

"So, you're suggesting we should help Dorsten?"

"I'm saying it's the only way he thought you would win. And he doesn't think you'll do it." Sasha sat back, startled by how much he'd just said. That wasn't part of the plan. He was just supposed to warn Hamo that they were in danger, not help plan a way to defeat Father.

The change in his countenance must have been obvious. After a prolonged silence, Sasha looked up to find both men staring at him.

"Thank you for sharing that, Sasha," King Darien was the first to speak.

"I didn't actually mean to say all that." He continued under his breath, "Now I really don't have a home."

"You might when this is all over and done with," Hamo must have heard him and answered.

"Unfortunately, Dorsten is not exactly on good terms with us." King Darien's lips pressed together in a tight smile, "Yes, it turns out they weren't thrilled to have one of their prisoners broken out from beneath their noses by a certain emissary of mine."

"I can't imagine who would do such a thing," Hamo replied, maintaining a perfectly straight face.

For the first time in weeks, Sasha had to look down at his hands to hide a smile that crept over his face. He wondered how much of the story King Darien knew. He wondered if he knew that Sasha was the said prisoner.

"Me either. No one I sent over there would demonstrate such a blatant disrespect for Dorstenian judgement." Both King Darien and Hamo started laughing. "You know, I could never officially condone Stephan's actions, but I'm glad you were able to get your daughters back. That doesn't resolve the tensions between our two countries, though. I'm afraid, Sasha, that your father was right. There's not much we can do to help Dorsten. We have our own borders to protect. I can't justify throwing away troops protecting theirs."

"But then he'll win." Sasha was surprised by how much that acknowledgement disturbed him. He turned to Hamo. "You were willing to do anything to get your daughters back. They're in more danger now than they were before. If he wins, you know what he'll do. There has to be a way."

"It's not the same. If he comes here, we will fight."

Sasha shook his head in disbelief.

"Then I need to go. I need to get as far away from here as I can, because if he wins, if he finds me...," He didn't need to finish, couldn't finish.

He'd been a fool thinking he could change anything. Father was right. Compassion was weakness. People couldn't stop hating each other. Father would win. And this time, Sasha was on the wrong side. He was on the wrong side because he'd chosen compassion. He shoved his chair away from the table and without waiting for either of them to speak, walked out.

Letting the door shut behind him he slid to the floor, his back against the wall. He couldn't push away the sick feeling of his mistake. He'd thrown everything away, lost any chance he had of being accepted by Father, and for what? Dorsten would fall. That didn't bother him much until he remembered that Drogo was there. Dival would be conquered. He cared about that mostly because he was in it. But so was Hamo, and Edith, and even Stephan. And now that he knew them even a little bit, the thought of what would happen to them sickened him.

The door opening next to him wasn't enough to get his attention, but Hamo standing in front of him was. Still, he didn't look up.

"Come on. It's late," Hamo said. "We should get something to eat and go to sleep."

Sasha begrudgingly rose to his feet.

"He's calling a war council meeting tomorrow. He wants you to be there."

"I need to go. I wasn't joking about that. I need to get back and get Dagmar and go somewhere where he can't find me."

"I'll take you back after tomorrow."

Chapter 51

DAGMAR LISTENED TO THE words of Taliea's song. Two years. Two long, lonely years since she'd heard her own language. Clinging to the sound of each word, she only gradually became aware of being noticed.

With horror, Dagmar realized her mistake. Not only had she drawn unnecessary attention to herself, but the young man in the room now had a perfectly good view of her face. Quickly turning her head to the side and allowing her long, loose hair to fall like a curtain over it, she shrank back. If her master found out, she would be cast out. The woman in charge of the companion slaves in training had made it very clear what happened to one that was cast out.

A hand on her shoulder made her jump. The singing woman knelt in front of her, gently brushing the tangled length of hair away.

"You understand me?" the woman asked, her voice soft.

"Yes," Dagmar whispered. She wasn't sure how her master felt about her talking in her native language, or about her talking to these people at all. They hadn't been allowed to communicate in any other language when she'd been kept with the other female slaves. But the only thing her master had said before leaving was for her to do as they told her.

"It's alright. You don't have to be frightened. No one here will hurt you."

Dagmar wished she could believe her. How many times had she been told those very words though, or had heard them said to another slave? Countless, and each time the words were false. Always they were a precursor to a particularly painful punishment.

"Where are you from?"

"Sondaru."

"That is my homeland as well. You're from a coastal town?"

"Pinjaru."

"How long ago were you taken, child?"

"Two years ago."

"Tell me about it." The woman's voice didn't carry the crisp note of command Dagmar was used to, but the compulsion to obey was strong anyway.

"They came in ships," she started, "in the middle of the night. They surrounded the whole village and then they started killing. They only left a handful of us alive. The rest they killed and then set fire to the village."

"Did you have any family that survived?"

"A sister and two brothers. But my brothers they killed on the ship because they tried to jump overboard."

"What about your sister? Is she still alive?"

"She belongs to a master like I do. He picked her a year ago."

"I'm so sorry you've had to go through that. You're safe here, though. No one will hurt you. My name is Taliea, and these people here are my friends. They will take care of you. You're free here."

A great, choking sob escaped Dagmar and then another. Her shoulders shook and when Taliea put her arms around her and held her, she did not resist. After a few seconds, her own hands clung to Taliea with a grip that defied ever being broken. And all the while she wept. Dagmar hadn't cried when she'd watched her parents cut down inside their own home. She hadn't cried when her brothers were slain before her eyes on the ship. For the last two years she'd bottled up her tears, afraid of what would be done to her if she were to give vent to them. Taliea's words broke that dam, and she couldn't stop crying now.

It was some time before Dagmar spent her tears. When her crying was nothing more than a few hiccupping breaths, Taliea slowly released her and pushed a handkerchief into her hand. Shakily, Dagmar wiped her face clean. She still had to be careful touching the bruise her master had given her.

The others in the room were talking although she couldn't understand them. Dagmar was glad. It meant they weren't all watching her.

"Dagmar, would you like to come with me to my house for now?" Taliea was kneeling in front of her again.

Dagmar panicked. She wasn't asked what she wanted, ever. And what would Sasha think?

"I can't."

"Of course, you can. It would be better for you. You and I can understand each other."

"But Master Sasha told me to wait here. He's coming back for me. He promised he wasn't going to give me away."

"I don't understand. You want to stay with him?"

"He's better than others. He doesn't make me sleep with him. And he's only hit me once when I disobeyed. He told me to stay here, and I don't want to make him angry."

"I see." Taliea's face was troubled and for a frightening moment Dagmar thought she was going to be angry and that all the kindness had only been an act to trick her. "Well, if you can't come stay with me, I'll do my best to visit you as often as I can. How's that?"

"Why?" Dagmar's large, blue eyes were perplexed.

"Because you need a friend. Now, come eat with us."

Dagmar followed her to the table.

Chapter 52

THE STIFLING AND WELL-REGULATED order of Father's war meetings was sadly lacking here, Sasha decided. He rubbed his temples, trying to push away the dull headache that hung over him. No one at one of Father's meetings would dream of arguing with him, or interrupting, or even speaking at all without permission. Those rules weren't in place here.

His own knowledge of the language was inadequate to keep up with multiple conversations at once, and his mind was too scattered to try to focus on just one. The overwhelming opinion in the room was the same as the one King Darien and Hamo expressed the night before. That much he gathered from the fragments he picked up throughout the morning.

Hamo said they would go home after this. Sasha smiled grimly to himself as he thought of how meaningless the word home was to him now. He didn't have one anymore. He'd thrown it away. He'd had half an idea that if Father was stopped, he could stay here in this country. The idea was less appealing with each passing minute.

He'd go back with Hamo and get Dagmar. No doubt Hamo and Edith would insist he leave Dagmar behind. But she was in as much danger as he was if Father succeeded. Since saving her from freezing to death, the thought of her being hurt by Father, or anyone else for that matter, grated against him sorely. They would leave. Find a ship that could take them somewhere, anywhere where his father would not find him. The plan floated around in his mind, desperate and reckless.

278

He had to get away. All he could think about was what happened to Boris, and what had happened to a nameless brother so many years before.

A lull in the voices made him look up, and he was startled to find everyone staring at him. He'd missed something. That much was obvious. He met Hamo's eyes with a question in his own. Hamo had an odd look on his face watching him, one Sasha had seen before but couldn't quite remember where or when.

"If you would care to, Sasha, please share with us what it is that we can expect from Chief Gundar and his army?" King Darien repeated the question Sasha had missed a moment ago.

Sasha's eyes lingered where they were for another second as it came to him exactly when he'd seen that look on Hamo's face. It was the night Meredith and Ophelia had found their way back to him. The night Sasha was so sure he was going to die. He'd woken up from nightmares that night, and Hamo had been looking at him, watching him with that very same expression. And Sasha understood. Hamo was trying to decide.

"They'll destroy everything. Burn towns and villages to the ground. Make slaves out of whoever they think is strong enough or pretty enough. You won't have a life like you do now." The words were ugly here, in the presence of so many people, and Sasha felt a shame he never had before for ever wanting to participate in such things.

"You seem very familiar with what they do. Care to explain?" a man sitting at the far end of the table asked.

Sasha froze. King Darien had told him before they came in here that he was not to tell anyone who he was or who he was related to.

"Sasha comes from Aruuk. He's the one who brought us warning. Based on corroborating information I received from other sources, we can trust what he tells us. The question is what we're going to do about it." King Darien's tone defied further questioning of Sasha. Sasha sank back in his chair, relieved. Too many questions and it was going to be just like another time in another castle that he would rather not remember.

Again, the chaos of voices erupted. Once again, Sasha had the uneasy sensation that he was being stared at and looked over to find Hamo watching him. What was wrong with him? Sasha squirmed and looked back down at his hands in his lap, confused.

"I think we should go." The voice was quiet, but firm. "We should go to Dorsten and fight them there."

"With all due respect, Hamo, I don't think it's any of our business helping Dorsten out." It was the same man who had begun to question Sasha.

"It's not." The room had fallen silent now, everyone intent on Hamo's words. "But it is our business to protect our own. Twenty-six years ago, we fought against soldiers from Aruuk. I fought against them. If they do make it to the Void, if they have the freedom of movement inside that place, we won't be able to stop them. And we need to stop them. I've seen what they do."

"Our borders are well protected. If we allow them to destroy Dorsten, we never have to worry about our neighbors again."

"Did you fight against them?" Hamo turned directly to him.

"No, I did not. In my capacity as an assistant to the king's secretary, I was exempted from military service."

"Our borders mean nothing to them. And Sasha's right. When they come, and they will if we don't stop them in Dorsten, they will destroy everything."

"The only thing you've wanted since you came here was to put an end to the fighting, and now you're asking us to start it again, and help our former enemies no less?"

"That's true. But fighting an endless war over something none of us could remember is different than doing whatever it takes to protect our own. Some things are worth fighting for."

Sasha glanced around the room, trying to gauge the effect Hamo's words were having on the rest of the men. The man at the far end still looked unconvinced, but most of the others were at least considering what he was saying. A flicker of hope rose within Sasha. Maybe he wouldn't have to run away again after all.

"Before we decide to help the Dorstenians, we should remember that Lord Bayner might not take seriously any warning we give him, or any help we offer. He's not exactly happy with us right now," King Darien interjected. "And showing up with even a small fighting force on their doorstep is going to look, and most likely be taken as, an act of war. He would view it as a threat, not help."

"He won't if I go. He just needs to be told ahead of time. He'll listen to me. He has a very good reason to listen to me," Hamo said.

Sasha wondered what reason Hamo could possibly have that would make Lord Bayner listen to anything he said. The lord certainly hadn't seemed like someone who would feel compelled to hear anyone out.

"Then I call for a vote," King Darien's voice echoed off the chamber walls. "You'll wait outside, Sasha."

Sasha nodded, grateful to be excused from the prospect of a tedious and disappointing vote. Despite the cold, he wandered out to the courtyard. There were few people out there and no one bothered him when he sat down on one of the stone benches.

He hadn't been out there long at all when Hamo found him.

"Are we going back now?"

"We are. And you should know, they voted to go."

It took longer than it should have for Sasha to absorb the true meaning of Hamo's words but when he did there was a sense of relief far greater than anything he'd experienced in the last few weeks.

True to Hamo's word, they started out less than an hour later.

"I have to come with you, don't I?" Sasha didn't need to bother asking but did it anyway.

"I'm not leaving you with them. Unless you have another place to stay, then yes. I could always ask if Stephan..."

"No, I'd rather go," Sasha hurried to cut him off.

"Are you afraid of him?" Hamo asked, laughing.

"No. I just don't really want to stay with him."

"You're scared of him."

"He held a knife to my throat, and made fun of me, and he told me himself that he wasn't going to let me go at the end," Sasha defended himself.

"According to Meri, that's exactly what you did to her. Only, you also pulled her hair."

"I know, I know. It was. I guess I just never thought about what it would be like to have it done to me. It was terrifying." Sasha shuddered at the memory.

"I guess you're coming with me then. Which is fine, because once Stephan hears about this, he's going to want to come too. The only problem is," Hamo frowned a little as he thought about it, "you're going to have to keep out of sight. As far as I know, you're still supposed to hang. I can't imagine Lord Bayner issuing a pardon after we broke you out."

Sasha's hand traveled nervously to his neck. He'd forgotten that part. Maybe he should try to find somewhere else to stay. Except he didn't have any money. Or any friends. Or the faintest idea of where to look.

"I wouldn't worry too much about it. You can always stay up at Drogo's as long as the two of you are on good terms. No one ever bothers him up there."

"I suppose so." His hand lingered on his neck, trying to imagine what it would feel like having the rough rope resting against his skin, tightening and taking away his breath. A shiver ran up his spine at the thought. He didn't want to go.

By the time they finally reached the house, Sasha had fully resigned himself to yet another long trip. At least this time he wouldn't be the one responsible for keeping them alive. That was far more work than he had bargained for. It would be easier too, this time, since the weather was slowly starting to change. Perhaps the wind in the plains had died down a bit.

Sasha hung back when they arrived to Hamo's house, and offered to take the horses to the barn, not out of generosity but in an attempt to avoid the little ache that inevitably came at seeing the overwhelming amount of happiness and excitement everyone exhibited, and to stay out of Meredith's glare for as long as possible. Hamo said it would be a few days before they left. It would be a long few days.

When he finished, everyone else was already inside and Sasha hesitated, staring at the closed door. It felt intrusive to just throw it open and come in. Was he supposed to knock? An great desire to not appear foolish or impolite tugged at him. They already thought so little of him. Raising a tentative hand, he knocked lightly, barely making enough noise to hear himself. No one answered. Taking a deep breath, he lifted the latch and opened the door slowly.

Inside, there was no sign of either Hamo or Edith, but the smell of food cooking reminded Sasha that he was hungry. All the girls were congregated in the sitting room, making that the last place Sasha wanted to go. He slipped inside quietly and headed for the dining table. He stopped mid stride when he saw Dagmar already sitting there with another woman, a stranger. Neither noticed him right away, giving him a chance to listen in on their conversation. Only, he couldn't understand what they were saying. The words were softer, almost musical, like no other language he'd ever heard.

For the first time, it occurred to Sasha that he had no idea where Dagmar was from. It hadn't even crossed his mind to find out. In fact, it had never crossed his mind that she'd had any life at all before becoming his.

His staring eventually captured the attention of the woman who looked up. She smiled politely.

"You must be Sasha. I'm Taliea. I've heard a lot about you."

Edith had said the same thing when they were introduced. Sasha could only imagine what they had heard about him, especially if this woman was getting her stories from Dagmar. He glanced toward Dagmar now. Her face was turned to him, her eyes widening with fright.

"What was she saying?" Sasha blurted out.

Taliea bit her lip, considering. Sasha was almost sorry he'd asked. Why couldn't they believe that he'd been a better master than most? He could tell them stories of what his older brothers had bragged about doing to their female slaves, and then they would think better of him.

"She was telling me about her home. And about you."

He looked back at Dagmar, who hung her head a little. Her entire demeanor had shifted at the reminder of his existence. Did she really fear and hate him that much? He'd only hit her that once, and he'd saved her life.

"I'm sure that was interesting," Sasha answered more harshly than he meant to.

"Actually, it was."

Sasha longed to ask what she had said about him but couldn't bring himself to do it.

"What'd she tell you about her home?"

"You should ask her sometime. You might find it interesting," she said with a smile.

Sasha nodded and sat down next to Dagmar, waiting to be given a clear idea of what to do with himself. The longer Sasha sat there, the more out of place he felt. He didn't belong here. No matter how much he wanted to be different, he wasn't. Not to these people.

A commotion from the sitting room drew him out of the pool of his own self-pity and he looked up through the open door to see a young man coming in.

"Uncle Al," one of the smaller girls cried out before grabbing his hand and pulling him into the house. "Taliea's here."

"I know, Nora. Why do you think I'm here?" Aldrid tousled Nora's hair, laughing. "Is your father home yet?"

"Just got back a little while ago," Ophelia said. "Somethings up, though, and he's talking to Mother."

"I see."

Sasha wasn't left sitting alone with Dagmar for much longer. Within a few minutes of Aldrid's arrival, everyone was gathered at the table. Dagmar sucked in a startled breath when Hamo and Aldrid came in and quickly loosened her veil from where it was twisted up around her head.

"She shouldn't have to do that," Meredith said, watching from across the table.

"It's fine, Meri. It makes her feel safe," Hamo answered before Sasha had a chance to say anything. Sasha's face grew puzzled. He hadn't expected Hamo to say something like that.

"It's not like you or Uncle Al seeing her face is going to hurt her." Sasha nearly choked at Meredith's audacity.

"She doesn't know that, and until she does, it's fine."

"So, I heard something's up?" Al interrupted the conversation. "What's it all about?"

"I have to go away for a bit."

"Where?"

"Dorsten. Tell you about it in a bit." Hamo shot a warning glance toward the younger girls who were listening with rapt attention.

"Need someone to come with you?"

"Well, I already have him for company," Hamo nodded toward Sasha, "But I wouldn't say no to more. Are you volunteering?"

"I might be. Sounds fun. You know, I haven't been that way since Stephan and I found you. I've heard the Void looks quite different now that we've stopped killing each other in it."

Sasha sat quietly through supper, saying nothing to anyone. The longer he spent around these people the worse his own loneliness grew. It was as if he was standing outside on a cold night looking in a window at a warm fire. He could see it, hear it even, but he felt no warmth from it. It wasn't his.

Chapter 53

MUDDY PATCHES WERE BEGINNING to show amidst the snow on the day before they were to leave. Sasha was in the woods, accompanied by Dagmar. He'd decided to talk to her out here in the refuge of the silent trees rather than in front of everyone at the house. He'd put it off as long as he could. Hamo said he couldn't wait any longer, and Sasha reluctantly agreed. It was time to say goodbye to the last thing he could truly claim as his.

Now that he was out here, though, he stalled, struggling to even know how to start or what to say. The only times he'd ever addressed Dagmar it was to give her an order. Even now, she followed him meekly at his command, not daring to question why he was taking her out here.

Spying a fallen log off to the side, Sasha made his way over to it and sat down, motioning for Dagmar to do the same. He took a deep breath. The air held a teasing hint of warmth to it.

"Dagmar, do you like it here?"

Dagmar looked at him, a mixture of anxiety and bewilderment in her blue eyes. She wasn't used to being asked about anything, and Sasha could see her trying to decide what answer she would give to keep him happy.

"It's alright if you do. I'm not angry about it. Do you?"

"Yes, Master Sasha. They are very...," she stopped, lowering her eyes, afraid of saying too much.

"They're kind?"

Dagmar nodded.

"You don't," Sasha hesitated, the words sticking like a lump in the back of his throat, "You don't need to call me that anymore, Dagmar. I'm not your master here, not anymore."

Her eyes, hurt and frightened, darted back up to his face. "But you said..."

"I'm not giving you away. You don't belong to anyone. You're free."

"I don't understand."

"You're free. You can go wherever you want. Do whatever you want." He swept his hand out. "You don't have to listen to me anymore."

"They said we could never be set free."

"Well, they lied," Sasha said in frustration. "They're not here. And if they don't find you, they can't do anything about your being free."

Dagmar was quiet for several long minutes, her face changing rapidly as she sorted through Sasha's words. Sasha leaned forward, resting his elbows on his knees, his chin cupped in his hands, staring glumly at the muddy brown earth before him. Now that the deed was done, he couldn't say he was entirely unhappy about it, but there was a finality to it that weighed on him.

"Thank you, Sasha," Dagmar spoke stiffly, hesitating over his name just slightly as she forced herself to leave the word master off. "You have been... kind... to me."

Sasha turned in surprise. Her eyes were brimming with tears, but there was something missing. The haunted look he'd seen in her eyes from the first day he'd lifted the veil off her face was gone.

"You can go back now, if you want," Sasha said.

"Thank you," Dagmar repeated. She stood, looking at him like she wanted to say more, but decided against it. Sasha watched her go. Taliea was at the house, so it would only be a matter of time before everyone there knew what he'd done.

Sasha spent another minute or so alone, trying to decide whether it would be better to go back now, or wait until any reaction over the news subsided. It was getting cold just sitting here. The fallen tree was wet and uncomfortable. He got up and started back through the woods.

He wandered around a bit before going all the way back. He was glad they were leaving in the morning. The constant reminder of what he didn't have was growing more painful with each passing day.

Sasha wasn't homesick, for home had never been all that welcoming. He wasn't exactly lonely, either, since he'd never had much experience with friends. He didn't know what he was. It was an emptiness that he couldn't quite put a finger on, but keenly felt every time he saw the others laughing or talking or just living. There was something so whole, so complete in their lives that he was missing. Even Dagmar was welcomed into it. Everyone felt sorry for her because she'd lost her home and family. No one seemed to realize that he'd lost his too. Probably because you chose to leave, Sasha told himself, kicking at the ground.

"Are you lost?" A man's voice rang out through the trees and Sasha spun around to find Aldrid standing there, watching him.

"I don't think so," Sasha said, looking at his surroundings a little uncertainly. He didn't think he'd wandered that far. His eyes fell on the bulging sack in Aldrid's hand. "What are you doing?"

"Checking my traps before we leave. Want to come along? I've just got a few left."

Sasha shrugged. His only interaction with Aldrid had been brief, limited to the first night he and Hamo had returned. Still, staying away from everyone else was more appealing than going back. He fell in step beside Aldrid.

The next hour proved to be the most pleasant he'd spent since leaving home. No, since before that. The emptiness had been just as present at home as it was here, just not quite as large. Aldrid kept up a running conversation that revolved around simple things like the weather, and Sasha asked a few questions about trapping that he answered. Not once, for even the tiniest second, did Aldrid remind Sasha of how sorely out of place he was.

"Come on, we'd better hurry if we're going to make it back before dark." Aldrid straightened from where he'd been kneeling, releasing an empty trap. When Sasha had asked earlier why he didn't just leave them, he said they would likely be gone so long that there was no point in leaving them. Sasha carried a bundle of traps they had collected over his shoulder. He wasn't even sure what compelled him to offer his help, it just sort of happened.

"Are you coming with us tomorrow for sure?" Sasha asked.

"Yes. I don't want to miss out on all the fun."

"I don't think it's going to be fun."

"I know." Al laughed, then grew serious. "But it's got to be done, and I'd rather go than sit around back here doing nothing."

"I'd rather not go," Sasha confided spontaneously, then bit his lip wishing he hadn't said it. He wasn't sure he could take a lecture on how little he ought to be trusted right now.

"No way for you to stay here, huh?"

"Hamo says I can't stay here, so I guess not."

"Makes sense, I suppose." Aldrid caught the involuntary slump of Sasha's shoulders out of the corner of his eye. "Look, I know probably no one's told you this, but leaving home the way you did and coming here just to warn us was a really brave thing to do. They'll stop seeing you as an enemy eventually. Just give it time."

"You think so?"

"I'm sure of it. Just wait and see."

"Thank you."

The house came into view and their pace quickened. Sasha came in behind Aldrid, dropping his eyes to avoid both the real and imagined stares. The littlest girls were loud and rambunctious in greeting their uncle. Sasha slipped quietly in and found a seat in the corner of the room. Dagmar looked up from where she was sitting Taliea at his entrance, the old, familiar fear crossing her face briefly before disappearing. He turned away, shutting his eyes and leaning his head back against the wall behind him.

Tomorrow he would leave. Tomorrow he wouldn't have to face this chasm between him and everyone else anymore. He couldn't wait for tomorrow.

Chapter 54

STEPHAN WAS COMING WITH THEM. Sasha groaned internally. He could already hear the jokes that would be made at his expense. He didn't have long to wait.

"You're not planning on trying to take off again, are you?" Stephan asked after they had only been on the road for half an hour.

"Why would I do that after coming all this way?" Sasha replied hotly.

"You don't have much of a sense of humor, do you?" Stephan asked, laughing and shaking his head a little.

Sasha wisely decided to remain silent. He continued in silence as the three men carried on a conversation about things Sasha had no idea about. Slowly, he let his horse fall behind so that it was abreast of the horse pulling a small cart.

For most of the day he stayed back there, ignored by and ignoring his three companions. It reminded him of his trip with Stephan and Hamo, except this time they didn't even need his directions. He might as well have been a shadow for all the attention they showed him.

"Hey, Sasha," Al called out to him when they stopped to make camp for the night. "Can you get a fire started?"

Sasha was glad he'd mastered the ability to build a fire on his journey with Dagmar. It saved him a good deal of humiliation now. He unloaded some of the wood they had brought with them in the cart and got to work while the others went about their own tasks.

Maybe mastered was too strong of a word for it, he thought as his efforts to produce a flame floundered.

"Have you never made a fire before?" Stephan stood over his shoulder, watching him and Sasha felt the blood rush to his face.

"I have," he said through gritted teeth. "I just haven't had to do it a lot. There was always a slave to do it for me."

"That's what comes of always having someone do all your work for you. Well, first of all," Stephan knelt next to him, his voice annoyingly condescending to Sasha's burning ears, "You're going to need something like dried grass or twigs for kindling to get it started. The logs are too big to catch right away."

Sasha sighed. Stephan was right, of course. He'd forgotten that little detail that he had unwittingly learned the first night he and Dagmar were traveling. He went in search of kindling.

Fortunately, starting the fire was the only thing he had to do. It would have been more embarrassing than he could bear to have been asked to cook something. He sat apart from the group, giving up a little bit of the fire's warmth for the comfort of distance. After eating, he got his own blankets and laid down, too disheartened to try to stay up and talk. They wouldn't talk to him anyway.

Sasha dozed for a short while before the voices awakened him. The others were still awake. He almost fell back asleep before he understood what they were talking about. Or rather who. Sasha stiffened.

"I'm just saying you're being awfully hard on him." He recognized Aldrid's voice. "He gave up everything to come here and try to make things right."

"You know what he did to the girls, Al. And he lied to us," Stephan said.

"I stole from you, and from a lot of other people, and you still gave me a chance," Al responded quietly.

"That's different. You were younger..."

"And raised to know better. Mother never once condoned what I did. You know that's not true for him. And he wasn't lying about the girl. Taliea said Dagmar told her the same thing."

"One good thing doesn't undo the bad. I never let it with you."

"You also didn't dangle it over my head at every opportunity. Come on, Stephan, you know what I'm saying is true. It's like you're punishing him over and over for the same thing."

Stephan grunted. For a minute Sasha thought they had gone to bed because both had fallen silent. He hadn't heard Hamo at all and wasn't sure he wanted to. It was one thing to hear that Stephan still held everything against him. It would be devastating if Hamo still did after he had told him everything.

"This has to do with how you feel about the northerners, does it?"

"You know how I feel about them, and you know why, Al. They're cruel cowards."

"And he left that. But the way you two are treating him is going to make him want to go back. Nobody should have to want to go back to that kind of life."

"Al, I don't hold any of that against him, but I'm not in a hurry to trust him either. He did kidnap my daughters," Hamo finally spoke up and Sasha almost gave himself away.

"I know. You don't have to trust him, but he needs help. I mean, Hamo, you let Forbes go. A man who tried to murder you, multiple times."

"I can't do anything else for him," Hamo said.

"You could have left him behind. You know King Darien would have seen to it that he was taken care of. Instead, you're dragging him back to the place he's supposed to be hanged and right in the path of his father."

"Well, it's too late to change that. What else are you wanting us to do?"

"Give him a chance to win. He's killing himself trying. At some point it's got to be good enough. It was for me, remember, Stephan?"

The trio lapsed into silence, but Sasha didn't dare assume they had fallen asleep. He lay as quietly as he could, fighting to keep his breathing even and under control.

He was so very thankful Aldrid had come with them. It was nice having someone on your side. His brief hour with Aldrid must have revealed something of his turmoil to this man who was apparently a former thief. Perhaps that's why Aldrid was so quick to come to his defense. Now he just wished he knew how Stephan and Hamo were taking the younger man's words. But they remained silent.

Sasha couldn't remember falling asleep after that. When he woke to the sound of the others up and moving about, his head ached with how poorly he'd slept. Part of him longed to tell Aldrid thank you for taking up his part. The wiser half of him knew it would be a terrible mistake to let any of them know that he'd overheard the discussion.

It wouldn't matter, in the end, anyway. Sasha had made up his mind riding in silence the day before that when all of this was over, he would either be dead because Father won, or he'd move on and find some place where no one knew him and start over - alone.

With that resolution on his mind, the days passed quickly. So quickly, in fact, that Sasha wasn't fully prepared to reach Dorsten when they did. It had taken Dagmar and him at least two days longer to cross the great plains. At the thought of Dagmar, Sasha began to wonder what she would do or where she would go now that she was free. She got on well with everyone at Hamo's house, but Taliea was the only one who understood her. Maybe she would stay with Taliea for a while.

His thoughts were rudely interrupted when his eyes caught sight of something flying towards him and Stephan's voice reached his ears.

"Put that on and keep the hood over your face." Sasha snatched the spinning bundle of cloth out of the air before it smacked him in the face. It was a cloak. "Don't want anyone recognizing you before we've had a chance to clear things up."

Sasha nodded his understanding and fastened the cloak in place, pulling the hood up and letting it overshadow most of his features. They would be riding in just as the sun went down and hopefully no one at the border would be looking too hard at the faces of everyone who passed through.

The hood worked its magic as they stopped at the opening in the forest. The two men who questioned them about their business assumed he was just cold and didn't bother him further.

"How, exactly, are you planning on clearing things up, seeing as how you messed things up so badly last time you were here?" Aldrid asked when they were on their way again, moving toward the town.

"I have a plan for that," Stephan said. Sasha could almost hear him grinning. "Just follow my lead."

The dark outline of the mountains and the castle nestled into the forefront rose up before them as the woods slipped away behind them.

Sasha jerked on his reins sharply, pulling his horse to an abrupt stop. The panic rising in his chest was so like what he felt being trapped in a tight space he couldn't quell it. What if someone recognized him? He could be dead in a matter of hours. If Lord Bayner did get his hands on him again, he certainly wouldn't wait a week before exterminating him. Or maybe he would. He'd hinted at more painful methods of dealing with stubborn captives. Perhaps he would torture him first, worse than before. The memory of those awful days drove his panic to the surface.

"You alright?" Hamo had stopped and waited for him now.

Sasha nodded, biting his lip. He desperately didn't want to go, but if he said anything now, Stephan would probably make a joke out of it. He nudged his horse forward again. When he came abreast of Hamo's, Hamo spoke again quietly, "I'm not going to let them hang you, Sasha. I promise."

Sasha might have shrugged it off as a thoughtful gesture, except for the last two words. However much Hamo might not trust him, he trusted Hamo. Hamo had let him go on a promise, a promise he would have been fully justified in breaking.

Aside from a few main streets and a handful of windows, the town was dark. The darkness was a mercy, giving Sasha the invisibility he needed to not only stay concealed, but also to hide the sick look of fear on his face from his companions.

"Here it is," Stephan said after almost half an hour of riding up one street and down another. He pulled to a stop in front of a large stone house. It was in one of the more spacious parts of town, with a small yard in the front, and a stable in the back.

"I thought we were going to the castle?" Aldrid gave voice to the same question Sasha had been thinking but didn't dare ask.

"We are. This is how we're going to get in."

"Breaking in through someone's house? Interesting."

"No." Stephan turned his back to Aldrid and knocked on the door.

It took two or three times of knocking, each with increasing volume, before Sasha noticed a flicker of light in an upper window. Someone had just lit a candle. A few moments later, the door opened. Sasha clapped a hand over his mouth to suppress the startled yelp that threatened to come out. In the flickering light of a candle stood Norman. This was Stephan's plan? Sasha's heart hit the ground. He'd be turned over to the lord for sure.

"Norman, it's good to see you," Stephan started cheerfully, ignoring the cold look in his brother's eyes.

"Wish I could say the same. Seeing as how you almost lost me my job and my head last time you were here, I suppose you came back to apologize."

"Sure," Stephan maintained his cheerful tone. "I apologize for any trouble I caused you. Can we come in now?"

"Who's we?" Norman tried to peer past him into the mostly dark street. Sasha lowered his head.

"Well, Hamo and some friends of mine."

Norman reluctantly stepped aside and let them in. Sasha kept his head down, hood up, and tried to avoid the light of the single candle.

"Got some place we can talk to you?"

"Stephan, what's this all about?" Norman asked as he led the way to another room. As they passed by the foot of the stairs a woman's voice called softly down, asking who was there. Norman answered, "It's just some friends of mine. Nothing to worry about."

The hearth in the sitting room held still glowing embers that were quickly stirred up into a fire. It was harder to avoid detection with the added light, but Sasha managed to stay mostly behind everyone else.

"You know, if I hadn't had such a good alibi the night you decided to break that boy out of the dungeon, Lord Bayner would have had my head."

"I know. I also only did it because I knew you had a good alibi."

"You're not wanting to see the lord, are you? Because he won't see you. He's sworn vengeance on you for making him look like a fool in front of everyone."

"See, now I thought he did that all on his own."

Norman managed a small, tight smile in response to Stephan's words.

"If you thought he was a fool before, you should have seen when I had to report the condemned as missing an hour before his execution was to take place. A lot of people were looking forward to seeing that. Now why are you here?"

"Got a map?"

Norman scowled but disappeared from the room only to return a moment later with a map in his hand. He laid it out on a small desk.

"You're about to come under attack, here," Stephan pointed to where the pass opened up out of the mountains near the capitol.

"We haven't picked up any kind of news like that. What makes you think we're in danger?"

"He does," Stephan gestured behind himself to where Sasha stood.

Norman looked past Stephan and took in the smaller figure standing behind him. Sasha would have gladly melted into the floor as his throat constricted and the blood drained from his face. He was beginning to question Stephan's motivation in bringing him to this place. Stephan was the one who wasn't going to let him go. Maybe this was his way of undoing what he saw as Hamo's mistake.

"You brought *him* here?" The shock in Norman's raised voice reverberated through the still room. "You know what happens if the lord finds out, don't you?"

"I did and I do." Stephan grew very serious. "And if you're ready to listen to what I have to say, I'll tell you why."

Norman sank into a chair, rubbing the bridge of his nose. He waved a feeble hand for Stephan to continue. It took Stephan only a few minutes to relay the same news that Sasha had ridden days to deliver in the first place. Norman didn't interrupt, although he did lean forward to study the map as Stephan spoke, his face darkening as his brother spoke.

"So, we're here to offer you help. Not just you. Your whole country."

"Why?"

"Because it's the only way we can see saving ours. They mean to have both."

"How did you find out about all this?"

"Sasha came and told us."

"Wait." Norman turned to Sasha. "So, you knew about all this? You knew and you still went through all that questioning just so you could turn around and tell them now? Why didn't you just tell Lord Bayner and make him stop torturing you? It would have made your life a whole lot easier."

"I didn't know anything when he questioned me. Torturing me couldn't make me remember something I never knew," Sasha answered.

Norman shrugged, shaking his head in disbelief. "You deserved it anyway, after what you and the others did to those poor villagers."

Sasha didn't say anything in his own defense. The memory of the charred rubble and shriveled, burnt corpses blurred his vision. It was horrible. What they had done was cruel. And he had been sorry at the time for missing out on it.

"Alright, so you're offering aid in fighting against Aruuk. But I don't think Lord Bayner's going to allow it. He's angry about what happened with him," Norman nodded toward Sasha, "I might be able to convince him to give you an audience but..."

"He'll cooperate if I talk to him," Hamo spoke for the first time.

"What makes you so sure of that?"

"I know something about him."

"What?"

Hamo hesitated. "He kept slaves."

"No." Norman was incredulous. "He wouldn't do that. It's against the law."

"I can prove it."

"How?"

Hamo glanced at Stephan, who shrugged, before rolling up the cuff of his right sleeve. Sasha knew at once what he was doing. There, only a few inches above his hand, faded with time yet still visible. It was a brand. The universal mark of a slave. Norman apparently knew it too. And he recognized the symbol of the brand. He let out a low whistle.

"That liar," he said, leaning back in his chair. "How long ago?"

"Twenty-six years ago was when I was taken. He kept me for nine years."

Norman's face went a shade paler than normal, and he blew out a long breath.

"No wonder he's been so careful to stay on your good side in all those meetings."

"I guess he figures it would be kind of embarrassing for everyone to find out about it," Hamo said.

"Not embarrassing. Fatal. He's not a king. Just a protectorate, and at this point not a very popular one. If word got out about this, he'd lose his position and he'd be hung. That's the penalty for it and people dislike him enough to make sure it's carried out."

"He was going to hang me for something he did himself?" Sasha said quietly to himself. Aldrid, standing the nearest to him, overheard him and met his eyes with a sympathetic smile.

Norman sat lost in thought for several moments.

"We'll need a plan," he said at last. "Even if we convince him to accept your country's help, without a good plan it won't mean a thing. He's a terrible strategist, but he thinks he's not."

"I've been thinking about that." Aldrid moved toward the desk with the map. "Aruuk has no idea we know, right?" He glanced at Sasha for confirmation.

"Unless Father figured out where I went. As far as he knows I'm with the army on the coast."

"So, they think they have the advantage of surprise. They don't. We do. Now, if I were setting a trap for an animal, I would put it in the place the animal feels safest. Somewhere they're not expecting danger. We can do the same thing with them. Where would they be the least likely to expect trouble?" He directed his question at Sasha but both Sasha and Norman answered.

"The mountains."

"Right, the mountains. Look," he drew his finger down the large pass that led into Dorsten, "this is the only place you could fit an army through. It also happens to be a great spot for a trap, an ambush."

For the next hour, the five hovered over the map, constructing the skeleton of a battle plan. At last, Norman seemed satisfied with it. He folded up the map, as well as a piece of paper he'd drawn different notes on and tucked them under his arm.

"How long did you say we have?" he addressed Sasha directly.

"They'll march as soon as the Spring Market is complete. We have maybe two or three weeks to prepare."

"Our own army will be here in less than a week," Stephan added.

"Well, let's go see what the lord has to say about all this." Norman started towards the door. "Actually, you can't come, Sasha. That would be a disaster. And, unfortunately, I don't trust you enough to leave you here by yourself."

"I'll stay back with him," Aldrid said, then added with a smile. "If you trust me to, that is."

"You sure?"

"I'm sure. On the list of people I never want to meet in my life, Lord Bayner is right at the top. Good luck talking to him, though."

Chapter 55

MEREDITH SWUNG HER DANGLING legs back and forth as she sat on the top rail of the fence, trying to blink away the angry tears that burned her eyes. It didn't matter how Father explained it, or how many times Mother said it was necessary, she hated it. First Sasha had taken her and Phelie away from Father, and now he was taking Father away from them.

It wasn't fair, she thought. There were other people who could have gone. Father wasn't the only one on the war council, and he wasn't the only one who had a hand in the peace between Dorsten and Dival.

"Meri!" Taliea called out to her. "Do you want to come with Dagmar and I?"

That was the other thing. Meredith knew it was wrong. Meredith knew she shouldn't feel the way she did. But the little worm of jealousy that had first crept up on her when Taliea and Dagmar discovered their shared nationality just wouldn't go away. Meredith tried to tell herself that Dagmar had gone through so much and it was only right for her to have such a good friend as Taliea. She had no good reason to refuse Taliea's invitation this time. She pushed herself off the fence and hurried to catch up to them.

"Where are you going?"

"Walking to town." When Taliea spoke of town she meant the little nearby village of Hallann that held a small number of merchants and traders. "It's such a beautiful day, and I thought it would be a good way to keep our minds off of things."

Meredith glanced to the side, catching the brief shadow that flitted across Taliea's face as she spoke. It was because Uncle Al was gone this time. Meredith pushed away her own troubled thoughts. Taliea had always tried to keep her spirits up, she would attempt to do the same now.

"It is really a nice day for a walk," she said, smiling brightly and linking her arm into Taliea's. "Let me guess, you want to buy some things for the wedding?"

"Actually, I was thinking we could get some things for Dagmar. The only clothes she has are the ones she was wearing, and I'm pretty sure some of those were Sasha's. The rest aren't fit to wear anywhere but a bedroom." Which is exactly what they were supposed to be for, thought Meredith. "I think, now that she's free, it's high time she had some things of her own."

Dagmar's eyes followed them intently as they spoke. Already she was beginning to pick up words and phrases of their language. Meredith shoved aside her jealousy long enough to meet her eyes with a smile.

The walk was a pleasant one. Meredith pointed out the crocuses that were just pushing their white and purple heads out of the remnants of snow. In the bright spring sunshine, with the warmth on her face and the fresh, faintly earthy scent in the air, it was easy to be happy and forget that Father was gone.

Before she knew it, they had reached Hallann. The streets here were dirt, or mud, not stone like the ones in Bren. Meredith stepped carefully around the puddles of water standing in the street.

"Let's try in there, shall we?" Taliea led the way to the weaver's shop.

Meredith was still the poorer seamstress between Ophelia and her, but she loved going to the weaver's. The colors showcased haphazardly in the shelves were a beautiful sight. The textures were a pleasure to run her fingers across. Of course, the shops in Bren had a much wider variety of both colors and textures, but this was still fun. Meredith had always had a good eye for color, and which ones looked good on different people. Forgetting her troubles easily now, she hurried to the first shelf and pulled out at least half a dozen bolts of brightly colored cloth.

"Here, Dagmar," she called to the girl, making sure to use her name so that she would know she was being addressed. Dagmar made her way over, her eyes darting all about the place, trying to take it all in. Meredith held a length of the first cloth, a deep purple, and draped it over Dagmar's shoulder and under her chin. She stepped back, her eyes narrowing appraisingly.

"That's pretty," Taliea commented, and then spoke a few words with Dagmar. Meredith watched as the girl's face went from confusion to shy pleasure. She reached out a tentative hand and brushed a single finger across a bolt of dark blue.

"You like that one?" Meredith asked and Taliea translated. Dagmar slowly nodded her head and Meredith scooped it up, unraveling a length of it and draping it around her like she'd done with the purple. Against her tan skin and blue eyes, the color was stunning. Meredith grinned.

An hour later, they exited the shop. Meredith carried the parcel of fabrics and ribbons as they continued down the street.

"Where to now?" she asked.

"The baker's."

Another of Meredith's favorite places. Inside, the smell of yeast and fruits mingled together in a sweet aroma. Again, Taliea spoke to Dagmar. Dagmar's eyes widened as she looked at the possibilities in front of her. After a moment she whispered to Taliea, her finger pointing bashfully toward a pastry filled with fruit and sweet cream.

Outside the bakery, Meredith took a bite of the still warm pastry. Dagmar closed her eyes blissfully as she tasted hers. A faint smile tugged at the corners of her mouth and then spread. Meredith realized it was the first time she'd seen Dagmar smile. She smiled back at her.

By late afternoon, they were ready to go home. Each carried at least one package, and Meredith was sure it was the first time Dagmar had done anything at all like that.

"I think she really enjoyed that," Meredith commented.

"I thought she would. I wanted to show her she can make her own choices now. I would say it's been a success, wouldn't you?"

"Well, she smiled."

"So have you."

"Was that part of your goal?"

"Perhaps. It doesn't do anyone any good to sit around brooding over things they can't change. It helped me too."

A whining sound from the side of the road interrupted them. Dagmar spotted it first and pointed it out, speaking rapidly to Taliea. Meredith followed her finger and saw the little black and white bundle of fur. She walked over and crouched down next to it.

"It's a puppy. And it's hurt," she added when she saw that deep red staining it's white fur. "If I carry it home, can we fix it up?"

Dagmar knelt next to her, gently scratching the whimpering animal under the chin. Both girls looked back at Taliea.

"It's not me you have to clear that by, Meri. What is your mother going to say if you bring that thing home?"

"I'll tell her it's for Dagmar. Then she'll let me take care of it."

"If you think so."

Meredith slipped her jacket off and fixed a carrier of sorts for the puppy. Dagmar watched her until she lifted it up, then she held her hands out imploringly.

"You want to carry it?"

Taliea translated and Dagmar nodded. Shrugging, Meredith passed it off. Dagmar took the bundle and held it close to her, fondling the ear that flopped outside. When the puppy stuck its muzzle out and licked her hand, she giggled.

"And now she's laughing. I'd say that's a very good day." Meredith laughed as well.

Chapter 56

SASHA LET OUT A LONG, SLOW breath, watching the way it hung in the cool morning air.

This was it.

Either Father would win today, and Sasha would die, or his new allies would win, and Sasha would start a brand-new life. He still hadn't decided where. His fingers ran up and down the taut bowstring absently.

This was it.

His very first, and hopefully last, battle. For having spent his entire life learning to fight and preparing for raiding and war, Sasha felt woefully unready for this moment. He shouldn't have told Hamo he wanted to do this. Hamo was leery of the idea from the beginning.

"You'll be fighting your own people, Sasha. Are you sure you can do that? You don't have to. You don't have to do this to prove anything to anyone." Except, Sasha was pretty sure he did.

"I've already betrayed them and helped plot their defeat. Besides, if he wins, I *have* to die. I'm not going to be taken alive by him. It'd be easier to die in a battle."

Now, in the tense quiet of the morning, he was regretting his decision. He shut his eyes. It would be over quickly, he told himself. The trap was perfect. They had no idea they were walking into it. Surrounded by the best archers either country could muster on both sides of the long, narrow defile, they would have nowhere to run. It was Aldrid's idea to create a controlled avalanche at either end of the defile, locking whoever was down there in. It would work. They would win.

Sasha felt beads of sweat forming on his forehead and the palms of his hands were getting sticky. He took turns wiping one and then the other on his pant leg. Archery was what he was best at, so it made sense for him to be here. It made more sense knowing that the men hiding in the rocks around him were mostly from Dival and could not possibly recognize him as the condemned escapee that Lord Bayner wanted so badly to get his hands on.

The whispers of the other men, most of whom knew each other just added one more layer to Sasha's already thick blanket of loneliness. These men would fight together. They would look out for each other. They were, in every sense of the word, comrades. He wasn't. No one would have his back. No one would scour the battlefield searching for his wounded or dead body.

He was alone.

A rustle behind him sent him spinning around. Norman was back there. He commanded the regular foot soldiers, should the archers' positions be overrun. Norman was too preoccupied with squinting into the thick fog that clung to the mountains to notice Sasha, which was fine with Sasha. The man was uncommonly like Stephan, Sasha thought. He was comfortable around neither of them.

Sasha squirmed. The sharp rocks dug into his knees and shins. Sasha shifted into a different position. He was bored. He reached behind him and fingered the feathered ends of his arrows, mindlessly counting them. Three dozen. Exactly what he had put in there the night before. He wondered if he would end up using all of them. Three dozen was a lot of men to kill. Sasha tried to push away the image of the man he'd shot in the back. It was the only time he'd used his bow against a person.

"Don't think about it," he whispered to himself, "Just do it. If they win, you die."

When he caught sight of the signal flag just to the left of their position, Sasha tensed. This was it. They were coming. *Don't think about it. Just do it. Don't think about it.* He pulled an arrow out. *Just do it. If they win.* He nocked it onto his string. *I die.* He adjusted his fingers' hold. *Don't think about it.* Boris was going to be in the front ranks. *Just do it.* He couldn't protect Boris. *If they win.* Odds were, he wouldn't even recognize him from up here. *I die.*

Sasha took a deep breath. And then another, forcing his lungs to slow down, willing his heart to stop racing.

The first sounds of an army on the march reached his ears. The tramp of men and the clang of metal. As if on cue, the thick fog evaporated, revealing the column of the long-awaited enemy. His people.

Sasha's heart thudded against his ribs, threatening to pound its way straight out of his chest. He tightened his grip on the limb of the bow. He slowly let the tension out of his clenched hand, wishing it would leave the rest of his body as well.

Further into the defile they came, oblivious to their own danger. Sasha had an almost irrepressible urge to stand up and shout out a warning. These were his people. Sasha fought down the urge. They were coming to murder and enslave innocent people. He didn't want to be a part of that ever again. Deeper and deeper they marched into the trap. The trap that was so perfectly set. Dorsten dangled like the bait on the other side of the pass.

Sasha cast one last glance at the men around him. The whispers were gone. Grim faced men peered out from behind their hiding places, waiting for the signal that would spring the trap. The signal that would ignite the slaughter.

Sasha looked to the left where he knew the signal flag would come up when they were to open fire. A flash of red. A shrill whistle. And the mountainside came silently alive. It wasn't until the first volley of arrows sailed into the thin column below that the men in the pass became aware of their position. The noise that erupted was unearthly. Echoing off the steep, impassable sides of the mountains swelled. Cries of pain mingled with yells of surprise. Anger mixed with commands.

Sasha tried to block out the sounds. Especially the sounds of pain. He drew his string back, aiming only halfheartedly at the squirming mass of humanity that was just now realizing its plight. He held his breath and released. He watched the arrow snaking through the air. It was lost from sight amidst the hundreds of others. Sasha knew it didn't miss, though. There was no way anyone could miss a target this big.

Another arrow was on his string. His fingers pulling back. His breath steadying. He didn't need to think. He could just do it. He let the string slide forward, off his fingertips. Another arrow. Another shot. Don't think about it, just do it. If they win, I die.

In the distance to the left, the ground trembled. A low rumble, growing in intensity, came in beneath the shouts and cries of the trapped men. A cloud of dust filled the far end of the pass. The trap was sprung. Sasha didn't allow himself to think. Another arrow. Another shot. It was getting easier. He was growing numb to everything happening around him. Numb to everything except the bow in his hands and the arrows he sent flying towards the bottom of the pass.

The sun rose higher. Sasha reached behind his back. His fingers closed around nothing but air. Empty, again. Still numb to anything going on beyond his immediate surroundings, he crawled back to where they had barrels full of arrows to replenish the archers. With meticulous care that defied the moment entirely, Sasha started counting out exactly thirty-six more arrows and sliding them into his quiver, checking each one before selecting it.

A shout followed by the loud clang of metal striking metal finally broke through the numbness. Sasha spun around. His brain refused to believe what his eyes saw. Only twenty yards away, right where his position had been, a chaotic skirmish was taking place. Sasha's eyes darted about, taking it in without understanding. There were around twenty Aruuken men there. Left with no way out, their desperation had driven them to scale the steep mountain side. Norman and his own men had moved forward to engage them. Sasha's eyes widened in horror as he realized he was looking right at Norman. And he was about to watch him die. Norman was bleeding from one arm already as a man bore down on him, his sword poised to strike him down.

Sasha's fingers worked before his mind quite caught up. The arrow was already in the air before he registered what he'd done. It was close enough that he could see the Aruuken's face. It was one of his oldest half-brothers, one whose name utterly escaped him now. He watched the arrow slide straight into his shoulder. Saw the man's eyes widen with pain and surprise, and then fix on Sasha.

Sasha scrambled backwards. His bow was the only weapon he had. He stumbled against a barrel and the man was on him. It was falling backwards that mostly spared him the first blow. Rather than decapitating him as was intended, the sword slid from his shoulder at the base of his neck down to his chest, leaving a bright red trail as it descended. Sasha watched in horror as the blade pierced an inch, two inches into his own chest. He gasped as air rushed from him. The pain came a moment later.

His vision swimming, he barely scrambled backward in time to avoid another deadly blow. This time, the pain was instant and intense. The sword cut deep into his leg, reaching the bone. Sasha screamed, but no sound came out. Satisfied, his half-brother turned away and rejoined the fight.

Sasha sucked in air, but it was not enough. Between the black dots that danced before his eyes, he saw his own blood gushing from both his chest and leg. It was his leg that was draining him fastest. Sasha reached a limp hand forward, his brain telling him he had to put pressure on it, or he would die. He. Would. Die.

"You traitor!" The words screamed in his face barely registered. Sasha looked up. Boris. His brother's face was twisted in rage. "How could you?"

Sasha tried to speak. The black in his eyes was thickening. Each breath was an agonized gasp. He was dying. Boris raised his sword. He was dying. And Boris would be the one to kill him. Sasha felt his life leaving him with the flow of blood. He didn't want to die. Not like this. Not alone. Not staring into Boris' hate-filled face.

His eyes clouded over entirely. The noise of battle turned into a dull roar in his ears. Even the pain disappeared with the loss of consciousness.

No one would care. No one would be bothered by his passing. All the good he had tried to do didn't matter. It all ended in dark, lonely death.

Chapter 57

THE BATTLEFIELD, IF IT COULD be called that, reeked of blood and death. Hamo swallowed down the bile that had risen at the stench. The fight hadn't even reached the spot he was in. Aldrid's trap had been perfect. Baited and drawn in, lulled to complacency by their own confidence, the Aruukens were slaughtered. What was left of their army, the part that had escaped the trap, had fled. A significant portion of the Dorstenian army had pursued, hunting down groups of stragglers for many hours.

Hamo surveyed the scene before him. Twenty-six years ago, he'd fought these people. They were cruel. Merciless. Ruthless. And yet, gazing out at the rocky ground littered with their dead and dying, they were human.

Hamo picked his way forward, avoiding the spots slick with blood and gore. He'd seen all this before. He remembered holding a man like one of these twenty-six years ago, killed by his own hand. He'd hated himself and everything about war in that moment. Letting his gaze pass over a mutilated corpse, he realized he still hated everything about war. The pitiful sounds of the dying were harder to block out than the sights and smells. The cries were endless. Even without knowing their tongue, Hamo was sure what most of them were asking for. The most basic human desire of all. The desire to live.

Hamo shook his head in disgust. He wasn't sure why he even came down here. He didn't want to be reminded that the enemy they had spent all morning destroying were in fact human beings and not soulless monsters.

He started back up the slope, his thoughts drawn again to the day he'd killed his first man in battle. That day was awful. Father had been there. Promising Hamo that he would never face his greatest fear. Promising him he wouldn't have to die alone. Hamo stopped and frowned. He looked up at the positions the archers had held. They had lined the entire pass on both sides. Most suffered few casualties, although there were a few places where the enemy grew desperate enough to try to climb their way out. Some succeeded.

Hamo started up again, his steps quicker, more purposeful this time. He made his way up out of the pass, and through the milling group of men. Here and there, wounded were being brought in. Hamo gave each one that he saw a brief glance before moving on. He caught sight of Aldrid moving to intercept him.

"You look like you're going somewhere?" Al asked, a half-smile disguising his disgust for the sight in front of them.

"I am. You haven't seen Sasha come back, have you?"

"No. But that doesn't mean anything, there's a lot of men around here, and he's supposed to be avoiding being seen."

"I know." Hamo started off again, Al trailing behind him.

"I have to be honest, I almost wish it hadn't worked as well as it did," Aldrid said quietly as they followed the trail that ran along the top of the pass. "What a horrible way to die."

"It is."

"You're worried about him."

"I am. I shouldn't have made him come. And I definitely shouldn't have allowed him to fight." Hamo shouldered past a group of men carrying their wounded friend toward the makeshift infirmary.

He reached the area he knew Sasha had been. He had picked it out himself because he didn't want him being recognized by someone from Dorsten. Pausing, he took in the spot. Bodies sprawled across the ground. Men from both sides lay twisted up in the gruesome distortions of death. This was one of the spots the enemy had broken through.

Hamo moved to the first body. Turning it over gently, he grimaced at the sight. Whoever it was, they were no longer recognizable by their face. It was nothing but a bloody mass of gore. Aldrid made a sick sound behind him before moving on to check other bodies. Thirty minutes of searching, and helping those that they could, failed to produce the one person they were looking for.

"Maybe he's already back with the others at camp. It's getting dark. No one's going to want to be stuck out here at night," Aldrid said.

"Maybe. We didn't pass him coming up here, did we?"

"I don't think so."

Hamo turned slowly around, taking in the entire area one last time before heading back.

"Al, look." Hamo hurried toward the overturned barrel, and the body that was just barely visible behind it.

Even before the face came into view, Hamo knew who it was.

"He's dead," Aldrid said after taking one look at Sasha's lifeless gray face. The copious pool of blood staining his clothes and the ground around him was shocking.

Hamo knelt in the blood-soaked dirt, his hand going straight to Sasha's neck, his fingers feeling for a pulse he was sure was already gone. He shook his head, taking in the gaping hole in his chest, blood bubbling gently out of it rhythmically. And his leg. Hamo's face grew puzzled. Sasha's leg had bled profusely. But it had been stopped. Someone had bound a belt around it, cutting off the fatal flow of blood. A flutter against his fingertips startled Hamo.

"Go, get someone to help us carry him down. He needs a surgeon," Hamo almost yelled the words at his brother. He reached for the tunic of a dead soldier nearby and pulled it off. Using it to push against the sucking wound in his lung, he pulled Sasha's own belt free and used it to hold the balled-up cloth in place. "Come on, Sasha. Don't die on me now. We won. You can't die."

By the time Aldrid returned a few minutes later with a couple of men, Hamo had taken the cloak off another dead body and had Sasha wrapped up in it. Together, the four men lifted his limp body onto a stretcher and carried him toward the infirmary that had been set up in preparation for the battle.

It was dark by the time they reached it. Torches and lanterns kept the area around the large tents well-lit despite the night. They set the stretcher down a short distance from the nearest tent.

"What if someone recognizes him?" Aldrid whispered to Hamo.

"He'll die unless a surgeon can drain and close his lung. We'll just have to risk it."

"I guess you can always just threaten the lord with telling his people the truth."

"I will if I have to. Wait here with him, I'm going to find a surgeon."

Hamo wasn't long in finding one. Recognizable both by the amount of blood splattered on them, and the thick white aprons they wore, several of them hurried about the inside of the tent, tending to men. Hamo approached the first.

"We have someone outside that needs help."

"So does everyone else," the man snapped, then looked like he regretted it. "I'm sorry, sir. There's a lot of wounded men that need tending. There's only so much I can do. What're your friend's wounds?"

"Chest and leg. He's got a punctured lung and he's lost a lot of blood."

The surgeon nodded along as Hamo spoke, his hands never ceasing from their task.

"Bring him in here, and put him right there," he jerked his chin to an empty spot on the floor. "I'll see what I can do for him. If he's lost too much blood, it won't be much."

"Thank you."

"And once you put him there, I don't need you hanging around. It's cramped enough in here as it is."

Having deposited Sasha where the surgeon told them to, Hamo stepped outside of the tent. The sight of several wounded Aruukens inside the tent made him feel a little easier about leaving Sasha in there. Not everyone was looking for vengeance at least. Hamo looked around the circle of tents, each one overflowing with wounded. He was tired.

"Guess who never showed up to the fight?" Stephan pushed through a cluster of men to approach them.

"I have no idea."

"Lord Bayner. You should hear what people are saying." He glanced around and lowered his voice, "This might not end well for everyone. People are starting to talk about how the lord doesn't care what happens to them. That it took the rightful king to save them. There's talk of replacing him. Where's Sasha?"

"He's dying," Hamo answered dully. "In there."

"Dying? What happened?"

"Position was overrun. He got wounded," Aldrid answered.

"I see. I'm sorry to hear that. Do you think it was a good idea putting him in there? What if someone recognizes him?"

"It's the only chance he's got. He's in bad shape, not something we could just throw a bandage on and call it good, you know," Aldrid said.

"I see. You two should get some rest. You look terrible."

"I'm going to wait a bit, see what the surgeon says," Hamo said.

It wasn't until many hours later that the surgeon emerged from the tent. He seemed surprised to find Hamo still waiting outside.

"Is he..."

"He's barely alive at the moment. Whoever tied off his leg probably saved his life. If he pulls through the night, he's got a chance."

"Thanks."

"You can go in and see him now if you like. Just don't wake him and don't try to get him to talk or move if he does happen to wake up on his own."

Hamo slipped inside the tent and Aldrid followed. It was noisy, just like out on the battlefield. He made his way to the side of Sasha's stretcher and sat down. The boy's face was still a pasty gray making his black hair stand out starkly as it stuck to his clammy skin. His lips were completely colorless from lack of blood. Several blankets covered him, but his skin was still chilled. He was turned on his side and propped up so that the blood would continue to drain from the punctured lung. His leg was encased in a thick bandage. Spots of red were visible against the white as blood continued to seep through.

"I'm going to get some sleep. I'll come back in a few hours if you want, and you can get some rest while I sit with him," Aldrid offered.

Hamo nodded, settling back against the side of the tent and eventually falling asleep.

An urgent voice came from directly in front of him. "Hamo, wake up."

Hamo opened his eyes. It took him a second to realize he'd fallen asleep sitting up next to Sasha's stretcher. Norman crouched down in front of him, his right arm in a sling.

"What time is it?" Hamo asked.

"Around four in the morning. Listen to me, you've got to go," Norman lowered his voice to a barely audible whisper, glancing quickly around the tent to make sure no one was listening. Hamo strained to catch his words. "You have to get that boy and get him out of here. The lord's gone crazy. There's been talk through the night about how people don't think he's fit to rule any more. Anyway, he's lost it. Flew into a rage. I don't know who or how, but someone told him you brought Sasha back and he's vowing vengeance on both of you. I don't think he cares any more about people finding anything out, either. He's just completely lost it. Says the whole thing was set up to make him look bad, and that you're the one behind it. He wants you dead."

Hamo stared at Norman, not quite understanding him. He rubbed a tired hand over his face.

"Look, Sasha saved my life. He shot the man trying to kill me. I'll help you get him to the border, and then you've got to move as fast as you can. It's one thing for Lord Bayner to kill the boy. But if he kills you too, like he's saying he wants to, it'll be war."

"He can't be moved," Hamo argued.

"Lord Bayner's already sent his personal guard after him, and you. Either he moves or he dies."

Hamo looked down at Sasha. He hadn't moved even a little throughout the night. His face was still colorless, his breathing still dangerously shallow and slow. By all appearances, he was dying. He'd faced the same thing with his own father twenty-six years ago. Certain death or probable death.

"Alright. Do you know where Stephan or Al are?"

"Waiting for you outside. I found them first. Stephan's got a wagon and team. I have a few men I can trust. We'll get you as far as the border safely, but you're on your own after that."

Hamo let out a heavy sigh as he got to his feet. He hated these decisions.

"Help me get him to the wagon."

There was no one else awake in the tent at the moment, and in a few seconds Sasha's unconscious body was lying in the back of the wagon. Stephan had furnished it with as much bedding as he could lay his hands on and Hamo arranged it so that Sasha was still propped up on his side. He slid a small pillow beneath his head, eliciting the first sign of life they'd had from the boy in the form of a soft moan.

"Alright, he's ready." Hamo nodded to Stephan sitting in the front of the wagon.

None of the handful of men still awake challenged their movements. Norman was a familiar and trusted face, and their total victory during the day rendered them unsuspicious. Even so, Hamo pulled one of the blankets over Sasha's face enough that it was concealed from any inquisitive eyes while still giving him space to breathe. As the light of camp fell behind them, Hamo turned to Norman, riding next to the side of the wagon.

"So, what exactly happened?"

"By the time I made it back to report, someone else had already reached him and told him about Sasha. He was furious, as you can imagine. Went off on a tirade about how you set him up. Said this whole thing was nothing but a way to incite his own people to insurrection. Before I was there thirty minutes, he'd convinced himself that Sasha was your spy, that your King sent his army not to help us but to overthrow us, and that you and the others were stirring up his own people against him."

"None of which is true," Aldrid commented. "Is he always like that?"

"He's always been an egotistical leader who likes having his own way. It's gotten worse over time. The worst of it is, there have been rumors. I don't know who started them. But there's a significant group of people calling for his removal from power. The fact that he holed up in the castle while we fought hasn't worked in his favor either. There are men saying that since Darien is the only heir from either Dorsten or Dival, that he is entitled to the rule of both countries."

"And what do you think?" Stephan turned partially in his seat to look at his brother.

"That's not something I'm free to talk about," Norman answered quietly.

The sun rose on the little caravan, revealing just how far they had come in those few hours. They were nearing the last stretch of the pass. Soon they would be in the open country beyond the mountains, in plain sight of the town as they moved toward the forest and border.

"How long do you think it will be before they find out we've left?" Aldrid asked, searching the pass behind them.

"A while," Norman said, his voice oddly tight.

"How's that? You said he'd already sent his men."

Norman didn't answer.

"You were the men sent," Stephan said.

Norman remained tightlipped, only the briefest flicker of acknowledgement in his eyes.

Hamo pulled back the blankets enough to reveal Sasha's face. There was no change. His hand touched his neck, feeling the feeble pulse that beat there. At least he'd made it through the night. Now he just had to make it home. Studying the blood drained face now, Hamo seriously doubted the chances of such a thing.

Hours later, and still without pursuit, the forest, just budding with green in the warm spring air closed in around them. Then they were through it, the Void stretched out before them like a vast sea of brown and green. A hand signal from Norman stopped the four soldiers accompanying them well inside the tree line, but he rode a little way out with them.

"I'm sorry it's come to this," Norman said as they stopped briefly to bid him farewell. "You deserve better for what you've done, saving not just your own people but ours. He deserves better." He glanced toward the still form in the back of the wagon. "I can't say anything for sure, but I don't think we'll be under a protectorate for much longer."

"Thank you, Norman," Aldrid said for them all. "We won't forget this."

"I doubt I'll be by for a visit any time soon, but you're welcome at my place," Stephan added.

"I'll keep it in mind. Here," Norman untied a leather saddle bag from off his horse and tossed it lightly to Hamo, "I'm sorry it's all I could get my hands on. Good luck to you all. I hope he makes it." Norman raised his hand briefly before wheeling his mount around and disappearing into the woods.

"Well, that's it, then." Stephan sighed, then lifted the reins and brought them back down again with a slap. The horses started forward again. "Let's get home."

Waves of pain rolled over Sasha, pushing him down, deeper and deeper into the abyss of nothingness. Every time he tried to surface, the waves redoubled their efforts. He was too weary to fight them off, to push through them. There was just blackness. Blackness and pain and cold. Sasha gave up.

Above him, Hamo loosened the ties holding the saddle bag closed. Inside, a bag of dried herbs, a tin of ointment, and several white rolls of bandages were the sole contents.

Hamo cupped a pinch of the herbs in the palm of his hand to study them. Their scent was anchored to an uncomfortable memory. It drug him back to Drogo's quarters, lying flat on his stomach, his back shredded by Forbes' whip, pain coursing through his body. The drink Drogo gave him smelled the same. The drink had driven away the monstrous pain. It had lulled him to sleep. The ointment was just as familiar, and for all the same reasons. Drogo had slathered it across the open, bloody stripes, staving off the chance of infection.

It may have been all Norman could get his hands on, but Hamo thought it would be enough. Hoped it would be enough. His torn up back had been painful, not life threatening.

Sasha stirred slightly beside him for the first time, a second faint moan reaching Hamo's ears.

"Can we keep moving or should we stop?" Stephan asked.

"Keep moving, I guess. We should probably get as much distance as we can between us and Dorsten."

Hamo pulled the blankets down enough to get a good look at the bandage covering Sasha's chest. It was soaked with blood. Hamo hoped it was just the blood that had seeped into his lungs and was now draining out. Sasha couldn't afford to lose any more blood. Carefully, trying to keep his hands steady in spite of the lurching of the wagon beneath him, he undid the dressing and applied a clean one. He moved down to Sasha's leg, relieved to find that the only blood on this bandage was dried and brown. It had been hours since this wound bled.

They pressed on through the day. It wasn't until the sun was low in the sky that Hamo suggested stopping. They'd left in too much of a hurry to bring anything with them to burn, so the fire, built from grass, died quickly and was barely enough to heat the water Hamo mixed the herbs into.

Sasha was closer to consciousness than he had been all day. Even with his eyes shut, his face twisted in a grimace of pain. A raspy cough was followed by a breathless moan. His blue eyes fluttered open. His hand reached jerkily for his chest, and he tried to lift his head up.

"Lie still, Sasha." Hamo's hand pushed him gently back down. Sasha's eyes closed for a moment, and then blinked open again, fear clouding them. His breathing quickened in panic. "It's alright. We're going to take care of you. We're going to get you home."

Pain, and something unreadable, flooded his face and his breathing grew more labored for several minutes.

"Don't have... home," Sasha whispered hoarsely through ragged, gasping breaths.

Hamo opened his mouth to answer but couldn't. He lifted Sasha's head slightly. Placing the rim of the cup against his still colorless lips, he poured the pain numbing beverage down his throat. Sasha coughed again, sucking in shallow gulps of air as he spewed the bitter liquid out. A hoarse whimper escaped his lips.

"Swallow it. It will help," Hamo said as he coaxed more into his mouth. Sasha swallowed slowly. Within a few minutes, the grimace on his face softened. His breath still came in ragged gasps, but the rest of his body relaxed as the pain slid away.

"How's he doing?" Aldrid leaned over the side of the wagon.

"Still breathing."

"I can hear that. He sounds awful, doesn't he?"

"You were right. I shouldn't have brought him. The only reason he even fought was because he thought he had to prove himself. He's going to die, and it'll be my fault."

"You know I usually love hearing that I'm right about something," Al smiled sadly, "But I think I'm just sorry this happened at all."

Hamo nodded.

"Why don't you let me sit with him for a bit while you get some sleep?" Al offered.

"Get me if he wakes up, would you?"

"Sure." Aldrid climbed up into the back of the wagon, trading places with Hamo. "You know, aside from the fact that it's not you laying there, this feels a bit like old times. Running away, trying to keep somebody alive, all because Lord Bayner is such an awful person. I'm really starting to hate that man."

"Well, you managed to keep me alive. Maybe we'll manage to keep him alive, too."

"Sure we will."

Hamo wished for just a fraction of Aldrid's optimism.

He wished for it even more as the next few days went by. The thread of life that Sasha dangled from frayed dangerously. On the third morning, they woke to find him flushed and feverish. The fourth evening he began coughing up blood and mucus. He didn't speak again since his three words to Hamo on the first day. On the fifth day, as they reentered Dival, Sasha opened glassy, dazed eyes and raved deliriously. No one could understand him as he slipped back into his native tongue.

Somewhere, deep beneath the surface of feverish pain, Sasha's dreams darkened. Phantoms of his past blended in a dissonant melody of fear and torment. He wanted to scream at times, he wanted to cry, he wanted to beg the dreams to go away. But he never had enough air to do it. He was suffocating. Trapped in this shadowland. Not alive, but not dead either. Swallowed up by the smothering darkness. It was inescapable. And he was terrified of it.

Chapter 58

MEREDITH BOUNCED BABY DROGO on her knee while Mother put the younger girls to bed. Sitting on the floor near the light of the fire, her knees drawn up to her chest with a book resting across them, Ophelia was lost in her reading.

"You should be asleep," Meredith whispered to Drogo. His dark eyes stared back at her, unblinking. "Yes, you should be. What are you thinking keeping us all awake like this?"

Drogo stuck his fist into his mouth and Meredith smiled at him.

"Meri, did you hear that?" Ophelia looked up suddenly from her book.

Meredith cocked her head, listening. The faint sound of wagon wheels was just audible. She started to say something to Phelie when the front door flew open.

"Uncle Al? What's..."

"Oh, good. You're still up. Go get Taliea. Tell her we need her right away." Uncle Al barely finished the words before turning around and running back out, leaving the door hanging wide open. Meredith felt the blood drain from her face. Needing Taliea meant only one thing. And if they were coming here, it was because of Father.

"Here, I'll take him. Go." Ophelia snatched Drogo out of her arms and Meredith sprinted out the door.

Even in the dark, she knew every step of the way there. She ran for as long as she could, then settled into a brisk walk. A light in the front window told her Taliea was still up as well. Pushing herself into a jog again, she reached the door and pounded on it.

"Meri? What's wrong? You look like you've seen a ghost," Taliea asked as she pulled the door open.

Meredith tried to catch her breath before speaking. "Uncle Al sent me. They're back and he says he needs you. I think it might be Father. Please, come quickly."

Taliea's eyebrows knit together with concern. She motioned Meredith into the house and started moving around quickly.

"Of course, I'll come. Did he say what was wrong?"

"No."

"Hmmm." Taliea pulled a satchel off a hook and went to the shelf that lined the far wall. Swiftly she selected several jars off the shelf and put them in the satchel. Dagmar, who chose to stay with Taliea most nights, came into the room. She rubbed her eyes and yawned before speaking to Taliea. When Taliea started out the door, Dagmar pulled a shawl over her shoulders and followed.

The return trip seemed agonizingly slow. Meredith was tempted to dash ahead but restrained herself. At last, the house came into sight. A wagon, the horses still hitched to it and apparently forgotten for the moment, stood just in front of the still open door. Meredith gave the bed of the wagon a cursory glance before going inside. Aside from a few blankets, it was empty.

Inside the front room, Ophelia stood, Drogo still in her arms. Meredith met her eyes and was surprised to find her twin not as devastated as she was. Priscilla, newly awakened, stood next to her. Her wide eyes never left the bedroom door.

"Where...," Taliea started to ask.

"In there. I told them to put him in my bed. Sorry, Meri," Ophelia answered, the expression on her face unreadable to Meredith.

A hoarse scream followed by a murmur of voices came from her bedroom as Meredith trailed behind Taliea towards it.

Even with his back to her, kneeling by the bed, Meredith recognized Father. Relief gave way to curiosity. Grandfather was there too, and Uncle Al. Meredith's curiosity grew. Mother stood off to the side, one hand over her mouth.

Father was holding someone down on the bed with Uncle Al's help. Meredith could see the person's legs thrashing, kicking off the blankets that had been covering him. Taliea moved to the bed, setting her satchel down on the little table next to the head of the bed.

Meredith stepped to the side enough to see past Grandfather. The figure on the bed started coughing, a horrible, rasping cough that ended in a gurgle of fluid. Meredith's own hand flew to her mouth as she recognized Sasha. Dark blood flecked the skin around his mouth. His blue eyes were wide open but glazed, not seeing anything in the room. Aside from the feverish flush in his cheeks, his skin was a deathly pallor. Another breathless scream came from him.

With Father and Uncle Al still holding him down, Taliea pulled away the bloody bandage that covered his chest, revealing not only a long, shallow gash from his neck to his chest but also a deep, bloody hole through his lung. Blood bubbled up from it, and angry red lines sprawled like a web across his skin. Meredith saw Mother's face go green and Mother stepped toward the door. Meredith decided it was a good time for her to leave as well.

Out in the sitting room, Ophelia had rocked Drogo to sleep and laid him in his cradle, and now she and Dagmar sat together on the couch. Priscilla sat on the floor in front of the fire, staring into it, trying to stay awake.

Stephan came out behind Meredith and shut the door, muffling the horrible sounds Sasha was making. Meredith couldn't decide if they were supposed to be words or if it was merely garbled nonsense produced by his delirium. Probably a mixture of both. As agonized as they sounded, she was glad she couldn't understand.

"Dagmar, what's wrong?" Mother asked and Meredith looked over to see that tears had filled the former slave girl's eyes, her expression deeply disturbed.

"He cries," Dagmar's face scrunched up in a thoughtful frown as she tried to find the words in their language, "want mother."

"I kind of wish I didn't know that," Ophelia said.

Now Meredith wished she could clamp her hands over her ears and forever block out the words. She preferred not knowing, too.

"Edith, I'm going to head home. But if there's anything you need, anything, send one of the girls for me. I don't know what Taliea will be able to do for him, if anything, but if you think it's too much for the little ones, I'm sure Alina wouldn't mind keeping them for a few days," Stephan said quietly.

"I don't know how he's even still alive." Edith's face had yet to return to a normal color. "Why did you bring him here? I mean, surely, they had healers and surgeons over there. Moving him had to have made it worse."

"It did. But we didn't have a choice. I'll leave it for Hamo to tell you, but we really had to bring him. It was the only chance he had."

"Poor thing. Crying for his mother, too." Edith shook her head. "It's awful."

Meredith sat down in a chair opposite Ophelia and Dagmar. Her eyes went again to Dagmar's face. The girl pitied for her former master. Meredith could see it all over her stricken face. Meredith wouldn't have believed it possible. All she felt for him was a dull sense of horror at seeing someone in so much pain.

Meredith jumped a little as another cry, this one louder than the last, filled the house and ended in the same wet coughing, retching sound, only this time the coughing didn't stop right away. Meredith heard Father's voice raised but couldn't understand what he was saying. Dagmar buried her face in her hands. It had to be awful, Meredith thought, understanding every tortured word.

The bedroom door was flung open, and Taliea came out.

"Edith, can you put some water on to boil." Meredith watched as Mother hurried to the stove. "Meri, I need you to go back to my house and get some things for me. Can you do that?"

Meredith nodded mutely. She would do anything to get away from the scene.

"Good." Taliea rattled off a list that included several different medicines, a scalpel, her suturing supplies, and a handful of other items. Meredith made a mental note of each, trying to remember where Taliea kept them all. Meredith had never seen Taliea worried or flustered. Listening to her now, she realized her friend was both. "The faster you get them, the better."

Meredith was more than happy to leave the house and the pitiful sounds behind. She was halfway across the clearing before she realized Ophelia was just behind her.

"I can't just sit there and listen to that," Ophelia said, catching up to her side. "Who would have thought we'd be trying to save his life a few months after he kidnapped us?"

"Not me. Does it make you feel sorry for him?"

"A little. I mean, even Dagmar doesn't hate him right now. I think she feels bad for him. He really must have treated her better than she thought he would."

Aside from the dying fire in the hearth, Taliea's house was dark. Meredith found a candle and lit it from the fire. Moving around the familiar room, Meredith grabbed one thing after another from Taliea's list and shoved it into her sister's arms. Ophelia, in turn, packed them into a bag. Meredith reached for the last thing Taliea had told her to get and froze. A jar full of dried white berries. Snowkiss. Did Taliea really need that?

"What's taking you so long? Taliea said to hurry," Ophelia spoke up behind her.

"Nothing." Meredith brushed her doubts aside and grabbed the jar. "This is it. Let's go."

A part of her that Meredith didn't want to admit existed at the moment hoped that it would all be over by the time they got home. It would be easier that way. And merciful. They could say they tried everything they could to save him, but that it was too late. She would be able to feel like she'd magnanimously forgave Sasha by helping him, but that he was too far gone to truly be saved. It really would be kinder. She'd seen the gaping hole in his chest, the froth of blood and pus oozing from it. She'd seen the feverish seizures that wracked his body. He wouldn't survive. It would be a mercy for him to die sooner rather than suffer longer.

Stepping inside the house, she knew he was still alive. The screams were faded to whimpers. Meredith took a deep breath before opening the bedroom door. Taliea glanced up from where she was bending over the body. He still convulsed wildly. They had rolled him onto his side, and Meredith felt sick as she saw the fluid draining away from his lung.

"Oh, good. You're back. Did you get everything?"

Meredith nodded, holding out the bag. Taliea dumped the contents on the small table and sorted through them quickly.

"Here, Meri. I need you to do one more thing for me. Take this," Taliea held out a jar and pushed it into Meredith's hands, "Crush one of them up and add just a few grains of it to the tea your mother has ready."

Meredith stared at the jar, shaking her head.

"I can't. I killed people with this," she cried, holding the container back out to Taliea. "What if I put too much in?"

"Meri," Father looked up at her for the first time, "Please do it. You won't put too much in."

Meredith couldn't argue with Father, not right now. She took the jar and went to the kitchen. A cup sat on the table, steam curling up from the reddish-brown liquid. Meredith carefully crushed one of the berries. It crumbled easily into a coarse powder. Pinching up just the tiniest amount, Meredith held it over the cup. She hesitated. She put a few grains back on the counter with the rest of the berries. She went back to the cup. Slowly, she let the powder slip from between her thumb and forefinger and watched it dissolve immediately. As soon as it disappeared, Meredith was sure she'd put too much in. Maybe she should tell Taliea to only give him a sip or two.

"Meri, is it ready?" Taliea opened the bedroom door and called softly.

"I'm bringing it now."

Meredith handed the cup off to Taliea and anxiously watched as Father lifted Sasha up enough for Taliea to pour it into his mouth. Their first few attempts ended with the tea spilling down his chin. Meredith noticed his body was trembling violently now and it was difficult to keep the cup in place. At last, he swallowed some of it.

Meredith held her breath. It had taken the guards several minutes before the berries took effect. Time seemed suspended. Sasha still shook, he still thrashed, his body still fought some unknown horror. His breathless voice still murmured and cried out softly. Meredith was beginning to think she hadn't put enough in, when she watched his entire body go slack. He lay still and quiet.

"Please tell me I didn't just kill him," Meredith whispered. It certainly looked as if he was devoid of life.

"You didn't," Father said. "He's still breathing."

Now Meredith could hear it too. Wheezing, shallow breaths drawn painfully into his lungs. He lay limp in Father's arms as Father lowered him once more on to the pillow. Meredith withdrew to the sitting room before Taliea could ask her to do anything else. Even with Sasha quiet, and the hour very late, it was a long time before Meredith succumbed to sleep, curled up in a chair.

A brilliant shaft of morning sunlight rested on Meredith's face. Although not enough to wake her entirely, it was enough to make her conscious of how uncomfortable she was. Half asleep, she shifted, and nearly fell out of the chair.

Blinking against the bright light, Meredith sat up all the way and looked around her. Ophelia and Dagmar were the only other ones in the room, and they were both asleep as well. Rubbing a hand over her stiff neck Meredith let her feet slide back down to the floor. The house was quiet. Strangely quiet.

Meredith yawned and stood up, tiptoeing into the kitchen. It was empty. Meredith's forehead crinkled up in a puzzled frown. Mother and Father never slept this late. With another yawn, Meredith tried to sort through last night. She must have fallen asleep very late, and even then, Mother and Father were still up. No wonder they weren't awake yet.

Mother had banked up the fire in the stove late last night to heat water for Taliea. There was only a little work required for Meredith to get it going again. Filling the kettle with water, she said it on the stove.

"What's going on?" Nora stood in the kitchen doorway, still rubbing her eyes.

"Shhh, everyone's still sleeping."

"I know. That's why I asked." Nora looked peeved. She came all the way into the kitchen and sat down. "I had a weird dream last night."

Meredith lowered the tea strainer into the pot and poured hot water over it.

"What was it about?" she asked absently.

"I was laying there in my bed, and someone kept screaming over and over. Only I couldn't understand what they were saying. I was so scared in my dream, but I couldn't move. And in my dream, I could hear Father saying everything was going to be alright."

"Uh...that wasn't a dream, Nora." Meredith noticed the counter with the jar of dried berries still sitting on it. She'd forgotten to put it up last night. She closed it up again and set it out of the little ones' reach.

"Yes, it was."

"No, it wasn't. You woke up and you didn't even realize it. Father came home last night..."

"He did? Where is he? Where is everybody?"

"They're sleeping. They brought someone back with them who was hurt really, really bad. That's the screaming you heard." Meredith poured Nora and herself a cup of tea and added a generous drizzle of honey.

"Who'd they bring back? It wasn't Uncle Al, was it?" Nora blinked back tears as she sipped her too hot tea.

"No. That boy that came here a few weeks ago."

"The one you glare at all the time?"

"I do not."

Elenora shrugged. "So, why are they all still asleep?"

"We didn't go to bed until really late."

"Is that why Scilla's asleep in our room?"

"I guess so. Phelie told Father to put him in ours. Come on, finish that," Meredith motioned to the cup in front of her, "and let's get some of the chores done before anyone wakes up. It'll be a nice surprise."

"Not for me, it won't," Nora grumbled but gulped down the remains of her tea.

Together, Meredith and Elenora went out to the barn.

Meredith had just finished up and was stooping down to scratch Stitch when the barn door opened.

"Father!" Elenora ran past her, almost knocking her over. Meredith looked up and met Father's eyes. Nora jumped up and wrapped her arms around his neck. "You came home!"

"I told you I would. What are you two doing out here?" Father still looked and sounded tired. Meredith wondered when he had finally gone to bed the night before.

"Meri and I were doing the chores since no one else was awake. We did it to surprise you."

"That's a nice surprise." Father smiled, but Meredith could see it never really reached his eyes. Looking at him now, Meredith realized he was weary from more than just last night. He must have spent the last several days and nights trying to keep Sasha alive. "Let's go inside and eat."

Meredith walked with Father back to the house while Nora ran ahead.

"He's dying, isn't he?" she kept her voice low.

"I don't know." Father's face clouded over. "He's in really bad shape. I honestly don't know how he's still alive. I just hope he stays that way."

"You really feel sorry for him, don't you?"

"Meri, he's hurt because he insisted on fighting against his own countrymen. I think that's proof enough that he's changed, don't you?"

Meredith frowned but didn't answer. Father spoke of Sasha as if he were some sort of hero, not remembering that he was the cause of all their recent troubles.

Breakfast was somber. The littlest girls were unaware of what was wrong but felt the tension anyway. In the unusually quiet house, Sasha's moans were clearly heard. Meredith glanced toward her bedroom door. Taliea was still in there. She had offered to stay while Father got some rest. Meredith pushed herself away from the table and fixed a plate of food.

Pushing the door open softly, Meredith stuck her head in first. Taliea was sitting in a chair next to Ophelia's bed.

"Want something to eat?" Meredith whispered. She wasn't sure if talking would disturb Sasha or not. Her eyes wandered over to where he lay. His face was white still. He moved restlessly, his hands clutching at nothing but air, his lips moving but only occasionally making any sound. "How is he?"

"Still alive. Not much better than that." Taliea took the plate of food and took a bite. "He does keep saying the same thing over and over. He's been mumbling it off and on most of the morning since the medicine wore off. I wish I knew what it was."

"Dagmar would know. She knew he was calling for his mother last night."

"She would, wouldn't she? I hadn't thought of that. I wonder if she'd be willing to come in here and translate a little, not that I'd blame her if she wasn't."

Meredith smiled a little. "Well, she'd need you to ask her, because she doesn't understand us that well either."

"All these languages! Sit in here for a minute while I go talk to her."

Before Meredith could protest, Taliea was gone. Meredith sat on the edge of her own bed. She tried to ignore Sasha's increased restlessness. His face twisted up in a grimace, but his eyes remained closed. He murmured something she couldn't understand. He repeated it, his voice hoarse, his breath coming in quick, harsh gasps between each syllable. His voice broke into a fit of coughing that brought blood up. He was asking for something, she was sure. She could hear the pleading in his tone.

The door swung open, and Dagmar timidly followed Taliea into the room. Her eyes widened in horror as she took in the sight. She whispered something in Taliea's ear and Taliea shook her head.

Dagmar stepped up to the side of the bed and gingerly lowered herself onto the edge of it. She said something softly to Sasha. Sasha stirred once more at her voice, this time the words coming out in a desperate cry. Dagmar listened, leaning closer to him to catch each word. And she answered. Whatever she said to him, some of the tension left Sasha's body. Dagmar turned to Taliea and translated.

"Of course. I should have guessed," Taliea said, turning to the small bedside table and picked up the half-filled glass of water. "Hold his head up a little, Meri."

Meredith did as she was told, a little startled at the heat radiating off him.

"He's sick," she said, watching as he gulped down the water.

"Very. He got blood in his lung, and it never had the chance to drain fully. It became infected. I flushed his lung out last night, but it hasn't seemed to do any good yet. I'll have to do it again, I'm afraid." Taliea poured more water into the cup and let him drink it as well. "Meri, I gave your mother some leaves to make tea out of last night. Do you think you could make some more?"

For days, nothing changed. Mother decided to have the youngest girls stay with their grandparents, leaving their room free for Meredith and Ophelia. Meredith wondered how long they were going to try to keep him alive. In eight days, his fever hadn't broken, his wounds were reopened so often she was sure they would never be able to heal, and he never once woke up. In eight days, the only thing they had accomplished was exhausting themselves. There had yet to be any sign that it was worth it.

Chapter 59

NIGHTMARE FOLLOWED hideous nightmare. Darkness and shadow swirled around inside him. There was never enough air. Never enough warmth. Never enough water.

He floundered in the darkness, trapped inside. There were times when the nightmares faded. When the deep blackness, the endless nothingness was all he knew. But always the dark dreams returned, dragging him back into the prison of fear and torment. Trapping him inside a black hole he could not escape.

Sasha opened his eyes in yet another dream. They were coming for him. Father was coming for him. He would be punished. He could hear their footsteps ringing down the corridor. He could see the steely cold of Father's eyes meeting his own. And blood. There was blood everywhere. His blood. Sasha scrambled back. More blood. He was drowning in a sea of it.

This time there was pain accompanying it. Real pain. Not surreal, nightmarish pain. Real, throbbing pain. He was on his hands and knees, crawling. The pain grew. His vision swam in his dream. He could hear Father coming up behind him. His lungs were screaming for air. But he couldn't breathe. He had to get away. He had to escape the torment he knew was coming. A hand settled on his shoulder. It wasn't from his dream. Sasha wanted to scream. But he didn't have enough breath.

"Sasha?"

A voice coming from somewhere beyond the dream slipped into his consciousness. Sasha fought towards it. If only they would keep speaking, whoever it was. If only he could keep hold of the strand of reality, they were holding out to him, he could pull himself up out of this pit of nightmares.

"What are you doing?"

The voice spoke again. This time Sasha was nearer. He could almost reach it. If he could just manage to force his eyes open. If he could just lift his own hand up to meet the one on his shoulder. But what if he didn't want to? What if the hand really belonged to Father? Fear, stoked by a thousand bad dreams, coursed through him. He could feel the panic rising, the way it always did.

"It's alright. You're alright. Come on. You can't be out of bed."

There it was again. Sasha tried to take a deep breath. It ended in a fit of coughing that tore through his lungs. The searing pain drove his eyes open for real at last. It was dark, mostly. A faint, flickering light, somewhere behind him, cast strange shadows. Sasha blinked. The coughing started again. He doubled over, his lungs burning. A feeble hand brought to his mouth came away wet with an almost black substance. Blood.

"Sasha, what are you doing?"

"Have... to... get... away," Sasha got the words out between coughs. "He's... going to... punish..."

The hand on his shoulder moved. Someone was kneeling in front of him, their face a blur to his eyes. Sasha pulled away. He was half convinced that this person was the one he was supposed to be getting away from.

"Sasha, no one is going to hurt you. You're safe. I'm going to help you get back into bed, alright?"

Sasha's befuddled brain tried to process the words. If he was somewhere safe, then he truly had no idea where he was.

The man who had been speaking shifted once again, and Sasha felt himself being lifted to his feet and half carried. The deep, throbbing pain began again, and this time Sasha could discern where it was coming from. His leg. It refused to bear any weight at all, leaving

Sasha entirely dependent on this man who promised him safety.

Sasha felt himself being lowered. He was sitting, then laying back on a bed. He started coughing again, and the man rolled him onto his side, wiping away the blood Sasha brought up. Sasha gasped, wondering why he couldn't draw in a full breath.

"Take it easy," the man said. "Here, try to drink this."

Sasha felt the cool rim of a cup touching his cracked, parched lips. The liquid brushed against them, and he let it fill his mouth. Water. Delicious, sweet, refreshing water. He guzzled it down. When the man pulled it away, he tried to lift his hand up to bring it back.

"I'll give you more. I just have to refill it."

Again, the cup was set to his lips. Again, he drank deeply, satisfying a thirst that had plagued him for what seemed like an eternity. At last, it was enough. At least, it was all he had the strength to swallow.

His eyes, which he hadn't been able to keep open for more than a few seconds, now refused to open altogether. A cool, moist cloth touched his forehead. Sasha sighed. It was wonderful. Even as his hold on reality slipped once more, he relaxed, basking in the cool relief.

The warmth of sunlight resting on his face forced Sasha's eyes open. He squinted, the light painful against his eyes. He'd never known them to be so sensitive. Turning his head away from the bright light, Sasha became aware of the dampness surrounding him. The bedding he was laying in was wet. It took him several minutes to realize that they were dampened by his own sweat. That was strange, he thought. The room certainly didn't seem that warm.

Weakly, he tried to lift his head. It flopped back against his pillow almost immediately.

"Sasha, you're awake." It was the man's voice from last night, or at least, Sasha thought it was from last night. He didn't actually know how much time had passed since that strange encounter in the dark. All he did know was that the darkness he had succumbed to after that was restful for the first time. There were no more nightmares, no more dreams. Just sleep.

Sasha turned his head toward the voice, blinking painfully at the dazzling sunlight. He stared for a minute before he recognized his companion.

"Hamo?" His own voice wouldn't rise above a hoarse whisper no matter how much effort he put into it.

Hamo leaned forward in his chair, resting a hand on Sasha's forehead. Sasha was surprised to read the concern on the man's face.

"Your fever's broken." He leaned back again, pulling his hand away.

"What happened?"

"You were wounded," Hamo continued on to explain but Sasha only half heard him. A memory stirred in his mind. The last thing he remembered seeing before the darkness. He was going to die, in that memory. He was sure of it. He was going to be killed. The image of Boris' face, contorted in bitter hatred for him filled his vision. Boris had been there, ready to kill him. Then why was he still alive?

"He didn't kill me," Sasha whispered, interrupting Hamo.

"Who didn't kill you?"

"Boris." Speaking this much made him terribly out of breath. "He was going to kill me. He didn't."

Hamo started to answer, but a fit of coughing from Sasha interrupted him. Pain erupted in his chest. His hand over his mouth came away wet with blood. Sasha lay back on his pillow staring at the dark stain in the palm of his hand. So that part from the previous night's dream was real. Hamo wiped the blood from his hand.

"Here, drink this," Hamo lifted his head up to meet a cup, "and try to go back to sleep. You need to rest."

Sasha swallowed the warm, bitter contents and felt himself slipping back into the darkness. He gave up fighting it almost immediately. The pain in his chest subsided with the light. All thoughts of Boris, and what had happened faded away. He was asleep again.

Hands on his body pulled Sasha back out of his slumber. Opening his eyes, he didn't have to look around to find who was in the room. She was bending over him, doing something to his chest. Something that hurt. Sasha moaned. He didn't recognize her, although he had the vague idea that he should have. He lifted a hand to push her away and the movement caught her attention.

"It's alright, Sasha." She brushed his hand easily away. He whimpered a little at the pain. "I know, I know, it hurts. I have to do this, though."

Sasha tried lifting his head up off the pillow enough to see what she was doing. For the first time since he was wounded, he caught sight of his own injury. His stomach revolted at the sight. Remembering the blood he coughed up earlier, Sasha's eyes searched the woman's face.

"Am I dying?"

The woman paused what she was doing and met his eyes. She smiled as she gently pushed back the hair that clung to his forehead. The gesture reminded Sasha painfully of Mother.

"I don't think so. Not now."

"But I was?" he croaked.

"You were very close to it." The woman reached for a cup sitting somewhere out of Sasha's line of vision and held it up for him to drink. The same bitter liquid filled his mouth that Hamo had given him earlier. Sasha swallowed obediently and went back to sleep.

Chapter 60

SASHA LAY, A FEEBLE, PALE invalid, propped up by several pillows and trying to make sense of everything. Since he had been completely unaware of anything that happened to him for nearly a month, and even in the last few days had spent more time asleep than awake, it was a difficult puzzle to sort. Aside from brief waking moments and a handful of painful, energy sapping words that he mostly couldn't remember after the fact exchanged with Hamo and Taliea, he had slept, lulled by the bitter drink they insisted on giving him. He couldn't complain. It held the pain at bay and the pain was otherwise unbearable.

Sitting here now, without the effects of the medicine, he hurt. Every breath was like a knife through his lungs. His leg throbbed. And it was more than just his injuries. The fever left a dull ache throughout his body.

After sitting there for only a few minutes, it occurred to Sasha that it was the longest he'd been able to keep his eyes open. Not that it was much. He was incapable of moving his own body still. In his entire life, he had never been this weak, this utterly helpless. He would be sitting in just this position until someone came in and helped him move.

Sasha's attempts at piecing together the events of his life in the past few weeks were cut short when Hamo came in and sat down in the chair next to the bed, a cup of broth in his hands. Sasha drank it willingly, savoring its richness, then leaned back against the soft pillows, a deep furrow on his brow.

"What happened?"

Hamo sighed a little. In the last week, Sasha had asked the same question almost every time he was awake and Hamo was in the room. His memory simply wasn't up to the task of holding onto the story Hamo had patiently repeated.

"You were wounded in the battle. Aldrid and I found you several hours later."

"You looked for me?"

"Yes. You didn't honestly think we'd just leave you there, did you?"

Sasha nodded as much as he had the strength for. It had been his dying thought. He remembered that much. Laying on the ground, blood gushing from him, watching Boris get ready to run his sword through his heart. Those pieces were all there. Along with the memory of thinking no one cared whether he lived or died. And that no one would come looking for him. That he was alone. Forgotten. Forsaken.

"I'm sorry you thought that, Sasha," Hamo said quietly. "I'm really sorry you even felt like you had to fight. I should have found a way to leave you here."

"But you came back for me. No one's ever come back for me." Sasha realized just how true his words were after he spoke. Not even his own brothers had come back to look for him when he fell down the ravine. It was like he never even existed to them.

"Well, we would have been too late if someone hadn't already helped you."

"What do you mean?" Sasha stifled a yawn. He desperately wanted Hamo to keep telling him what had happened, and he knew if Hamo thought he was too tired, he would make him lay down and go to sleep again.

"You would have bled to death long before we got to you, except someone tied your leg off and stopped the bleeding."

"Who?"

Hamo shrugged. "It had to have been done just after you were wounded, or it wouldn't have been in time."

Sasha struggled to keep his eyes open as he took in Hamo's words. He owed his life to some stranger. Most likely, he would never find out who. He also owed his life, again, to the man sitting next to him.

"Thank you," Sasha whispered.

"For what?"

"Saving me. For not leaving me to die." Sasha couldn't keep his eyes open any longer. Whatever Hamo said in response was lost to sleep.

The pattern continued for days. More sleeping than waking. But it slowly shifted. Sasha managed to stay awake a little longer each day. He was able to lift his own head up. Then he was able to feed himself. There were stretches of time when he was left alone, and in the last day or two, Sasha had attempted standing up. He only tried it when no one else was in the room, sensing that both Hamo and Taliea would tell him he wasn't ready. So far, he had only managed to sit up and swing his legs over the side of the bed.

He had just laid back down from such an effort when the sounds of talking and laughter floated into the room. It was like that most evenings. Sasha tried to shut it out. It still didn't belong to him. This evening was harder than usual. He was restless and bored. The bed was uncomfortable after so many days of being stuck in it. He tossed and turned, trying to fall asleep so that he wouldn't have to listen to everyone but him enjoying their lives. It failed. The more he tried to ignore it, the more he noticed it. Aching for that companionship, Sasha squeezed his eyes shut.

His heavy sigh was cut off by the door opening. Sasha pushed himself up on his elbow to see who it was, wincing a little at the pain it caused in his chest. Hamo came over to his bedside.

"Tired of lying in bed?"

Sasha nodded.

"Want to come out and sit a bit? It'll change up the scene at least."

Sasha hesitated. He was miserably bored laying in here, but if he went out there, it would just be uncomfortable and awkward like the few days he'd spent at the house between trips. He wasn't sure he was ready to be either glared at or deliberately ignored.

Hamo didn't give him the chance to answer, though. He slid his arm beneath Sasha and sat him up.

"Come on. It'll do you some good," Hamo said as he helped Sasha to his feet for the first time.

Sasha's legs trembled beneath his weight, and pain shot through the injured one. Sasha gasped at the pain but found it bearable. Leaning heavily on Hamo, he made it to the doorway. Beyond, he could see the family gathered in the sitting room. No one was even looking in his direction. That helped a little, he supposed.

Hamo helped him over to a chair and pulled a stool over for him to prop his injured leg on. Sasha leaned back against it, watching. The scene was a comfortable one and for once, Sasha's presence didn't mar it. No one tensed at his entrance.

Sitting on the floor near the fireplace, the two smallest girls were engrossed in some game of their own imagination. Ophelia was sitting in a corner, a book in her hands, looking up every now and then to laugh at something Meredith and another girl were doing.

Meredith held the baby on her lap, while the other girl knelt on the floor in front of them. A little bundle of black and white fur wriggled on the kneeling girl's lap. Using her fingers, she teased the puppy into jumping and putting its paws on Meredith's knees. As the black and white head came up, the baby on Meredith's lap laughed.

Sasha's eyes widened as he watched them. Dagmar was the one kneeling on the floor. Only, he'd never seen this Dagmar before. She giggled at the baby's laughter. When she turned to look at Ophelia, there was no fear in her eyes. Watching her now, Sasha wasn't sure how he had ever thought her pretty before. There was nothing pretty about the cringing shell she had been. She looked alive now, animated and enthusiastic.

"How are you feeling, Sasha?" Edith was sitting nearby, her hands busy with sewing.

Sasha almost regretted Edith's addressing him. Out of the corner of his eye, he saw Dagmar stiffen and look suddenly unsure. Someday, he hoped, she would be able to be around him without being a little afraid of him.

"I'm alright."

"You know, you gave us quite the scare there for a few days." Edith smiled as she spoke, clearly trying to put him at ease.

"I'm sorry." Sasha lowered his eyes.

"I didn't mean it like that. We're all very glad you've pulled through."

Aldrid and Taliea's arrival prevented Sasha from having to come up with a response. Sasha sank back against the chair, noticing that Dagmar had gone back to their game with the baby.

"We stopped by to check on him," Taliea was saying, then caught sight of Sasha. "I guess I don't need to ask if you're feeling better."

Aldrid clapped his hand on Sasha's shoulder and sat down in the chair next to him. "Finally up and about, huh? Maybe now Hamo will stop worrying over you. It's about time, too. I assume you've heard about what's going on?" Aldrid turned his attention to Hamo.

"I've heard," Hamo answered. "I'll be leaving in the morning, most likely."

"I have to come with you, don't I?" Sasha asked softly, his heart sinking at the prospect. That must be why Hamo wanted him up and about. He needed him ready for another trip.

"What? No. You're not going anywhere." Hamo brushed off his concern.

Sasha stared at him, uncomprehending at first, then turned away blinking rapidly. Hamo was leaving him behind. Leaving him with his family. Hamo was trusting him.

Chapter 61

A FEW MORE STEPS AND HE would reach the fence. Sasha gritted his teeth and took another step forward.

It was the farthest he'd made it since being wounded and it wasn't very far at all. He had hoped, once he got out of bed the first time, that his recovery would speed up.

Now, three weeks after that hope, he was beginning to doubt he would ever be fully on his feet again. The fence was within arm's reach now and he stretched out his hand to grab the top rail. Inside the paddock, a little black mare swatted flies with her tail.

Sasha leaned against the fence, arms hooked over it to support him, watching her. His breath came in short, heavy gasps. With a start, he realized it was his own horse, ridden all the way from Aruuk. Whistling softly, he called the beast to him. Still chewing a mouthful of grass, she lifted her head over the fence and let him scratch it.

"I guess I didn't give everything up from home. You're still here." He laughed a little as she nibbled on his sleeve.

"Well, look who finally got out of bed." The voice directly behind Sasha was horribly familiar. Startled both by the nearness and identity of the speaker, Sasha spun around and very nearly collapsed, grimacing at the pain that shot up his leg. Stephan grinned down at him. "Heard you were ready to go on another road trip, right?"

Sasha paled. Hamo was already gone. Stephan couldn't possibly mean Sasha was going somewhere with him, could he?

"You really don't have much of a sense of humor, do you, son?" Stephan leaned against a spot on the fence next to him, a thick envelope in one hand. "I'm just messing with you."

Sasha bit his tongue, sure that any response would just spur Stephan on.

"I wasn't sure you were even going to make it to the fence just now."

"You were watching me?" Sasha turned back around, facing the fence and rubbing the mare's broad forehead.

"Saw you as I was coming up the drive. Still hurts pretty bad, huh?"

"Only if I'm not careful. Mostly, I just can't breathe. And everything makes me tired."

"I suppose that makes sense. You were in a bad way when we brought you here. I'm glad you're on the other side of that now."

"You are?" Sasha blurted the words out, not even trying to mask his disbelief. He regretted it immediately. Why would he goad Stephan like that? He cast a sidelong glance at the big man, trying to gauge his reaction. Stephan's face was serious as he stared out over the landscape.

"I am, really. Goodness, boy, none of us wanted you dead. You can't possibly think that, not after we drug you all the way back here just so Lord Bayner wouldn't get his hands on you." Stephan paused, then seeing that Sasha remained doubtful, continued, "It's the knife, isn't it? You're still scared of me because of that, aren't you?"

Sasha squirmed a little and studiously avoided Stephan's eyes. "Maybe. And you said yourself you weren't going to let me go, you were going to take me back to hang. And you made fun of me. And you said that the one good thing I did couldn't undo all the bad things I had done. You didn't want to give me a second chance."

"So, you did hear all that. I thought you were still awake," Stephan said quietly. Sasha hung his head. He hadn't meant to say all that just now, and he certainly hadn't meant to disclose his eavesdropping. "Sasha, however much I didn't trust you, I truly never wished you dead. Maybe I was a little hard on you. I think you proved me wrong. I shouldn't have made it so that dying was the only way you could see to doing that."

Sasha didn't trust himself to say anything. It was the last thing he had expected to hear from Stephan.

"Now, I'm forgetting why I came all this way in the first place." Stephan lifted the envelope up for Sasha to take. "Hamo will be home tomorrow or the day after at the latest, but he wanted me to go ahead and give you this. Said it might make you feel a bit better."

Sasha took it, wondering what Hamo thought would make him feel better. He stared at it. He turned it over in his hand, staring at it in bewilderment. There was lettering on the outside, but it wasn't like the lettering they used in Aruuk. Sasha grimaced, knowing what was about to happen.

"Well, aren't you going to open it and see what it says? Because I'm curious, even if you're not."

"I can't read it," Sasha whispered, his face growing hot.

"What?"

"I can't read the words. That's not how we write in Aruuk. I never learned how to read this."

Stephan looked to be on the verge of making a joke, then thought better of it. "Want me to read it to you?"

"Please?"

Stephan tore the envelope open and perused its contents silently, Sasha's anxious eyes never leaving his face as his expression grew more and more surprised. Stephan let out a low whistle and reread the words.

"What? What does it say?" Sasha couldn't decide if it was a good sort of surprise or a bad sort of surprise.

"It says, '*In recognition of the service rendered to both Dival and Dorsten, as Sovereign of these newly united nations, I, King Darien, issue this pardon to one, Sasha Gundarson, for any and all crimes hitherto committed against the people of Dorsten. No further punishment of said crimes may be inflicted on the*

pardoned, nor shall any new record be made of them.'
That's the first one," Stephan slid that paper
underneath another one and continued reading, "This
one says, *'I, King Darien, grant the full rights of
Divalian citizenship to Sasha Gundarson.'*"

"What does it mean?"

"Seriously? I think it's pretty clear what it means.
King Darien pardoned you and made you a citizen.
Looks like you have a new home."

"But my sentence. That wasn't here. That was in
Dorsten. He can't pardon that, can he?"

"You missed a lot while you were out of it, didn't
you? Dorsten, Dival, they're not separate anymore. Not
like they were anyway."

"How?"

"People of Dorsten got tired of Lord Bayner and of
not having a real king. When we showed up to help
them fight, they decided it was time to go back to the
old crown. Darien was the only true heir to either
throne. They just signed the union the day before
yesterday. They're two different provinces now of the
same kingdom. Hamo must have asked King Darien for
this, though," Stephan gave the papers a little shake,
"because the king wasn't going to mess with any
sentences Lord Bayner had already handed down. He
said there would be enough to sort out without going
back and undoing things."

"He asked for this, for me?" Sasha took the papers
and held them, staring at the unusual lettering. A new
home. A new life. He didn't need to read those letters
to understand the importance of Hamo's gift. They
were the two things he had so desperately longed for.
Now they were his.

"Must have. He's also got to be just about the only
person in our history who has gotten the king to sign
two of these pardons. They don't usually come very
easily."

"Who else did he get the king to pardon?"

"His brother, Al. Come on," Stephan put his arm
around Sasha's shoulders, steadying him, "I'll give you
a hand back to the house and you can show everyone."

"What did Aldrid do?" Sasha asked, leaning heavily against Stephan.

"Stole, from a lot of people. He also did something very brave that probably saved us a lot of lives, and most certainly saved his brother's."

"Really?"

"It's why Hamo asked for the pardon in the first place."

They reached the house and Sasha found a place to sit and recover for a bit.

"Look at this, Edith." Stephan took the papers from Sasha's hand. "Your husband has a lot of sway with the king. At this rate, I think he could ask him for just about anything and Darien would give it to him."

"What is it?" Edith's hands were white with flour as she kneaded bread dough. Stephan held them up for her to read.

"That's wonderful! I guess you won't have to worry about getting in trouble anymore. Did Hamo send those?"

"Yes." Sasha looked suitably embarrassed when Ophelia came in and wanted to see as well.

She pursed her lips as her eyes traveled over the words. "Aren't these hard to get? I thought you had to petition the king, and he only gave it to important people."

Stephan laughed outright and even Edith tried to hide a smile at Ophelia's words. She stared at them for a moment before she laughed as well.

"That didn't come out right, did it? Either that, or I guess that makes you an important person, Sasha. I bet it's nice not having to worry about being hung anymore."

"Really nice." Sasha caught sight of Meredith standing in the doorway and dropped his gaze. Everyone else might have forgiven him and moved on, including King Darien apparently, but she certainly hadn't.

Chapter 62

W HAT ABOUT THESE ONES?" Elenora held
up a cluster of bright orange flowers.
"No. Blue and purple, Nora. I've only said
that how many times?" Meredith looked up from where
she was filling her own basket.

Uncle Aldrid and Taliea's wedding had to be perfect,
and orange wasn't a perfect color for a wedding. Nora
pouted for a moment and then continued her search. A
branch breaking behind her caught Meredith's
attention and she turned around to see who was
coming.

Her face betrayed her initial surprise when she
realized it was Sasha. He'd been up and about the house
for a few weeks now, but she'd managed to avoid him
for the most part. It was easier to feel forgiving and
generous to someone who was dying, she'd decided.
Now that he was safely recovering, it was easier to
remember what he'd done to make her dislike him in
the first place.

"Hi, Sasha," Elenora said. "Do you want to help us?"

Annoyance flashed across Meredith's face when her
sister spoke. Everyone else in the house was like that.
Talking to him, trying to include him. No one
remembered what he had done to her and Ophelia. She
turned back to what she was doing while Sasha paused
and caught his breath before trying to answer.

"What are you doing?" he asked finally.

"Picking flowers for the wedding. It was supposed to
be last month, but they decided to wait because you
were dying."

Meredith cleared her throat loudly, hoping to catch her younger sister's attention. Elenora looked up and her bright eyes went wide with horror as she clapped a hand over her own mouth.

"I wasn't supposed to tell you that, though. We were supposed to keep it a secret so that you wouldn't feel bad," She hurried to say while Meredith groaned internally.

"Oh. Well, I," Sasha stammered, at a complete loss.

"Just pretend you don't know," Nora suggested.

"Sure."

"And you can help us, if you want. Meredith only wants purple and blue ones, but I think the orange ones are pretty too. Don't you?"

"I guess so?"

"See, Meri? We should get orange, too. Sasha thinks so."

"I didn't actually say..."

Meredith rolled her eyes. She should have asked Phelie to come with her instead. Ophelia at least would have recognized and appreciated her efforts in choosing the right colors. And Ophelia might not have been so quick to engage Sasha in conversation. Although, she wasn't so sure about that after watching her sister laughing in the kitchen with him and Mother and Grandfather. Even she seemed to have forgotten what Sasha had done.

"I'm sure Sasha doesn't want to help us pick flowers, Nora." Meredith could feel her sister's eyes on her at the sound of her voice. It was a little harsher than she intended.

"Why did you come out here then?" Nora turned to Sasha again.

"Just to get out of the house for a bit."

"Wish you'd stay out of the house," Meredith whispered under her breath. She really didn't intend for anyone else to hear her, but glancing at Elenora, it was clear her younger sister had. She didn't dare look at Sasha to find out if he had.

If he did, he didn't respond. Meredith could hear him walking away and let out a sigh of relief.

"Why are you so mean to him?" Nora asked after a few minutes of silence.

"I'm not."

"If Father saw you, he'd say you're being mean. And he told all of us to be nice to him."

"I shouldn't have to be nice to someone like him. He kidnapped Phelie and me. He hurt me," Meredith said defensively. It was true that Father told them all when Sasha first began recovering that they were to treat him well.

"He said he was sorry."

"That doesn't mean anything."

"Yes, it does. If I fight with Scilla or Adel and then I say I'm sorry it makes everything better and we're friends again. And you say you're sorry all the time for the same thing."

Meredith froze, absorbing the unintended sting of Elenora's words. She opened her mouth to argue, to say that it was different, but the words refused to come.

"I think he's sad that you won't forgive him. Just like I'd be sad if Scilla didn't forgive me," Elenora continued, heedless of Meredith's reaction. "When do you think we have enough flowers?"

Elenora's abrupt shift in the conversation caught Meredith off guard. She remained speechless for a long moment, trying to push away Nora's previous words.

"You can be done now," she said at last. "I'll finish up by myself."

As Elenora disappeared in the direction of home, Meredith abandoned any pretense of doing anything productive. She sat back on her heels, staring into the trees, her thoughts a long way off. They wandered back to the day she and Phelie were at the old mining camp. The first time she had seen Sasha. He'd laughed at her, hurt her, hurt Phelie.

She should still be angry about all of that, Meredith insisted. She had every right to be. All the fear of that day came flooding back, watching her sister lay still on the ground, begging to be untied so that she could help Phelie. It was the worst day of her life, and he was responsible for it, for all of it.

Her memory wandered back to another day. Seeing Father there in the mountains, knowing that she was safe at last, knowing that Father hadn't abandoned them at all. It was a moment she loved to relive. Pure in its happiness, it marked the end to the worst few weeks she'd ever known.

Sasha's face, when he recognized her, came to mind. He was terrified. Even in the shadows she had seen it. His face was sick with fear thinking that he was going to be killed. When Father went to free him the following morning, she'd seen the way he was trembling, certain that it was his end that Father was coming to deliver. His fear had been every bit as real as hers had been.

Rising to her feet so quickly that she went dizzy for a moment, Meredith picked up her basket and started for home. There was so much she needed to do; she didn't have time to unravel all the emotions that Elenora had unwittingly set in motion.

The house was empty, except for Mother and baby Drogo. Meredith set down her basket on the kitchen table, and sat down, her hands idle in her lap as she watched Mother busy at the stove.

"What's the worst thing someone's ever done to you?" she asked suddenly.

Mother stopped stirring and turned to face her. Studying Meredith's troubled face for a moment, she wiped her hands clean on her apron and sat down across from her.

"This isn't about me, is it?" Mother said softly.

"I don't want to stop being angry at him. He deserves it," Meredith blurted out.

"I see. Well, Meri, no one has ever done anything quite like that to me. But they did to your father, and worse."

"I know."

"Do you know what he did about it?"

"No." Meredith bit her lip. "But I have a feeling it wasn't what I'm doing."

"It wasn't. He let the man go who had hurt him. Said he couldn't live with himself if he didn't. See, Meri, forgiving isn't just for the other person. It helps you, too. Have you noticed you're the only one who spends all of their time being angry and missing out because of it?"

"Maybe," Meredith said, thinking of the evenings she had spent in her room because she didn't want to sit in the same room as Sasha.

"You're also the only one who can change that." Mother stood up again and returned to her work.

Meredith sat for a while longer, picking leaves off the stems of the freshly picked flowers and tearing them into little bits. Finally, she got up and wandered outside, in search of her sisters to distract her. They weren't to be found in the yard, but as Meredith turned toward the barn, she caught sight of a figure leaning against the paddock fence. Even though his back was to her, she knew it was Sasha.

He didn't hear her come up behind him as he stood, arms hooked over the fence, one hand idly rubbing the face of the black horse Father kept in there. His horse, she realized. Just about the only thing here that was his.

"She's really pretty, isn't she?" Meredith wrapped her own arms over the fence rail.

He jumped a little, startled by her voice so close, and only looked at her briefly before turning away.

"She is."

Meredith reached out and patted the animal's sleek neck. The horse turned and nibbled at her sleeve, and she smiled a little. Sasha let go of the fence and took a step toward the house.

"Wait," Meredith stopped him.

He faced her again, his face drawn into a puzzled expression, his eyes wary and uncertain.

"I'm glad you're feeling better."

He stared at her, disbelieving and speechless.

"Look, I know I haven't been very nice." Meredith twisted a strand of hair on her finger. "I'm sorry."

"Really?"

"Really. I am. I mean, you almost died, and all I could think about was how much better it would be if you did. That's a really horrible thing to think about anyone."

"You wanted me to die?"

"I sort of did." Meredith realized just how harsh her words sounded. "But I don't anymore."

"You just don't want me here?"

"I didn't say...," Meredith stopped. She had said exactly that, and he had heard her. "Alright, so maybe I did say that." Ugh, why can't I just say it, Meredith berated herself, cringing inwardly at her clumsy attempts. "I'm sorry, Sasha. For saying that, and for thinking that. And I'm not angry about what you did anymore. I mean, I still wish it hadn't happened. I just don't want to be mad all the time. Can we just start over?"

"Sure, I think." Sasha's eyes had lost some of their wariness. "I, um, I think I should go inside and rest for a bit." He started to go but turned back one last time. His eyes met hers without looking away. "Thank you."

Chapter 63

SASHA LEANED TOWARD STEPHAN for at least the tenth time since the wedding started.

"What are they doing now?" he whispered.

Stephan sighed quietly but otherwise ignored him, and Sasha made a mental note to just ask when it was all over. He didn't understand any of it, so the explanation needed would no doubt be lengthy. The ceremony was like nothing he'd ever seen. There was a lot said about love, most of which was completely foreign to him. Commitment was mentioned, another idea Sasha hadn't heard much about. Whatever it was all about, Aldrid and Taliea seemed happy, happier than anyone Sasha had ever seen.

He looked around. The flowers Meredith and Elenora had been picking yesterday turned the whole place every shade of blue and purple, giving off a sweet fragrance.

There were people Sasha had never seen before there. A sister of Hamo and Aldrid's that he hadn't known existed and her family. Friends and neighbors. Sasha's head was swimming by the time he'd met a quarter of them.

When the meal started after the ceremony, Sasha found a corner to hide in. He sat down on a bench along the wall, watching the celebration, the old feelings of loneliness pushing to the surface. He hadn't felt that much since his recovery.

"Hey," one of the twins said and sat down next to him. Sasha stared at her, trying to decide which one it was since he had lost the only tool he had for telling the difference between them. They both wore their hair up today. The girl laughed. "You could just ask. I'm Phelie. Are you alright?"

Sasha nodded. "What are they doing?"

"Um, dancing. It's fun. Haven't you ever danced before?" She cocked her head, staring at him with a barely concealed smile.

"No. We don't do that sort of thing in Aruuk."

"Boring place. Want to come get some food?"

"You want me to?"

"Well, Father sort of told us to make sure you weren't left sitting in a corner all by yourself, feeling left out." Ophelia shrugged. "You don't have to look so offended about it. None of us mind. Honestly."

Sasha smiled a little. He could almost hear Hamo saying the same thing. Looking at Ophelia now, she certainly didn't look overburdened with talking to him. Maybe she really didn't mind. And it was nice to be included.

"Alright. I'm kind of hungry."

"So, what are you going to do, now that you're officially pardoned and all?" Ophelia asked, keeping the conversation going as they made their way to the table of food.

"I hadn't really thought about it." Sasha hesitated. He had actually been giving it quite a bit of thought, especially during the long, lonely hours of just lying in his bed. He just wasn't sure if he was ready to tell anyone. On an impulse, stemming perhaps from Ophelia's open friendliness, he decided to confide. "Actually, I have an idea. I think I want to find my mother, and my sister, Agathe."

"The ones your father sold?"

Sasha nodded.

"Do you have any idea where they are?"

"No. But I know someone who would." Sasha's face darkened as he spoke.

"You don't mean...Sasha, that's a terrible idea. He'll kill you if he finds you, won't he?"

"I know."

"And anyway, how would you go about doing that? Maybe you should, I don't know, learn a trade. Earn some money first. That's actually what I meant when I asked you what your plans were. It might make a search for them a little easier."

Sasha nodded again, lost in thought. Ophelia was right. But now that he'd said his idea out loud, it wasn't going to just go away. He had to do it. He had to find Mother. He had to find Agathe. He owed it to them.

Epilogue

THE NOISE OF BATTLE FADED with the afternoon. The noise of the dying took its place. To the shadow crouching behind a rock, neither made much difference.

When a group of soldiers ran by, the figure pressed itself closer to the rock. He watched as the pursuers caught up with the pursued. A single man against a half dozen. The scene was barbaric, but not shocking to the young man hiding in the shadows. Naturally, the single man died, although in the end he had begged to be spared. It was no more than Boris expected. It was why he was hiding, waiting. That, and the motionless body a few yards in front of him. He should have left it hours ago but couldn't bring himself to.

As the fiery orange glow of the setting sun draped itself across the mountainside, Boris saw two more men approaching. They were not pursuing. Boris watched as one by one, they searched the bodies in the grove of trees. He heard their foreign words. Even without understanding their words, he understood their purpose. They were looking for someone. One person, out of all the masses of dead and wounded on the battlefield. Boris almost laughed at the idea. They were giving up now, he thought, peering through the shadows to where they stood, gazing around in defeat. Then one of them said something and pointed in the direction of Boris' hiding place. Boris felt his skin crawl as they approached. They had seen him. He pressed himself as close to the rock as he could get, not daring to look out again.

Their voices carried easily on the night air, but he could not understand them. What he did understand was that they weren't coming any closer. Peering out from behind the rock, Boris inhaled sharply. They had found the one they were looking for. It was none other than the still figure he had kept watch over all afternoon.

His brother.

The traitor.

The reason he was hiding, hoping to just survive the night. His brother, Sasha, whom he could not bring himself to kill. His own sword still stood in the ground near Sasha's body, its point embedded in the rocky earth.

These men were taking care of Sasha. Lifting him onto a stretcher, carrying him away to safety.

Curiosity got the better of Boris. Keeping to the shadows, which were thankfully deepening with every passing minute, and staying far enough behind to not make any noise that they would hear, he crept after them. Why was his brother so important to these people that they would come in search of just him?

Boris followed them to the circle of tents overflowing with wounded. It was harder to stay in the dark here. Torches lit the place brightly, and men moved about all over the place. Boris decided he had risked enough coming this far. Sasha was still alive. He couldn't afford to hang around and find out anything else.

He backed away. And into a group of enemy soldiers. Before he could draw a weapon, he was thrown to the ground, a sword poised above his throat. Boris thought of the man he'd watched beg for his life earlier that day. It hadn't done him any good and Boris wasn't about to meet his end groveling. Boris closed his eyes, waiting for the blade to finish him.

Other titles by S. T. Hobbs

The Divalian Chronicles –

Prequel ~ The Thief and the Slave

Book 1 ~ The Traitor's Alliance

Book 2 ~ The Last Chief

Book 3 ~ The Courier's Apprentice

Book 4 ~ The King's Successor

The Oracle's Odyssey –

Book 1 ~ The Forgotten Curse

Book 2 ~ The Fallen Gates

Book 3 ~ (Coming soon) The Fates' Finale